CAMINO WANDERING

TARA MARLOW

Wildlig
PUBLISHI

Dedicated to my mother, Gai Soper.

THE MOST CRACKPOT IDEA EVER

SAINT JEAN PIED DE PORT

AUBREY LAY, heart pounding and suffering from an anxiety level she'd never experienced before. What the hell was she thinking? Did she honestly believe she could walk the entire length of northern Spain? What if she injured herself? Who would help her? Was she kidding herself, believing she could do this? She'd never been super fit, not even in her younger days. But now? Now she was fifty and her body ached at the prospect of the distance. Eight hundred bloody kilometres. Fuckity fuck, fuck.

Fact was, she was falling apart before the walk had even begun. At least mentally. What was her Plan B? What if she didn't walk the Camino de Santiago?

She rolled over on to her side and placed her hand over her pounding heart. She'd come halfway around the world to do this bloody walk. She had to do it. Besides, she'd been talking about walking the Camino for... well, months. Ever since her son Simon had shown her that bloody movie, the Martin Sheen one.

People were watching, waiting for her to fail. People at home. Friends online. She could sense their expectations, waiting for her to quit. Yes, she had to do this, if only to prove them wrong. Because, if she didn't, they won the judgement game.

Fuck. Fuckity fuck, fuck. She flipped on to her back once more.

Besides, she thought, with a waiting list at her next night's accommodation, she had little chance of getting a bed if she changed her mind.

There was no choice. She had to swallow this angst and get on with it. Aubrey sat up on the soft double bed and placed her feet on the plain wooden floor. She looked around at the room in her albergue. Albergue. She'd have to get used to that word. It was what they called hostels on the Camino. She rolled the word on her tongue. The albergue she was now in, in Saint Jean Pied de Port in the south of France, offered private rooms, along with dorms. Most albergues on the Camino were just dorms. That she knew from her research. She'd opted for a private room for this part of her journey and was relieved she had.

She looked around the room. It was clean, basic, filled with everything a pilgrim needed, she supposed. A bed with minimal linens, a simple wooden chair, and a small bathroom containing a minuscule sink, toilet, and a decent-sized shower. It was simple, but at least she could privately deal with her pre-Camino panic.

She looked back to the rustic wooden chair in the room's corner. On the seat lay her nylon shopping bag, which held her pilgrim necessities: her English passport, European cash, a travel pack of tissues, a small stash of Nurofen, Chapstick, her Ray-Ban sunglasses and her Pilgrim Credential. She'd stopped in the Pilgrim Office the night before to pick up her Credential, a crucial part of her walk. It was the document that proved she was a pilgrim to be stamped by albergues and restaurants along the way. It would allow her both access to the albergues and ultimately, proof of her pilgrimage once she reached Santiago de Compostela. If she ever reached it, she mused.

To the left of the chair, her pristine maroon Deuter backpack sat in a large black bucket on the floor. For bedbug containment, she had surmised the night before. Her backpack was spewing open with all of its contents. She wasn't ready to contain herself to a compact space just yet, and just the thought of sharing a dorm room full of people took her anxiety to new heights. With a shake of her head, she was relieved to have booked a private room.

Fuckity fuck, fuck was right.

Aubrey threw herself back on the bed. She was bone tired just envisioning the walk. It wasn't just the Camino. She cried when her twenty-three-year-old son had dropped her off at Melbourne airport. Not cried. Sobbed. She felt like she was leaving home, never to return. A part of her wished that was the case. There was so much she wanted to leave behind, but this adventure was only for three months. Besides, she was returning to her European roots. Well, her English roots anyway. That had exhausted her too. Seeing her dad for the first time in years had almost broken her completely. Her beautiful dad. He looked old and lonely, like a worn-out pair of boots that had been discarded into the back of the closet.

Aubrey sat back up and reached over to the nightstand for her iPhone, disconnected it from the charger and unlocked it. She looked at the clock to see what time it was at home. Seeing it was early evening, she clicked over to FaceTime to call her son.

"Hi, Mum. Where are you?"

"Hi, love. I'm in Saint Jean Pied de Port. I got in about seven last night. Sorry I didn't call you. Did you get my text?"

"Yeah, I got it. I wasn't sure if you were starting your walk today or tomorrow." Simon hesitated. "Are you okay?"

"Yes, love, I'm fine. It was a bit of an ordeal getting here from London yesterday. That rain from the last few weeks has done a number on transport. The rail line from Biarritz to Saint Jean was closed, so I had to work out a shuttle," she said, knowing she was rambling. "And, of course, by the time I'd stopped by the Pilgrim Office and checked in to my albergue, I was just too tired to call you. Sorry about that."

"It's fine Mum. You sound a bit, I don't know … worried. Are you okay?"

She paused before answering, "Yes, I'm alright. Anxious I suppose." It was hard to admit this to her son. She hated him knowing she was having second thoughts.

"Why? You seemed so excited by this walk."

3

"Oh, I know," she said, remembering her eagerness of this adventure had blocked everything else that was going on in her life.

"How was London?" asked Simon. "How was Granddad?"

Aubrey sighed. "Hard. He looks sad, lost. It's been hard for him since Granny died. I should have stayed longer."

"Is that why you're anxious? Or..." he prodded.

Aubrey looked down and tried to smooth some wrinkles from her shirt, hesitating on her answer. She shifted focus back to the screen.

"No, it's not that," she said, not wanting to admit what was going through her mind. "I'm just worried about how much I've committed to. Whether I can do this. Eight hundred kilometres is a long way. It's like walking from Melbourne to Sydney."

"Yeah, I know. But you can do this. Put one foot in front of the other and before you know it, you'll be in Santiago," her son said.

"If only I had your spirit."

"Mum. I know you can do this. You need to do this. We both know you do. Besides, once you get going, you'll be fine," said Simon, with the confidence of youth.

"We'll see." She looked out through the French doors into the courtyard beyond; the light was peppering the opposing wall.

"We have a deal, remember?" he prodded. She remembered. She asked him not to let her quit, no matter what she said.

"You're right. One day at a time," she said, trying to boost her confidence for what lay ahead. "Okay, I need to get going. I need to pick up some snacks. Tomorrow is only eight kilometres, but it's all uphill and the next day it's longer."

"Okay. I'll let you get to it."

"Thanks love. How's everything there? Sorry, should have asked."

"All is fine. Don't worry," he said, but Aubrey also knew her son wouldn't tell her if there was a disaster either. She knew he could handle anything that might come up. "Mum, you've got this. I know you do."

"Thanks love. I needed to hear that," she said, looking down, now stretching out the wrinkles in her black merino t-shirt. "I'll reach out again when I can. From what I read Wi-Fi is sporadic over the next few days."

"No worries. Just be careful. I'll be thinking of you, sending you positive vibes. Love you Mum! Mwah."

"Love you too." She paused, before adding, "Thanks again for the support." She blew an air kiss into the phone before hanging up.

"Yes. I can do this," she said aloud. If only she believed that. Each time she considered the walk, she felt unsure, nervous. Was it just about the walk, she wondered? She thought about Simon. He had been her rock in so much of her life, especially over the last two years.

Five minutes later, Aubrey stepped out of her albergue to join a few other backpackers in the street. Some carried the look of lost sheep, eyes wide and bulging. Others looked determined, like they'd been here before and knew exactly what they were doing. Aubrey felt akin with the lost sheep crowd.

As she walked the compact streets of the Middle Age hamlet, she wondered about the stories that lay behind the thick walls. The ancient stone buildings, stuccoed with white-wash and capped with red tiles, lined the street. Colourful shutters bordered the open windows, their residents chatting with their neighbour across the way. It was an almost party atmosphere, and it was barely nine in the morning.

Her map led her to the supermarket in the newer part of town. The market was much bigger than she imagined, and she had to remind herself of the limited space in her pack. Keeping herself in check, she purchased roasted almonds, a couple of apples, some dried bananas and a robust amount of trail mix.

Aubrey walked back to the old part of the city. She needed to buy trekking poles. Given the cost of them in Australia, plus the hassle of getting them to France, buying them here made sense. She read the St Jean Pied de Port Pilgrim Shop offered everything a pilgrim needed, so she'd start there. They had everything from the trekking poles she needed, to buffs, to even new boots. Although she couldn't imagine starting this walk wearing new shoes of any kind. Talk about priming yourself for blisters straight off the mark!

When Aubrey stepped into the shop, a petite smiling woman greeted her in French. Crap, she thought. She should have brushed up on her French before arriving. She had taken a Spanish class, figuring she could get by on her rusty high school French, but she had not imagined a full transaction with it. Her face must have given away her panic. The woman asked, with a knowing smile, if she spoke English. Aubrey looked embarrassed, nodded and mumbled "Petit Francais", or little French, and a very grateful "Merci."

The shopkeeper was gracious. She spent the next ten minutes explaining the right poles for her. She left Aubrey to try them for herself, when another pilgrim walked in. The shopkeeper offered the same greeting as she had with Aubrey, and it made Aubrey smile when the pilgrim reacted the same as she had. Like a stunned fish, she chuckled. They must get this all day, every day.

With poles and a poncho purchased, a decision she made at the last minute, Aubrey headed back to her albergue. She wanted to explore the town more, but she was so tempted to curl up on the bed for the afternoon. She wasn't jetlagged. Just emotionally exhausted. Best to keep moving, she thought, so she spent the next few hours wandering the town. She headed up the hill to La Citadelle, once a 17th Century French Military building. Now the fort was a school. The views were spectacular. She could see the details in the village below. But it was the surrounding Pyrenees countryside that had her heart in her throat. Tomorrow she would climb those mountains. The following day, she'd be on the other side. It was enough to give her an anxiety attack.

2

WILL I EVER GET TO ORISSON?

SAINT JEAN PIED DE PORT TO ORISSON

AT SEVEN-THIRTY THE NEXT MORNING, dressed in her green Columbia hiking pants, black merino top and zip-up hoodie, Aubrey stared into the bathroom mirror. A ghastly sight stared back at her. Her cognac-coloured eyes looked drained. The bags under them would have exceeded her airline weight allowance. She leaned in and noticed her eyes no longer showed a red tint, which was an improvement from the day before. She moved her head to the right, keeping her eyes forward and looked at her long, curly auburn hair. Sadly now, thanks to the travel shampoo bar she'd used the night before, it was frizzy, and bed headed. She raked her fingers through the curls, unknotting the tangles, then bunched it high on her head and secured the knot with a hair elastic. Then, she reached for her toothbrush.

Once done, she leaned into the mirror. The stream of sunlight from the nearby window was glinting off the small stud in her freckle-spattered nose. On closer inspection, she realised there was not much she could do with her drawn, dried-out face, other than washing it and slathering it with moisturiser. She just hoped that helped. She knew her moisturiser was a luxury on the Camino, but she didn't care. This stuff saved her skin.

At ten past eight, Aubrey left her room. She made her way down the heavy wooden stairs where she received a wave from the lovely albergue hostess and a 'Bon Camino'. Ah yes, French again. She was eager to get to Spain so she could understand the language better.

She was dragging this morning. She intended on leaving at seven, but her body had rejected the idea. Being with her dad for a week had drained her more than she'd realised. She'd walk it off, she thought. But she knew there was so much more than worrying about her dad's health to walk off. That was just the tip of the iceberg.

She laced up her hiking shoes. Her trekking poles, now wrapped in the bright yellow duct tape she'd brought from home, sat in the corner bucket. They were at least identifiable, she thought, as they stared at her, egging her on. She could almost hear them whisper to her to get this show on the road. If only she felt that enthusiasm.

Her Camino journey was to begin. She was as ready as she'd ever be. She grabbed the poles, opened the door and felt the cool breeze of the morning hit her. She stepped outside and on to the cobbled street.

"One step at a time," she whispered to no-one. She looked down at her phone and saw it was eight-twenty-three. Shit. She really needed to get going.

The street was quieter than she expected, unlike the morning before. It was like there was a lull between crowds. She saw four other pilgrims as she began walking down the wet, cobblestone hill. Two, with their heads down, seemed focused on getting their journey started, maybe later than they'd planned, like she. The other couple were standing in the middle of the bridge, facing the town and looking up. As she passed them, she turned and saw they were staring up at a statue of the Virgin Mary embedded in the church's archway. She remembered reading how Catholic pilgrims offered a quick prayer to the statue, asking Mary to watch over them on their pilgrimage. Not being religious herself, Aubrey walked past and then, seeing the morning light reflecting on the river, stopped for a quick photo, careful not to disturb those praying.

As she continued toward the old city gates, an elderly woman, dressed in a traditional Basque dress, tights and sturdy shoes, smiled at her and offered a quiet 'Bon Camino'. Aubrey smiled in return. Somehow, this made it real. She was doing this.

At the city gates, she looked behind her for one last view of the quaint village. She wanted to savour this moment. Her journey was beginning. With a deep breath, she turned and started up the first hill.

AT FIVE FEET, TEN INCHES AND CARRYING BOOBS AND HIPS TO THE ENVY OF many young women, Aubrey now struggled with her backpack. She had spent a considerable amount of time in the Paddy Palin shop. The shop assistant explained how to adjust every strap and buckle to ensure the pack fit comfortably and correctly. This morning however, all that knowledge escaped her. Now the shoulder straps were digging into her shoulders like Satan was pulling her down to greet him in Hell. She bent over, tightened the hip straps a little more, and found some relief.

Despite her pain, she relished the beautiful morning. A light rain shower fell the night before, making everything look fresh and in bloom. As she reached the split that would take her either to Orisson or Valcarlos, she stopped to catch her breath. The hill had her heart racing, but only because she had foolishly tried to keep up with a younger, fitter couple, who were seemingly sprinting up the incline. She needed to find her own pace!

She walked to the sign that pointed toward Roncesvalles, via the Napoleon Route, and laughed. Twenty-four kilometres? No thanks, she thought, relieved she was only going to Orisson today. But she knew she had a long way to go. Eight kilometres, most of that uphill, a trek that was sure to take her hours.

Pilgrims passed her at a rapid rate. Some with a perky wave, others a quick smile. She had to contain her competitive nature and not attempt to keep up with them. The hills were making her pant more than she wanted. After an hour into the walk, she stopped and took a long drink of her water. Looking around, she took a deep breath in and inhaled the French countryside. Even by mid-morning, she found fog still hugging the valleys, and winding its way over the surrounding hills. It was a stunning sight, almost postcard perfect. She admired the French cottages nestled into the lush green hills. And she laughed when a group of sheep stared at her through the fence, looking to her for, well, something. When she saw other sheep continuing to eat, uninterested at the foot traffic nearby, she pointed at them and said to the sheep still staring at her, 'Look! There's the good stuff'.

A few people walked in front or behind her. There were fewer than she expected. She was glad now she had been late to start. If she had left earlier, she was sure to have seen those hiking the entire way to Roncesvalles and tempted to walk a faster pace, like she had before. She enjoyed her slower pace, giving herself the opportunity to enjoy the scenery. And, she had to admit, she needed the solitude. It gave her time to think.

The birds sang to Aubrey as she walked. She felt as if they were following her, keeping her company. Maybe they were. Maybe she had a beautiful spirit walking with her. It would be lovely if that was the case. She'd rather think that than why that spirit would be lingering. She didn't want to go there. She couldn't go back to that dark place.

She focused on the countryside, dotted with white stucco cottages with deep terracotta tiled roofs, as she continued up the mountain. The further she climbed, the more incredible the scenery became. A sense of balance came to her. Smelling the blossoms and hearing the twitter of the birds filled her soul. The mass of wildflowers blanketing the fields were utterly breathtaking. With each stop, she looked around and felt Mother Nature showering her with love. And there were plenty of stops. The elevation change was harder than she thought it would be.

The line from some movie popped into her head, over and over: 'Beautiful, wish you were here!' Each time it popped into her head she considered her children. She wished they could have shared this experience with her. But it was because of them that she was here in France, undertaking this interminable walk.

After a major climb, and an elbow turn in the road, she groaned out loud. Not another bloody hill. Yet another steep incline stretched out before her. She soldiered on, realising she would get nowhere complaining. A few minutes on, she noticed a large herd of sheep coming toward her, dominating the road. Pilgrims she'd not seen before began scrambling to the side, trying to get out of the way. But within seconds, they were pulling their phones out of hidden pockets trying to capture the moment.

"He must think we're a bunch of imbeciles," she mumbled. "Surely, most people had seen sheep in their lifetime." But this scene was so quintessentially French, she understood the admiration. The old shepherd, bumbling along with his crooked, wooden staff, was whistling quietly while his working dogs did their job around him. Aubrey took advantage of the wait and removed her backpack. She took a drink of her water and grabbed an apple from her top pouch. She popped the apple into her mouth with a crunch and picked her backpack up once more. The chuckling shepherd waved as he walked past, greeting each of the pilgrims with a 'Bon Camino'.

The sign at Hunto said two kilometres and listed thirty minutes to walk it. But when the trail branched off and left the asphalt behind, she saw switchbacks ahead of her and decided it would take her more than the estimated time. She'd been walking for two-and-a-half hours already and took a break before tackling the switchbacks.

She found a large log under a tree. It looked to be a spot the locals had created for tired pilgrims, or a spot which tired pilgrims had created for themselves. Either way, she was thankful. She unhitched her backpack, letting the weight slide down her leg. Once her bum hit the log, exhaustion flooded in, nearly overwhelming her. She opened the top pouch of her pack to find her trail mix. She needed energy.

"Are you okay?" A deep baritone voice asked her. She jumped at the sound. She was surprised to see a good-looking hiker approaching, approximating him to be in his late twenties. His American accent was distinctive. As he got closer, she noticed his tousled brown hair, flicked with grey, with matching grey in the whisper of a five o'clock shadow. He must be in his thirties then, she thought, possibly forties. She hesitated, disconcerted by his good looks and the intensity his umber-coloured eyes.

"Oh," she said, catching her delayed response, brushing invisible specks from her lap. "Yes, I'm okay. Just needed a pick me up," and held up her trail mix as she sat with her legs stretched out before her.

"Beautiful day for a walk," he said, and turned to admire the views beyond the fence. She noticed how at ease he was with his backpack. She only wished she was with hers.

"Breathtaking, isn't it?" she said. He laughed at that, turning back toward her.

"Ha! You can say that again! Where are you from?" the American asked. "England?"

"Originally, yes. But I live in Australia now." She paused. "Melbourne. You?"

"You've come a long way," he said. She nodded. "I'm from New York. Well, not originally." He smiled, the authenticity and warmth of it took her by surprise. The smile was so genuine. "How far are you walking?"

"Today? Or overall? It's a bit of a crazy adventure isn't it?" she asked, popping a few more nuts into her mouth. He laughed again, his face lighting up. Another nut dropped to her lap. She looked down and stared at it.

"Are you going to Santiago?" he asked. She looked back up at him and nodded.

"Me too," he said. "That's the goal anyway."

"I just need to get to Orisson first. I don't know if it's exhaustion or exertion, but I am dragging today." She closed the bag to her trail mix.

"I bet. It's a long way to come for this walk," he said and took a long swig of his water.

"Yes. Plus, I'm a Slow Stroller," referencing a popular Facebook group, one of many her son encouraged her to join. "I'll get there eventually. I'm in no rush."

"Well, I'm straight off the train from Bayonne and I still have to get to Roncesvalles today, so I'll leave you to it."

"Wow. That's a long day. I wish you luck!" She said, grabbing water from the side pocket of her backpack.

"Thanks. Buen Camino!" he wished her, and with a wave, he continued walking.

"Buen Camino," she repeated, and watched him go.

She thought of her son, Simon. He'd be like this guy, she imagined. Fit, eager to keep going. Simon had the unlimited energy of a twenty-three-year-old. She thought then of her daughter, Cass. While Cass would have found France and Spain both fascinating and beautiful, she could not imagine her walking eight hundred kilometres. Aubrey sighed. This journey would be difficult if she kept thinking 'what if?'. But she would never have imagined she'd be doing this without either of her children. And yet, here she was. She stood, shook her head, working hard to keep the tears at bay. Time to push on.

When she reached the top of the switchbacks, she saw a sign displaying the mountain range, showing just how far she'd come. So far, so good, she thought and took a moment to congratulate herself. As she admired the views, she looked down at the trail she'd just followed. The incline had been challenging in parts, and she was pleased with herself that she'd taken her time and made it. But she was not done yet and she was already wanting to unload herself of her backpack for the day. She was tired of carrying it. Hell, she was ready to throw it over the damn mountain!

She turned back only to see the road continue ahead.

Bloody hell. How much further? This has to be the longest two kilo-metres in history, she thought. She hoisted the pack back on. It wasn't terribly heavy. She'd packed frugally but throughout the morning, she worried that she hadn't packed properly. What if she hadn't packed enough to keep warm if the weather turned? It had been chilly when she left this morning and she'd managed fine. She brought two sets of clothes so she could always wear it all if it came down to that. But what if she couldn't wash? Or if it rained and things didn't dry? There had been substantial rain over the last few weeks. That had been the tipping point that had prompted her to purchase the poncho. What if she experienced snow or sleet? Would her poncho hold up? It hadn't been cheap, and her pants were water resistant. At these insane worries, she laughed. Clearly, when she packed, she had not thought things through on the cold and wet-weather front. Oh well. She would have to be fine with what she had.

When Aubrey rounded the corner, she saw a restaurant with a large patio jutting out, overlooking the spectacular Pyrenees mountains. The place was packed with pilgrims, just like her. There were tables full of people enjoying lunch in the sunshine. This had to be Orisson, she thought. She checked her phone. It was a little after one in the afternoon and she knew of no other place until Roncesvalles. If it was, she'd made better time than she estimated.

As she approached the restaurant, she saw the guy from New York putting refilled bottles of water into his pack. He waved in recognition, then hitched his pack back up on to his shoulders, turned and continued onwards up the road. She silently wished him luck once more.

Aubrey walked inside to the very crowded, dimly lit restaurant, hoping to find out where she could check in. Pilgrims were everywhere. The bar to the right was busy with one girl pulling beers, and another writing passport information into a large ledger. Ah-ha! Check-in. She dropped her pack with a stack of others near the bar and pulled out her passport and credential, then laid her trekking poles against her pack. Joining the queue, she turned to look back into the restaurant.

"Crazy, isn't it?" A tall woman, with straight, shoulder-length grey hair, dressed head to toe in black, stood nearby at the bar. She smiled hesitantly over at Aubrey, her sea green eyes expressing her wonderment. She looked natural and chic. And, Aubrey noticed, she had a very distinct Australian accent. Aubrey smiled back.

"Yes! Are you Australian?"

"I am," the woman said, slightly more confident now, and nodded to the passport in Aubrey's hand. "Are you English?"

Her voice was soft and quiet against the intense noise in the bar. She leaned toward the bar and took a beer from the bartender, handing over five euros. She offered a quick "Merci" when given her change, then looked back at Aubrey.

"I'm originally from London, but I live in Australia now. Melbourne. You?" Aubrey asked.

"Really? Wow, small world! I'm from Tasmania," she said. "Did you just arrive?"

"Yes." Aubrey said as she inched her way forward in the queue, still with two more ahead of her to check in.

"I got here about an hour ago. They've been non-stop the whole time I've been here." The woman took a sip of her beer and sighed. Aubrey inched up one more place.

"I'm Georgina," the woman said.

"Aubrey," she replied.

"When you've checked in, come join me. I'm sitting outside on the patio with another woman I met about twenty minutes ago. She's from Australia too. I think she's regional. Somewhere north of Sydney?" She took another sip of her beer. "To be honest, I'm surprised there aren't more people sitting outside. I mean, the views are amazing." She pointed her thumb toward those huddled around tables inside with a look on her face that seemed to express the people sitting there were nuts. Aubrey laughed.

"I will definitely find you," she said, just as she edged to the front of the queue and the albergue hostess asked for her credential and passport.

"Bonjour!" said Aubrey, with a broad, goofy smile on her face, expressing both gratitude and relief that she had overcome the first hurdle.

3

SKETCHY KNEES, SKETCHY STORIES

ORISSON

AUBREY HEADED OUTSIDE into the sunshine, the sudden light just a little too bright. With her sunglasses somewhere deep in her bag, she shielded her eyes with her hands, while trying not to spill her beer or drop her tortilla.

"Merci," she said gratefully to the pilgrim holding the door open. She walked across the road to the large deck. She found Georgina sitting against the far railing, her back to the bar. Another woman sat across from her with her feet propped on a chair, icing a knee.

"Hello," Aubrey said, looking at Georgina.

"Hi Aubrey! Please, join us." Georgina scooted over to give Aubrey room, accidentally knocking the chair behind. She offered a quick 'sorry' and a smile for the intrusion.

"Sorry it took me so long. They had to show me to the dorm." Georgina introduced her to Pam, who gave Aubrey a wave. The woman looked like a sweet little granny, her glasses sitting precariously on the tip of her nose. Pam had short, blonde/brown choppy hair, which gave her the appearance of looking younger, but Aubrey estimated her to be in her mid-sixties. Maybe it was her glasses that aged her? Or the sadness in her eyes.

Pulling out the chair to sit, Aubrey pointed at the ice-packed knee, but Pam ignored her inquisitive look.

"Which room did they put you in?" asked Pam, her voice gruff, strong, and very Australian. She was definitely from the bush, Aubrey decided, just as Georgina had guessed.

"Up there, above the bar, the room with about twelve bunks," Aubrey said, pointing to the stairs between the buildings. "The room straight ahead. I think I got the last of the beds. The room was rather full already. Backpacks spread out everywhere."

"I was the first one in one of the downstairs rooms," Georgina said, pointing below the enormous patio area. "There's probably ten beds in it and one bathroom. That's going to be interesting. It's probably full now as well." She scooted her chair over to give Aubrey a little more wiggle room. "And I have no doubt there are backpack explosions there too. It will take some getting used to. I've done nothing like this before," said Georgina. Aubrey nodded.

"Which room are you in?" said Aubrey, looking over at Pam.

"Same room as you, I think. I'm at the end against the wall. Like Georgina, I was the first one in that room. I got here around eleven."

"Wow! What time did you leave?"

"Six-thirty. I'm an early bird but a slow walker."

"I usually am too, but I couldn't get it together this morning. I left at half past eight," Aubrey said. She noticed Georgina look at her watch.

"Before I forget, do you know where to do laundry?" she asked, looking at Pam and then at Georgina.

"There is a hand wash with a line up the back," said Pam. "But there's a washing service in Roncesvalles at the monastery tomorrow. I'm waiting for that."

"Good to know. Thank you," said Aubrey. Pam played with the ice pack on her knee.

"What happened to your knee? Are you okay?" Aubrey asked, taking a swig of her ice-cold beer, licking the foam from her top lip.

"I had my knee go out from under me when I was boarding my

plane to Biarritz. And now, it wants to give out whenever I add any actual weight to it. Climbing stairs is really tough. It's always been sketchy, but it's never gone out on me," Pam said. Aubrey looked over at the knee. Pam had wrapped her travel towel around the ice, but the water had seeped through to her black hiking pants. There was a large wet spot now where the ice pack had been.

"Sketchy?" said Aubrey. "That is an interesting description."

"Yeah. As in, my knee is shit. Done for," said Pam, and put the ice pack back on it, even though she'd just taken it away. "I mean, it's often swollen after a lengthy walk. But now, I'm anxious about making it all the way to Santiago." Aubrey could relate.

"Oh well. I'm here now. So, I guess I'll just take it one step at a time. See how I do," added Pam.

"That must have been scary, happening on your way here?" said Georgina.

"I'm thinking the Universe is trying to tell me something. Like, what the hell are you doing you stupid woman?!"

"Surely not," said Aubrey.

"With the ice pack and Nurofen, it should ease it a little, right?" Georgina asked. Aubrey looked around at the other pilgrims sitting on the patio.

"It doesn't seem you're the only one nursing some injury," Aubrey said. There were quite a few people treating blisters, some with ice on their ankles. You could smell the various forms of liniment when the wind picked up the scent. It hadn't been that hard of a day, she thought, but who knew where they had walked from. Many looked to have walked a lot further than Saint Jean Pied de Port.

"I met a girl today who had walked from Le Puy," Aubrey said, turning back to face Pam. "I saw her feet when I stopped at Hunto. I've never seen so many blisters. She had blisters on blisters. I think boots were the cause. She said she had taken a rest day in Saint Jean but, if you ask me, she'd need at least two or three to clear them altogether." She took another long draw on her beer.

"Shit, that would be painful. I hope I don't get blisters. The knee is bad enough to deal with! Although, I have to admit, I have a shitload of stuff in my backpack, in case I do," Pam said. She then laughed thunderously, a sound so booming coming from her small stature, the sound surprised Aubrey.

"For all I read online in the Facebook forums, I ignored everything that said, 'don't over pack'," Pam added, then reached for her water.

"Those online forums were great for information though. I learned a lot," said Georgina.

"I didn't read much of them at all," said Aubrey. "The forums got a little too opinionated for me. It was hard to navigate what information would apply."

Pam laughed again. "I think I was on every forum out there. My head is full of shit I learned. And I have notes galore on my phone. But I hear what you're saying, some people were dictators!"

"God yes. There were so many opinions. I didn't know what was right or misguided," said Georgina. "But I was mostly interested in the weather, and I looked for information from those ahead of us. I was having a bit of a panic attack yesterday," admitted Georgina, looking worried. "I couldn't decide which route to take because of the rain. Either this one or the valley route."

"The rain has been horrendous, that's for sure. But I think everyone is concerned about the weather," Pam said, as Georgina scooted her chair back a little, now the people behind had moved. Aubrey settled back into her chair, crossed one leg over the other. The sun was at her back, and she was enjoying the warmth from the sunshine.

"I read there was a man rescued from a river last week," said Pam. "It scared him so much he went home. It was that, or he was just sick of being wet. Nevertheless, with the combination, it would be enough to make anyone question what they were doing."

"Yes, I heard about that too," Georgina said. Aubrey could feel the immense amount of stress coming from the woman. "I think an enormous part of my anxiety has been reading about other pilgrim's experiences. Flooding is rampant and now trails are questionable."

"It is a worry," said Pam, taking the ice pack off her knee, and placing it on the table. "But we can only use common sense as we go."

"So, where are you from?" Aubrey asked Pam, thinking a change of subject might be an excellent strategy. Pam paused, taking in the change of subject.

"North of Sydney. You?" asked Pam. "You sound English. A bit of a posh accent there." She'd heard that before from Australians.

"Originally from London, but I've been living in Melbourne for thirty years. I'm thinking of moving though."

"Back to England?" asked Pam.

"No. Staying in Australia. I've lived in Australia far longer than I ever lived in England. I'm considering the Victorian highlands."

"That's a nice area," said Pam.

"Where north of Sydney? I have friends up that way," asked Aubrey.

"Hunter Valley, but I just moved north of Newcastle. Sometimes it's easier to just say Sydney."

"I get that," said Georgina. "I tell people I'm from Hobart, although I live an hour from there on the east coast."

"What do you do, when you're not walking in France?" asked Pam, her attention returning to Aubrey.

Aubrey hesitated. This is where her story got sticky. "I'm between jobs at the moment. That's part of why I'm here. To work out what's next. I just sold a dress shop in Melbourne." Better to keep it simple, she thought. "You?" Aubrey looked at Pam, then at Georgina.

Pam answered first, "I'm a retired teacher. Thirty-five years."

"Wow!" said Georgina.

"And you?" asked Pam, looking at Georgina.

"I own a café."

"Oh, that's lovely. On the east coast?" asked Aubrey.

"Yes. Orford."

"I spent a month driving a campervan around Tasmania late last year," said Aubrey. "Sadly, I don't remember Orford."

"Well, if you drove from Hobart and took the coastal route north, you would have gone through Orford." Aubrey thought it was likely she had stopped at Georgina's café.

The sun felt warm against her back, but at this altitude, the breeze was cool.

Aubrey looked around when she heard an increase in chairs scraping. The patio was clearing, with some re-hitching their backpacks to continue onwards to Roncesvalles, while others headed to the dorm areas to rest or do washing. Some pilgrims remained, sharing their stories with others, just as they were. Others sat with a beer at their side, writing in their journals. One couple sat opposite each other at a table, a bottle of white wine between them, saying nothing but enjoying the sunshine and the scenery. Aubrey appreciated their laid-back vibe.

Aubrey saw Georgina look at her watch again, right before she stood up from her chair.

"Do you ladies want another drink? I'm getting another beer. And, if I can, something to eat. What do you have, Aubrey? That looks good," said Georgina, looking down at Aubrey's already half eaten dish.

"It's called a Tortilla de Patatas. It's like a baked omelette. It's got some ham, potato and onion in it... It's delicious."

"Yum. I'm getting one. So? Another beer?" Georgina asked again.

"Yes, thanks. That would be great. Helps with the tired legs! Self-medication, I think they call it?" Aubrey said with a smile, reaching for her purse to pay for her beer.

"Pam?"

"Why the fuck not?" Aubrey laughed at the unexpected language coming from this grandmotherly figure. "Sure, I'll have one." She went to pull money out of her backpack.

"My shout." Georgina said, holding up her hand to stop any further movement toward payment. She leaned down and lowered her voice until it was barely a whisper.

"I'm just thankful for some conversation in English. It's been twenty-five years since I was in France." She stood upright, "And I'm grateful for the tip about washing. Thanks for that. Saves me time and, it gives me the opportunity to enjoy this view!" She sighed. "It's just so beautiful."

Aubrey looked back at the valley again and noticed how the clouds looked like cotton balls floating through the sky. She turned to say something to Georgina about it, but she had already walked across the road toward the bar by the time she turned around.

"You owned a dress shop, you said?" Pam asked. Bollocks. She was hoping to ask Pam a question. Her own story was one she was not sure of anymore.

"Yes. I've just sold it. So, what's your story?" she countered, but Pam had a look of utter confusion, then fear, cross her face. Aubrey guessed she wasn't used to answering questions about herself. "What grade did you teach?"

"Primary. First grade."

"Kids are cute at that age. When did you retire?" Aubrey asked, then drank the last of her now warm beer. She rummaged through her nylon bag, hanging on the back of her chair, to look for her Chapstick.

"End of last year," Pam said, as Aubrey applied her Chapstick. Pam repositioned herself in her chair, the chair scraping noisily along the patio floor, just as Georgina came back to the table. She balanced three beers in one hand and a slice of Tortilla de Patatas in the other. Pam looked relieved at Georgina's return.

"You look like a pro, handling all that," said Aubrey, taking one of the beers from the table.

"Thank goodness there was someone to open the door! Here you go," said Georgina, moving a beer in front of Pam.

"Cheers!" said Pam, holding her beer up in the centre of the table.

"To our first successful day on the Camino. We're doing it!" said Aubrey, clinking glasses with a smile on her face, then taking a long sip from her beer.

Half an hour later, they headed back to their dorms but made plans to meet for dinner. Georgina took the glasses inside with Aubrey's help, while Pam hobbled up to her dorm alone.

"She's a bit of an odd duck," said Georgina of Pam, once they reached the door, "but she's got a wicked sense of humour." Aubrey had to agree. There was something about Pam she could not quite put her finger on, but she sensed an angry vibe from her. Something was buried within Pam. But, like herself, she was not ready to open up on day one either. With the glasses returned, she waved to Georgina and headed up the stairs to her dorm.

When Aubrey entered the room, it was abuzz with noise and rustling, mixed with some accents she couldn't quite place. Dutch maybe? Some Irish in there somewhere. Aubrey expected the room to be quiet, too tired from the climb for joviality. Excitement seemed to rule instead. Everyone was chatting and sorting through backpacks, prepping for the following day. Pam included.

Aubrey rummaged through her pack, looking for her shower things. She looked over to see Pam surrounded by dry bags of various shapes and sizes. She looked focused as she pulled socks, a zippered jacket and wet gear from the sacks and meticulously hung them over her bed rail. Aubrey chuckled. She was nowhere near that organised, so Aubrey left her to it. With travel towel and nylon bag in hand, which now included her toiletries, she headed to the shower. Halfway there, she returned to grab the token for the shower she'd left on her pillow. Yes. Organised was not something she could claim to be anymore. More like scattered. Like her life.

4

A CHANGE OF LIFE, A CHANGE OF SCENERY AND A FRESH ADVENTURE

ORISSON

SHOWERED, Aubrey took some time to write in her journal. She looked down at her phone and saw it was just after six. Shit. She was late. She tucked her journal away and grabbed her nylon bag and ran downstairs.

When she walked into the heavily wooded room, it surprised her at how busy it was. The bar area to her right was jumping, with wait staff bustling, trying to get people's drink orders sorted and dinner prep finished.

Inside the restaurant, the bright yellow walls held a homey feel. Chatter and laughter filled the room. Aubrey scanned the room. The long tables were lined with pilgrims, many drinking wine or beer. Jackets hung on the back of almost every chair. Some faces looked intense, trying to understand the foreign accent being spoken to them from across the table. Some heads nodded in understanding but how anyone heard anything was indeed a mystery. The place was loud.

Aubrey finally saw Georgina. She was sitting about a third of the way from the end of a table, which spanned the length of the room. Her back was against the wall. She was nodding at something Pam said, who sat across the table from her. Georgina looked up and waved, pointing to the open seat to her left. Relieved, Aubrey headed that way. Given the crowd, she was happy to find the seat saved for her, even if it was wedged against the wall. She was a little more curvaceous than Georgina, so she resigned to the fact that she'd have to contort her body to squeeze in.

"Sorry I'm late. I got distracted with my journal. Then, just as I was leaving, I had to put on warmer clothes. It's freezing outside!" Aubrey said as she hitched up her long, multi-patterned skirt, exposing leggings underneath, to climb into the seat. "Thanks for saving a seat for me. Wow, it's so busy in here!"

"It was busy when I got here at five-thirty. When they started making up the tables for dinner, I grabbed three seats, just in case we couldn't get any together later. People swarmed around me!" Pam said, trying to keep her voice down, but it was hard with the volume level of the room.

"Thanks Pam. Do either of you know what's on the menu? I mean, I don't care, I would eat anything. But that Tortilla only went so far and I'm hungry," said Aubrey, placing her hands on her stomach, her rings pinging against the silver belt buckle she wore over her black merino shirt.

"I think we all are," smiled Pam. "I read online that it's a three-course meal. A very rustic dinner. Typical of the Basque region. Soup, I think. Maybe pork and some beans for the main course? And then dessert. Not sure what that is. Oh, and wine." She lifted her almost empty glass of red wine in toast and drained the rest.

"Thank goodness there's wine," said Aubrey. "My legs stiffened up after lying down a while. How's the knee?"

"Nothing more wine won't fix!" Pam said, laughing. Aubrey noticed how quickly Pam's face went from a curmudgeonly-looking scowl to absolute delight with a quick joke. Her piercing, cornflower-blue eyes sparkled, and her dimples ran deep.

"You have a beautiful smile Pam," said Aubrey.

"Oh." And the scowl returned.

"I'm sorry. I didn't mean to make you uncomfortable," she said and sat back in her chair. "It's an old habit from retail days." Questioning eyes looked at Aubrey from both Pam and Georgina. "I've been told I need to stop giving people compliments when I notice things that I like about them. It's not very English, I have been told."

"Oh, hell no! Never stop giving compliments. I mean, I'm not..." Pam hesitated. "Well, yes, I'm uncomfortable," she said and smiled this time. "But that's because I'm not used to people telling me things like that. So... thank you."

Pam jumped in her seat when a server reached past her to put more wine on the table, like the quick movement scared her. But Aubrey noticed Pam recover quickly.

"Ah, just in time. Nothing like wine to relax you!" Pam said, with a nervous smile. Then she grabbed the carafe and filled their glasses to three quarters, before passing it on to those around them.

"Don't know when that'll be coming around again, so had to make sure we had plenty!" said Pam, a cheeky grin replacing the nervous one.

"Cheers lovelies. To being uncomfortable!" said Aubrey. They laughed and clinked their glasses.

"Ooh, not bad!" said Georgina, after taking a sip. "Okay, so cheesy question time. What brought you to the Camino, Aubrey?"

"Oh, ah. Change of life, change of scenery, and a fresh adventure." Aubrey said and lifted the glass to take another long sip. The wine was pretty good.

"Sounds about right," said Georgina and turned to look at Pam, who was still drinking deeply from her own glass. "What about you Pam?"

"Oh, you know... Change of life, change of scenery, fresh adventure." Her laughter was crisp and bright.

"I think we're all in this for the same reason then," said Georgina.

"So, the shop you owned. Was it the style you're wearing? Boho, I think it's called?" Georgina asked.

Aubrey laughed. God, no. Her style was so different now than it had once been.

"No, it was a high-end shop. Designer labels," Aubrey responded.

"Wow, nice. You have a unique style. I like it." Georgina leaned in

26

closer, "although I'm not sure I could do a nose piercing. Did it hurt?" Aubrey smiled and touched her nose.

"No. Not at all. It was my fiftieth birthday present to myself." Aubrey turned in her chair, leaning closer to Georgina. The guy next to her was loud. "What about you, Georgina? How long have you had your café?"

"Oh, I don't know," she chuckled. "Forever. Something like twenty years?"

"Wow. That's a long time. I had my shop in Melbourne for a long time too. It felt like a lifetime. Maybe it just seemed like I lost a lifetime there?" She took another sip of her wine, trying to drown out the memory of that part of her life.

"My daughter is running the café at the moment. She's a master baker. So, it works out," said Georgina.

"How old is she?" asked Aubrey, trying to hide the sadness in her voice. Georgina pepped up at the mention of her daughter.

"She's twenty-three. A little younger from when I started the business. It may be time to hand it over to her. I don't know yet. I'm giving her a test run while I do this. Baby steps." This surprised Aubrey. Twenty-three was awfully young to be running a business on her own, but thinking back on her own history, Aubrey had been on her own for years by then.

Georgina's stomach grumbled loud enough to make her laugh, covering her stomach. She looked down at her watch.

"Same," laughed Aubrey, holding her hand against her rumbling stomach. "Maybe have a piece of bread?" She leaned over to pick up a piece of bread from the nearby basket, her silver bangles jiggling.

"Thanks but I already had three pieces before you got here."

"Pam. Do you have any kids?" Aubrey asked, trying to re-engage her in the conversation.

"No." And it was obvious from her tone that that was the end of that discussion with her.

They heard cheers go up across the room. Large metal bowls were being placed family style on to the tables. Aubrey watched as people peered in, trying to determine what was within.

"Where are you from?" came a strong Irish accent from across the table, the question posed to Pam. Aubrey sighed in relief. She found it more challenging to talk to Pam than Georgina. Pam seemed to close off conversations or ask questions herself, which made Aubrey equally uncomfortable.

The server placed the soup bowl in front of Georgina, who scooped broth into her bowl.

"Vegetable soup. I think." Georgina said, handing the spoon to Aubrey.

"It could be gruel at this point. I don't think I'd care." After they finished their soup, a bland dish of pork and beans was served. It needed more spice they agreed, but it was filling, and Aubrey suspected that was the point.

"God help the room tonight," joked Pam. "There will be a lot of 'toot-tooting' going on, I imagine." She added more beans to her plate. Before long, dessert was placed in front of them.

"May I have your attention please!" a booming French accent rose from the bar. All looked up, and the room quietened down. "Welcome to the Orisson Refuge." Cheers and clapping echoed around the room. The Frenchman explained it was a family-run business that welcomed Pilgrims from all over the world.

"We have a tradition here at Orisson. You are beginning your Camino journey or adding to your Way, if this is not your first pilgrimage. For many it is. We ask that you stand, say your name, where you are from and why you walk the Camino. Who would like to start?"

A hand went up from the end of their table and the pilgrim stood. Brave, thought Aubrey.

"Hello. My name is Melissa and I'm from New Hampshire in the United States. I'm here with my husband, Brad. This is our fourth Camino." Clapping ensued. "I am walking the Camino again because I see the Camino a little like childbirth. You forget the pain and agony of the experience after a while, and just remember the joy. Then, after some time, like childbirth, you want to repeat the experience. And so, here we are." And with that, she sat down, encouraging her husband to take his turn, with applause filling the room.

"I hate this stuff," whispered Georgina.

"Me too," said Pam, "but we don't have a lot of choice. So, suck it up Buttercup." She winked at them both.

"Did you know about this?" asked Aubrey, remembering Pam saying that she'd read a lot beforehand.

"I read about it, but I wasn't sure."

"And you didn't think to warn us?" asked Georgina, just as it was her turn. She smiled at the person next to her, anxiety written all over her face. "Here goes."

"Um. Hi. I'm Georgina. I'm from Tasmania, Australia." Aubrey saw a blush spread across Georgina's cheeks. "I am walking the Camino, my first one, because I read about the Camino on a blog a few years ago and I guess, well, it called to me." Then Georgina sat abruptly down, her cheeks now on fire.

"Your turn Aubrey," she whispered, relief written all over her face. Aubrey stood, her invisible mask of confidence firmly in place.

"Hello. I'm Aubrey. I'm from England but have lived in Australia for thirty years. I'm walking the Camino for a change of life, a change of scenery, and a fresh adventure. What else? Oh, yes. It's my first Camino and I am hoping to walk to Santiago, without dying first, or breaking something in the meantime." To laughter and applause, and a few agreeable nods, she sat down. She could talk about fashion and product all day, but it had been years since she'd been in the spotlight like this. She wasn't comfortable with this kind of attention. Especially lately.

Eventually, it came around to the other side of the table. Pam's turn.

"Your turn, Buttercup. We did it, so can you," joked Aubrey. She and Georgina raised their glass to her.

Pam stood and displayed what Aubrey saw as Pam's own mask. She faced the room.

"Hello. I'm Pam. Also, from Australia. This is my first Camino. I've just retired and thought a long wander would be a suitable way to kick it off." And with that, she abruptly sat.

"Well that was telling. Not." Aubrey whispered to Georgina, watching as Pam took a huge gulp from her wine.

"Fuck," said Pam. "Not doing that shit again." Aubrey laughed, still taken aback at the language that came from this woman's mouth.

"Oh my, Pam. You swear like a sailor!" said Aubrey.

"Well, you try being around first graders for thirty-five years and see what comes out of your mouth."

"Great point!" Aubrey said, laughing. "Don't hold back on our account!"

"I don't hold back anymore, on anyone's account. I learned that the hard way."

5

UP TO MY KNEES IN ADVENTURE

ORRISON TO RONCESVALLES

Aubrey lay awake with her anxiety bubbling. The cacophony of snoring woke her from a deep sleep. She thought over the immense amount of rain and sleet reported over the last two weeks on the Camino. The Pilgrim office in Saint Jean Pied de Port reported that the Orisson owner 'knew his mountain' and he would shuttle people to the Valcarlos route, the valley route, if he needed to. She had asked about the weather when she'd checked in yesterday but was told, with a shrug and a smile, that everything seemed okay. What kind of answer was that? How were they to go on with that kind of information? So, now, here she was, wide awake at god-thirty, and wondering how this day would pan out. Georgina's anxiety yesterday had not helped.

Aubrey was eager to get walking but knew it would be stupid to leave in the dark. Especially going up over a mountain range, when she had little actual hiking experience. Besides, it was too bloody cold. She snuggled down under her blanket, thankful for the warmth and comfort.

The surrounding noise, like a symphony of snorers who'd gone rogue without their conductor, was anything but comforting. And someone desperately needed a CPaP machine. Their breathing was frightening to listen to. She tried, but she couldn't pinpoint which pilgrim it was coming from.

Then, someone let out a sound-barrier smashing fart, so strong, her bed rumbled. She couldn't help but giggle. It was the loudest fart she had ever heard. Was it the guy next to her on the top bunk? Or the woman in the bunk below him? Then the odour hit her. Jesus, Mary and Joseph! It was offensive! She pulled her blanket up again and covered her mouth, trying not to let the nausea take over. Even the guy sleeping in the bed above her groaned, then rolled over.

Aubrey grabbed her phone from under her pillowcase and hit the button to check the time. It showed just after three. Shit. It was still hours until the sun was up and even longer until breakfast. This was one day she couldn't skip out on food.

Fine, she'd try to go back to sleep, remembering she had earplugs in her toiletry bag under the bed. As quietly as she could, she grabbed the earplug case, popped it open and wiggled the earplugs into her ears, hoping to God they worked!

SHE SENSED THE ROOM WAKING BEFORE SHE OPENED HER EYES. SHE rolled over to face the room, slowly opened one eye, only to slam it shut again. A broad, older man crawled down the stairs of the bunk bed across from her. A vision of sagging, white cotton briefs was not the way anyone wished to be greeted in the morning. She waited until he'd walked toward the bathroom before she opened her eyes again. She checked her phone. Five minutes to seven. Brilliant! Time to go.

She saw the surrounding space was clear. She stealthily put her bra on, then sat up and wriggled into her pants. Standing, she took a quick peek at the bunk above her, but the bed was empty. Huh. She hadn't felt the bed move when the guy got down, let alone hear him grab his stuff. The earplugs had worked. That, or she was more tired than she thought. She tugged her down blanket back into its case and wrestled it back into the bottom section of her backpack. Then, grabbing her valuables and toiletry kit, she secured them all into her nylon bag, before heading to the bathroom.

It was just after seven-fifteen when she arrived at the refuge's restaurant. The air was crisp, fog lay thick in the valley below, and a layer of ice covered everything. She had fifteen minutes to eat breakfast before they closed the kitchen. She dropped her backpack with the mass of others, leaned her trekking poles against the pack and walked inside. Pam was with Georgina, already seated at one of the long tables.

"Good Morning!" she said with enthusiasm. Apparently, too much enthusiasm for Pam, who gave her a quick wave, her other hand propping her head up.

"Did you see how beautiful it is out there?" said Georgina, clearly more of a morning person. Aubrey nodded. "Wish I had my actual camera. I must have spent a half hour taking photos."

"Hmm. I should get some shots myself, but I need coffee first," said Aubrey.

"The coffee is not great. I feel I have to warn you," said Georgina, grimacing as she took a sip from her…. wait, was that a bowl? She watched as Georgina took a sip. Yup. She was drinking her coffee, not from a cup, but from a bowl.

"But" Georgina sighed, "it's caffeine."

"Over by the bar," mumbled Pam, but not moving from her rested position.

"Thanks. I'll be right back." She headed over to the bar but could not find where they'd placed the coffee.

"Café?" The voice boomed from behind her. She jumped a mile high.

"Shit!" she screamed, suddenly embarrassed. "Sorry. You scared me. My language. I'm very sorry," she said, her hand on her heart. The older gentleman with the baritone smiled at her.

"No problem," he said, in a heavy French accent. "Sorry to have frightened you. Are you looking for café? Ah, coffee?"

"I am," she said, returning the smile.

"It is here," he said, and pointed at the area behind her. "They also can do a hot chocolate if you prefer. Ask at the bar."

"Oh, lovely. Thank you." Embarrassed, she grabbed a coffee in her own bowl, and returned to the table.

She sat next to Pam and Aubrey sampled the strong-smelling coffee. It kicked back.

"Wow! This is strong enough to stand on its own two legs," she said.

"It is strong, I'll give it that," said Georgina, laughing at Aubrey's reaction. She noticed Georgina grimace again as she took tentative sips. "It's too bitter."

"Well, it'll get me started," Aubrey said, reaching for some bread from the basket in the middle of the table.

"I was just telling Pam an interesting story," said Georgina.

"Oh?" asked Aubrey, breaking the lengthy piece of bread in half.

"I heard about it in the dorm this morning. About that guy over there." Georgina nodded her head toward a guy sitting alone at the end of the table on the other side of the room. "Apparently, he got so drunk last night that he lost his day pack with all their valuables. Passport, credit cards, credential. Even his camera and an iPad."

"Oh wow," said Aubrey. Georgina had Pam's sleepy attention now. It also looked like her coffee was finally kicking in.

"His wife told him this morning that she would keep walking. He had to stay behind and find the daypack. Now he's in the doghouse. That's what she has told everyone. Poor man. That's the wife over there at the end of our table. The one shooting daggers at him."

Aubrey took another sip of her coffee, following the story with her eyes.

"Oops. How'd he lose the backpack?" asked Pam, grabbing a piece of bread, while Aubrey started slaying jam over the top of hers.

"That's the funny part. Well, okay, probably the sad part. He was so drunk he rolled down part of the mountain. The server from last night rescued him. She heard a voice when she walked to her car late last night. She had her flashlight and shone it in that direction and saw him splayed out. Seems like this isn't the first time it's happened." Georgina chuckled and grabbed another piece of bread from the basket and scooped out some jam onto the bread. "The server returned inside, got the kitchen hand, and they hauled him back to his dorm room. When the wife got up to go to the toilet in the middle of the night, she saw her husband laid out in the corridor. So, she just left him there. She didn't know until this morning that the backpack was missing. Not until she asked him where it was."

"Shit," said Pam. "I hope he finds the pack. But she won't get far either. She needs her documents."

"No, she won't," Georgina said, before taking an enormous bite.

"So, just to warn you both, I'm a slow walker. You girls are younger than me, so if you need to go ahead, go for it. I don't want to slow you down," said Pam, taking her juice glass and draining it.

"I'm a slow walker too. Age has nothing to do with it. How old are you Pam, if you don't mind me asking?" asked Aubrey.

"Don't mind at all. I'm fifty-eight."

"I didn't think you looked retirement age," said Aubrey.

"I retired early. I loved teaching, loved my kids... well, most of them. But I was ready for a fresh start," said Pam and took another sip of her coffee.

"I'm forty-nine and I'm slow too," Georgina said and looked over at Aubrey. "What about you, Aubrey? You said you got your nose piercing at fifty, so that makes you..." said Georgina.

"Fifty," she said with her mouth full, breaking the rules of etiquette from her childhood.

"Are you okay to walk together then?" Pam asked. Georgina nodded, as did Aubrey. "Will be good to walk this long stretch together. Seventeen kilometres is a long way to Roncesvalles, with no services. And, you know, this is the part where people tend to die," Pam said and bit into her bread.

"Yeah, I read that too," said Georgina solemnly then perking back up again. "I just want to brush my teeth before we go. I won't be more than a few minutes. Oh! And I still need to pick up the sandwich I ordered last night." She finished her coffee, but not before shaking her head one last time. "Ugh. I'm done here."

"I forgot about the sandwiches," said Aubrey, trying not to fixate on the death part. "Thanks for the reminder. That would have been terrible had I left mine behind."

"I'll grab your sandwich for you if you like," Georgina said. "Still looks awfully crowded up there at the bar."

"That's brilliant, thanks! I won't be long."

"More time to take photos. For that, I'm happy to wait," said Georgina, and stood from the table.

WITH HER JACKET ZIPPED, BEANIE AND GLOVES ON, BACKPACK LOADED, and water bladder filled, Aubrey was ready to go. Georgina was on the iced-over patio, to take some last shots of the fog in the valley.

"I'm a bit worried I'll be too slow for you," said Pam as she was loading the last of her backpack. "I am the definition of a Slow Stroller," she said, pointing to a patch on her backpack of a turtle, "but I'm okay with that." It made Aubrey smile.

"I'm perfectly happy to go slow and take all of this in," Aubrey said, looking beyond the patio at the shadowed mountain range, fog filling its crevices. The sun was barely peeking from above the ridge. She saw Georgina turn then, being careful on the ice-covered patio, and return to them.

"Sorry to keep you waiting," Georgina said. She looked at her watch. "Seven-forty. Not bad."

With packs on and trekking poles adjusted, Pam did a double tap of her trekking poles, and with a wave goodbye to Orisson, they began following the yellow arrows, showing the way toward Roncesvalles.

"I just find this all so…" said Pam, after a few minutes of the three of them walking in silence. "I just can't catch my breath."

"From the views, or from the cold?" asked Aubrey, with genuine concern in her voice.

"Oh, from the views. Although it's bloody cold. I have mornings like this where I live, but we don't have these views, that's for sure," said Pam.

"It's stunning, isn't it?" said Georgina. "I mean, these mountains! They are spectacular. I'm just glad to have layered up! Suddenly I'm not as worried about packing so much crap."

"Oh, you and me both," said Pam. "I was in pain walking yesterday with my backpack. I have way too much shit in this thing, but I figure I will need it at some stage. I layered up this morning too, but I'm hoping it warms up some." Aubrey stayed quiet. She noticed their packs were considerably larger than hers.

Suddenly Georgina slipped, saving herself with her poles.

"Oh! Be careful!" said Aubrey.

"Ice. Black ice, by the looks of it," said Pam.

Georgina started walking again. "Now I'm even more thankful I bought these trekking poles in Saint Jean."

"Slow and steady. We'll get there," said Pam. They halted conversation while they concentrated on their steps. Footprints were visible on the road from pilgrims who'd started before them. Heavy frost covered everything. Before long, they had crested the hill, and the sun was shining, thawing out the road. On the other side of the mountain, large patches of snow covered the mountaintop, but they would melt by the end of the day.

"So where in the Hunter Valley did you live?" Georgina asked Pam when they'd found their stride again.

"A place called Broke, which is ironic because originally the place was that, for a long time. But now it's a popular wine region. There's also a lot of coal mining in the area. So, really, far from being broke."

"How long did you live there?" asked Aubrey.

"All my life," Pam said and pulled off her gloves and stuck them in her pocket, jostling her trekking poles as she did. "Until last year."

"Wow," said Aubrey, "I can't imagine living in one place." They all slowed down a bit to allow Pam to readjust herself.

"Yeah. I mean, I moved away to Armidale for Uni, but then went back to the Hunter and started teaching."

"Are you married?" asked Georgina.

"No," said Pam, but the way she said it, the abruptness of her tone, made Aubrey wonder if there was more to the story.

"And you, Aubrey?" Georgina asked, but now with a more cautious tone in her voice.

"Was. Old news," Aubrey said, and saw Pam smile at her response. "What about you Georgina?"

"Still am. Still old news." They all chuckled. "It's complicated," Georgina said, sounding sad.

"And Aubrey, you said you lived in Melbourne, but not anymore?" asked Pam. Aubrey wasn't sure how much she wanted to say about her life. It was, like Georgina's answer, complicated. But she had to determine what her answer was, and fast.

"Well, like Georgina said, it's complicated. For the last year, I've been travelling a bit, living in a campervan, trying to find a new place to live. I'm needing a change, although I would like to stay in Victoria. The Victorian Highlands area is at the top of the list right now. It seems like it's calling to me. But I don't know yet."

"I'd love to do something like that. Travelling around in a campervan, I mean," said Georgina wistfully.

"Yes, it's been a lot of fun. I've not done anything like that before. And, after the last few years, I needed to do something different. Time to get out of my head," said Aubrey, afraid to say anything more.

"I hear that," said Pam. "I did some travelling after I left Broke. Went to America and then England. You know, places I'd always dreamed of seeing. It was eye opening, that's for sure. And now, France and Spain. The language thing is a challenge for me, but it's fun to see how other people live." Her enthusiasm was bubbling. It seemed her coffee had kicked in.

A few kilometres on, they reached a crest and saw the Vierge d'Orisson, or the Virgin of Orisson, off in the near distance. The vistas of the valley below were magnificent. The fog in the valley, just beginning to dissipate from the sunshine, provided an ethereal glow to the scene.

"Look at these views!" exclaimed Georgina. "I'm sorry. I gush, but I just can't believe how beautiful it is here. I am going to walk over to the statue and take some photos. You guys can continue on without me if you aren't ready to stop yet." The woman was very polite, Aubrey thought.

"No. I'm good to stop," said Pam. "There looks to be a bunch of rocks over there to sit on. My knee is nudging me. Suddenly my knees are feeling like hinges that have gone rusty. I need to grab some Nurofen from my pack and have some water." She headed straight for the rocks, removing her pack as soon as she reached them. Pam pulled out a small plastic bag from the top of her pack. It held a tissue pack, a wipe for her glasses, some Nurofen, a jar of Vaseline and Band-Aids. A quick medical kit, Aubrey surmised.

Aubrey decided to stick with them. She followed Pam and rested her trekking poles on the rock to the side and slid her pack down to the ground. She stretched out her back, raising her arms up. Taking a seat near Pam, they sat in silence, enjoying the rest stop as much as the surrounding scenery. Two Asian pilgrims joined them. After a couple of quick snaps of the Virgin of Orisson, they wished them a Buen Camino and left, just as Georgina returned to them with a smile plastered on her face.

"Incredible, isn't it?" Georgina said. Her voice was breathless. She turned around and opened her arms, her face directed toward the sky, and took a deep breath in. Upon exhaling, she turned again and smiled. "I hope you don't mind waiting a bit longer. My ankle has just started niggling at me, but the photos were too pressing." She took a seat next to Pam and pulled out her water and Nurofen.

"Ankle? Are you alright?" Aubrey asked.

"Yeah, I'm okay. I sprained my ankle at home a few weeks ago. It's getting better. I've got it strapped up and slathered with Tiger Balm. It's just not used to this excessive walking while carrying a ten-kilogram backpack."

"Ten kilos?" gasped Aubrey. It surprised her that Georgina was carrying such a heavy pack.

"Mine's that heavy too," said Pam. "Or thereabouts. Maybe eleven. It's still too heavy."

"Wow," said Aubrey. Georgina and Pam both stared at her. And here she was worrying at home that hers would be too heavy.

"How heavy is yours?" Georgina asked Aubrey, taking a drink of her water.

"Seven."

"What?! How!?" Georgina exclaimed, her voice going up a few octaves, looking at Aubrey with dismay. Aubrey shrugged.

"Fuck. Clearly then, I need to do something about the weight in my bloody pack," grumbled Pam. "I was worried about being cold. And snow. And the rain. So, I packed an extra pair of pants, a fleece... too much."

"I hear that," said Georgina. As they rested, a group of twenty-something hikers practically ran past them.

"Time to move. I'm stiffening up," said Pam, who stood and grabbed her backpack. Georgina followed suit. Aubrey stood and stifled a groan. Yeah, she was stiffening up too. Sitting on cold rocks hadn't helped.

Aubrey pulled some dried fruit from her pack before hoisting it on. They began walking, and she offered some of the mix to Pam and Georgina. Another group of young hikers passed them at a much faster pace than Aubrey could ever imagine going.

"What is it with these kids? I feel a hundred years old," said Pam.

"Me too," said Georgina, then stopped suddenly in her tracks. "Hey. Do you hear that?"

Georgina turned and looked at the surrounding mountains. "There." Aubrey looked in the direction Georgina was pointing. Stocky, chocolate-coloured horses stood about a hundred meters away. Bells hung around their neck. Their winter coats, thick and long, glistened in the sunlight.

"Oh! Aren't they beautiful?" said Pam. "I read horses were here. Didn't think I'd see them, though. I read the shepherds place the bells around their necks so they can find them. The horses can run free in the Pyrenees. They used to be endangered, but not anymore."

"It's such a soothing sound, don't you think?" Aubrey closed her eyes and listened to the bells as the horses munched away at the grass. She opened her eyes again just as Georgina reached for her phone to take photos. Aubrey was happy to watch the horses chuff their way through the grass while Georgina snapped away. The horses seemed oblivious to the pilgrims trudging up the hill.

"Sounds like you've read a lot about the Camino," said Aubrey to Pam, when they continued up the mountain.

"Yeah, I read a bunch of memoirs. Followed a few blogs. Some things stuck, plenty didn't. I wrote a lot of things down so I would have it when I got here. Should have listened more to the 'don't pack too much' comments though. Sounds like you read the right thread." Pam said, nodding to Aubrey.

"You'll laugh at what I did pack. Not the practical stuff. I packed accessories," Aubrey said as she jingled her hands holding her trekking poles. She had multiple silver bracelets on her right wrist and three leather bands on her left. "Once in fashion, it's hard to let that go. I think I left out half of what I will need."

"Maybe. Maybe not," said Georgina, "I'm used to the cold, but not the heat and I didn't know how hot it would get, especially on the plains part. The Meseta, I think it's called. Plus, I packed for wet weather and blisters. Still, I don't know."

"Oh, but I bought a poncho," joked Aubrey.

"Good, you might need it at some point!" said Georgina, smiling over at Aubrey as they continued up the paved road. Aubrey moved to the side where there was a softer surface on the grassy verge.

"How did you guys go buying for this adventure? I had such a hard time finding the right gear," said Georgina. "You'd think with Tasmania being an outdoor Mecca, that there'd be a lot of options for women. It's not so much a problem if you are like these young, skinny things, bounding up around us, but I can't wear anything that skin-tight!"

"I had the same issue," said Pam. "I am bigger and shorter than you both. My options were very limited. Newcastle's options were horrendous. I had to take a special trip down to Sydney. Even then I look like an old hessian bag thrown together."

"Oh Pam, no you don't," said Georgina. "I do know what you mean though. I flew to Melbourne. Even then, I had to buy some stuff online. I see you, Aubrey, and believe you have it right."

"What? Me?" she said, shocked at the comment. Hiking gear was not her fashion choice by any stretch!

"Yeah. The sandals you were wearing after your shower last night. You said you can use them in the shower and around town?" asked Georgina. Aubrey nodded. "Well, I packed both sandals and rubber thongs, flip-flops, for the shower. And I still don't know if I should have."

"Me too! Wish I'd known about the ones you brought!" said Pam.

"And so nice! I am a complete fashion disaster next to you, especially last night." added Georgina. Aubrey groaned. "But even today, you look so well put together."

"You don't look like a fashion disaster Georgina. You're rather chic in all your black and your gorgeous silver hair," said Aubrey. She hated how these women saw themselves. The Camino was far from a fashion runway for anyone, but these two women looked comfortable and wore what was practical.

"Unlike me," said Pam, before Aubrey could compliment her. "I'm lumpier than a bag of spring potatoes. I'm the short, fat one out of the three of us." Aubrey saw Georgina shake her head, reflecting her own opinion.

"I would not call you, or anyone, fat," Aubrey said. "It's one thing I hate about the fashion industry. The whole Yummy Mummy ideal is so unrealistic."

"The what?" asked Pam, genuine confusion etched on her face.

"You've not heard of that before? Yummy Mummies?" Aubrey asked. Pam shook her head. Aubrey pointed at the gaggle walking past them. They were in lycra from head to toe, little backpacks attached to the back of their skinny bodies.

"That is a Yummy Mummy," said Aubrey, "Or at least, mothers who look like that. The kind who shops in those kinds of outfits."

"Yeah, I'm so far from that," said Pam. "I've never been particularly into fashion and it wasn't something I considered when I was packing either. I wouldn't stand up to the fashion stakes anyway. Look at you both. You're both tall and, yes, what some would call curvaceous, but my five-foot, three-inch frame just doesn't stand up. I'm the little old Nana next to you two."

"I wasn't considering fashion when I packed either," said Georgina, "I only brought black because it hides the dirt!"

"Well, I don't have many clothes for this walk," Aubrey said. "In fact, you've seen my entire wardrobe already." Today, Aubrey's auburn hair was contained in a braid under her beanie. She wore the same green hiking pants she'd worn the day before, held up by a thick belt that sported a chunky silver buckle. Under her black zip up hoodie was a black, long sleeve merino shirt. She wasn't used to wearing hiking pants but knew her days of lycra were long gone.

They plodded further up, leveraging their poles as the wind howled around them, silent in their tromping for a while. They stopped more than once to admire the views. Valleys below still had morning mist hovering, and the sky was now a brilliant blue. The intensity of the sun gave Aubrey a headache, so she dug into the top of her pack for her sunglasses. The relief was instant, but she'd have to dig her hat out eventually to protect her skin as well.

The Pyrenees mountains were spectacular, but when the track left the road, they left the views of France behind. They followed a snow-lined trail through a dense forest area. Before long, they were at the Fontaine de Roland refilling their water. They each took photos at the border, laughing at how it was nothing but a cattle grid. Most pilgrims simply walked over it; unaware they were stepping from France into Spain.

"It's a little slippery in this section. Watch your step," said Aubrey as she led the threesome into another forested area. There was snow on the sides of the trail, and a thick layer of leaves which deceptively covered the thick mud beneath. Clouds had rolled in and the surrounding mist gave the forest area a mystical aura.

Ahead, they saw Bomberos, or Spanish firemen, clearing snow from the path. Pam stopped to watch, and before long, Georgina was taking photos. The men were impressive. They were like firemen on steroids, as they flung their hoes into the compacted ice. They tossed solid blocks aside as if they weighed nothing. They watched for some minutes as the two men cleared the path, heaving the chunks of snow and ice over the fence and down the mountain. It was Georgina that got them going again. Good thing too, Pam admitted, she could have watched them all day.

About four hours into their day's walk, Pam announced she was ready to find a spot to eat their lunch. They found a lovely patch of dry rock under some trees and pulled out their baguettes from Orisson, thankful they had remembered to pick them up. They were back on the trail after a short time. They still had some distance to go.

"THIS MUD IS SQUIDGY," SAID PAM, USING HER POLES TO KEEP HER balance as they traipsed through another muddy section. Aubrey heard Georgina laugh just ahead of her.

"That's a funny way to describe it. But, yes, it is," said Aubrey.

Just after they passed the emergency hut, Aubrey sensed someone behind her, so she moved to the side to let them pass. She called out 'hiker coming' to Georgina and Pam ahead of her. Snow had made the trail path narrow. Pam, just in front of her, stepped into a section cleared of snow.

"Buen Camino," the middle-aged pilgrim mumbled. He was dressed in a large hoodie, hood up, his hands in his pockets and a daypack hanging off his slumped shoulders. He moved past them quickly. After some distance, Georgina turned and offered a huge grin.

"That was the husband who lost his backpack at Orisson," she whispered, a smirk on her face. "Guess he found it."

When they reached the apex, Aubrey could not see the ground at all. The downward slope was covered in snow. Pam's face reflected her own hesitation. How the hell were they supposed to navigate this? Some keen beans were coming up behind them, just plunging in. There was a trail of sorts on the right side of the hill and on the left side, a trail of mud.

"What are you thinking?" Aubrey asked Georgina. Georgina laughed as she surveyed the area.

"Honestly? What the hell was I thinking, believing I could do this walk?!" Georgina said. Pam looked pensive.

"Well, we're here. We can do this. Do you want snow or mud?" Pam asked. They watched a couple trudge through the knee-deep snow. Aubrey watched a woman, wearing wet weather pants, slide down on her bottom in the mud to the left. "I vote snow. It isn't a lot," said Pam with conviction. Georgina looked uncertain.

"Agreed. We need to just take it slow." Aubrey led the way down the snow-covered hill, her poles sinking into the white powder, bringing each leg up high, before plunging them back into the snow. Her feet planted on to what seemed like solid ground until it wasn't. She squealed as she slipped.

"Shit! Are you okay?" asked Pam, who stopped behind her. Aubrey turned around with care, a massive smile plastered on her face.

"Oh yes. Just up to my knees in adventure!" she beamed, then turned again and continued. "But watch your footing through here."

They made their way down the slope slowly, their legs soaked up to their knees. But they had managed it. When they reached the bottom, Pam laughed heartily, her arms raised in the air, as she looked back at the trail in triumph.

"That was fucking nuts," Pam declared.

"This is even crazier. Look!" exclaimed Georgina. They were standing in front of the sign the pilgrim office had warned Aubrey about. The office insisted she take the road, the easier route that winds gradually down the mountain. The other option, the more popular route it seemed today, was the more direct route. Straight down. Aubrey saw thick snow covering the road. She couldn't even see where the verge began. Those behind them weren't hesitating in going straight down the mountain.

"We could slide down the road, possibly slip on ice under that snow. Or we go like snails down the mountain. We made it through that," said Aubrey as she pointed back at the knee-deep snow. "I think if we're careful we can get down the mountain. We just need to take our time." Georgina looked at her watch.

"Sure. Why not," Pam said and plunged ahead. Aubrey and Georgina laughed behind her, then followed. Using her trekking poles to keep her balance, Aubrey navigated the rocks methodically. A young group of men ran past them, bouncing themselves off the rocks. Pam stopped in her tracks, shaking her head. She turned to Aubrey and Georgina behind her and said, "There's just no fucking way I would do that."

At the base of the steepest descent, they followed the switchbacks down, finally getting to a flat section. Pam stopped.

"Are you okay?" asked Georgina. Aubrey's own knees were screaming, so she knew Pam's had to be. Time to rest, she thought, as she saw Georgina look at her watch again. They were racing against the clock, but the sun wasn't close to setting yet, so she knew they had enough time. Pam was looking around.

"Yes. I'm fine. My knees feel like they're stuffed with cotton wool, about to burst into flames at any moment, but they're keeping up." Pam continued looking around a bit more desperate. She looked at them both, hesitant to speak before urgency won out.

"But I need to pee. I can't wait anymore. I'm sorry, but I'm going behind that tree," she said, pointing ahead. "Will you guys watch out while I go?"

"Of course," said Aubrey. "And I'm next. I have to go too!" Pam dropped her pack, leaned her poles against a tree, pulled a plastic bag containing toilet paper from the top pocket of her backpack, and ducked behind a tree.

Aubrey headed off behind a nearby tree when Pam returned. After making sure the tree hid her, she pulled her pants down and sighed in relief. She hadn't realised just how much she needed to go until that very moment. Just as she was pulling her pants back up, a millennial hiked past, right in front of her, but he didn't seem to see Aubrey at all. She quickly picked up her soiled tissue with her Ziploc bag and re-zipped it.

"Did you see that guy? Where in hell did he come from?" asked Aubrey, as she came out from behind the tree. Pam and Georgina were standing next to the backpacks, shocked, shaking their heads.

"I'm so sorry. He was past us before we even saw him. I think he took a shortcut." Georgina said, absolute horror written all over her face.

Pam started laughing as Aubrey popped the Ziplock bag into her side pocket to dispose of later.

"Oh, don't worry about it. I don't think he saw anything. And if he did, oh well. I'm just glad I finished peeing first. I think he would have been more embarrassed than me!" she said. Pam's laughter got louder, and she was soon laughing too. Georgina looked at them both, gobsmacked. Then she giggled.

"Don't make me laugh," said Georgina. "I'll wet myself. I'm off to the bush. Wish me luck and hopefully, no perverts!" Pam doubled over with unbridled amusement. Georgina dashed behind a different tree.

They were still laughing about Aubrey's encounter when they continued on, prompting a conversation about the crazy gadgets they'd read about online, including the Shewee.

. . .

"THERE IT IS!" PAM DECLARED AND DID A LITTLE JIG, WHICH MADE AUBREY chuckle. They had finally arrived in Roncesvalles. Aubrey felt relief. They had walked over the Pyrenees! She also felt proud of herself as she looked up at the massively imposing stone monastery before her. It was grander than she had imagined. Georgina checked her watch.

"What time is it?" Aubrey asked, still in awe as she gazed high at the stonework.

"It's almost four thirty," said Georgina, exhaustion running through her voice. "Oh my god, I am so tired!"

"Me too! I just want to sit down somewhere. Let's find the check in," Pam said. Aubrey walked the path behind them. She looked across to the grassy area and saw people lying about, soaking up the sunshine. She smiled.

When they reached the worn steps to the entrance door, Pam stopped after the first step. "Shit! My knees are screaming." She gave Aubrey a pained look.

"Shall I push you from behind?" joked Aubrey.

"Fuck, yes. Wouldn't hurt!" said Pam. She continued working her way up the stairs, using her poles as leverage. A sailor's ears would burn if he could have heard the expletives Pam gushed as she made her way to the top of the stairs, but she eventually got there.

Thirty minutes later, they checked in and climbed the flight of stairs up to the dorm area, albeit at a snail's pace. When she saw the stairs continued up, she sighed in relief, grateful their beds were on the first floor. They were assigned a bed number and found the bunk beds in pods of four, all segregated into the massive cavern of a room. Aubrey was assigned the pod next to Pam and Georgina. In her pod, sleeping bags were on three of the beds. Still, she scored the lower bunk she requested when booking. Georgina had forgotten to ask and was given a top bunk. She didn't care, she said, she was just happy for a bed.

It was all rather efficient. The dorm provided lockers at the back of the pod behind the bedheads. Outlets were available nearby to charge their devices. Before she could pull anything from her pack, Pam was in her pod, inspecting her bed, instructing how to look for bed bugs.

"Hadn't even thought to check," Aubrey admitted, watching Pam as she lifted the mattress, scrutinizing it. If she was honest, she was too damn exhausted to worry about it. She already knew how to inspect for the ferocious little beasts, but she was too damn tired to say anything to Pam. So she let her continue her mission, thankful all the same that Pam was looking out for her.

A few minutes later, loaded with her toiletries, towel and change of clothes, she headed for the showers. Pam, chatting with Georgina as they sorted through their packs for their buried clothes, stopped her as she went past.

"You remembered not to buy a dinner ticket at check-in. Right?" Pam asked. Aubrey nodded. Pam continued, lowering her voice, "Apparently the restaurants who do the pilgrim meals for the monastery are not too great. It's what the forums said, anyway."

"I'm happy to go anywhere where there is alcohol and food right now," said Aubrey, with a chuckle.

"I hear that!" laughed Pam. "We'll hit the hotel restaurant, if you're okay with that?" Pam looked to Aubrey with the question, then over to Georgina. They both nodded. "I read it's good. And there's a bar there so we can have a beer or wine first."

"Sounds good to me," said Georgina, now grabbing her towel. Aubrey nodded and stepped back from the pod.

"Enjoy the shower. We're not far behind you," Georgina said, looking ready but Pam had yet to get anything out of her pack. Aubrey headed to the bathrooms, pleased to see there were multiple stalls and no lines.

After a soul-rejuvenating hot shower, she stood at the line of mirrors. She wore her multi-coloured boho skirt with black leggings underneath, black t-shirt, and her silver-buckled belt hanging around her waist. She braided her long, auburn hair to the side. Returning to an empty pod, she put on some long silver earrings, her mass of silver bracelets on one hand, and her leather bands on the other. She popped her hiking clothes into her nylon bag for the laundry. She laid out her down blanket on the bed, popped her earplugs into her pillowcase for later, then hung her wet towel over the end of her bed. Standing, she grabbed the nylon bag, a charger for her almost dead phone, her jacket, and walked to the common area at the end of the hall to wait for Pam and Georgina.

"Look at you. How can you look that good after our walk today?" Pam asked, walking into the common area, just as Aubrey ended a phone call with her son. "I feel like a total dog next to you," Pam continued.

Aubrey looked at her with a scowl and quickly complimented Pam on her haircut. She said she was jealous of the wash and go style that suited Pam so well. Pam blushed and, Aubrey hoped the comment made her feel a little better about herself. The woman was small with a shapely figure, but she was beautiful, especially with her piercing blue eyes and her infectious smile, when she let herself relax.

"Come on, let's go to the bar," Pam announced, leading them down the stairs. Going down was slow and painful. Aubrey's legs were on fire and she knew Pam's knees weren't great. Georgina had said nothing about her ankle, but she saw her limping slightly now. Luckily the restaurant had an elevator.

"I'll buy the first round. I'm guessing we'll be having more than one?" Aubrey asked. Georgina and Pam both agreed without hesitation. Aubrey headed to the bar. She returned with three cold beers and took a seat in the leather chair, opposite Pam.

"We made it," Pam said, her sigh expressing her pleasure to be sitting. "Seventeen kilometres is a long way without a lot of stops. It was a bit challenging with everything still so wet."

"But we did it. I know my knees have expressed their displeasure. How are yours Pam?" Aubrey asked, crossing one leg over the other, settling in.

"Like I've just jumped out of a twenty-story building and landed knees first on to concrete," she said, which made them grimace. "Tender, but I slathered them with Tiger Balm." Pam looked at Georgina. "Thanks for the share. The Tiger Balm seems to be working."

"I put some on my ankle too," Georgina said. "It's a little swollen after that descent."

"We will smell like a pair of oldies in a nursing home," said Pam. "The odour will surely scare all the bedbugs away. But truly, I really don't care what we smell like. Better than before the showers, I'm sure," said Pam. "Here's to cheers. Another day on the Camino!" And they clinked glasses, each taking a well-deserved drink.

Aubrey sat back in her chair and closed her eyes. There were only a few pilgrims in the bar with them, so the place was relatively quiet. She thought of their accomplishment. She was astonished she'd made it over the Pyrenees without incident. She was so sure she'd fall or have some other disaster. But she didn't want to verbalise that, in case she jinxed something.

"I booked us in for six-thirty at the restaurant," she said, her eyes still closed. She opened them to find Georgina staring at her watch. "Hope that's okay."

Aubrey had noticed that by the time she'd hung up on her call with Simon, it was already after five-thirty. Now, it'd be closer to six and she was hungry!

"That's great!" said Pam. "Thanks for doing that." Georgina nodded her thanks too.

"One lady in the bathroom was telling me about the lengthy line to check-in when she arrived around three-thirty," said Pam. "They announced that anyone without a reservation was out of luck. They would have to keep walking. She said the monastery was offering help with forward plans or to arrange taxis if needed."

"Ugh. I can't imagine having to stand in line. Luckily we had all reserved a bed!" said Georgina.

"I couldn't walk any further today. Even if you paid me a million dollars," said Pam. Aubrey listened as Pam told them another Facebook forum story. Aubrey sat back and thought how lucky she was to have met them both. She was more surprised when she realised it had been only twenty-four hours since they'd met. She felt like she'd known them for years already. She just wondered if she was ready to tell them the real reason she was walking the Camino.

6

SKIPPING THE DARK STUFF

GOOD MORNING. Time to Get Up. The Camino is Waiting.

The damn sing-song voice was coming from somewhere, like an insistent alarm clock for pilgrims. If someone would please shut that person up, she could go back to sleep. But the singsong was getting closer. She could now hear the accompanying footsteps approaching her pod. The lights were now on, and the room was reacting to the words.

She reached under her pillow for her phone and clicked the activate button. It was just after six in the morning. Are you freaking kidding me?

But the two younger guys and the older woman sharing her pod were moving, putting on clothes, grabbing toiletry kits and making their way to the bathroom. Happy to have the pod to herself, if only for a few minutes, she stretched out under her down blanket and took advantage of the quiet. Her muscles were tight and sore, but some yoga would help that.

She reached for her clean pants and bra at the end of the bunk and slipped them on. Just as she finished, the guys returned, greeting her with a 'buenos dias'. Then, with an eagerness of only the young, they packed up and were out in less than five minutes. The elderly Dutch woman returned a few minutes later and, by then, Aubrey was ready for the bathroom herself.

"Good Morning," Aubrey said with a smile. "It looks to be a glorious day for a walk."

"Yes, it does," said the Dutch woman she'd met the night before. "It will be a slow walk for me, but I will enjoy it."

Aubrey nodded, remembering how pleased she was to discover at least one of her pod-mates spoke English. They exchanged Camino pleasantries when they settled in for the night. The Dutch woman shared she was only walking to Logroño. She had walked the Camino five times before, explaining she did it in two-week increments. But now, at eighty-two, she figured this would most likely be her last Camino. She'd been a lovely pod-mate, and a good balance to the two young Spaniards.

"The bathroom is busy, but people are moving quickly," the woman warned. Aubrey thanked her and went off to the bathroom. She poked her head into Pam and Georgina's pod. They were still laying on their beds, their bunkmates having just left.

"Good morning lovelies," Aubrey said quietly. "I'm just heading to the bathroom now, so I'll wait for you downstairs. I'm going to do some stretching before we leave. My body is tight today."

"Mine too," said Pam as she unzipped her sleeping bag. "Come on Georgina. Time to get walking."

"Two minutes more," Georgina mumbled. Aubrey left them to continue to the bathroom.

Forty minutes later, standing downstairs in the lobby area, Aubrey watched as pilgrims made their way to breakfast, or headed back on the Camino. She looked back toward the stairs and saw Pam and Georgina hobbling toward her.

"Sorry to keep you waiting so long. It took us longer to wrap our limbs than we thought," said Pam.

"Are you okay?" Aubrey asked, looking down at Pam's knee. She saw they were both leaning a little heavier on their trekking poles.

"Nothing that a nice little wander won't fix," said Pam, "although if I'm honest, my knee was screaming at me in all kinds of languages this morning." Georgina nodded in agreement.

"I'm all for taking it slow," said Aubrey. They stepped outside and on to the shaded cobblestone courtyard, before walking through the portico, past the entrance to the bar, the chapel on the left, and stepped into filtered sunlight as they made their way to the street.

"Oh! Look at that gorgeous sunrise!" Georgina whispered. The sun was just poking its face out. They walked a few more feet so as not to be looking right into it. Aubrey breathed in, energised by the view. The church broke the sunlight, and the rays reached around and touched the paddocks across the street.

"Let's get this show on the road, shall we?" said Pam.

"Yes, but first a photo op! I want you ladies over there!" said Georgina, pointing at the sign stating it was 790 kilometres to Santiago. There was a short line of other pilgrims planning the same thing. Aubrey had seen pictures of this sign online, so she knew it was an opportunity not to pass up.

"Did you guys hear that damn sing-song alarm this morning?" asked Aubrey, as they stood in line.

"Are you talking about the wakeup call? That glorious: 'Good Morning. Time to Get Up. The Camino is waiting,'" Pam sang. Aubrey laughed at Pam's awful rendition. "Oh, I loved it! I had heard they sometimes pipe in music. This was much nicer. More personal. Better than I imagined," Pam continued.

"A little nicer than them shouting: Get up and get the hell out!" responded a pilgrim behind them. All the English-speaking pilgrims in line laughed out loud. Aubrey took note that when Pam laughed, her dimples pierced her cheeks, and her eyes sparkled more than the morning mist in the sunlight. She also noticed how much more awake Pam was this morning, more than she'd had been the previous morning in Orisson. The Camino energy had kicked in.

Georgina's sea-green eyes were surveying the surrounding paddocks. Her silver hair, this morning in a ponytail, shone in the morning light, with strands straying against her black outfit. She was an attractive woman, and shy, although not with her photography, Aubrey thought.

This morning, Aubrey felt like the slob of the group. She tried to pull herself together a bit for the photo. Her green pants were wrinkled. She tried to smooth them out but remembered what she'd looked like in the mirror that morning and gave up. She'd look shocking in the photo no matter what. Her face was puffy, and her hair had not complied to her coaxing when she'd tried to braid it earlier. She had, instead, tossed it into a topknot and thrown her buff on to keep the strands off her face. And her eyes had the bloodshot red back. Yep, she was the grungy one today.

They got to the front of the queue and Georgina styled the photo, taking several with Pam and Aubrey together and alone. Aubrey got one of Georgina under much protest. Eventually, they asked a pilgrim holding a serious camera in his hand to take a photo of the three of them together. Happy to oblige, he snapped their beaming faces all lined up at the 'Santiago 790 km' sign. Then, returning the favour for their photographer and his wife, they were off.

"Please send a copy to us Georgina, even if I do look a mess!" said Aubrey. "I want to remember everything about this Camino and that will help me when I'm old and docile."

"You and me both!" said Pam, taking the lead on the trail.

The sunlight filtered through the forest, its rays highlighting the saplings beneath the huge pines, while the mist danced around the trunks. Birdsong followed their easy stroll.

Aubrey realised she had not heard Georgina's footsteps behind her in a little while. She stopped, stepped to the side to let a few others pass, only to reveal Georgina with her phone out, taking photos of the sunlight through the trees.

"I'll catch up," she called. Pam had also stopped. Aubrey suggested they wait. Pam agreed, saying she felt in no rush. Once Georgina had caught back up with too many apologies, Aubrey told her to take as many photos as she wanted. It was a gorgeous morning, and she was happy to savour it.

After the three kilometre stretch from Roncesvalles, they reached the witchy haunt of Burguete and admired the witch's cauldron mural. They found a café across from it and stopped for breakfast. Pam, who was quickly becoming their own Camino Information Guide, advised them to skip breakfast in Roncesvalles, and find breakfast a little further along.

When they opened the doors of the café, Aubrey found they weren't the only ones with that idea, but she was relieved to find it was not overrun. Pam explained that many pilgrims may have chosen the cold toast and coffee a Roncesvalles ticket would have provided. Lucky for them, they'd skipped that choice.

As they waited for their café con leche and tortilla de patata, they exchanged stories of their bunkmates. Georgina and Pam had shared a pod with two large, older Spaniards who had imbibed a little too heavily over dinner, according to Pam, and had snored up the dust bunnies.

"And I must be the fart magnet," Pam said. "Once again, I had a guy blowing the partitions apart with his bloody loud flatulence." She then explained that she had a woman in Orisson who was farting all night. Aubrey shared her own Orisson farting experience.

"That was the woman above me! Oh! The smell!" said Pam. Aubrey laughed. She spotted Georgina screw up her nose after a sip of her café con leche.

"Not good?" Aubrey took a sip of her coffee. It was okay. Not worth a nose scrunching though, she thought.

"It's not Australia good, but it'll do," said Georgina. "Besides, it's caffeine. It'll be fine." She took a bite of her tortilla. "But wow. Now, that's good."

With full bellies and backpacks adjusted, Pam double tapped her poles on the ground as they headed off. They followed the main village road until they saw the telling yellow arrow, high on a stone building. The arrow was pointing to the right, down toward a bridge. There, they passed an ATM and a vending machine. But the vending machine was not full of sodas as they would have expected, but medical supplies. Lots of stuff for blisters and sore muscles, Pam observed, commenting at the ingenious thinking.

When they walked over the rickety wooden bridge, Pam pointed to the water below, flowing at a fast pace. She threw Aubrey and Georgina a worried glance. Aubrey sensed what she was thinking. She'd thought the same. There had been flooding over the last few weeks and even now, with the water subsiding, they would have to be vigilant. They walked past several dairy sheds on the right, packed full of bellowing bovines. Pam walked up to pat one cow, only for it to lunge at her.

"It seems Spanish cows are not like the docile ones we have in the Hunter," she declared.

Their morning got a little more challenging as they began another ascent, walking up a long slow hill, but with the scenery to distract them, the climb passed easily. The beautiful countryside both entertained and impressed them. They laughed at two fornicating horses, one having had quite enough of the other, and Georgina took photos of wildflowers just popping into bloom. Walking through patches of rocky terrain and down through some mud, they took their time. They hobbled over bricked pavement, sore on their sensitive feet, despite their well-soled shoes, and headed up and over more rocky hills, passing the time with easy conversation.

Pam declared it was the descents that were harder on her knee. It was tough going in patches, but Aubrey was surprised at how refreshed she felt. She was a little stiff from the day before, but her stretching had helped immeasurably. She was in her element with the weather and the terrain. It reminded her a lot of the Victorian highlands. She'd be happy with this kind of lifestyle every day, she pondered, when they walked in silence for a while.

When they reached Bizkareta, they stopped at the café on the hill for another coffee and a second breakfast, as Pam called it. They dropped their packs, and Aubrey and Georgina went inside to order, Pam holding the table for them outside.

"I can't pass up a good pastry anymore," Aubrey said, placing Pam's coffee and pastry in front of her. "Once upon a time I would have punished myself at the gym for the extra calories. Now, I've earned this delicious thing fair and square!" Pam raised her coffee in salute. Aubrey cut into her chocolate filled pastry. Georgina took a tentative sip of her coffee, then another. Aubrey waited for her reaction. She didn't say anything but there was no nose wrinkling either.

"So, Georgina, how's this coffee? Any better?" asked Aubrey.

"Better. Still, not great, but better." Pam and Aubrey smiled at each other. Georgina looked at them and laid her cup back down.

"I know, I am a coffee snob." Georgina said, as she cut a slice of her chocolate croissant, looking up at them. "It's what happens when you own a café. You refine your tastes, and if you care, you choose only the best beans. That's the reason my business has survived for twenty years." This was a very confident Georgina they hadn't seen before. She apologised about so much but not about this.

"You don't have to explain. I just think it's funny," said Aubrey. "You've got to know your product to be successful. I get that."

"Yeah. There have been a few places pop up here and there, but the locals stick with me. I had one guy come through about a year ago. He told me he owned a café in Melbourne himself. He said he'd be back because he liked my coffee. Turns out, we were using the same roaster," Georgina said, then took a bite of her pastry. She sat back in her chair and groaned.

"Oh? It's good?" Aubrey asked. Pam started in on her pastry, reacting the same way as Georgina.

"So, who did you say was looking after the café while you're here?" Pam asked, picking up her coffee. "Your daughter?"

"Yeah, Nicole. She's currently my baker but I've put the training wheels on her to see how she does running the place for three months. I'm nervous, to be honest," picking up her coffee and holding it with two hands as she spoke, "but I think she'll be fine. She has my best friend there with her to help if she needs it. My friend Bec has worked at the café since I opened. I talked to them last night, and they said all was well."

"Are you looking to hand over the reins then?" asked Pam, placing her knife and fork side by side after devouring her pastry.

"Considering it. I think I'm ready to do something different. Nicole is eager. Owning a bakery is her dream. She's been a tremendous asset for my café already. She is the only twenty-three-year-old I know who has her head screwed on firmly and knows exactly what she wants. Where she gets her confidence from, I have no clue," said Georgina as Aubrey felt a knife to her gut, thinking of her own daughter.

"Anyway, she seems like the best fit. I don't know. It's something I am thinking through while I'm here." She placed her coffee cup down and finished up her pastry. Aubrey just stared at Georgina, her thoughts cloudy. Realising it, she shook the dark thoughts from her mind, took a deep breath and decided she needed to change the direction of the conversation.

"What about your photography?" asked Aubrey. "You seem keen and based on the photos you showed us last night of the first two days, you have an eye. I've seen that quality in art exhibits in Melbourne and Sydney before. And London, too. You should think about doing something with that."

"No, no. It's just a hobby," Georgina said just a little too quickly. Aubrey sensed Georgina's discomfort at her compliment. Georgina ran her hand through her hair. She'd seen her do that the night before when an older gentleman in the hotel bar complemented her on the colour of her eyes. It was obviously a nervous gesture.

"I think you're better than a hobbyist. You have a keen eye. You should embrace your gift." Georgina continued with the hair fondling. Yes, it was definitely a nervous gesture, she thought. "Well lovelies, are you ready to continue?" asked Aubrey.

Pam, groaning as she stood, announced that while sitting was good, stiffening up was not. They walked to their backpacks leaning against the wall nearby. With a quick lift, Aubrey had her pack on and strapped in no time. Pam and Georgina both struggled with theirs.

"What do you have in those packs? Bricks? They seem mighty heavy," Aubrey asked.

"Too fucking heavy," said Pam as she adjusted her shoulder straps. "How heavy is yours again?"

"Seven kilograms." Pam stopped in her tracks.

"How?" She looked bewildered. They were both looking at her with genuine intrigue.

"I laid out everything I thought I would need. I looked at each item and asked myself if it was something I could do without. I knocked out a lot doing that," she said.

"I did that too, but I guess not as thoroughly. There are a few things I kept in because I had such a hard time finding things in the first place," Pam said. They continued walking, Pam setting the pace once more. They were working their way through some muddy patches, each navigating the best way around it, all using their trekking poles for balance.

"I get it. I am a size sixteen and being tall doesn't help either."

"You are so not a size sixteen," said Georgina, shaking her head in disbelief.

"Actually, I am. Trust me, I know the struggle to prepare for this walk. It's why I have one pair of pants with me."

"One?!" Pam shrieked loud enough to chase off a flock of foraging sparrows.

"Yes. One pair of pants, a pair of leggings and my skirt. One short-sleeve shirt, a singlet, a long sleeve merino, a zip up jumper and this windbreaker jacket. I wasn't kidding when I said you've seen the entire range of my Camino wardrobe. I have one pair of sandals and these trainers. That's it."

"Well, I definitely over packed!" said Georgina. "I'm with Pam. They do not make hiking gear for women with substance. And I am not one of those people who wear workout gear year-round. God, I hate that fashion trend. What did you call them Aubrey?" asked Georgina, as they made their way up the steep incline.

"The Yummy Mummies," Aubrey said. They stopped halfway up a hill, all out of breath from talking and walking.

"Yes," Aubrey reached into Georgina's side pack pocket and handed her the water bottle, before doing the same for Pam. It was a process they had devised the day before. So far it worked great. Otherwise, both Pam and Georgina had to remove their backpacks to retrieve their water bottles.

"You know, I used to be one of them," said Aubrey, sucking on the water tube from her hydration pack. Pam looked confused. "I used to be a size eight. I starved myself to death for years. Used to spend two hours every day at the gym. An hour in the morning doing cardio, and then an hour at night toning."

"Bloody hell," Pam said, as serendipitously, two women practically sprinted by them, their tiny bottoms cocooned in lycra.

"Yep, that was me. Right there. At the gym anyway. And you may well think, what the hell happened?"

"Well, no. I would assume you ate a carb one day and realised what you'd missed out on," said Pam. Aubrey and Georgina both laughed at that.

"Whatever happened, you look great," said Georgina, nodding for them to keep walking. "I want your style when I grow up." Aubrey didn't know why. Georgina had great style of her own and she wondered if Georgina knew it.

"Thanks. I like yours too. But my style has changed a lot over the last few years. When I became a van girl, as they say, my inner bohemian came out."

"Sounds like leaving the city was the right move for you," said Georgina.

"Yes. I'm much happier, and definitely freer, than I was in Melbourne."

"And you can be when your backpack is only seven kilos! I still can't get over that," Pam said.

"I can help you if you like. I'll crack the whip. You can send stuff home or leave it in a donation box at an albergue. The donation box in Roncesvalles was overflowing with stuff. Better than carrying it eight hundred kilometres," said Aubrey.

"I may take you up on that," said Pam. Georgina nodded in agreement, as she bent to tighten her hip straps a bit.

Two hours later, on the peak of a hill, they saw a food truck doing a roaring business.

"Time for a stop," said Pam. Aubrey nodded, seeing Georgina gaze down at her watch. She had no intention of asking her what time it was. The only time she cared about was the time right now. Pam was right. It was time for a break, and the strawberries looked too enticing to pass up.

As they made their way down the hill into Zubiri, it was slow going. Pam's knees were hurting, but she was quick to make jokes about it.

"Did I tell you that two surgeons worked on my knee?" She chuckled, "It was a joint operation." That started them laughing, but she had more.

"Yeah, my other doctor is addicted to hitting his patients on the knee to test their reflexes. He really gets a kick out of it." The jokes took their minds off the descent. Pam was turning out to be the queen of puns and what she called 'dad jokes'.

She felt a connection with Pam and Georgina now, or who she thought of as the Lovelies. Because they were lovely, genuine, down-to-earth women. She was happy to walk with them. She wasn't eager to dig back into the grim stuff that had spiralled her for the last two years. Not yet. She was happy for conversation and light-hearted banter, but she was sure that would change again soon too.

As they walked into Zubiri, twenty-three kilometres from where they had begun their day, Aubrey was looking forward to the private room they had booked. She was tired, sure, but more, she was sick of the snorers already. And she was ready for a private bathroom. She was fine sharing with two other women. It was definitely better than ten.

As they walked over the Puente de la Rabia in search of their albergue, Aubrey thought of how well she gelled with these two women. She had to keep her mind from going dark when she took her focus off the scenery and the company. She had enjoyed her solo walk the first day, loved the freedom to set her own pace, but she had to be conscious of letting her mind wander too far. She'd done a lot of therapy and had worked through a lot of baggage. But with too much time to ponder, it was not a healthy thing for her. She wasn't eager to do that again.

7

ALWAYS BE PREPARED

ZUBIRI TO LARRASOAÑA

GEORGINA LOOKED DOWN at her watch for the third time in the same number of minutes. She and Pam had agreed to leave early. Georgina was eager to catch the sunrise. But Pam was dawdling, doing God only knew what. Aubrey wanted to do a yoga session and told them not to wait. Instead, she planned to meet them at their first stop, further up the track. Pam had been nursing her knee the night before through copious amounts of wine and now, as a result, she was dragging. The descent into Zubiri had been rough.

"I'm almost there," grumbled Pam. "Just need to brush my teeth. And go to the toilet." Georgina was obviously biting her tongue as she watched Pam head to the bathroom. Aubrey offered to walk with Pam to let Georgina go ahead, but Pam was insistent on leaving early too.

"She's like a little old woman sometimes, isn't she?" said Aubrey, as Pam closed the door to the bathroom. "You can't be angry at her. It's just how she is. But it's funny. She's so meticulous about getting every-thing out the night before. I noticed it in Orisson and in Roncesvalles. But by the morning, she spends time just..."

"Faffing around," finished Georgina, looking at her watch again. Aubrey chuckled.

"She'll be ready soon," Aubrey said, thinking Georgina needed a distraction. "So, where am I meeting you? Larra... something."

"Larrasoaña, I think it is. Something like that. First bar on the right," Georgina said. When Pam finally came out of the bathroom, she added, "you have my mobile if you're a while."

"We'll wait for you. I'm not in a hurry today," Pam said and looked up at Georgina and asked if she was ready. Aubrey bit her lip, trying not to laugh.

"Ready and waiting," said Georgina, trying hard not to let the impatience come through, but to Aubrey, it was loud and clear.

"See you soon!" chirped Pam and, with a wave, they left.

With the front door closed, Aubrey stretched and glanced over at her phone. It was just before seven and, to her relief, there were no urgent messages from home. That was good. It meant things were calm. Simon had sounded relaxed when she'd spoken to him. She just hoped that wasn't a cover.

By the time she was out the door, it was just before eight. The sun had risen, and it was turning out to be a beautiful morning. But it was still cold, and frost covered the ground. Her thoughts turned to Pam's mood this morning. She'd been cranky. Aubrey was thankful she'd delayed her departure. She didn't need the negative vibe. She was looking forward to having a little time to herself. She loved walking with the Lovelies, but this time alone was good too.

She noticed how the frost clung to the beautifully woven spider webs, revealing the intricate detail. It was a work of art. Aubrey channelled Georgina's photographic abilities and took photos at various angles as they glistened in the filtered sunlight.

Aubrey passed a huge industrial plant, something she found to be an eyesore against the landscape. She sniffed the air, it smelled damp, but free of any chemical she could place. She followed the perimeter road. They had tacked AstroTurf to the fence around the plant, somehow trying to give it some semblance of green. They'd failed miserably. She also tried and failed to determine what kind of plant it was. Eventually, she came to a board informing her that it was a magnesium plant. She laughed, missing her personal Camino Information Guide. Pam would have known the answer.

The stone path, inching its way slowly up the hill, tested her lung capacity. At the top, she found a small hamlet named Ilarratz. She stopped in the shelter, set in the middle of town, and pulled out the pastry she'd bought the previous afternoon. The hamlet was straight out of a fairy tale. While picking apart the pastry, she admired the robust wooden beams set into the old stone buildings. Wagon wheels hung on stuccoed walls, and shrubs grew in pots beneath them, levelled out on the hilly path by wooden blocks. Baskets of flowers slipped over, while climbing roses creeped along behind them. Quaint, she thought. She took a long drink of water and noticed a few stray cats appear, begging for food. They seemed to multiply when she gave attention to one, then another.

She thought about her children. God, she missed them terribly. Aubrey had mentioned Simon to the Lovelies. But not Cass. Aubrey reached up to her throat. She felt pressure in her chest and made herself take a deep breath. She wished Cass were here with her. She knew Cass would pull out her sketchpad and pencils, trying to capture the essence of the place. She was talented with her magic sticks, as she liked to call them. The pressure in her chest remained, thinking of her daughter. Aubrey knew nothing would make it go away unless she refocused her thoughts. After a few snapshots, she packed her pastry away and ventured onward.

The Abbey lay before her on the right. Pam had mentioned it the night before, something she'd noted in her book from her forum notes. When they'd left that morning, she told Aubrey to look out for it. The Abbey was rustic but looked as if an impressive deal of restoration was in the works. She was disappointed to see a closed sign displayed across the fence. Pam had explained that a pilgrim now owned The Abbey. He had bought it some years ago and after a lot of renovation efforts, had uncovered some secrets to the place. She made a mental note to ask Pam what she knew of it. What a shame she couldn't see it for herself, she thought. But as she continued, she noticed the planter boxes further along the road filled with daffodils just sprouting. Spring was well and truly here.

. . .

By the time she made it to Larrasoaña, she was ready for a break. Following Georgina's instructions, she found the only bar open at the far end of town. Flags flew above the outdoor seating area. She felt a touch of nostalgia seeing the enormous Australian flag waving proudly. She walked around the back to find Pam hunched over some guy's foot. Georgina looked on with interest.

"Bloody hell. What reality show have I just walked into? Doctors Without Borders? Pam, what are you doing?!" Aubrey asked, as she slid her backpack down against the wall.

"Helping Ben with his blisters," said Pam, focused on the task at hand.

"Hey, it's you!" the guy said. It was the New Yorker she'd met on day one.

"Hi! The guy from Orisson! Or rather, just before there?" He nodded, "I thought you'd be long gone by now."

"Sadly, no. Caught a nasty case of blister-itis," and pointed down to the foot currently in Pam's lap.

"Ouch!" Aubrey said. He had two massive blister clusters, one on his heel, the other on his big toe. She rested her hand on the back of Pam's chair.

"Yeah. You could say that again," Ben said. He winced when Pam accidently poked a sensitive spot. Recovering quickly, he smiled broadly up at Aubrey.

"Pam and Georgina were just telling me about you. They were saying they were walking with an Englishwoman who lived in Australia. They were trying to describe you. Georgina thinks you look a little like Kate Winslet, but Pam argues you look more like an actress from the West Wing. Toby's wife or something? Anyway, I wondered if it was you."

"Kate Winslet? Oh, I wish," she said, just as she saw the guy wince again. "Probably the accent."

"And the red hair. And the same build," added Georgina. "I'm thinking nostalgically. Kate Winslet from her *Titanic* days. Or, in *The Dressmaker*."

"I wish I looked that young. But I'm happy to take that compliment," she said. Georgina smiled over at her.

"Welcome, Señorita! May I give you a glass of wine?" the owner asked, a beaming smile on his weathered face as he approached the table.

"It's a little too early for me for wine but… maybe a café con leche?" asked Aubrey.

"Of course! Please sit. I bring to you," the owner offered.

"Dos, por favor," said Pam, holding up two fingers. She pointed to her bum bag, signalling Aubrey to grab her money.

"No problem. No money now," he said. "Please, sit. Rest. Welcome."

Aubrey smiled at the man, thanked him, then turned back to the doctoring in front of her. "You guys look intent there," she said.

"Are your shoes too tight or… what happened?" asked Aubrey.

"I'm wearing boots that are too small. And they're not airing enough overnight. And I don't have the right socks. Take your pick. I need to buy another pair of shoes in Pamplona tomorrow. It'll be slow going at this rate." He took a sharp breath at something Pam was doing to his foot.

"I stopped here yesterday to give my feet a chance to heal a little. Ended up staying in the Municipal further along. I've been here since eight this morning, chatting with Pedro," he said, pointing at the large Spaniard walking toward them, cups in hand. "I'm glad you guys came along. I'm sure Pedro has better things to do than chat with me."

Pedro placed the cups in front of them, along with a chopped-up croissant to share.

"Disfrutar. Enjoy," said Pedro, as he stepped back from the table.

"Oh, thank you! That's so nice of you," said Georgina, smiling appreciatively.

"I have bread in the oven. I just put it in. It won't be ready for an hour, but it's worth waiting for," said Pedro, his hands on his hips.

"It is. I had it yesterday. He makes it here, fresh, in his shop," said Ben.

"Where are you from?" Pedro asked, pointing proudly to all of his flags. Georgina pointed to the Australian flag.

"Australia," she said and smiled as she pointed to each of them.

"Ah, Australia. Beautiful. Well, let me know when you are ready for wine. On the house. My welcome to you." And with that, he left them to it.

"He's been plying me with the stuff since yesterday. It's not the worst wine I've tasted," admitted Ben, smiling over at Pedro. But Georgina and Aubrey were intent on watching Pam work on Ben's feet. Her instincts as a nurturing teacher seemed to have kicked in. She asked him how he was dressing his feet each day.

"Holy shit Pam. Is that your first aid kit?" Aubrey asked, when she saw Pam reach for gauze in the kit. Pam nodded. "Wow. Is there an operating table in there as well?" Pam smiled, then put Ben's foot down, picked up his other, and gave it a thorough inspection. She treated his blisters while educating them on how to manage their feet for the Camino. She explained the positives and negatives of petroleum jelly, toe socks, and wrapping toes with tape. Clearly, Pam was the expert on the subject. Aubrey was just relieved that none of them had developed any blisters so far. Thinking that, she wondered if she'd just jinxed them. Wouldn't matter...Pam would fix them up.

Aubrey watched in amazement at how efficient Pam was using string, betadine and a needle. Pam lanced the blister with the doused needle, carefully cleared the seeping goo, gently applied tea tree anti-septic cream and wrapped his heel in fresh new gauze. Ben sat back in his chair and spoke words of immense appreciation. All the while, Pam moved on to his toes, explaining what she was doing and why she was doing it.

"Do you know each other from Australia?" Ben asked, flinching a little as Pam popped another blister.

"No, we met at Orisson," Georgina said, leaning forward in her chair to watch Pam's work more closely.

"Thankfully," said Aubrey, also immersed in what Pam was doing. "Pam, you are amazing. How do you know what to do?"

"Well, I've had to do this before, at school. I used to help the school nurse, but mostly from the..."

"Forums," Georgina and Aubrey finished in unison. They looked at each other and laughed. Ben, meanwhile, looked at them with confusion. "Pam is a sucker for a good Camino forum. She's our very own Camino Information Guide."

"Ah. Well, she's learned something from them. Pam, thank you. You're a godsend," he said.

"Nah. But you can buy me a beer at some point. How's that?" She finished up the last of the gauze wrap and sat back.

"That first aid kit has got to be two kilos of your pack alone," said Aubrey.

"Yeah, probably," said Pam. The sun was hitting Aubrey's eyes through the gap in the shade cloth.

"Wow, that sun has heated up fast," Aubrey said, and took a seat at the table next to Ben, opposite Pam and Georgina. The Nurse Pam show was over.

"Twenty-four degrees Celsius, I read," announced Pam. Pam had taken to checking the weather every morning. It was part of her daily ritual.

"You know, I saw that Pedro had a fresh juice machine," Aubrey said. "I'm going in. Anyone else?" With nods all around, Aubrey got up and Georgina went with her to help carry the drinks back.

"Hola. Quatro jugo, por favor?" Aubrey said, pointing to the machine.

"Zumo de naranja?" Aubrey nodded and gestured four with her fingers.

"Si! I bring to you." Pedro looked at Aubrey and smiled as she released her breath.

"God, that bread smells amazing. I'm hanging around long enough for that at least," declared Aubrey. "I can't pass up fresh bread."

THEY FINISHED THEIR JUICE, WHICH AUBREY EXCLAIMED WAS BETTER THAN any café con leche they'd had so far, then enjoyed Pedro's freshly baked bocadillas. They turned out to be massive baguettes, filled with jamon, which Ben explained was delicious premium ham, freshly picked tomato still warm from the sun, and drizzled with extra virgin olive oil. They were moaning with pleasure after the first bite. It was one of the most delicious meals they'd tasted so far.

They shared their stories with Ben, of where they were from, and what had brought them to the Camino. Then, they told tales of the people they had met along the way. Ben had even heard about the backpack incident at Orisson, although Aubrey couldn't work out how, given he had been a day ahead of them. The Camino wire, Pam had joked.

They learned that Ben lived in New York with his husband Kanmi, a chef. He was walking the Camino as a much-needed break from running their company. And, he admitted, he was also walking to deliberate whether he was ready to take the next step in his life.

"The next step?" asked Pam.

"Kids," said Ben. Aubrey saw something cross Pam's face that she couldn't quite place. Aubrey would ask Pam later what the look meant. Ben continued. "We have a wonderful friend who offered to be a surrogate for us, but I am the one holding back. I need to make sure I'm ready." He picked up his glass and drained the last of his juice.

"It's an enormous step," said Georgina. "Kids are a lifelong commitment."

"Yeah, they are," said Aubrey. "And if you're already involved in a busy company, you've got to determine what's the priority. I had that reality check in Melbourne."

"Oh?" said Ben. She felt all eyes on her.

"Yeah, I had a very successful business, and I travelled a lot. It was pretty full on. My then-husband was in corporate finance and had his own world of crazy, so we had to juggle childcare," Aubrey said. "We managed the day-to-day stuff with the help of a great nanny. That helped a lot. But a lot was sacrificed." Aubrey felt as if she was describing someone else's life, it seemed so long ago.

"It took me a long time to realise what the priorities were. It was a very hard lesson to learn," Aubrey said. She felt tears welling up. She took a deep breath, a coping strategy her therapist had taught her. "In hindsight, if just one of us had had a crazy job, that would have been okay, I think. But we both worked long hours. The family suffered. I see that now." She could feel the tension mounting around the table. Aubrey looked up. "Believe me when I say you have to be ready to be completely present. That's all."

Ben nodded.

"Is that why you moved out of Melbourne?" asked Georgina. Aubrey looked at her, confused before catching on. "More time with the family?"

"Oh, no. I just... needed a change." She picked at crumbs on her plate while everyone waited for her to expand on her comment. Shifting gears, she continued. "I think today is such a beautiful day, we should just settle in and stay. My feet are protesting wholeheartedly, and I don't think they want to move another step," Aubrey said. She wanted out of this conversation and fast. She needed, more than anything, to shut down the emotion that had broiled to the surface. "What do you think, Lovelies? It would be hard to continue, now it's warming up. Don't you think?"

"Yeah," said Pam. "To be honest, my knees feel like they've locked up and I can't find the key." Aubrey looked over at Georgina. Georgina shrugged.

"Ben?" He pointed to his bandaged feet, showing he wasn't going anywhere, anytime soon.

"Good, it's settled. Time for beer then?"

8

SORTING THROUGH THE CRAP

LARRASOANA

THEY PAID Pedro at the bar, then wandered across the street to the albergue where Ben was staying. Since the Municipal only allowed one-night stays, he'd had to find another place. Pedro had directed him here. When he'd shown the hospitalero, or the albergue host, his blistered feet, he allowed him to leave his backpack. But he had directed him to return later to check in.

"Hola," said the hospitalero when they walked in the door. He looked at Ben. "Ah, yes. Your bed is ready. I show you." He looked at the others.

"Reservation?" he asked. They shook their heads.

"Do you have beds for my friends?" asked Ben.

"Si. Yes. But I have only four beds available. Come. Please. Take off your shoes." He turned and showed them a closet where they could store their hiking shoes and poles. From all the signs posted indicating where shoes and poles should go, Aubrey hoped this guy's fastidiousness about cleanliness spoke to the rest of the place.

After providing their passport information, getting their credential stamped and paying their albergue dues, including dinner, they followed the hospitalero as he bounded up the stairs in front of them. The stairs went on forever. Aubrey could see Pam was in pain. She used the banister to pull herself up. Ben walked up on the edges of his feet. For Aubrey, the soles of her feet were protesting. Georgina seemed to be the only one not having an issue. They reached the top floor and were shown a room at the end of the hall. The host pointed at two bunk beds.

"Okay?" he asked. They all nodded, although Aubrey wondered why he'd assigned beds to them. The room was otherwise empty.

"Dibs on a lower bunk," said Pam.

"I'm happy for a top bunk," said Ben.

"Yes, me too," said Aubrey. "That way I know someone won't step on my head in the middle of the night when they have to go to the toilet." Aubrey noticed Georgina hesitate before thanking her for the lower bed.

"Just watch your step in the middle of the night," said Georgina, and began checking her mattress for bed bugs.

"It's okay. I have a retail bladder. I can hold it for hours! Once I'm up there, I'm up there for the night!" Aubrey laughed, then began inspecting her mattress too. Pam and Georgina followed suit.

"What are you guys doing?" asked Ben, watching them all inspect their beds.

"Checking for bed bugs. Don't you?" asked Pam, like it was the most natural thing in the world.

"Um, no. I just assume the place is clean," Ben said.

"It may look clean, but you don't know what someone is bringing in on their backpacks from the previous place," said Pam. "They may have stayed in a bug infested five-star hotel for all you know." Pam stood, satisfied her bed was clean. "Do you want me to show you what to look for?"

"There she goes..." said Aubrey to Georgina, then turned and watched Pam. She was like a little mother hen. "Listen to her Ben. You will be glad to have met her. Goodness knows I'd be scratching my arms off if it wasn't for Pam to remind me to check," said Aubrey, while Georgina wandered off to find the bathrooms.

Aubrey sat on the floor and started unloading her pack. Ben had headed off to do some hand washing in the bathroom, so she had a little extra space. She looked up and saw that Pam had her massive medical kit on the bed, her toiletry bag beside it. Aubrey watched as she pulled layer after layer from her pack, trying to find something, which she guessed was at the bottom.

"Do you want to go through your pack Pam? I can help you lighten your load," offered Aubrey. She was happy to help the Lovelies. She was less worried now, knowing she had gotten through the last few days with her basic possessions. Maybe she had it right after all?

"Ugh. Yes, I'd love the help," said Pam.

"You know, that's not a bad idea," said Georgina, walking back into the room. "Would you do that for me too? I need to get rid of some stuff. My shoulders are killing me."

"You may not be carrying your pack the right way either. Let's start with what you have. Who wants to go first?" she asked. Aubrey had her stuff out and ready for a shower on the bed. It was the same t-shirt, skirt and sandals she wore every night.

"Go shower first. We'll wait," said Pam.

"Okay. Then while I'm gone, pull everything out of your pack you've not used yet. We're into our fourth night already and we're over the Pyrenees, so anything you haven't worn yet, apart from wet weather gear, you most likely won't need. So, start there. I'll be back in a few minutes."

When Aubrey walked back into the room, she placed her wet sandals from the shower in the window alcove, allowing the breeze and sunlight to dry them. She wrapped her hair with her neon green travel towel, auburn tendrils sticking out here and there. After placing her toiletry kit on her top bunk, she looked around at the piles surrounding both Georgina and Pam.

"Are you finding this as hard as I am?" Georgina asked Pam.

"Yes. I am worried that I'll be cold, and I'm worried about the rain," Pam said.

"Have you been cold yet?" asked Aubrey.

"Well, no. I haven't."

"And what have you been wearing to keep warm?" asked Aubrey.

Pam looked pensive. "Singlet, t-shirt, merino long sleeve, and my puffer jacket, when I need it."

"And if you are walking along and it rains, what do you grab?" asked Aubrey.

"My poncho."

"Not your rain jacket?"

"No. But..." Aubrey looked at her with a knowing smile. Pam looked down again at her rain jacket. "What if it's a downpour?"

"Well, you would either get out of it until it blew over, if you could, or you would be fine with rain pants and your poncho." Aubrey walked over and touched the poncho. "That poncho is top of the line, Pam. Nothing is getting in that. But keep the waterproof jacket if you want to. It would be good for the lighter rainy days."

"Okay," Pam said, with a distinct question in her voice. "What about pants?"

"How many pair do you have?" asked Aubrey.

"Three. Plus, leggings to sleep in," said Pam.

"I have two plus leggings," said Georgina. Ben walked back into the room.

"You need two pair of pants. Total. Leggings and one pair, or two pair, then sleep in undies."

"Man, she's a whip cracker!" said Ben, and hung his damp towel from the bed railing near Pam. He sat on the single chair in the room, watching the show. "Pam is too, for that matter. How have you survived with these two, Georgina?"

"I'm just pleased to follow along," she said with a smile. "Aubrey, what about socks? Just tell me and I'll send home whatever you tell me to."

"Keep three pair," said Aubrey, smiling at the look of horror on Pam's face. "Total. I'd say two but throw in three in case you need to change them mid-day, or if you lose a pair and can't replace them immediately. You know, like if you're in the middle of the Meseta, for example."

"How do you know all this?" said Pam in awe. "I read everything I could, and no one was this specific. Where were you when I was packing?"

CAMINO WANDERING

"I have been long distance walking before. But, with those hikes, I had to carry my food as well. But I read something that said, 'We find out quickly that our stuff won't save us. It only makes us suffer.' And it's true. You two have been talking about the weight of your packs since you started. It's probably not helping your knee at all either."

Pam nodded.

"They say the Camino provides and today, it provided Aubrey to us, to remind us that, like life, we need to lighten the load," she said.

"I'm happy to help lighten your load any day Pam." Aubrey said, smiling gently at her.

"Ben, how heavy is your pack?" asked Georgina, as she moved items to a pile at the end of her bed.

"Eight kilos, plus water. But I have an iPad in there. I promised my husband that I'd bring it to keep in touch, and to check in with the business here and there. Leaving him with the business almost caused a meltdown."

"It's a lot," said Aubrey, pulling the towel off her hair. "The business, not the weight of the pack. You look like you can handle that kind of weight."

"Yeah, it's not bad. I knew going in that I would carry extra, and that's fine. Speaking of, I'm heading downstairs to call him. It should be late enough by now. You ladies have fun," he said, and hobbled to the door in his bandaged feet.

"He's very cute," said Pam, when he left the room. "I'd do him if I were a gay man." Aubrey and Georgina both cackled.

"God, Pam. That kind of talk can get you into trouble," said Aubrey. Pam shrugged. Aubrey just shook her head.

It had been a delightful way to spend the day, chilling out in the bar. She liked Ben a lot. Sure, they were all probably old enough to be his mother. He reminded her a little of her son, Simon. He seemed to be the genuine article, she thought, and turned her attention back to the piles around Georgina and Pam.

"Okay, so we both have a pile of shit to send home," Pam said. "I have a fleece, half this medical crap, a pair of pants, leggings, socks, underwear, a swimsuit, and two... wait, no. Three shirts. Wow. What do you have, Georgina?"

"An extra jumper, thermal underwear, a beanie, two pair of pants, two shirts, and some toiletry stuff I will donate. I don't need it all and I can get what I need as I go."

"Outstanding work, Lovelies. How do you feel?"

"Lost," said Pam at the same time Georgina said, "Free."

"Well Pam, we'll work on that for you," said Aubrey, "I think you'll find it freeing too after tomorrow."

"We can send stuff home from Pamplona," said Pam to Georgina. "It's only about fifteen kilometres tomorrow, with what my app says." Georgina nodded and started returning her pile to the bottom of her pack.

At dinner, a plethora of accents surrounded them. Wine was flowing, and they'd already finished their first course. Ben and Aubrey sat together, facing Georgina and Pam.

"So, where do you live in Australia? At the beach, like the advertisements have us foreigners believe?" Ben asked, picking at the peppers on his plate.

"Kind of. I live in a small village on a bay, but we do have a beach property," said Georgina.

"I'm coastal now too," said Pam, "but I was born and raised on a farm. I only moved away recently. Still a country girl at heart though."

"And you Aubrey?" asked Ben.

"City girl mainly but, unlike these two, I'm considering moving to the country," laughed Aubrey. "I grew up in London, but I moved to Melbourne in my twenties. I do like Melbourne. It'll be hard to leave. It's a fun place to live."

"Yeah, I agree. I went to Uni there. Loved it," said Georgina, then looked down at her shirt to pick off some breadcrumbs. "That was a million years ago, and it wasn't for long. Three years."

"Why did you move back to Tasmania? Didn't Melbourne make you want to stay?" Aubrey asked.

"Oh, long story," she said and gave Pam a sideward glance. Clearly, there was more to it.

"And you Pam?" asked Ben, who was either ignoring Georgina's glances or not noticing them. "You recently moved to the coast? Have you lived in the country all your life before then?"

"Yep. I've never lived in a city before. Even went to University in the country. What about you Ben? I couldn't imagine living in New York City. The noise alone would do me in." Aubrey was noticing a pattern with Pam. She seemed a master at deflecting questions.

"I'm not originally from the city either. I moved to New York about fifteen years ago, for business school. I'm originally from Utah."

"Really?" asked Pam. Aubrey was surprised too. He came across so much like a New York City kind of guy.

"Yeah. I grew up in a Mormon family. But, you know, being gay and Mormon didn't quite gel, so I moved to New York and have never looked back. But I miss the big skies." The host placed their next course on the table.

"Did your family disown you?" asked Georgina, her voice quiet. "You said it didn't gel."

"Some, but not all of them," said Ben and picked up his wine.

"When did you get married?" Georgina asked.

"About two years ago, but we've been together for ten. Are you all married?" He looked to each of them.

"Not anymore," said Aubrey. "Divorced for about a year."

"No," said Pam, shaking her head.

"Yes," said Georgina. Aubrey looked up to see Georgina wince when she added, "Twenty-eight years." Aubrey knew Georgina had mentioned being married at Orisson, but other than her 'Yes, married. Old news' comment on the way to Roncesvalles, she'd not mentioned her husband at all. In fact, she had not even mentioned his name. Aubrey realised there had to be a lot more to Georgina's story that she wasn't sharing. Seems they were all holding back.

9

THE CAMINO WHISPERS

LARRASOANA TO PAMPLONA

AN ITALIAN COUPLE shared the dorm room with them that night. Their snoring had been horrendous. Then, too early, shining their headlamps around the room and rustling plastic inside their packs, they prepared to leave. Bright light blinded Aubrey every time they moved in and out of the pitch-black room. It seemed like an eternity. Aubrey couldn't understand how some pilgrims could be so inconsiderate. Why couldn't they get their shit together outside?

Georgina stirred in the bed below her. When the Italians finally departed, Pam muttered, 'thank fucking god'. Aubrey stuck her arm out with a big thumbs up. Pamplona, their next stop, was only fifteen kilometres away and with their accommodation secure, and Ben's battered feet still a problem, they agreed to take their time to get there. Aubrey was looking forward to the private room she had booked. She needed peace and quiet.

Aubrey stretched, then reached for her pants hanging over the end of the bedhead. After pulling them on, she swung her legs around to the ladder and carefully made her way down.

"Noooo. Not yet. I don't want to get up yet Mum!" said Georgina.

"Then don't," said Aubrey, grabbing her toiletry bag and towel to head to the bathroom.

"If that was sleep, then I'd like a refund," said Pam softly. "I don't think they will kick us out until eight, thank god." Pam snuggled back down in her sleeping bag. Aubrey was surprised. Normally, Pam was the early bird.

Aubrey stood in front of the bathroom mirror, amazed to see how rested she looked, no thanks to the bloody Italians. Her eyes shone bright and clear. The puffy, bloodshot eyes she'd been sporting days before, had disappeared. She thought of Georgina as she raked her hands through her curly hair, gathering it up into a messy bun. It was clear she wasn't ready to share her story yet. Fair enough. They were all skirting their stories, but it seemed odd that she hadn't mentioned her husband before. Georgina was not shy about mentioning her well-adjusted, confident daughter. Aubrey wondered why she felt stung by this. It was almost…what? Fucking annoying, she thought. She splashed water on her face. Aggravated, she towelled off and stared at her reflection. They all had stories they weren't ready to share. Trust was a fragile thing.

Thirty minutes later, they were up and ready to go. Pam did her usual faffing around, but she made sure Ben had his blisters treated properly. She then helped Georgina dress a small blister on her little toe. And when Aubrey mentioned how stiff her legs felt, even after stretching, Pam delved into her pack and pulled out her stash of Berroca tablets. She'd found them while cleaning out her pack. She instructed each of them to pop the tablets into their first water of the day. The magnesium would help ease the muscle fatigue, she explained. Pam was their mother hen, Aubrey thought, thankful for the care and attention she provided. She could easily forgive the occasional faffing about.

Downstairs, they headed to the shoe room, while Pam headed off to see what might be available for breakfast. The hospitalero hadn't mentioned anything about it the night before.

"Oh, shit!" exclaimed Pam, not getting far at all. Georgina walked her way, but Pam blocked her, trying to hide what was behind her back.

"We need to go. Now!" Pam shot Aubrey wide googly eyes, looking for help to block Georgina, but it was no use. Georgina pushed past her.

"Yeah. No," Georgina said, turning on her heel and walking back toward the shoe room. "Not doing that. Not now. Not ever."

"What?! What is it?" Aubrey asked, leaping past to see what was so offensive. When she saw the offending object, she burst out laughing.

"It's…" Aubrey began as she placed her hand over her heart, "Oh God, the worst! It's a vending machine… for coffee!"

Aubrey and Pam both howled with laughter. Ben, already putting his shoes on, looked at Aubrey uncertainly, not getting the joke. Pam had seen his look.

"Georgina is a major coffee snob. M.A.J.O.R," she explained. She was still laughing, but Georgina smiled.

"Whatever. Yes. Yes, I am a snob," she said, reaching down to lace her shoes. "But I own a bloody café! I am allowed," she said, grabbing her pack and her poles, and heading out the door.

Pam and Aubrey were still laughing as they left.

THE TRAIL LED THEM ALONG A NARROW PATH BESIDE A RIVER. THEY WERE careful to sidestep the mud. Pam grumbled about the raging current and the torn-up path. She had mentioned her worry before. She was a barrel of stress by the time they reached a clearing. Fortunately, a small café presented itself about four kilometres along.

Georgina checked her watch.

"Look at that. It's coffee time!" Aubrey teased with a grin.

Georgina just rolled her eyes and carried on down the stairs to the café, listening to Aubrey and Pam laugh playfully at her expense. Georgina took a peek inside.

"Inside or out?" she asked.

"It's rather wet. Are there tables inside?" Ben asked.

"Yeah. One big one at the back. I think we can all fit."

"You snag it, I'll order for you," said Aubrey to Georgina. "Café con leche?"

"Yes please. And tortilla if they have any. Thanks."

They left their backpacks outside with the mass of others and placed their poles in the bucket nearby. Aubrey had given Pam and Georgina some of her yellow duct tape, so their poles stood out. It was busy inside, but Georgina snagged the table before others had a chance.

When they were all seated, Aubrey and Pam looked at Georgina expectantly, awaiting her judgement.

"Oh, just drink your damn coffees," Georgina said, taking a sip and wrinkling her nose at the offending taste. Pam and Aubrey relished her reaction, enjoying the show.

"How are the blisters holding up?" Pam asked Ben. He'd been keeping pace with them, not that they were much faster than snails.

"Better. What would I have done without your help?" he asked.

"The woman has a wealth of knowledge. She used to be a teacher," volunteered Aubrey.

"Somehow, I can see that," Ben said, smiling over at Pam. "I can imagine you wrangling a bunch of rowdy teenagers," he said.

"Nope. First Graders," said Pam, taking a bite of her tortilla.

WITH FULL BELLIES, THEY WERE BACK ON THE TRAIL. PAM SUGGESTED A slight detour to a 13th Century church in Zabaldika she was eager to visit.

"The church is run by nuns," Pam said, looking down at the notes on her phone as they finished their coffees. "They welcome pilgrims to come and say a prayer and ring the bell in the tower. The bronze bell is the oldest in all of Navarra," she explained. After listening to her description, they all agreed it was worth the diversion. Pam was interested in the history, she shared, not the religious aspect. Aubrey remembered Pam's reaction in Roncesvalles about attending Mass. She looked quite relieved when she and Georgina admitted they were too tired to attend. But Pam's reaction, then and now, piqued Aubrey's curiosity. Did Pam have something against the Catholic church?

They walked through a park that ran beside the river, rather than taking the narrow trail on the hillside. Pam was excited when they found a public toilet.

"Make sure you take your own toilet paper," said Pam, the first one to use the facilities. "There isn't any." Aubrey appreciated the tip since she had been caught short a few times already.

A little further along from the park, Pam looked down at her notes a final time, before pointing to a steep rocky trail. There, at the top of the hill, was the Abbey. It reminded Aubrey of a smaller version of Roncesvalles with its ancient worn stones.

They followed the building around to the front, placing their packs on the long wooden bench running along the church wall. Just outside the entrance, a small, conservatively dressed woman greeted them in Spanish but switched to English once she heard their butchered reply. She asked each of them which country they were from, then gestured for them to follow her. They walked through the arched doorway and into the principal part of the church. It was intimate and very quiet. Aubrey felt a sense of peace. The nun handed them each two pieces of paper. Aubrey whispered thanks and made her way to a pew on the other side of the church while Ben and Georgina took their seats on the other side of the room. Surprisingly, she saw Pam go directly to get her credential stamp. To each their own, she thought.

Sitting on the wooden bench, Aubrey looked up. The altarpiece before her was large and imposing. She wasn't sure who she was seeing, but she did recognise Mary Magdalene and John the Baptist. And Jesus, of course. She started reading the blessing the nun had handed her. Tears gathered in her eyes and emotion welled within her as she read the Beatitudes of the Pilgrim. When she reached the ninth blessing, she took a quick breath in, feeling the words speak to her.

"BLESSED ARE YOU PILGRIM, IF ON THE WAY YOU MEET YOURSELF AND GIFT yourself with time, without rushing, so as not to disregard the image in your heart."

AUBREY THOUGHT OF THE LAST FEW AWFUL YEARS. THEY HAD BEEN BEYOND difficult. Melbourne reminded her of everything that happened. She needed out. Travelling had helped. Exiting her toxic marriage helped too. But she was still reeling. That she knew. Now, here, she was feeling the pain all over again. Dark thoughts, she chided herself. A moment later, she heard the bell toll from above.

Aubrey folded the piece of paper and slipped it into her nylon bag. Georgina remained on the other side of the church, tears on her cheeks as she read the blessing herself. Aubrey turned in the pew and saw Pam and Ben coming down the stairs. Pam held her eye for a moment, then pointed outside. Aubrey nodded.

She stood and walked to the back of the church, where she asked for a stamp in her pilgrim credential and, after receiving permission from the nun, walked slowly toward the staircase. The worn stone stairs rose upward in a tight circular pattern. The steps were steep. She wondered how much pain Pam suffered with her sketchy knee. Aubrey knew she would find the determination to get there if she was keen enough. The other pilgrims at the top kindly waited for her to ascend.

With a smile of thanks, she looked around the compact space. She took photos of the roof's construction, then of the countryside beyond with her phone. She reminded herself to capture the church on her way out as well. There were two bells, but she noticed one was off limits. The other, she was welcome to ring. She ran her hand down the rope and felt a tickle on the back of her neck.

Hello, she thought. I'm glad you're here.

With a deep breath, Aubrey closed her eyes and pulled hard on the rope. She listened to the perfect pitch ring out into the countryside. The sound went on for a long time. She stood still, her hand still on the rope, feeling emotion flow over her, tears turning to sobs. She let herself feel it all. She felt in harmony with the bell as it returned to its original place, quiet and spent.

When she descended, she saw Georgina still sitting in the pew. She placed a light hand on her shoulder, leaned down and whispered, "We'll wait for you outside. But do go up and ring the bell. I highly recommend it. It's very cleansing." She squeezed her shoulder and left the church.

Ben and Pam were sitting in the garden, snacking on trail mix and dried fruit. They looked relaxed and unhurried. She joined them in the sunshine while they waited for Georgina.

"I'm sorry for taking so long," said Georgina, as she walked quickly toward them a little while later.

"No problem. Happy to be sitting in this gorgeous garden!" said Aubrey, knowing the distraction would be welcomed in the emotional moment. "Look at those daffodils sprouting."

"To beautiful new beginnings" said Pam, raising her water bottle to them. The sentiment made Aubrey smile. She was ready for a new beginning. She sensed Georgina was ready for something new in her life too.

BY MID-AFTERNOON, WEARY FROM THE HEAT, THEY REACHED PAMPLONA. The yellow arrows helped navigate their way through the city streets. Tired, Aubrey was thankful the Camino had its own identifying navigation system.

Eventually, the yellow arrows pointed them to the medieval wall surrounding the old city. Georgina insisted on taking photos at the city's commanding gate, before Ben left them to find his accommodation. His blisters were on fire, he admitted. They made plans to meet up with him later in the piazza. When Georgina snapped the last of her photos, Pam announced it was beer time.

"Yes!" said Aubrey excitedly, and they followed the yellow arrows up the hill and into the Old City. This part of Pamplona looked to be straight out of a history book. Aubrey giddily thought for a moment that she could hear bulls thundering in the distance, but that was another time of year. Instead, she admired the colourful buildings lining their path. Balconies jutted out, flags flew to support the region, or the country. Tuscan yellow-coloured buildings glowed like gold in the sunlight and their peach counterparts looked almost whimsical. Flowers appeared to reach out to greet one another, they seemed so close. But the cobblestoned streets were eerily quiet. Georgina looked at her watch.

"It's siesta," Aubrey said.

"Oh! You're right," said Georgina, looking in amazement at the emptiness.

"I love the siesta concept," said Aubrey with a sigh. "I think that's one piece of the Camino I will most definitely take home with me."

AFTER A ROUND OF BEERS, FINDING THE HOTEL PROVED MORE OF A challenge than they'd expected. The confusing maze of streets was a lot to take in. All the streets looked the same. They searched Google maps, but it sent them in the wrong direction. For an hour, they walked lane after lane.

Fuckity fuck, fuck, Aubrey thought. They were well and truly lost and tiring quickly. Pam suggested they stop in the official Tourist Information Centre, which she'd spotted when they first entered the old city. That got them on the right track and in front of their hotel in five minutes.

"What time did we say we were meeting Ben?" asked Aubrey, as they waited to check in.

"I don't know. I think I lost my marbles in the street when we got lost," said Pam. Aubrey chuckled.

"We told Ben six o'clock," Georgina said, looking at her watch. "It's now a quarter to five."

"Then I'm going to lie down for a bit before we meet him," Pam said. "I know I said it was fifteen kilometres today, but I think it was more like twenty. They say you need to listen to your body, but I'm telling you, mine just points and laughs. I think I'd like a quick dinner and an early night. I'm fucking tired." Georgina nodded.

"I agree," said Aubrey. "With all that pavement, my feet are about to fall off. I'll text Ben and let him know that we'll meet him for a quick dinner."

Minutes later, they cheered when they saw an elevator to take them to their rooms.

"Good. I couldn't make it up the stairs," said Pam "and I'm only on the second floor."

Aubrey's key revealed she was on the third floor. So was Georgina.

They all squeezed into the miniscule elevator, backpacks and poles piled up. It seemed like they had to hold their breath just to fit. At the second floor, they reshuffled, and with a wave, Pam headed to her room. On the third floor, Aubrey and Georgina found their rooms in opposite directions. As Georgina turned to leave, Aubrey grabbed her arm.

"Are you okay?" she asked. When Georgina hesitated, Aubrey reached over and gave her an awkward hug, backpacks and poles in their way.

"Be kind to yourself, Georgina. This isn't an easy journey," Aubrey smiled and turned, making her way to her room. She knew that while her lips spoke the words, her heart had yet to catch up. She needed to heed her own advice.

10

THE JOY OF DOING NOTHING

PAMPLONA

AUBREY RELISHED the privacy of her own room when she woke the next morning. It was quiet outside. She stretched, slightly embarrassed she had slept naked. It was something she had not done in a long time. She'd taken another long hot shower after dinner. By the time she finished she was so achingly tired, she climbed straight into bed, disregarding the clean underwear in the bottom of her backpack. So, here she was.

She looked over at the side table. The clock read nine-thirty. Holy shit, she thought. She was supposed to be meeting Georgina and Pam at ten.

As Aubrey rushed to get ready, she had worried thoughts about Georgina. Even though they'd been walking together for almost a week, she was still a bit of a mystery. She kept her private life just that, except for boasting about how great her daughter was. But for the rest, she was quiet. She was more of a listener. Still, Aubrey felt there was something missing. As a café owner, you'd think she'd like to ask a lot of questions. But she didn't. Instead, she kept to herself. Maybe it was her marriage? Georgina admitted to being married when they walked to Roncesvalles and again in Larrasoaña, but she'd not spoken of her husband before or since. That seemed strange. Aubrey's friends spoke of their husbands all the time. What was Georgina not saying?

Her thoughts turned to Pam. Remembering back to the first night when Georgina asked if she was married. Pam froze at the question. Then, when Ben had asked in Larrasoaña, Pam had looked panicked. Something had happened to her, she thought. Something traumatic. She didn't know how she knew, but Aubrey could feel it in her bones.

LATER THAT AFTERNOON, AFTER HER ERRANDS WERE COMPLETE AND enjoying lunch with The Lovelies, Aubrey headed back to her hotel room. After managing some yoga, she lay down on the bed to write in her journal. She was tuning back into her intuition and she was eager to capture her thoughts about Georgina and Pam.

The phone buzzed beside her. She opened her eyes from the nap she had not meant to take, picked up her phone and looked at the time.

Fuckity fuck. They planned to meet Ben in the piazza for dinner. Now, seeing the time, Aubrey sent a quick message to Georgina, telling her she was running late, but she'd meet them there.

No problem came the immediate answer. *We'll be late too.*

Are you still at the hotel?

No. But we'll see you in the piazza soon. Will you text B and let him know?

Okay, she had some time. She slowly plied herself off the bed and headed to the bathroom. Her head was there, but her body was protesting. She felt aches from head to toe.

Ten minutes later, she walked into a hive of activity in the piazza. A casual football game was in progress. Pilgrims and tourists mingled in clusters, chatting away. Multi-generational families sat together, enjoying a picnic. A group of teenagers danced around a boom box. The atmosphere was carnival-like. This was Spain. This was what she had always imagined. This is how it should be. The joy bounced from group to group.

"Aubrey!" She followed the sound and found Ben, his arm

stretched out along the back of a bench, the other waving for her attention. He looked completely at ease. She smiled at his familiar face. She had only known Ben for a brief time, but it was amazing how easy it was to get to know someone quickly. She realised in that moment that she knew more about Ben than she knew of Georgina and Pam and she'd been with them since day one. She needed to change that.

"What an atmosphere!" she said, as she approached him. He nodded with a smile, patting the seat next to him. Nearby, children were playing football with an older gentleman when their ball rolled their way. Ben hopped up and caught the ball and, with some fancy footwork, popped the ball up into the air and somehow kicked it around the back of him and toward the children. The kids gawked in awe and the gentleman applauded in approval. Ben bowed and headed back toward Aubrey.

"That is some skill," she said, admiring his quick feet.

"Yeah, soccer scholarship to college, but I injured my knee after a year. I focused on business management after that," he said, taking the seat again next to her.

"Another skill you can share with your kids," she said.

"Yeah," Ben said, and he rubbed his thigh nervously.

"Here's Georgina and Pam. Wait, what do they have in their hand?" he asked.

Pam and Georgina came toward them, giggling like two teenagers, a cheeky twinkle in their eye.

"A box of wine. Oh, no," Aubrey said, laughing at the spectacle of the two women.

"What are you two up to? You look like two schoolgirls who've snuck out on a Saturday night to drink and smoke cigarettes with their friends," Aubrey laughed. It was true. Pam had a conspiratorial wickedness about her. Georgina, on the other hand, looked like her innocent best friend, happy to be along for the ride.

"We thought the best way to experience this amazing piazza was to be one with the locals. Look around. We're not the only ones," Pam said as Georgina handed out half-filled cups. With a cheeky grin, she raised her glass.

"To another day on the Camino," Pam said, and they all touched their plastic cups together. "Even if we didn't walk today, we're here."

Ben offered the bench to Pam and Georgina, saying he was happy to sit on the ground beside them. For a while, they sat back drinking their wines, quietly watching the scene before them. Mothers casually pushing strollers while their older children rode scooters. Older women linked arms with their sons. Old men smoked cigars, ambling along with canes. And teenagers congregated, eating ice creams out of cups. It was a magical atmosphere.

"You know, this wine isn't half bad. Especially for a goon bag," said Georgina.

"A what?" gasped Ben.

"A goon bag. That's what we call a box of wine in Australia," said Georgina, blushing. "Not sure how it came about, but that's the slang for it."

"It's a very bogan thing to do," said Pam.

"A what? A bogan?" Ben shook his head. "And here I thought coming to Spain, I'd be learning Spanish, not Australian."

Aubrey leaned over to him. "Bogan is kind of the equivalent of 'white trash' in America," she said. Ben laughed, finally understanding.

"You all amaze me. I'm glad to be here with you," he said.

"Oh, stick with us kid, we'll teach you all kinds of things," teased Pam.

On their second cup of red wine, they watched a guy set up several plastic containers and pour a soapy mixture into them. He then handed wands to the small children gathering around. He dunked his wand into the first container and when he pulled it out, a huge bubble began trailing. He waved his arm softly in the air and the bubble continued growing. Aubrey had never seen a bubble so large before.

"Wow! Look at that!" she said, pointing at the bubble.

Georgina jumped up to photograph the scene. Aubrey noticed her being careful not to capture the children. Pam said, in a quiet voice to Aubrey, that as a past teacher, she was happy to see Georgina's consideration of their privacy. It was something their school had been very conscientious about. Aubrey nodded. Looking around, it was easy to assume that the bubble act had to be a common occurrence. He'd need a permit to do it in Australia. Here though, he simply looked to the parents for permission before handing their child a wand.

All around them, people were laughing. Aubrey found this moment so joyous, she wanted to remember it forever. Such a sense of community and feeling of festivity was rare, she knew. She would cherish this moment for the rest of her life.

"Who's ready for food?" asked Georgina. "I'm eager to eat more tapas."

"Pintxos, remember," said Ben. Their waiter had corrected them at dinner the night before.

With that, Aubrey took the empty wine cask and cups and discarded them in a nearby bin. Walking back to Pam, she lightly rubbed Pam's shoulder and they walked together out of the piazza arm in arm.

11

HAVE YOU NEVER SEEN 'THE WAY'?

PAMPLONA- ZARIQUIEGUI

THEY MET Ben at eight the following morning in the piazza, then continued the search for yellow arrows, making their way out of Pamplona's old city.

"Oh, wow!" said Pam. "It's like night and day walking today. My backpack is so much lighter. I feel so free!" She walked with her arms swinging freely, skipping along for just a beat.

"Ow, that hurts. I need to remember I'm not fifteen anymore," she said. They all laughed.

"Mine feels light too!" agreed Georgina. "Thanks for your help Aubrey. It feels so much better." Pam was walking ahead, doing her jig again.

"I was nervous to send the box home, but not anymore," said Georgina. "My daughter scoffed at me when I told her to look out for it. Her way of telling me 'I told you so'."

"As kids do," said Aubrey, sharing her son's comments when she had her Camino packing all laid out on the bed. He'd teased her about all she was taking, reminding her of the travelling idiom: Pack half of what you think you need and take twice as much money.

"That's a good thought," said Ben. "I must tell Kanmi that. He packs three suitcases when we go on vacation. One suitcase is just for shoes!" That cracked them up.

As they made their way through the park, Aubrey noticed more people walking this morning. There were more locals than pilgrims. She realised it was Saturday morning. She had lost touch with time.

"I shared the photos we took yesterday with Nicole too. Who knew you could get a photo that makes you look like you're running with the bulls? And she was quick to remind me of a time, years ago, when I was literally running from a bull at home. Not the same, let me tell you!" said Georgina. Aubrey felt a stab of pain at her missed opportunity to share the experience with her son. She'd called but he didn't answer.

"I remember a time when I had my monthly cycle on the farm," Pam said, before suddenly looking at Ben, embarrassed.

"Go on. It doesn't bother me if it doesn't bother you," he said. "I'm Mormon remember? I have a multitude of sisters and three mothers." Pam raised her eyebrows but recovered before continuing.

"I was walking home across the paddock late one afternoon, rather than the road home. A male kangaroo came after me. Apparently, they can be attracted to the scent. Barely made it over the fence in time. Dad told me I was lucky. Learned my lesson. I didn't do that again."

"Wow, that would have been scary!" said Aubrey. Pam shrugged. She was a tough nut, thought Aubrey.

"Were you lonely growing up on the farm?" Ben asked. When Pam hesitated, Aubrey looked over at her. She had a look of confusion but then of deep contemplation, as if she didn't seem to know how to answer the question. Aubrey almost said something, but Pam spoke.

"No, I don't believe I was. I mean, I'd known people there all my life, but our life was really all about the farm. Some days were quiet, sure. It was just me and my parents, but..." She hesitated and Aubrey looked back over at her. Pam's face softened.

"I had joy early in my life. When I was a teenager," she said, and Pam's voice went quiet. "A boy. He almost saved me."

"From what?" asked Ben. Aubrey was curious about the answer too. Pam seemed like she was in her own world.

"It's the only time in my life I've ever been truly happy," Pam said, ignoring Ben's question. And before anyone could ask another question, her face took on a look of sadness, then anger, before she returned to the present. Ben looked at Aubrey for guidance. She shrugged.

"What about yours, Georgina," asked Ben.

"My childhood was very different from Pam's. I spent most of it at the beach or fishing with my dad."

"What about the property you mentioned?" asked Aubrey.

"It's my husband's property," answered Georgina but she quickly changed the subject when she saw the landscape ahead of them.

"Look at those massive fields of canola! Wow! The yellow is so vibrant. It almost looks like a swathe of bright sunshine across the hillside. It's so beautiful! Oh, I wish I brought my damn camera!" she said, disappointed.

"Is that what those flowers are?" asked Ben. "Canola? I've wondered."

"Yeah, for making canola oil. Just look at those flowers. Wow! And that colour, it's like..." said Georgina, reaching for her iPhone.

"... happiness in a field," answered Aubrey.

"Yes!" said Georgina as she captured the acres upon acres of yellow. Aubrey had seen fields for the last two days, but here it was vibrant and in masses like she'd never seen before.

When they made it to Cizur Manor, they were ready for breakfast but struggled to find a café open.

"It's Saturday. We've seen people all morning. Where'd they go? Surely there's a café!" said Pam.

"Looks like there's one over there," said Ben, pointing toward a hidden bar tucked off the road.

"Good eye," said Pam and started in that direction. Two at a time, they headed inside to order and use the toilets. The other two stayed at the outside table minding their backpacks. Ben came out laughing.

"You should see what's in the men's toilet. It is the funniest thing ever. I guess the gentlemen, ah, need a little aid?" He pulled out his phone and showed them the photo of a bullseye sticker inside the toilet's bowl. "I know, it's uncouth of me to take this shot, but I had to. It's hilarious."

"Share it with us?" Aubrey asked. Ben nodded. "I'm posting that on Facebook," said Aubrey. "My son will get a kick out of it. I spent years trying to teach him where to aim. He has it now at twenty-one, thank god." That had them laughing again.

"How's the coffee, Georgina?" asked Pam before even tasting hers.

"Honestly? Good. Either that or I'm getting used to these coffees. But I think this one is good. It's nice and strong." She took a delicate sip of the hot beverage without wrinkling her nose for once.

"The croissants are divine," said Aubrey, feeling like a five-year-old with an enormous smile on her face and a mouth full of croissant and crumbs. "I love carbs."

A young guy arrived when they were about halfway through their coffees. He pointed to the Australian flag on Pam's pack and exclaimed "Australia!" She nodded.

"Hello! I am Paolo. I am from Italy." The guy was tall, almost six feet, and lean. He had the arms of a bricklayer and a beautifully tanned face that sported laugh lines when he smiled. His hair was short, dark and curly, buried under a blue baseball cap turned backwards. The colour of the hat brought out his chocolate brown eyes. He looked like the poster boy for young Italian men.

"The café? Is it good?" They all looked pointedly at Georgina.

"Yes, it's good," she replied sheepishly.

"You are the expert, no?" He smiled at Georgina. Aubrey chuckled. Of course she was.

"She is," said Pam. Georgina sighed.

"I guess I am the expert in this crowd," she said.

"Then I will indulge. Grazie." He wandered into the café, leaving his pack at a nearby table.

"You guys! He's from Italy. He knows his coffee!" Georgina said.

"I'm from Melbourne. We're known as coffee snobs too, you know. But, compared to you, apparently not," said Aubrey, smiling. "It's better to defer to the one in the business."

Paolo returned and Aubrey invited him to join them. Georgina seemed embarrassed. But he was young and eager and a breath of fresh air.

"Where did you begin your Camino?" asked Ben.

"Pamplona! I walk to Santiago to meet the bella ragazza, ah, beautiful girls." Then he whispered, with a finger to his lips, "but don't tell Mamma!" He laughed naughtily. "Mamma thinks I walk for the religion, yes?"

"So, this is day one for you?" asked Aubrey as Paolo passed her his napkin, pointing to her lip. She was still covered in croissant crumbs after finishing the last on her plate. "Oh, thank you," she said, suddenly embarrassed by her lack of decorum.

"Si. I spent three nights in Pamplona. I was having so much fun, but then Mamma reminded me why I was here. She wishes for me to find my... path." His English impressed Aubrey, and she found him funny and rather cheeky.

"Sure! Pamplona is great," said Ben.

"Si. But the ragazze. Ah.... Like you tré belle donne," he smiled seductively at Aubrey, Georgina and then toward Pam.

"I think your Mamma is right to worry about you," said Pam. "You're a cheeky one, aren't you?" She smiled, rising from her chair. "I don't mean to be rude, but I want to keep going. Who's ready?"

When they were all loaded up, Paolo wished them a Buen Camino.

"Don't worry, you'll probably pass us if you don't pick up some poor girl in the meantime," said Pam, before waving him goodbye.

They walked together for a while in silence, climbing the long slow ascent, taking more photos of the blooming canola and the rolling green hills. Soon, Pamplona was just a vision in the background.

As they continued up the hill, Aubrey thought about Zabaldika. She wanted to ask Georgina what she was feeling in the church but didn't want to seem pushy. She didn't want her to feel uncomfortable and clam up even more than usual. Well, I didn't talk about my moment either, she thought. She considered whether she was ready when she caught sight of a butterfly flying past and turned to follow its flight.

"Oh! Turn around and look. That's Pamplona, right? Where we walked from this morning. It feels so far, doesn't it?" she said. They took a moment to take it all in. The fields of yellow were a blazing contrast to the bleak grey of the city beyond.

"We should probably push on. Those clouds look menacing and I don't think Zariquiegui is too far ahead," said Pam, reading the notes on her phone. Aubrey looked toward the nearby village and saw the dark grey clouds closing in quickly.

They had walked about fifty metres before hearing a voice behind them, "Ciao! Hola!"

Paolo had caught up to them. Aubrey was surprised it had taken him so long. Maybe he had met some girls to chat with along the way. There were plenty out walking today, she noticed.

"Hey Paolo," said Ben and the two walked ahead together, leaving the three women behind.

"Ben's probably happy to have a guy to talk to," said Pam.

"Maybe. But he was telling me yesterday that he enjoys walking with us. He likes our company, of course. But our pace really suits him given the condition of his feet," said Aubrey.

"He needs to keep an eye on those blisters, or he'll be going home," said Pam, her voice lowered.

"I think he realised that himself. He appreciates your help," said Aubrey. Georgina nodded. Mothering was what Pam did well, thought Aubrey.

"Well, we've lost them," said Aubrey. Paolo and Ben had increased their pace, lost in conversation about travel adventures.

"We're stopping at the next town, right?" asked Aubrey. "The village before the pilgrim statues on the hill? That's the place you want to take sunrise photos, isn't it, Georgina?"

"Yes. It's the Alto de Perdon. I hope that doesn't slow you all down. I know it means it's a short day today," she said.

"I don't mind. I'm not in any hurry," said Aubrey.

"Nope, me either," said Pam.

"Good. I think the statues will be pretty in the morning light," murmured Georgina.

"Ben knows we're stopping, right?" asked Pam.

"Yes, I think so," said Aubrey.

"THE CHURCH LOOKS FAMILIAR," SAID AUBREY AS SHE LEANED HER POLES against the bordering stone wall. "I feel like I have seen it before."

Aubrey stood staring at the church, while Georgina took photos of the doors. Pam was looking for notes on her phone.

"You probably have," said Georgina, looking over at her. "Did you watch the Martin Sheen movie, *The Way*?"

"Yes. Of course," said Aubrey.

"It's where Martin meets up again with the Canadian, and where Joost meets her for the first time. She's sitting on that rock wall there, smoking." Georgina said, pointing.

"Oh yes. I see it now." Aubrey said. Pam wandered over. "Look, it's the church from the movie, *The Way*."

"Hmm. Don't think I've seen that one," said Pam, distracted by whatever she was looking for on her phone.

"Really?!" said Aubrey and Georgina in unison, shock in both voices.

"No. Who's in it?" Pam asked, putting her phone away. Georgina and Aubrey looked at each other and started laughing.

"Martin Sheen," said Georgina. "Surely you've seen it. It's a movie about the Camino."

"Nope, haven't seen it. Only saw a documentary," said Pam, picking up her trekking poles again.

"Of all the people Pam, I thought you would have seen that movie," said Aubrey, shaking her head in disbelief, as they finally walked toward the bar. "It's the movie that prompted me to walk the Camino. Simon recommended it to me."

"I'll put it on my list when I get home then," said Pam. Aubrey and Georgina looked at each other, still shaking their heads. Aubrey assumed everyone who walked the Camino had seen that movie at least once.

"To be fair, I didn't watch it until a few months ago," admitted Georgina. "But I've seen it five times since." She pointed at Ben and Paolo sitting outside up ahead. They had bocadillas and beers in front of them.

"Hello boys!" said Aubrey. She sat on the edge of a seat at their table, her backpack still on. "Did you see the movie, *The Way*?"

"Sure," said Ben. He looked at Pam and Georgina as if to ask, what gives? Aubrey looked at Paolo.

"Si," said Paolo. Aubrey looked back at Pam with a raised eyebrow.

"Okay! Jesus. I'll watch it when I get back. I promise." Pam lay her trekking poles against the table.

"Have you not seen the movie?" Ben asked Pam, shocked.

"Nope," Pam said and removed her pack, sliding it to the ground. She thumbed in the church's direction. "The church is in one scene apparently."

"Yeah, where Sarah sees Boomer again," he responded. Aubrey laughed.

"I will watch it. I promise. When I get home. Now, are we checking in?" asked Pam.

"Ben? Are you continuing? Or sticking with us?" asked Aubrey.

"I can see if they have four beds?" asked Pam.

"I think I want to keep going. Although those clouds do look menacing." The clouds had darkened, and the wind had picked up. "I'm not sure I want to be around metal statues when that lightening comes over us."

"So, stay or go?" said Pam, her tone impatient. She glanced over at the people gathered near the door, ready to check in.

Ben looked at the three women individually and then at Paolo.

"I will stay. Paolo? Want to join the party?"

Lightning cracked above them.

"My Mamma would say that is a sign from God. Si, I will stay. I will see if they have room for me."

"Good. I'll see if I can push it to five. You guys will have to check in with your documents," said Pam.

"No problem." They downed their beers, grabbed their wrapped bocadillas, picked up their backpacks and walked inside to check in.

The hospitalero escorted them to an unassuming building around the corner from the bar. He asked them to remove their shoes on the ground floor and to leave their trekking poles in the huge metal canister tucked into the corner. Then, walking up the worn wooden steps, the host pointed to three shower cubicles, which looked like individual bathrooms on a cruise ship, all self-contained and with no ventilation. That'll be interesting, Aubrey thought. After showing Paolo a bed in one room to the left of the stairs, he showed Aubrey,

Pam, Ben and Georgina to their beds. They were tucked into a back room.

After settling into the new dorm, Aubrey, Pam and Georgina took some time journaling or napping. Paolo and Ben headed back to the bar just as the skies opened up with a deluge of rain. After a while, Aubrey got up to do some yoga.

"Lovelies, what do you think?" asked Aubrey, as she finished her last stretch. "Time for a beer or wine, before we decide on dinner?"

Georgina looked at her watch. She really made Aubrey laugh with this lifelong habit.

"I think so," said Pam, hoisting herself off the bed. "If I lie down any longer, I won't be getting back up."

With the storm blown over, they walked to a restaurant at the top of the hill. They checked the menu. They were early so ordered beers before settling in at a covered table outside.

"To another day on the Camino," said Aubrey, clinking glasses with her friends. The beer was refreshingly cold.

"So, Georgina, I've been wanting to ask you this and I hope you don't mind my nosiness. You mentioned you're married, but you haven't mentioned your husband at all. I'm curious why?" asked Aubrey. Pam pointed to her upper lip. Aubrey wiped the condensation off with her finger.

Georgina picked lint from her shirt. She looked up, nodded, then ran her hand through her ponytail. Stalling, Aubrey thought, and watched as Georgina picked at the coaster. Aubrey could feel the discomfort bouncing off her.

"I'm sure you've been wondering. I guess, well, I really didn't mean to not mention him. As I said, it's complicated." She looked like a kangaroo caught in headlights.

"You don't have to talk about it, if you don't want to," said Aubrey.

"No. It's okay. I... well, no, it's okay. I'm okay to talk about it." She took a deep breath and ran her hand through her ponytail once more. "We got married young. Early twenties. We kind of grew up knowing each other. Patrick is kind of the quintessential Aussie guy. A man's man, if you will." She took a sip of her beer.

"He's been running his family's farm since his dad died five years ago. He also has a fly in, fly out job in the mines on the mainland, two weeks out of the month. I have the café, so we barely see each other. Not much of a story, really."

"Sounds like it would be hard to maintain a marriage with that kind of schedule," said Aubrey.

"No harder than most," she mumbled.

"And you run the café full time, right?" asked Aubrey, her hands now wrapped around her beer. Pam sat back in her chair, listening.

"Yeah. Patrick's dad was a mean guy, very much a dictator about the farm. No one did it right. Patrick was the only son, so it all fell on him. He has four sisters. They all went to the mainland as soon as they could and haven't been back since. They don't even come back for holidays anymore. Their dad ran them off." She picked more at the coaster, not making eye contact at all.

"So, Patrick has been dealing with all of this since his dad died. His mum died about ten years ago and, after she went, his dad got worse. Seemed like she was the one that kept him in control. Once she was gone, his filter vanished. It really did a number on Patrick. He was happy to be away, to be off working in the mines. He had to take that work because the farm was losing money. It wasn't until his dad died that he realised how serious the money issues were."

"So, now he manages his fulltime mining job and the farm? Who manages the farm when he's away? Not you, surely. You'd have enough with the café I would imagine?" Aubrey asked.

"No. Not me. He employs a part time manager to look after the place when he's gone. It's mostly Patrick's deal more than it is mine. I just play the supportive wife." Now that was interesting, thought Aubrey. Georgina took another long drink of her beer and looked around. Aubrey followed. People were arriving for dinner. When Georgina went quiet, Pam suggested they move inside.

Walking toward the door, Aubrey found it wasn't what Georgina said that she was curious about. It was what she didn't say. She saw Georgina as shy, maybe even insecure, but certainly not submissive.

12

WHAT MESSAGE ARE YOU SENDING?

ZARIQUIEGUI TO PUENTE LA RIENA

IT WAS pitch black when she felt the bunk move. Pam and Georgina were leaving early to catch the sunrise at Alto dé Perdon. Aubrey had decided to hang back and walk with the boys instead. She'd gotten the impression over dinner last night that she'd upset Georgina by asking about her marriage. Best to give her some space, Aubrey thought.

She could hear Georgina and Pam quietly grabbing their stuff and leaving the room. They had been stealth about it. Aubrey thought back to the Italian's departure that morning in Larrasoaña and appreciated the contrast in the way her friends left. She could hear faint whispering from the other side of the door, then silence. She turned over and saw Ben sleeping soundly on the other side of the room. Within minutes, she heard the door close downstairs.

"Good luck, Georgina," she whispered. She knew Georgina was excited to take sunrise pictures against the metal pilgrim statues. Aubrey closed her eyes once more, but sleep eluded her. She wasn't prepared to pack up and follow Georgina and Pam in the dark either. So, she snuggled under her down blanket and thought of what Georgina had said about her husband.

Georgina described him as stoic and stubborn. A farm and an out-of-state job were a lot to take on, especially if he insisted on doing it all alone. When Aubrey thought of her ex-husband, Brendon, the words 'gutless wonder' leapt to mind. She loved that Australian saying. It said so much. Brendon was not like Patrick at all. If anything, he avoided responsibility, hiding behind his mother's skirt. Aubrey was glad the marriage was over, but more than that, she found the marriage embarrassed her. How could she not see his true character sooner? She sighed. She realised she'd not thought of Brendon at any length this entire journey. That said a lot.

Aubrey had been married to Brendon for twenty-three years, most of it a rollercoaster ride of crazy work schedules and bustling social lives. But his true character, the character she had ignored for so many years, had come to light only two years before. She had taken the blinders off. Or ripped them off, if she was honest with herself. If only she'd done so earlier. It would have saved a lot of mental anguish, that's for sure. And not only for her, but for... no. She wasn't going there.

She nuzzled back under the blanket and waited until the light was bright enough for her to see the room. Then, she dressed quickly, got down from the bunk, quietly grabbed her backpack and headed downstairs.

Moments later, standing outside of the albergue, she sent Ben a text.

Decided to head off to catch P & G. Will see you later. x Aubrey.

As SHE MADE HER WAY UP THE NARROW TRAIL, SHE COULD IMAGINE THE photographs Georgina was capturing right about now. She turned around and saw the most amazing sunrise peek its way over the hills. It was a glorious morning but freezing. The storm the day before had swept in an iciness to the region. Her breath clouding with condensation as she trudged up the hill, her nose running from the cold. Pam's weather app had saved her from a morning of misery, allowing her to dress appropriately. She'd thrown her tank top under her long shirt and put her t-shirt over the top, finishing it with her zip up hoodie. She threw on her windbreaker at the last minute. She'd remove layers as the day warmed.

By the time she reached the Alto, the sun was up, and Georgina and Pam were no longer there. But she savoured the brief minutes to herself before other pilgrims followed. The metal statue was beautiful. It captured the essence of pilgrims well. She asked the pilgrims coming up behind her if they would take her photo. She was suddenly missing her Camino family. She would have loved to have shared this moment with the Lovelies. But she had chosen not to join Pam and Georgina or wait for Ben and Paolo. She regretted her choice.

Satisfied with her time at the top, she slowly descended. The shale was extremely slippery. She heard the loud crunch coming up behind her, just enough of a warning before the cyclist zoomed past her.

"Jesus H. Christ! How about using your goddamn bell?" a voice screamed from behind her. Aubrey looked back and saw a tiny woman barrelling down the hill toward her. A stream of colourful language spewed from her. Language that would make even Pam blush. The pixie-like woman stood barely over five feet. She had spiked silver hair and a stance that Aubrey could only describe as lean and mean.

"I wanted to yell out to you, but I was trying to catch my breath," said the woman as she caught up. "Can you believe that punk?!" Her American accent was so high pitched, it screeched in Aubrey's ears.

"He scared the life out of me!" said Aubrey, her hand over her racing heart. She smiled. The woman looked like she wanted to kick the shit out of someone.

"Yeah, the little punks think they rule this god damn Camino. I've almost been hit twice today by cyclists. First time was this morning coming out of Cizur-Mayor in the dark, and I was even wearing a flashing light on my backpack. And now this!"

Aubrey shook her head before turning to continue down the trail.

"It's so slippery, especially after that rain we got last night," she warned, but the woman was nipping at her heels, so Aubrey stepped aside. "Go around me if you like."

And off the woman went. No Buen Camino, no nothing.

"Wow." Glad she'd avoided any more interaction with that dynamite pilgrim.

. . .

AUBREY FOUND PAM AND GEORGINA SEATED ON THE PATIO OF THE FIRST café she came to after her descent, just as arranged. Georgina had a coffee in front of her, Pam a pot of tea. Both looked relaxed and happy.

"Hello Lovelies."

"Aubrey!" said Georgina. "You're earlier than we expected. We've just ordered."

"What did you think of that descent?" asked Pam, not waiting for Aubrey's answer before continuing, "We took our time. It was slow going down that shale. My knees now feel like they have more rubber than a tyre factory." Aubrey smiled. "Georgina almost slid down on her bum. And not intentionally!"

"Oh, no! Are you okay Georgina? It was perilous, that's for sure," said Aubrey as she unloaded her backpack.

"You can say that again. Plus, I had a cyclist come up behind me and scare the bejesus out of me. That's when I slipped on the shale."

"Had the same thing happen to me. Then this pixie of a woman came barrelling down behind me, swearing after him. She was not a cheerful woman," Aubrey said, pulling her money purse and credential out of the top part of her backpack.

"I think the woman you're describing is inside," said Georgina. "Came in and there were two cyclists parked here when we arrived. They were just finishing up a coffee, and she unloaded on them."

"Short grey hair? Lean and mean? High pitched American accent?" asked Aubrey.

"That sounds just like her," said Georgina, placing her cup back into its saucer. Aubrey shook her head.

"Spitfire, that one," said Aubrey. "Okay, I'll be right back. What did you order?"

"Bacon and eggs!" announced Pam, an enormous grin on her face.

"Oh, yum!" It sounded just the thing for breakfast after the morning's hike. Aubrey walked inside and noticed the American woman seated at a table, looking as calm and collected as can be. Aubrey waved at her before placing her order and getting her credential stamped, but with no further conversation coming from the woman, Aubrey headed back outside.

"Cool as a cucumber she was. You'd never know the language that spouted from her mouth up there on the hill," Aubrey said, taking a seat.

"So, Ben and Paolo didn't join you?" asked Georgina.

"No, Ben was still asleep when I left but I sent him a text." They served Pam and Georgina their bacon and eggs, along with an enormous basket of bread. Aubrey's mouth watered as she inhaled the delicious aromas.

"How was the sunrise? Did you get the pictures you wanted?" she asked, grabbing a piece of bread when Georgina pushed the basket toward her.

"Gorgeous. It was the perfect morning with enough cloud to make the photos interesting. Here. Have a look." Whatever had Georgina brooding last night, the sunrise had brought her out of it. She took Georgina's unlocked phone and started scrolling through the photos.

"Georgina, you really have an amazing eye," Aubrey said. "These are stunning. Please, please do something more with your photography."

"Oh, they're okay. I wished for my camera this morning. The photos would have been a lot crisper," said Georgina as she took a mouthful of eggs.

"You're killing me Georgina," said Aubrey, just as they placed bacon and eggs in front of her. She reached for her cutlery.

"O.K. my mouth is salivating just looking at that. And the smell!" said Ben, as he and Paolo wandered in.

"Hello! Join us!" Aubrey said. The two men unloaded their packs. Paolo walked directly inside while Ben stopped to chat. "You made great time. You were both still zonked when I left." Ben laughed.

"Yeah, was pretty tired. Stayed up too late playing cards with Paolo and some other pilgrims staying at the other albergue." He looked down at their plates. "That looks amazing. I'm going in. Would you ladies like anything else?" With shakes of the head, Ben went inside. As he walked in, the American woman walked out.

"Buen Camino," offered Aubrey and got a wave.

"Don't know about you, but that's just rude," said Pam. "At least offer a return Buen Camino."

"Yeah. I agree. I said it to her on the trail and she just ignored me," said Aubrey, and they all fell silent to devour their breakfasts.

GEORGINA, AUBREY AND PAM DIVERTED TO SEE THE IGLESIA DE SANTA María de Eunate, a 12th-century Romanesque church that would take them another three kilometres further. Pam was giddy about the diversion, especially when she told them the history behind it. It was once believed that the church's origin is connected to the Templars, but its construction is the result of a family saga, juicier than a ripe orange, shared Pam.

"It's also built in the shape of an octagon, so if the drama doesn't get you, the unique architecture might." Pam promised to explain more once they arrived. Ben and Paolo decided to continue to Puente la Reina.

"Let's meet up later this afternoon," Ben suggested.

The day seemed never-ending as they walked the long, straight road toward the church. They wore wide-brimmed hats to block the intense sun. The swirling wind kicked up dust that lined the back of their throats. Aubrey was doubting the merits of this detour. When they arrived, a crowd had moved on, so they had the place to themselves. They walked through the archway to gaze at the octagonal wonder, then waited for Pam to read them the juicy background.

"Now, keep in mind, this is from a blog, but it's a good synopsis," she said and cleared her throat. "Following a series of adultery and ghastly murders, the remaining son built the monastery in remembrance of his mother, whom he poisoned. He buried her under the foundation as she was very influential in the spiritual realm and the promotion of the Brotherhood, which still exists today. Thousands of pilgrims have been granted hospice and a chance for spiritual reflection here since the early 12th century. The mystery surrounding the odd architecture, however, remains."

"Do you have any other details on the family?" asked Georgina, pulling out her phone to take closeup photos of the gargoyles.

"Yes, let me find it," said Pam, scanning her notes. "Here it is. It's a bit convoluted. Argentina, married to a French count, ran away with a handsome visitor to the castle. Pride hurt, the French count left and met Dona Sancha, who happened to be the stepdaughter of Argentina. The French Count became the lover of Dona Sancha, both of whom despised Argentina, so they beheaded her and the traitorous partner. Dona Sancha gave the Count a son who grew up hating his father. The son, when he became a teenager, arranged for his father's death in battle," Pam laughed, "as teenagers do. Anyway, reading on... Dona Sancha, as ambitious as her son, tried to then poison her son but the son learned of the evil plot and turned the tables. Dona Sancha drank the poison instead and died. Grief stricken, the son built the monastery and buried his mother underneath, where thousands of pilgrims have been granted hospice since."

"That puts a new perspective on it, doesn't it," stated Aubrey as they walked around the stone monument. Georgina snapped away with her iPhone, while Pam read.

"Look here's where the mason marked his stopping point," Georgina said excitedly, pointing at etches in the stonework. When they reached the entrance, Aubrey left Pam and Georgina to continue their tour. She walked inside the cool, darkened building. A sense of peace fell upon her. Then, she felt the presence.

"Hello. I've missed you," Aubrey whispered. She could feel a slight breeze cross her neck, just as she had in Zabaldika. She was glad for the company. The presence had come to her often, but more so since starting the walk. Her ex-husband called her crazy when she first mentioned the feeling. He'd even threatened to commit her. But her therapist had assured her it was normal. Aubrey didn't care who believed her. She knew what she felt. What she sensed. And she loved it. She had only wished... ugh, she needed to not go there.

She walked up to the front of the church and lit a candle for both her children. Neither had had easy childhoods. Aubrey carried a lot of guilt about that. Feeling tears on her cheeks, she slowly wiped them away, and sent a message into the Universe. Then, blowing her nose, she turned and walked back out into the sunlight.

Georgina and Pam sat beside their packs snacking on trail mix.

"What is it about these Spanish churches?" she asked, taking a small amount of trail mix from Georgina.

"Just be careful. Religion can ruin lives," said Pam, standing. Aubrey looked at Georgina with a raised eyebrow and, when Pam's back was turned, Georgina shrugged. Before she knew it, Pam had her backpack on and was heading up the hill, setting a pace that proved too fast for Aubrey's sore feet. She and Georgina let Pam go to walk off whatever angst was gnawing at her.

"How are you doing Georgina? I'm sorry if I upset you last night," Aubrey said. They were back on the trail. Georgina had been deep in her own thoughts. She smiled, then quickly swerved to avoid a pile of horse poo.

"I've been thinking about what you said last night about Patrick," Aubrey said.

"Oh?" she asked, pulling ahead on the narrow track before it widened again.

"I guess it made me think about my own marriage. I was a bit in the background," said Aubrey.

"I think Australian men are raised to be more dominant. Our generation seems to be that way anyway," said Georgina.

"Maybe, Brendon wasn't that way."

"You haven't talked about your marriage before either," Georgina said. "I didn't want to pry."

"Oh, you wouldn't be. And I'm sorry if you saw it as that, last night. Me, prying I mean." Georgina looked up and shook her head.

"You weren't prying. It's just something that I'm working through, that's all. I wasn't trying to hide it. I guess I'm just not one to talk about stuff like that. So, what was your marriage like?"

"Oh," Aubrey said, surprised, not sure she was ready to talk about her marital woes either. But she wanted to help Georgina if she could. "I guess it's fair to say the issues we had were not new. Divorcing Brendon was inevitable in hindsight." Georgina was quiet for a minute. Aubrey didn't know whether she should go on.

"I didn't see what was going on in my marriage because of work and then, well, other family stuff took over," Aubrey continued. Her voice cracked and she took a deep breath, trying to regain control of her emotions. She wanted to help Georgina, but she wasn't ready to talk about the rest.

"With my marriage, I kind of ignored what was going on. I guess you could say I had blinders on," Aubrey finally said, walking up the steep road toward an old village. Georgina walked with her head down. It was hard enough to climb the hill without words taking their breath away too.

"What made you take the blinders off?" Georgina asked finally.

"Um...." Shit, how did she explain this part? She hesitated, then said, "Therapy."

"What do you mean?" Georgina asked, confusion lined her face.

"Well, Brendon had everything I once looked for. A background my parents had approved of. Money to make life comfortable. Social standing in Melbourne, which was important to me back then, especially after my first marriage. Plus, he was a major romantic back then. He was all about grand gestures. But, with therapy, I saw the red flags I had missed. I was hesitant to leave him at first. The last straw for me was when he slept with a twenty-year-old. I decided then to confront him about it. He threw barbs at me. Told me what a pig I had become. He told me he couldn't even get it up with me anymore. Then he laughed." Aubrey remembered she'd never wanted to hit anyone before in her life until that moment.

"Idiot," said Georgina. "I mean, look at you. You're beautiful. What was he expecting of a wife in her late forties? A waif?"

"Apparently he was still looking for that twenty-something me and substituted me for another twenty-something." Georgina let out a breath that sounded more like a whoosh.

"After copious amounts of money spent on therapy, I confirmed for myself that I was doing just fine as I was. Granted, his words sent me to the gym. But I ultimately decided I was now fitter and healthier than I'd ever been. And, his image of women is, well, to be blunt, fucked up."

"Amen to that," said Georgina.

"So, long story short, after the affair and, well, some other things said, I realised I was better off on my own."

"Geez. What else did he do? I mean, having an affair and telling you he can't get it up around you would be enough justification," said Georgina.

"Yes, you'd think so. It all came down to who he was at his core. And, his priorities," Aubrey said. Georgina got the hint that she was ready to move past this conversation. "But I know this. Distance puts a lot of things into perspective. Maybe being away will give you some perspective too. I don't know, but I sense that there's more going on with you and Patrick than you said." Georgina nodded. "As my best friend told me just after I left Brendon, 'if you keep focusing on stupid shit, you get a stupid life.' That rang true for me."

"Love that. So true," she said, pointing to Pam sitting outside of a café, a pot of tea in front of her. "I guess I'm trying to sift through the shit to see what kind of life I have."

"Just make sure, Georgina, that you're focusing on the right things. Not the stupid shit," said Aubrey. Georgina squeezed her arm, just as they re-joined Pam. Whatever had been bothering Pam before didn't seem to be bothering her now.

THEY WALKED INTO PUENTE LA REINA FOLLOWING PAM'S GOOGLE directions to their albergue. Once more, it was quiet.

"Siesta!" Georgina declared, without even looking at her watch. Progress, Aubrey thought with a smile.

After they showered, they combined a load of laundry, and went in search of something to eat. They were directed to the old town by their host. He explained it was shaded and much cooler. As they walked across the square, they saw Ben and Paolo sitting with two younger women.

"Didn't take Paolo long," whispered Pam.

"Hello ladies. Joining us?" said Ben, waving them over.

"Why not," said Aubrey. Paolo retrieved chairs for everyone. Aubrey spotted the rawness on Ben's heels.

"Did you not heed Pam's advice this morning, Ben?"

"No, I did not." He bowed his head. "But I'll be okay."

"Let me know if you need help with those feet again," said Pam, mumbling 'silly boy' under her breath. She gave him a playful punch in the arm before taking a seat next to him.

"Georgina, Pam, Aubrey, this is Marinka and Hannah. We met in Pamplona, at the albergue." They nodded with confirmation.

"Lovely to meet you. Where are you from?" said Aubrey, scooting her chair further into the shade. The sun almost blinded her.

"Germany," said Marinka, turning to Hannah.

"The United States. And you? Are you from England?"

"Originally. I live in Australia now. We all do. We met on the first day at Orisson," said Aubrey. Paolo offered to take their drink orders.

"Is that where you started?" asked Hannah.

"Right before there. We started in Saint Jean Pied de Port. You?" asked Aubrey.

"I started in Pamplona but plan on walking to Santiago," said Hannah.

"Yes, us too. And you? Marinka is it?" asked Aubrey.

"Yes." She looked down at her lap, Aubrey picking up her shyness right away. "I began in Pamplona. I am walking only two weeks."

Paolo returned with a handful of beers then dashed inside for the rest.

"Here, let me give you money Paolo," said Pam when he returned. Aubrey had learned how Pam hated owing money to anyone. It prompted them all to reach for their cash.

"No. On me. That is the saying. Yes?" he said, raising his glass. "Cheers!" They all scrambled for their glasses.

"To another day on the Camino," said Pam, and they all cheered.

"Some of us clearly fared better," she added, giving a nudge to Ben. He looked sheepish, which made Aubrey smile.

"Oh look, it's Lean and Mean," said Aubrey quietly, nodding toward the other side of the plaza. Before she realised what she was doing, she waved. The small grey-haired woman she'd come across just after the Alto de Perdon began scurrying toward them, as if on a mission.

"Now you've done it," whispered Pam.

"Hello!" Aubrey said. The woman just stared as she stood behind Hannah and Marinka, her hands resting on the back of their chairs.

"God-damn fucking millennials. I have just checked into my albergue, and they have taken over the place. I wanted to sit quietly to journal, but no. They have turned it into a party zone. They think they own this god-damn Camino."

"Um," Aubrey stuttered. She looked over at Marinka, Hannah and Paolo, who all happened to be in the category this woman was bitching about.

"I'm going to go back and attempt to take a nap. Seriously though? These kids are killing me with their damn headphones and their fucking attitudes." And then, without waiting for a response, she turned on her heel and stalked away.

"What the hell was that?" Aubrey cried. The woman's anger was incredible. Everyone else looked as stunned as she felt. Although Pam had a look of utter fear. Aubrey reached over and shoulder bumped her, snapping her out of whatever was going through her head.

"This is going to sound bad. And I really don't mean to offend you when I say this," said Hannah, looking pointedly at Pam, "but I wanted to turn to her and say, 'Okay Boomer'."

They all cracked up. Pam, the only baby boomer amongst them, raised her beer in Hannah's direction, and laughed heartedly along with the rest of them.

13

ARE YOU HAPPY?

PUENTE LE REINA TO VILLATUERTA

THE SUN HAD BARELY RISEN when Aubrey, Georgina and Pam strolled into the sunrise. Their destination for the day was an albergue called La Casa Magica. Pam had shared the recommendation over dinner the night before. Everyone was eager to stay when she mentioned there were no bunk beds. The clincher was the home-cooked meal.

Ben decided he would stick with Paolo. Mostly because he wanted to protect the girls from Paolo's roving ways. Paolo had already recalled a few stories of his conquests on the Camino, jokingly whispering each time, 'don't tell Mamma'. Aubrey was relieved Ben was thinking of them. The girls seemed so young and innocent and she'd seen plenty of Paolo's in her lifetime. But for now, this morning, it was just her and the Lovelies.

"I love these mornings," said Georgina. "Everything looks so fresh. And it's quiet, except for the birds chattering."

"It's my favourite time of day," said Pam, as the three of them found a rhythm.

They walked in silence for an hour. Occasionally, one of them would point out the single red poppies on the side of the track, or the way the dew clung to a fence wire.

"Wait. Stop," whispered Georgina. She stopped so quickly, Aubrey slammed right into her pack. "Do you hear that?"

Aubrey listened and didn't hear a thing. Until she did.

"What is that?" she whispered.

"It's a cuckoo," said Georgina, turning toward her, a smile on her face.

"Then someone forgot to tell them they need to stop their little sing-song at twelve. It's still going!" said Pam. And it kept going, with the sound so far off they couldn't pinpoint which direction it even came from. The call ricocheted off the hills.

Apart from her excitement over the cuckoo, Georgina was quieter than normal. She looked deep in thought, and after their conversation yesterday, Aubrey hadn't wanted to disrupt her reflection. She'd been in that place herself.

"I have been thinking a lot about our dinner at Zariquiegui," said Pam after a while. "I wanted to ask you this question Georgina, and I hope you know it comes from a good place." Georgina looked over at Pam and by the intense look on Pam's face, Aubrey suddenly felt like she shouldn't be there. She didn't want Georgina to think she'd shared their conversation yesterday with Pam either.

"Okay," Georgina said tentatively.

"You mentioned your husband," said Pam. Georgina nodded. "Are you happy with him?"

Now, that was an interesting question thought Aubrey. Georgina was quiet for a little while.

"Sorry I asked," said Pam at Georgina's hesitation. Aubrey was curious about the answer herself.

"No, it's okay. I am just trying to find my answer," said Georgina. Her voice was soft. She took another minute. "I think the answer is no. I don't think I am."

"You seem to talk about him like he..." Pam hesitated, "well, I don't know. That's why I'm confused."

"It's hard with Patrick. He's had this pressure from his family. Pressure he puts on himself. He's pulled in a lot of directions."

"And where do you fit into that?" asked Pam. Pam was asking questions Aubrey had been afraid to ask Georgina yesterday.

"It's what I'm trying to work out to be honest," Georgina answered. Pam nodded.

"How long have you been married?" Pam asked.

"Twenty-six years. Together for twenty-eight," said Georgina.

"That's a long time," said Pam, going quiet for a few minutes before continuing. "Does he tell you what's going on?"

"Not always. As I said the other night, he spends a lot of time out of state working." Georgina adjusted the strap flapping on the side of her pack. Their pace had increased with the intensity of the conversation.

"But there's always the internet Georgina." Aubrey butted in, walking behind, keeping pace. "I mean, you're on the other side of the world and I see you chatting or videoing with your daughter constantly. It's clear you've a close connection with her." She heard the tone in her voice change when she mentioned Georgina's daughter. Luckily, Georgina didn't pick up on the note of jealousy.

"I do. I'm lucky for that," she said. Yes, she was, thought Aubrey. More than she knew.

"I've tried to get Patrick on board with technology," Georgina said a little while later, "but he's resistant. He prefers to talk on the phone. Those calls are always short and to the point, merely to relay information."

"That's got to be hard for you when he's away so much. And now, with you here…" said Aubrey, moving to walk side by side with them as the path widened.

"My marriage isn't easy," Georgina said. "We've always had our challenges. It started with his family not accepting me. His mother had her social connections. She made it very difficult when I first opened the café. Thank god for the tourists or I would never have made it. Patrick doesn't talk about feelings. Doing that makes you weak according to his father and that trickled down to him. So, trying to get him to talk about what I was feeling with his family, well, it was challenging. It's still difficult. Even with his parents gone, there's still a massive deal of resentment lingering.

Our communication has never been great." Georgina took a deep breath. "When he is home, the world evolves around him." Georgina looked pained and helpless. Oh, Aubrey knew what that was like.

They walked a little further in silence. The quiet between them was a mix of anticipation of what else Georgina might say, and time to process the information already out there. For Aubrey, she thought about how deeply she could relate.

"I feel like I'm lost in all of it," whispered Georgina eventually.

"Have you talked to him about that?" asked Pam.

"Yes. But he's stubborn." She took a deep breath before going on, "He goes into a funk for days. It's like a merry-go-round and I'm constantly dizzy."

Georgina's comment, about how the world evolved around him, had Aubrey thinking back to the last few years. She assumed Patrick suffered from some extent of anxiety with all that familial pressure. She could clearly see how much Georgina was struggling. Patrick's story was all too familiar. He was pushing everyone away, trying to deal with it himself. Aubrey had done the same thing.

"One thing I've learned over the years," Aubrey said, "is while you can be there for someone, it's up to them to make their own choices. It took about a year of therapy before I understood that." She smiled at Georgina. Georgina nodded. But then she noticed the confused look on Pam's face.

"I talked to Georgina for a bit yesterday, when we walked on our own," said Aubrey. "I realised what a gutless wonder my husband was after some eye-opening events." Pam looked up and laughed at that, while Georgina just smiled.

"Yeah," mumbled Pam to herself, then looking up again at Aubrey. "And that's when you divorced him?"

"Yes," said Aubrey. "My point, I suppose, is Patrick can do whatever he's going to do, but it's up to you Georgina to work out what you want. You need to work out what makes you happy. After yesterday, I was thinking about a line I read in a book that really stuck with me. It said: 'The life you have led doesn't have to be the only life you have.' I think it was Anna Quindlen who said it. I found it poignant."

Georgina simply nodded. They walked in silence after that, but Aubrey's mind was buzzing.

Whether Patrick was a man's man, or not, it seemed he put a lot of pressure on himself. And on their marriage. A carry-over from his upbringing for sure, Aubrey considered. There would be untold hours of therapy needed to unravel those kinds of issues. But Aubrey hoped Georgina didn't take it all on herself to help him manage it either. It really was up to him. The only thing Georgina needed to work out was whether she wanted to stand next to him. If he didn't want to put in the work to figure it all out, that was his problem. Talking about Patrick's issues was a little too close to home for Aubrey too.

They stopped for breakfast at Cirauqui. Aubrey was relieved to sit. Her feet were aching. Georgina admitted her feet were feeling weary too, while Pam complained about her knees.

"Well, look who it is! Hello ladies," said Ben. They were getting ready to leave when the boys showed up.

"Where are the girls?" asked Pam, looking past them. Aubrey looked too. She didn't see Marinka or Hannah either.

"Behind us," said Ben. "Hannah said she wasn't feeling great this morning. They'll meet us in Villatuerta."

"Do you think those girlies will be okay?" Pam asked Ben, when Paolo went off in search of a bathroom. "With Paolo I mean. He's a bit of a playboy."

"Sure, but I think Hannah has him worked out. She said she met a few of 'his kind' in Italy," said Ben. "Not sure about Marinka though. She's been pretty sheltered I think." Marinka was definitely a shy one.

The five of them arrived at Villatuerta a few hours later. Storms brewed once more. When Pam stopped to look for directions, Aubrey looked toward the sky. She felt the wind pick up and swirl around her head. Tiny raindrops fell on her cheeks and she knew they were in for a deluge of rain. As they stepped through the doors of Casa Magica, the skies opened. She just hoped Marinka and Hannah had a fast pace and good rain gear.

The host showed them a shared room offering no privacy at all. There was a double bed at one end, a single bed at the other, and a couch, which normally would have been fine. But the shower stood grandly in the middle of the room, the couch providing a front row seat to the show. And the toilet, the crown seat it may be, was also fully exposed at the far end of the room. They stood at the doorway for moment, mouths agape. As one, laughter erupted. The host looked a little offended when they politely declined the offered room. Paolo seemed to hesitate.

"Paolo, I bet that would be your kind of thing, especially with the girls," teased Pam, walking toward the dorm room they were offered instead. Paolo followed.

"Nah, Hannah wouldn't allow it. She would have stopped him in his tracks," said Ben. Paolo flashed his wicked smile.

Just as they put their packs down, the front door opened downstairs and they heard girls laughing. Aubrey and Paolo went down to investigate and found Marinka and Hannah puffing from exertion. Aubrey was relieved to see them, but she had to laugh when Paolo fussed over them. He helped them out of their packs and carried them upstairs for them while the girls dried off.

Later, Aubrey found Paolo laying in a hammock on the verandah. Rain was gently falling beside him. He seemed to enjoy the moment. When she approached, he jumped up to show her a vending machine filled with cans of beer. She was astounded she could buy a beer for a euro; the idea of it piqued her interest.

"Care to join me?" she asked. He nodded. She popped in two coins.

"Cheers," Paolo said when they returned outside. He tapped his can against hers.

"Tell me about yourself Paolo. What do you do for work?" she asked, popping the tab from the can, amused she was drinking a beer from a vending machine, but she was curious about this playboy. She sensed there was more to him than he portrayed.

"I am without a, what do you call it? A job?" he asked. She nodded. "For now, I have fun." The wicked twinkle in his eye returned. "And you? Are you a model? Maybe, a television star. You are bellissima, Aubrey."

"Bellissima?" she asked. "As in, beautiful?" He nodded. He was such a flirt. "Well, thank you. No. None of those. I am also without a job."

"What do you want?" he asked, taking a swig from the can.

"I don't know. I used to own a dress shop but," she hesitated, knowing she really didn't want to go there, "I have moved on. I am considering something creative."

"Like painting? Or writing a book?" he asked. She laughed at that. She was the least creative person with that version of the arts that she knew. Her skills were more on the practical side.

"Like accessories," she said, realising she was admitting this to someone else for the first time. "I'd love to do something like this," she said and jangled her bracelets at him. She felt like she was revealing a deep secret.

"Yes, she loves her accessories," said Pam, joining them. Aubrey hadn't heard Pam walk up behind them. She felt like she'd been caught by her schoolteacher with a secret note. When Pam sat down, the conversation shifted to aching limbs. Aubrey was disappointed with Pam's interruption. She was enjoying the conversation with Paolo.

Dinner that night consisted of homemade paella followed by natilla, a creamy custard, for their dessert. Most everyone at the table was in a festive mood, but Aubrey found herself reflective. She noticed that Georgina was quiet too. No, not quiet, she thought. Sad. Georgina had admitted to her, in a rare moment they were alone, that she'd been thinking a lot about Pam's question: whether she was happy. Georgina explained that her best friend had asked the same question only a year ago when things weren't going well at home. Back then, Georgina had scoffed at the question. Now, Georgina told Aubrey, it was hard to sort shit from the gold. Aubrey hugged her. Georgina clung to her for dear life. She could feel Georgina's tears hit her shoulder. The suffering seemed obvious once you turned the corner, Aubrey thought. She was getting there.

14

DANCING AROUND TRUTHS

VILLATUERTA TO VILLAMAYOR DE MONJARDIN

"WHERE ARE THE KIDS?" Pam asked, when they met downstairs.

"Left already. Paolo promised to behave," Ben said, lacing the last of his shoes.

"I hope so," Pam answered. "You're not walking with them today?"

"No. Still needing to nurse the feet and Paolo walks a mean pace."

"Where's Georgina?" asked Ben, standing and grabbing his pack.

"Left early too. Said she needed some time to think about things," Aubrey said. Ben nodded.

"I'll wait for you outside if you're okay that I walk with you today?" Ben asked.

"Of course. Anytime," said Aubrey. Pam looked at him as if he were crazy even asking the question. He was a part of them now.

It had not surprised Aubrey when Georgina told her she was leaving early, wanting a day to walk alone. She seemed to have a lot on her mind. They loaded their backpacks and found Ben standing in the sunshine, his face to the sky, basking in the morning light. With a double tap of Pam's poles, her sign she was ready to get the show on the road, they followed the yellow arrows out of town.

"So, tell me about your life in New York Ben. Is it as crazy as I imagine?" asked Pam, once they found their pace.

"New York is fabulous. It's exhilarating, exhausting and noisy. We're constantly on the go. Kanmi, is either buried in recipes or preparing food, if we're not travelling. It's a crazy life, but I wouldn't change it for anything."

"Seems like another planet to me," said Pam, her trekking poles now an extension of her arms.

"I have to admit, I miss the quiet days of Utah," said Ben.

"Do you miss your family?" asked Aubrey.

"My dad, no. But I miss my sisters and my mom, for sure. My sisters quietly keep in touch with me, keeping me in the loop, but it's dangerous for them. If my father ever found out... My mom is one of three wives, and submissive."

"That's got to be so different from your life in New York. How was it growing up?" Pam asked.

"Well, growing up Mormon was one thing. Knowing I was gay and Mormon, well, that was a whole other being. I escaped, and I don't use that word lightly, as soon as I could. I was fourteen when I left. My father had just discovered my truth, and he and two uncles beat me severely. It's a wonder I survived. My mother and her sister-wives nursed me. As soon as I was well enough, my mother got word to my aunt, who lives in upstate New York now. She flew to Utah and helped me escape. I don't know how they did it, but I'm so thankful they did. My aunt raised me from then on. She put me through college and has supported me like my mom never could."

"That's quite a story. So, I take it you've never been back?" asked Pam.

"No," Ben said this with great sadness. "I wish I could, for my sisters' sake. I would love to get them out of that environment." Pam stopped to free a pebble that had found its way inside her shoe. Ben held her upright as she pulled the shoe off.

"Thank you," she said as she found her footing again.

"You're welcome." They continued walking. "To be honest, I don't know how much of a Utah boy I am now. I love New York."

"I can't imagine it," said Pam. "I'd be running for the bush after a day looking for peace and quiet. I've never done well in the city. London had me cowering in my hotel for two days."

"If you ever decide to try New York you have a guest room waiting. You too Aubrey," Ben said.

"Thanks. I may take you up on it. Compared to New York, Melbourne is a quaint country town. I love New York," Aubrey said. "I've been many times, but it's always been for work. I'd love to go and be a tourist."

NOT FAR FROM VILLATUERTA, THEY STOOD OUTSIDE A BLACKSMITH'S SHOP. There was a long table holding some of his wares just outside the gates. Easy trinkets for the pilgrims, thought Aubrey, as she perused the table. Smart. She picked up a small shell on a leather band and knew it was the perfect thing for her backpack. And it was lightweight! She could even use it as a bookmark.

She poked her head inside the shed-like structure. A fire pit was roaring in the middle of the courtyard, iron tools heating in the centre. The blacksmith looked up from his work with a welcoming smile. He waved them over to show them what he was doing. White hot metal seared within the flame. Aubrey appreciated the art of his craftsmanship. His English was limited but his enthusiasm enthralled them. They each purchased a trinket for their backpacks and the blacksmith stamped their credentials, showing they had walked one hundred kilometres. With it all tucked into their packs, they trudged up the hill toward the infamous Camino 'wine fountain'.

As they approached, a busload of tourists descended on the fountain's courtyard.

"Please make way for the pilgrims," shouted the tour guide, but the words fell upon deaf ears. Aubrey had read the term tourigrinos many times, but now she saw how fitting it was. Here were tourists, curious about the Camino but not walking it like the traditional pilgrims. The tour guide continued his plea, but the tourists were not letting anyone get in the way of their wine! So, Aubrey, Pam and Ben lined up for their turn.

Pam detached her Camino shell from her pack. It was a scallop shell. All pilgrims had a Camino shell attached to their pack, a symbol identifying them as pilgrims. Pam stepped up to the wine spout and filled her shell, informing anyone who would listen that this was the tradition of the pilgrims. Ben and Aubrey followed suit.

As they sipped the rough red from their shells, Pam educated them on the fountain. It was built specifically for the pilgrims, filled daily with only one hundred litres of wine from the Bodega. Filling up bottles was considered poor form, as doing so risked other pilgrims missing out. Pam seemed rather put out with the tourigrinos filling their water bottles, but Ben reminded her everyone did the Camino their own way. Theirs was simply different. Pam scoffed at that notion but a few tourigrinos had taken note and filled their bottles with a minimal amount of wine.

Before long, they found themselves tourist attractions when the tourigrinos realised Aubrey, Pam and Ben were 'the genuine thing'. Cameras came out, and the tourigrinos asked many questions. Aubrey found it odd being the centre of attention. The three of them looked like scruffy vagrants compared to the tourists clad in their polo shirts and pressed khaki shorts. She stepped aside while Pam happily fielded their questions.

"Well, that was an experience," Pam said, waving goodbye to the tour group.

"You were a hit!" said Ben, as they made their way up the hill past the gates to the private entrance of the Bodega.

"Tell me Pam. What's your life like? Where are you from?" Ben asked.

"Originally from the Hunter Valley. It's about three hours north of Sydney. My town is small, smaller than Saint Jean I would say. I lived there for most of my life. I know everyone in the town, and they know me."

"How was that for you? My community growing up was the same," said Ben. "Wasn't always the best thing."

"Agree with you there. It's both good and bad. Everyone thinks they know everyone else's business. And, when people have an opinion about someone, it's hard to change their minds."

Oh, I know that mindset, thought Aubrey.

"I moved away a few years ago," said Pam, "I live closer to the coast now, further north."

"Do you still have family there, Pam?" asked Ben. Pam didn't answer right away. Aubrey looked over to Pam. She was either considering her answer or lost in memories.

"No, no family," she said finally. "My mum died twenty-odd years ago. My dad had his first stroke not long after that, so I admitted him into a nursing home. He died about five years ago. Fatal stroke."

"I'm so sorry," said Aubrey but when she looked at Pam, she saw anger. Rage even. Ben listened intently.

"Don't be sorry. I didn't visit him once I put him in the home. Just paid the bill," she said. Before they could respond, Pam continued. "I know how religion can steer your life, for good or for bad. They raised me in a very strict Catholic household. You did what you were told. You never bucked the system. If you did, you paid the price."

"Sounds like my childhood. It was very much like that. It's why I had to get out. I could not be gay and exist in that community," said Ben.

"I wish I'd fled when I had the chance. You were lucky Ben," said Pam. Aubrey looked across at Pam again and felt the intensity of Pam's emotions like they were her own.

"Look at where you are," Aubrey said. "You may have taken a rocky road to get here but look around. Look at the beauty and positiveness in where you are, right here, right now." Aubrey looked up toward the countryside stretched out in front of them. Field upon field of barley and wheat swayed in the breeze, as the hills undulated into the distance.

Pam took a deep breath and growled, "Now you're starting to sound like a fucking shrink."

THEY ARRIVED AT VILLAMAYOR DE MONJARDIN AND FOUND THEIR albergue. They were assigned a dorm room on the upper floor. Pam groaned, so Ben carried Pam's pack up the stairs. The room was compact. Five sets of bunks were crammed into the space. But they had lined one wall with lockers to keep backpacks off the floor. Pam nudged Aubrey. She nodded in the direction across the room.

"Holy shit," Aubrey whispered. A woman stretched out on a bottom bunk against the wall rested with headphones in. Her eyes were closed. "It's Lean and Mean."

"Don't make any noise. She'll bite your head off," said Pam, while making all the noise she could.

"Pam, you are terrible," said Aubrey, pulling her stuff out quietly to prepare for her shower.

"What?! It's fucking two in the afternoon. It's peak hour. People are arriving. People will make noise."

"I'll see you in a few," said Aubrey, shaking her head disapprovingly. She headed to the showers. All the stalls were occupied. While she waited, she thought about what Pam had shared. The religious trappings made sense, but locking your dad up and throwing away the key? That was harsh. What awful stuff had happened for Pam to do that? And her comment about opinions in a small town and changing their minds? She had to wonder who she was talking about.

Later, they headed to the village bar hoping to find Georgina. The bar was almost empty, and Georgina was not there. Pam and Aubrey settled into journaling, while Ben retrieved his iPad. He needed to check on the business.

"Ha! Business is up," he said chuckling. "Maybe I should go away more often?"

"How would Kanmi feel about that?" asked Aubrey, looking up from her journal.

"He's okay with it for now. Told me to get it out of my system before we have kids. I understand that. I can't imagine doing this walk and having young kids still at home." She had to agree. She couldn't either. But she wondered if she'd walked the Camino with her kids, would life be different now? No. Probably not.

They were all deep into their journals when Aubrey felt another nudge from Pam. She pointed with her pen toward the bar. Lean and Mean was up from her nap.

"We should probably invite her to join us," said Ben. "She's walking on her own. As a fellow countryman, I feel compelled to ask…"

"Go ahead," said Pam. "I'm curious about her story."

"Me too," said Aubrey.

Ben waved to her and pointed to the chair. With a nod, Lean and Mean walked toward them.

"Hi. I've seen you a few times on the trail. I'm Ben," offering his hand.

"Hi. Lee. Where are you from?" Lee asked Ben. Aubrey wanted to laugh. Lee acted as if she and Pam didn't even exist.

"New York. Utah originally. You?" Ben asked as she sat.

"Santa Fe. Originally from California," she said. Lee pointed her body toward Ben, her back to Pam, and her leg crossed away from Aubrey.

"Hi, I'm Aubrey. I'm from England. But I live in Australia. I first saw you after Alto de Perdon, near the pilgrim statue," she said, extending her hand as Lee did with Ben. Lee looked down at her hand before taking it. "And this is Pam. She's from Australia too." Lee then scooted around, finally acknowledging Pam.

"Oh yes. You've been walking with another woman," Lee said to Pam.

"Yes, Georgina," said Pam. "Also, from Australia."

"Where is Georgina?" asked Ben, picking his beer up.

"Not sure," said Aubrey, "I got a text about an hour ago to say she was okay. She'd catch up with us, but not sure when."

"Hope she's okay," said Pam.

"She'll be fine. I think she just wanted some time to herself."

"Fair enough," said Pam. Aubrey caught the worried look on Ben's face. She was worried too.

"So, where did you start your Camino, Lee?" asked Pam. Aubrey shifted her attention to the petite woman sitting across from her. Lee hadn't softened her manner, but her tone at least was a little more cordial.

"St. Jean. Walking to Santiago. Maybe Finistère. You?" Lee asked.

"Same. How are you finding it?" asked Pam.

"It's beautiful. The canola fields are terrific. The wildflowers, the sunrises, it's all gorgeous."

"Have to agree," said Pam. "And what about the people? Have you met some lovely people along the way?" Pam asked.

Aubrey was wondering what was happening here. Pam was riled about something. Was she intentionally provoking this woman? Aubrey looked over at Ben, but he was stuck back into his iPad, fingers flying across the keyboard.

"Everyone has been very nice," said Lee. Pam took a sip of her beer.

"Agreed," said Pam. "I feel very fortunate with the group we've gathered. Isn't it amazing how many youngsters are doing it? I think it's incredible that they can take time off, break from their routines, and do such a monumental walk," said Pam. She took a long sip of her beer, her lips slightly curled against the glass. Oh shit, Aubrey thought. It was like watching someone poking the devil with a stick to see if they'd go straight to hell. She had to stop Pam now. But was too late. She had unleashed the beast in Lee.

"If you're talking about the ones with headphones in, the ones that party in the dorms, the ones that don't care about giving us older folks a bottom bunk, then I'm not sure I agree with you. They say nothing to you as they go past, boom boxes blaring, singing at the top of their lungs." Pam had unleashed unbridled fury. Aubrey sat speechless. She never imagined Pam to be so mean, or heartless. She stared at Pam and, at first, saw fear cross Pam's face when the anger unfurled from Lee toward her, but then it changed just as quickly to amusement.

"Remember one thing. It's everyone's Camino. They have every right to be here, just as much as you do," said Pam, mimicking the words Ben used only hours before about the tourigrinos. "We're pilgrims. We're not meant to judge. You need to suck it up Buttercup."

"Pam," Aubrey whispered. Lee was silent, as if considering Pam's words. Aubrey realized she was seething. Before she could say anything to smooth the situation, Lee got up, jostling the table as she did. They all scrambled to save their beers from spilling. With her own beer in hand, Lee strode outside.

"Pam. Why did you do that?" asked Aubrey.

"Oops. I forgot how sensitive Americans can be. Present company excluded," said Pam with a smile that would only make the devil proud.

What the... what the hell was that? Aubrey stared at Pam who sat back at her chair and drained the last of her beer.

Well, fuck, fuck and fuckity fuck, thought Aubrey.

15

SECRETS AREN'T REALLY SECRETS

VILLAMAYOR DE MONJARDIN TO TORRES DEL RIO

AT HALF PAST SIX, Pam and Aubrey stepped out into the crisp cool morning. They could see their breath in the pre-dawn light as they followed the yellow arrows back to the Camino. The fog hung low across the landscape, and when she looked toward the budding sunrise, the view was otherworldly. The dew clung to the ground, giving everything the appearance of being freshly watered, with droplets clinging to the wire fences along the trail.

Ben left at six, wanting to arrive at Torres del Rio early to get some work done. Georgina had texted at dinner last night that she was ahead in Los Arcos, and she'd meet them in Torres del Rio, still twenty kilometres away. It surprised Aubrey at how much she missed her.

They wandered the path in silence. The trail was lined with barley and wheat on either side. Canola glowed dimly in the distance. Even the cuckoos were counting down, calling non-stop in the background. Aubrey smiled, remembering Georgina's amazement of the birds. She'd forever think of Pam and Georgina whenever she heard a cuckoo.

After another few kilometres, Aubrey was deep in thought about her conversation with Georgina. Had they said something that had spiralled her? Was she very upset? She worried she'd lost her Camino sister after only a hundred and twenty kilometres. Georgina hadn't given her the impression she was angry in her messages, just that she needed time to think. Aubrey had to give her that.

She thought about Georgina and the relationship she had with her daughter. She envied that. She'd missed so much of her own daughter's life growing up. She missed bonding to such a depth. She hated to think she was jealous of Georgina's relationship, but she finally admitted to herself that it was true. She couldn't do anything about the past with Cass and was thankful therapy had helped in recent years. She just hoped that Georgina appreciated the treasure she possessed.

As they walked toward Los Arcos, they noticed an odd plant growing straight up in the field they passed. After the third field, they still couldn't figure it out.

"What the fuck is that?" Pam asked. Curiosity getting the better of her, Pam strode out into the field, grabbed a stalk with both hands and gave it a good yank. It came out so easily she nearly toppled over. She held her trophy up in the air, grinning triumphantly.

"It's asparagus," she declared. Aubrey walked closer to the field to see. "It's the biggest fucking asparagus I've ever seen."

"Now what are you going to do with it?" laughed Aubrey.

"Try to replant it. It's got at least another foot left to grow!" said Pam, looking around. Aubrey laughed. The thing had to be twenty centimetres long. It was white and thicker than two thumbs side by side. Pam tried to replant it but failed miserably.

"Just hope a bird comes by and has a delicious lunch," she said, leaving it sticking out of the ground. "I feel bad now. What if the farmers needed that piece?" Pam asked when they continued walking.

"I'm sure you're not the first to do that," said Aubrey, trying to placate her. She felt bad too. As they continued walking, Aubrey became unsettled by the quiet. She desperately wanted to ask Pam about the conversation with Lee, but she didn't know how. It was obvious something had set Pam off, but she didn't know what. She could feel her anger blistering beneath the surface.

They arrived in Los Arcos just after nine o'clock. They agreed a second breakfast was in order since they'd only eaten a processed muffin and coffee before leaving that morning. They found a café in the piazza and walked inside to order.

"I'm getting bacon and eggs," announced Aubrey. "I mean, I love a good breakfast at home, but the bacon and eggs on the Camino are something else altogether. Don't you think?" Her mouth watered just thinking of them.

"Maybe it's the fact that we work for them that make them taste so much better?" Pam suggested.

"Add in the mix of fresh air," Aubrey added. They were rambling, she knew, but the place was packed, and she was hungry.

Pam seemed in a great mood today, almost joyful. She didn't want to bring her down, but Aubrey sensed an underlying anger in Pam she couldn't brush off. When they were halfway through breakfast, Aubrey hesitantly approached the subject of the night before.

"I was thinking about last night, with Lee," began Aubrey. Pam didn't look up from her plate. Instead, she studied it intensely, as if it might suddenly fly away. She gathered more egg on her fork before taking a large bite.

"Yeah," she said, when she finished her mouthful. "Probably shouldn't have done that," she said, going quiet again.

"I was really surprised you did," said Aubrey, finishing her coffee.

"Yeah," said Pam, but she said nothing further. Pam looked stricken with remorse, so Aubrey decided not to push her any further.

As they made their way to Torres del Rio the day was heating fast. The fields to the right of them looked like brownie batter left out in the sun too long. Huge mounds of cracked earth the size of boulders spread as far as she could see. And dry, so dry. She wondered what might grow in that type of soil. She was surprised an hour later when they came upon a field of flowering sweet peas. The contrast was startling. They talked about the wonders of smart irrigation and natural springs.

Just past the sweet peas, the dirt path ended at a paved road. The Camino's yellow arrows pointed left to the village on the rise. A few metres along, there was a bus stop to the left. A willowy brunette stood with her pack off, looking down at a blonde girl sitting in the shade.

Aubrey recognised them as Hannah and Marinka, the two girls that had been walking with Paolo. She thought they'd be way ahead of them by now.

They approached the girls with a wave. Hannah slammed her head between her knees in a quick second. She still had her backpack on. When Aubrey and Pam reached them, Hannah slowly raised her head. Her cheeks were bright red and blotchy. Marinka looked very concerned.

"Are you okay?" asked Aubrey. Marinka shook her head. Pam knelt down to Hannah.

"Hannah? Are you okay?" she asked. Hannah said she was very hot and suddenly nauseous.

"Do you have any water?" asked Pam.

"I ran out. Marinka just gave me the last of hers." Aubrey took her pack off. Pam did the same, then reached into her side pocket for the extra water.

"When did you last eat something?" asked Pam, passing her the full bottle of water.

"We had a juice in Los Arcos and shared a pastry," said Marinka.

"I don't think the next village is far. Drink some water," said Pam. "In small sips."

Hannah followed her instruction.

"Good," Pam said, "Now, let's get your pack off." Hannah nodded and both Marinka and Aubrey helped slide it off her shoulders.

"How about your shoes and socks?" asked Aubrey. "That will help you cool down faster." Hannah looked up at her, dazed, so Aubrey stepped around to untie her shoes and Hannah slipped them off.

"We're only a kilometre from the next town. How about we risk some water and pour it over Hannah's feet?" asked Aubrey. Pam nodded and took her water bottle and dribbled it over her feet. "Wiggle your toes. Let the air hit your feet. I learned this trick on another long-distance walk," Aubrey shared, smiling at a weary Hannah.

"Don't worry, your feet will dry before we put your shoes back on. We don't want you to get blisters too," Aubrey said smiling at Pam.

"I have something else that will help," Pam said. "While I grab it, fan her with my hat for a few moments, will you Marinka?"

Pam reached into her first aid kit and pulled out a neck cooling scarf. She cracked it and then placed it around Hannah's neck.

"How's that?" Pam asked.

"Better. Thank you." Hannah closed her eyes while Aubrey reached into the top pouch of her backpack.

"I have an energy bar which will at least give you a boost. May help your stomach too," she said and handed it to Hannah. Aubrey was surprised Hannah was taking their direction without question. She truly must not have been well. She watched as Hannah tentatively took a bite from the energy bar and sipped a little more water. Pam handed Marinka the last of her water, which she took gratefully. The girl looked pale. It was clear she was worried.

"Were you nauseous from the heat?" Pam asked Hannah. The young girl hesitated then nodded. They let her sit quietly for a few minutes.

"Better?" Pam asked. Hannah nodded. She looked better. The water and protein bar seemed to have helped.

"I'm really sorry to have bothered you guys," she finally said.

"It's no bother. Happy to help," said Pam, "Do you think you can walk into town?" Hannah nodded.

"She'll be okay," Aubrey whispered to Marinka. Relief washed over her face.

"Let's get your shoes back on," said Pam, "then we'll take our time strolling up that hill. I'm an expert at slow strolling." She got a smile from Hannah, which Aubrey sensed was the point of her lame joke. Marinka picked up Hannah's backpack but given the heat and the girl's worry, Aubrey suggested they carry it together, each carrying one strap.

"You can tell me how you came to walk the Camino," Pam said, tying the last of Hannah's shoe with a flourish. Aubrey knew Pam's knees were hurting her even before she bent down to help Hannah. The woman was a force to be reckoned with.

As they made their way up the hill to the village, Pam asked them about their Camino journey. Aubrey realised they'd not learned their stories yet.

"I was taking a gap year with some friends from school," said Hannah quietly. "We were travelling around France when I heard about the Camino. My boyfriend went back to the States, back to college. My friends wanted to head to the south of France to party. By then, I was pretty much done with that scene. So, I headed to Pamplona," said Hannah. She stopped to catch her breath. She hadn't quite fully recovered. Marinka picked up the cue.

"That is where we met. In Pamplona," said Marinka. "I planned this pilgrimage for two years and now I am doing it in two-week increments." Aubrey knew this was common for Europeans.

Aubrey was inspired by their adventurous spirit. They were both so young. Hannah said she was eighteen in answer to Aubrey's query. She was free of commitments, which was so different from Aubrey at that age. Aubrey guessed that Marinka was younger than Hannah, but Marinka surprised her when she said she was twenty-five. She had the shyness and reserved nature of one much younger, Aubrey thought. But she also had to have a bit of a rebellious streak to do this walk on her own.

AFTER ONE VERY LONG KILOMETRE IN THE INTENSE AFTERNOON SUN, THE four women walked into what they thought was Torres Del Rio. They were disappointed to discover that their destination was a kilometre further. Pam wailed "Fuuuckkk!" at the news which shocked the younger girls. But they continued on, quickly finding their accommodation after they dipped down to cross the river and then trudging up the short hill.

While Pam and the girls checked in, Aubrey entered the Wi-Fi passcode into her phone. There was a message from Georgina. Aubrey seriously had to get a SIM card in Logroño, she realised, relying on Wi-Fi was just not working. And Pam's Australian plan cost her a fortune, so that was no help either.

Aubrey responded to Georgina's text.

Just arrived in Torres del Rio. Georgina responded quickly.

Already in the bar. Come when you're ready.

She was eager to see Georgina again and relieved to know she was already here. They worried about her when they didn't see her at the albergue the previous night.

Thirty minutes later, Aubrey walked into the bar. She felt refreshed after her shower. She was wearing her long multicoloured skirt. But this time, given the heat, had paired it with her black tank top. Her wet, auburn hair was braided into a fishtail off to the side. She spotted Pam and Georgina chatting at a table across the way.

"Hello Lovelies," Aubrey said. Georgina smiled and stood to hug her.

"You look like a breath of fresh air that had just breezed into the room," she said as she released the embrace.

"Why the fuck can't I look like you after a shower?" said Pam, smiling at Aubrey from her chair.

"Why would you want to?" responded Aubrey, dropping her bag in the chair next to Pam. "You look radiant. Your skin is glowing, and your eyes are sparkling. You look... happy."

"Huh. Well must be the beer and sunshine," said Pam, her beer glass already half empty.

"Maybe," said Aubrey, "I know I'm done with sunshine for today. I saw Paolo and Ben downstairs in the pool. It looked inviting. But now, a cold beer sounds better. Another round?" She noticed how relaxed Georgina looked.

"I'll have one, thanks," said Pam, finishing her beer off in one long swig. "Can I give you my glass to take up there?"

"You can," she said, taking Pam's glass. "George?"

"I'm okay. I think I'm just going to wait for wine at dinner," said Georgina. "I already had a beer before you guys arrived. I would have had a nap, but I checked emails instead." Aubrey nodded and headed to the bar. She was happy to leave that part of the conversation to Pam. Aubrey knew Georgina would mention how well her daughter was handling things. She said it every time they talked of news from home. Aubrey sighed and handed over money to the bartender. She needed to let it go. She was happy Georgina had someone she could rely on like that.

"How are things at home?" Aubrey asked, caving in, when she returned with two beers in her hand. She passed one to Pam.

"I was just saying I should leave more often," said Georgina. "Everything is going smoothly."

"Like Ben. Same thing for him apparently. Maybe you should," said Pam, clinking glasses with Aubrey.

Thankfully, Pam changed the subject and told Georgina about Hannah's struggle.

Pam glanced over Aubrey's shoulder.

"Hello boys," she said. Ben and Paolo walked in, freshly showered.

"Pam, you know in modern society that calling us boys may be a little offensive," Ben said with a wink.

"Well just call me old-fashioned," Pam responded.

"Okay Boomer," Ben teased, and reached down and gave her a side hug.

"Oh! No, you didn't!" Pam laughed.

"You are the anti-stereotype. Trust me," Ben said.

"Where are the girls?" Pam asked, getting a shake of the head from Ben.

"Hannah's asleep," said Paolo. "Marinka said she would wake her for dinner."

"I think the heat wiped her out," said Ben. "Marinka said she almost fainted before you guys came along."

"We were just wondering if she's okay," said Aubrey. "We're worried. Is she dehydrated? Not eating enough?"

"Oh. I thought you knew," Ben said, looking at each of them with a questioning look. "She's pregnant."

"Paolo," said Pam, scorn quickly crossing her face.

Paolo held his hands up in a defensive stance. "No. No, not me. I swear."

Ben laughed. "No, it's her high school boyfriend's baby. She only found out right before the Camino."

"You know, the thought went through my mind when she was saying she was so tired, but I didn't want to think she'd..." said Aubrey. "Well. It makes sense."

"Yeah, she told me the other day," said Ben, "She's just getting used to the idea herself. I know she hasn't told her parents yet, but she said she was walking the Camino to work out what to do. This was supposed to be a fun gap year before starting college at NYU."

"Poor love," said Georgina, just as they announced dinner. As the line formed in front of the restaurant for the pilgrim communal dinner, Paolo sent a quick text to Marinka to let her know.

"Do we pretend we don't know and wait until she says something?" considered Aubrey.

"I think that may be best," said Ben. "I shouldn't have said something. I honestly thought you knew after today. She's embarrassed. If she didn't say anything when she had trouble, she may not be ready to."

"Sure. I just wish we'd known," said Pam, hesitating for a beat. "But then there's nothing different I would have done, I suppose. Glad to know now. Thanks Ben," she said and squeezed his arm. Marinka and Hannah joined them. Hannah was looking better than she had earlier that afternoon.

THE CONVERSATION AROUND THE TABLE WAS RAMBUNCTIOUS. AUBREY WAS glad to see Georgina laughing freely. She listened intently as Ben and Georgina talked about New York. She was happy to add her own stories of adventures when she'd travelled there for buying trips for the shop. When the Canadian couple at the table joined the conversation, talk turned to raising kids in the country versus in a city like New York.

"You know Pam, I have never asked you. Do you have kids? You mentioned your parents, but..." asked Ben, who sat directly across from her. Pam shook her head slowly. Aubrey could feel Pam tense beside her.

"Are you okay?" Aubrey whispered. She reached beneath the table and took Pam's hand. Pam let her take it, but then pulled away.

"I'm fine." Pam looked down, then reached over and took a gulp of wine. She looked directly at Ben. "I was pregnant once. I was a little older than Hannah. I told my parents, who, as I told you, were devout Catholics. I was about two months pregnant by then." Pam sat up a little straighter in her chair. "They told me I had to get married. So, I married the father a week later. A boy I had been seeing for about six months." She took another deep drink of her wine. "I lost the baby about two weeks later. We had no more children after that."

Aubrey looked at Ben. He looked as stunned at the news as she.

"Religion can steer your life without your permission," said Pam. "I married at twenty-one and stayed that way for thirty-five years," she said. She took a bite of the steak going cold before her. Aubrey almost dropped her fork.

"Wait. What? We all asked if you were married," said Aubrey, hearing the shock in her own voice.

"You all asked if I was married, yes," said Pam. "And now I'm not. Not anymore. My husband died five years ago."

"Oh Pam, I'm so sorry," said Aubrey, reaching for her hand again. Pam didn't take it this time.

"Don't be. I'm not. It's been the best five years of my life," Pam said and continued eating her cold, limp fries.

Aubrey sat frozen, her loaded fork balancing the long-forgotten pasta.

"Sorry," said Pam. "I should have at least told you that much before. I just don't like to talk about it. It was a very, very hard part of my life." Pam hesitated. "He was not an easy man to live with, let's put it that way."

"Sorry. I guess I'm just surprised," said Aubrey. "You've been so quiet when people have talked about their partners, marriages, children. I just assumed you were never married."

"Would have been easier," Pam mumbled.

"What's going on?" Georgina asked. She'd been engrossed in a conversation with the Canadians about Tasmania.

"Did you know that Pam was married?" asked Aubrey.

"Yes. She's a widow," said Georgina, looking over at Pam. Aubrey was taken aback that Georgina knew.

"Well, yes, I guess that's true. But she was married for thirty-five years," said Aubrey, looking from Georgina to Pam.

"Old news," said Pam. Aubrey saw Georgina nod. Clearly these two had had a conversation about it when she wasn't around. She wasn't sure how she felt about that. A bit hurt at being left out, perhaps. Pam was a straight shooter. She didn't hold back information. At least she hadn't thought so. She shook her head.

"I'm just so surprised," said Aubrey, sitting back in her chair.

"Well, now you know," Pam said. She scraped her chair back and stood up from the table. "I'm going to bed. I'll see you all on the trail tomorrow."

16

FEELING THE VIBE

TORRES DEL RIO TO LONGRONO

"Well, shit," said Aubrey as they watched Pam set off to her room.

"She'll be okay," said Georgina. "She'll share if she wants to and if she doesn't, we'll respect that. Everyone has their secrets." Aubrey thought this was an interesting turn of phrase, and she scooted over to take Pam's chair next to Georgina. She wasn't sure how to take Pam's news, but she had Georgina's attention for now.

"How are you doing Georgina? We missed you on the trail the last few days." She noticed Ben turn and start talking to Paolo, who was talking to Marinka. Hannah was picking at her food at the other end of the table.

"I'm fine," said Georgina. "You gave me some things to ponder. So did Pam." She lowered her voice, "Right now, I'm more worried about Hannah. Now we understand what's going on."

Aubrey turned to Hannah. She was still picking through her salad. She'd ordered the vegetarian meal, which didn't seem the best choice for her. Aubrey had seen her eating a burger two days before, so she knew she wasn't a vegetarian. She needed protein. Aubrey leaned over to Hannah and asked if she was okay. Hannah jumped, surprised out of her train of thought.

"Oh yeah. I'm okay. Just tired." Hannah smiled meekly. Aubrey thought she looked very pale. Georgina leaned over.

"Hannah, do you want some of my steak here? I won't eat it all and you should have more than salad," said Georgina.

"No, I'm okay. I am still a little nauseous," she said and placed her hand on her stomach. "But I'll be okay."

Ben piped in, "You should have some of Georgina's steak. It'll give you some energy for tomorrow."

"I'll be okay. Paolo gave me some of his protein bars," Hannah said. "I'll have those in the morning. Right now, I'm really tired. I think I'll just go to bed."

"Should you take a rest day in Logroño?" suggested Aubrey. "It's a twenty-kilometre day tomorrow. A rest day after seems like a grand idea. Doesn't it?"

Hannah looked at Ben and then over at Aubrey. "Yeah, I thought about that. Maybe."

"Pam and I were talking about that earlier," said Georgina. "We've been walking now for over two weeks. I'm ready for a break."

"Yes. Our stop in Pamplona was not what I would call a rest day. I could use a proper rest day too," said Aubrey.

"I agree," said Ben, looking pointedly at Hannah. Aubrey knew they were all pushing her hard, but they had her health in mind. Aubrey knew how taxing this time was in a pregnancy.

"We all could use a break," Ben continued.

"I will think about it, I promise. For now, I'm going to bed. Good-night everyone."

"I wanted to offer her my hotel room, but I didn't want to give away I knew," whispered Georgina to Aubrey.

"She'll be okay," said Ben. Georgina's whisper had been loud enough for Ben to hear. Aubrey looked toward Marinka. She was deep in a conversation with Paolo at the end of the table. "She needs to eat more. Something more solid," he mumbled as if to himself. She noticed movement at the end of the table. Marinka and Paolo stood to say goodnight and followed Hannah to the dorms. Aubrey suspected

Marinka's protectiveness was at play. They bid them goodnight. Aubrey exhaled deeply.

"Poor love," said Georgina. "I remember my morning sickness vividly. It crippled me. What was yours like Aubrey?"

Aubrey absorbed the jolt of the question before she could answer. Her pregnancies had been extremely difficult to say the least. She was told she would never have children, which is why she'd adopted. It had caused a lot of contention between Brendon and her. He planned to continue his lineage. Maybe he would now with his young lover, she thought. She came back to Georgina's question before she continued down that rough train of thought.

"I had horrendous morning sickness too. Luckily, it never lasted long. But then, neither did the pregnancies."

"Oh my god, I'm so sorry..." Georgina hesitated. "I didn't know..."

"It's okay. It's not a secret," said Aubrey, playing with Pam's abandoned spoon. She didn't mind talking about the fact she had adopted, but she rarely shared why she made that choice. Her pregnancies were a painful memory. Georgina looked worried. Ben just looked confused.

"It's okay George, really," She took her hand and squeezed. "I adopted my kids."

"Cool," said Ben. He looked at Georgina and hesitated, seemingly not sure whether to add to the conversation or leave it well alone. He opted for the easier route. "I'll walk with Hannah tomorrow and watch out for her. Marinka is trying to help, but..."

Aubrey smiled. She was grateful the conversation had changed back to Hannah.

"Yeah, she looked anxious when we came across them today," said Aubrey, "I don't believe she knows how to help her."

"I'll walk with you guys tomorrow, if that's okay Ben?" offered Aubrey. "Maybe she'll open up to me? At least I can talk to her about morning sickness, help answer some of her questions. This must terrify her."

"Good idea. I'll walk with Pam," said Georgina, "I'm sure Hannah doesn't need all of us hovering." Aubrey nodded. "But we won't be far if you need us."

"From what I've read and what the Camino Master told me earlier," Ben said, referring to Pam, "it's a hard walk tomorrow to Logroño."

"Should we meet in Viana? That's about halfway. We can see how things are?" suggested Georgina.

"Yes, that's a great idea. Do we know if Hannah has a place to stay yet?" asked Aubrey. Ben shook his head. "Georgina, Pam and I reserved beds at a private albergue. There are only about six beds to a room with its own bathroom. It may be a good idea for her, rather than staying in a full dorm."

"If it's too expensive, I'll cover her," said Ben generously.

"I'm happy to as well," Georgina said with a smile. "Let's see how she's feeling tomorrow and ask her. This is her Camino too, after all." Yes, Aubrey thought, realising that they may be making plans for Hannah she didn't want to make.

After dinner, Aubrey went upstairs. She was happy to have her own room and the opportunity for a good night sleep. The snorers the night before had been horrendous. She was pretty sure Lee (aka Lean and Mean), had been the worst offender. Pam had boasted about her silicone earplugs keeping the noise at bay. Aubrey figured hers would be okay, but after last night, she'd be buying some like Pam's in Logroño.

As she brushed her teeth, she thought about Pam's news. Married. Okay, married was one thing. But married for thirty-five years and not say anything, especially when she was asked? She said he wasn't an easy man to live with. But clearly, something deeper was going on with her. That was evident.

Aubrey slipped into bed. An aura of intense sadness, tipped with rage, simmered in Pam. Aubrey knew she wasn't reacting to something Pam had said. It was more of a premonition, her intuition at work. She sorted through everything she knew of Pam, but she couldn't put her finger on it. Her stomach churned, urging her to reconcile the confused feelings she was having. She breathed through it until her stomach finally settled, deciding to leave it for another day. The answers would come.

. . .

HER PHONED BEEPED. SHE UNFURLED HER ARM FROM THE BEDSHEET AND reached over to the side table. It was a text from Ben. He was downstairs with Hannah, Marinka and Paolo asking if they should wait for her.

Go ahead. Sorry. I'll meet you in Viana.

It was a few minutes after seven. She forgot to set an alarm. She texted Georgina to see where they were.

Waiting on Pam. Aubrey had to laugh at that.

Do you mind waiting for me too? I'll be about 10 mins.

No problem. Just saw Ben and Co leave. You oversleep?

Yep. THX. Will be there soon.

She was downstairs in less than ten minutes, backpack on. Pam still wasn't there. Georgina was getting antsy.

"Why don't you go on? I'll wait for Pam. We can catch up," suggested Aubrey.

"No. It's okay. I'll wait. It won't be as hot today. I checked the weather." Aubrey laughed. "I'm becoming Pam with the Camino Information. Did you hear the storm that came through last night? Bucketed down."

"No, not at all. It took me a long while to get to sleep last night, but once I was, I slept like the dead," Aubrey said.

"According to Ben, there was an Olympic snorer in the dorm last night," Georgina said.

"If people know they are huge snorers, why not get their own room? Do they not know?" she asked. She'd been wondering that for days.

"I guess they don't realise," said Georgina. "Oh, there's Pam. She doesn't look like she slept well at all."

"THE TOWN IS QUIET THIS MORNING," SAID AUBREY AS THEY MADE THEIR way through the narrow streets.

"But the sunrise, it's so pretty. Look at that, with those clouds," said Georgina. The clouds looked like an artist had taken a feather brush and softly painted them intense pink and red sky on a canvas. Georgina whipped out her phone to snap her morning photos while

Aubrey admired the scenery. The atmosphere was beautiful, serene, and there was a mist hanging in the air that kept everything looking mysterious. Pam was quiet. She'd yet to say a word.

They started up the trail and, like most mornings, kept to their own thoughts for the first thirty minutes or so. They passed sheep at the top of the hill, their heads poking through the fence, instantly making her think of the grass being greener on the other side metaphor.

"I..." Pam said... Aubrey looked over at her and when she didn't continue, kept the pace going. "I need to tell you something."

"It's okay," said Aubrey. "I'm very sorry about last night." Pam shook her head decisively.

"No, I need to tell you. Both of you. There's more to the story. In fact, I haven't shared it with anyone."

"Okay," said Georgina.

"So, I told you I was married for thirty-five years and that I lost the baby right after the wedding. The truth is," she took a deep breath before plunging in, "my husband beat me, and I lost the baby."

"Oh, shit..." said Aubrey. Both she and Georgina stopped in their tracks.

"There's more," said Pam, not stopping at all. Aubrey and Georgina scrambled to catch up.

"I got married because I was pregnant, as I said last night. I had only been out with one other boy, but my parents intervened, and we broke up. Later, while I was at University, I met Mick. Mick courted me, hard and fast. I believe he thought that my parents were rich, since they had all this property. But he was wrong about that. My mother inherited the land. My parents struggled all their life to keep it going. But my parents loved him. My dad thought he walked on water. Mick charmed them, just as he charmed me. He was, in their eyes, a good Catholic boy." Georgina groaned.

"Mick and I had sex, if you can call it that, only the once. That's all it took to get pregnant. When I told my mother, she said nothing. Instead, she went to the phone and rang my father. My father forced me to marry Mick because of my father's prominent position in the church. He wasn't having his unmarried daughter having a baby on her own or, God forbid, having an abortion. So, that was that. I was twenty-one, married, with a baby on the way." Pam took a big gulp of air but continued her story. Georgina and Aubrey could barely keep pace.

"About two weeks after the wedding, Mick heard I had slept with someone else. It wasn't true of course, but Mick didn't believe me. He'd made up his mind that I'd slept with my old boyfriend and then accused me of trapping him. He didn't trust me when I told him the truth. So, he beat me. I lost the baby and was in hospital for three days. He told people I'd been out riding, and the horse had thrown me."

"Why didn't you leave him?" asked Aubrey, aghast at this news.

"She was Catholic," said Georgina quietly, understanding.

"That's right. I told my mother what happened. She refused to listen. I wanted a divorce. I asked for an annulment. Anything to get away. But marriage was until death do you part in the eyes of the church and my parents. My mother screamed at me. Told me that divorce was a sin and how I would go to hell. I was still devout myself back then, so I believed her, and stayed," said Pam.

"Were you always devout? Did you consider a divorce later on?" asked Aubrey, regretting asking the moment the words popped out of her mouth. Her confusion was making Pam more tense.

"I asked him for a divorce about ten years into the marriage, but Mick was heavily involved in the church community. He just laughed at me. He refused to divorce me because, by then, he was on track to become a deacon."

Aubrey shook her head. "That is so messed up," she said.

"Oh, I agree. I attended church every week with him because, well, that's what I was expected to do. But I used to go through my shopping list in my head when they sang hymns, or I'd plan out my class lessons. I didn't want to be there. So, I would mentally disconnect from it all. Go into auto mode."

"Mick died five years ago," Pam said. "It's been a very blissful five years since. Until Zabaldika, I had not stepped into a church since Mick's funeral. And I only went in there because I am fascinated with old architecture. I was curious to see the church that hadn't been majorly renovated in hundreds of years. And then the bell... Well, that bell was pretty special. My grumpy knees were screaming afterwards, but it was worth it for the bell."

Aubrey sensed this to be the end of Pam's confession, especially when Pam slowed the pace. Aubrey didn't know how to respond. Georgina didn't look like she did either. It was a lot to take in, but then Georgina opened her mouth, closed it then took the plunge.

"That's why you never went to visit your dad?" Pam nodded. She looked spent, but she also looked as if a huge weight had been lifted. Aubrey could imagine the relief she must be feeling after coming clean with them. This is why she was so wound-up last night, Aubrey knew. She was deciding whether to tell them or not. It'd only been two weeks since she'd met them. That was a short amount of time to trust someone with your deepest darkest secrets. Aubrey thought about her own secrets and whether she trusted these women. She knew she did. But she was still sorting through her own baggage. So, if she was hesitant, maybe they all were? Pam had taken a huge leap, maybe it was time for her to do the same?

Pam shocked Aubrey when she said she wanted to stop at the San Pedro church in Viana before they joined the others. When they arrived, unsurprisingly, Pam was reluctant to go in.

"As I said, my time with the Catholic Church feels done," Pam said. She paused, taking a deep breath. "But part of my reason for walking the Camino is to put my anger at the church to rest." With another deep breath, she walked toward the doors with determination. As they entered, Georgina steered right, while Aubrey and Pam went left.

Aubrey immediately felt the bad vibe.

"I have a terrible sense about this place," she whispered to Pam. "Something. I don't know, I can't place it...." She shivered. "Something evil... I've got to get out of here. It's not good." Before Pam could say anything, Aubrey strode toward the door. When she opened the large wooden doors to the sunshine, the evil presence left her immediately. She waited for Pam and Georgina by the gate. Pam came out first. A few minutes later, Georgina followed.

"Sorry. I can't explain it. Something evil happened in there. I couldn't shake the terrible vibe," said Aubrey. She was surprised to find that her supernatural vibes were coming strongly now she was on this spiritual path. She'd experienced the supernatural before, but this was different. It had really shaken her.

Pam put a reassuring arm around her shoulder. "I get it. I keep telling you, religion can ruin lives, too often the innocent," said Pam. She tapped her poles twice before announcing: "Well, best not to dawdle. I'm hungry! Where are those youngsters? I read there is a brilliant place for lunch here. Vagual. It's Mediterranean."

"Anything that's not a pilgrim meal sounds great to me," said Georgina. Stale ham and cheese baguettes, or the ensalada mixta, a salad with canned tuna dumped on top was getting old fast. Pastries and bacon and eggs did little to make up for the usual pilgrim fare.

"Let's shake off the bad vibes and embrace the good ones," Pam said, looking pointedly at Aubrey. She nodded and began texting Ben to let him know where to meet them.

"As long as you're okay Aubrey?" asked Georgina. Aubrey nodded. She'd work it out. Seeing Hannah would be a good distraction. She was eager to see how she was feeling. "Then let's go."

They made their way along the cobblestone street to find the restaurant Pam had discovered. Ben texted they were waiting for them in a nearby bar but would meet them at the restaurant. Seems Hannah had her appetite back today.

AFTER THEIR DELICIOUS LUNCH, THEY WALKED AS A GROUP TOWARD Logroño. Aubrey was paired with Georgina while Ben and Pam chatted away about academics. Paolo, Marinka and Hannah led the way about twenty metres in front.

"I was thinking this morning," Aubrey said, "how do I manage to get up and do this every day? It has to be part of the Camino magic. I mean, yesterday, the heat made it really difficult. But usually, after a good night's sleep, I feel restored once more and ready to do it all over again."

"Yeah, just getting up and down these hills," Georgina said, "seems less of an effort now we're into it. I feel stronger. I am definitely noticing changes in my body."

"I feel my body toning up again. Who knew that to lose weight and tighten the body, all you need to do is walk two hundred kilometres in ten days, drink wine and beer and eat anything you want?" They both laughed at that idea.

"Yeah, probably not the best weight loss plan," said Georgina. "But if it means, you can walk through trails of wildflowers and see these kinds of views every day, I'm all in."

Aubrey had to agree. The scenery was amazing. She figured that would change eventually, that the walk would become monotonous. So far, the landscape just rolled from one fabulous scene into another. And, while her feet hurt and her legs ached at the end of every day, it was so much easier than it had been a hundred kilometres before. In no small part thanks to their little Camino Family. She felt lucky to share the journey with them.

"Oh! Do you smell that?" Georgina asked, leaning toward the bordering trees, nose first. "It smells like..."

"Almonds," Aubrey finished for her, just as Georgina stuck her nose into a cluster of blooming white flowers.

"Oh my god, it is! It's an almond tree. It smells amazing. Hey! You guys, wait up," Georgina called ahead. Everyone stopped and turned. She pointed excitedly at the rows of trees they were walking through.

"Smell!" she cried. Each of them stuck their noses into a nearby cluster of flowers. Paolo pulled back quickly, "Oh! And watch out for the bees," she called, laughing.

"Almonds," Georgina declared. "Incredible. I truly am loving this walk. From the daily cuckoos we keep hearing, to these wildflowers. I'm finally feeling like I'm figuring this thing out."

"Whatever you did on your night alone Georgina, it did you good. You seem happier," said Aubrey.

"Yeah. I'm getting there. I'm working through it," she said, somewhat sombre again, and they continued walking in an effort to catch the others. Aubrey was sorry to bring Georgina out of her Camino love bubble. When the path widened, she gestured to Georgina to link arms. Georgina chuckled when their trekking poles tangled, but they got it sorted and continued walking arm in arm.

The path took them through a forest, before coming out to a bridge spanning a major highway. Aubrey felt shellshocked at the speed of traffic after days of experiencing blissful narrow lanes and dirt trails. They continued up past an industrial area and, a few minutes later, Ben let out a whoop.

"What?" asked Pam.

"Do you know what that sign means?" Ben asked, pointing to what looked like a directional sign along the highway. It said 'Comunidad de La Rioja' or Rioja community. They all shook their heads. "We are now in the best wine region of Spain. One of the best in the world actually. The wine will flow tonight my friends!"

"Let's just fucking get there, shall we?" suggested Pam. "My knees feel like one of those toys where you press the button on the bottom, and it collapses at every joint. Plus, I have to pee!"

17

KIDS THESE DAYS

LONGRONO TO NAVARETTE

In Logroño, Aubrey, Pam and Georgina shared their six-pod room with Marinka and Hannah, while Ben and Paolo opted to stay at the Municipal albergue. They were all beaten by the heat and the distance, so they called it an early night after a quiet dinner.

The following morning Marinka and Hannah surprised the Lovelies when they announced they would continue walking. They tried to recommend a rest day, especially for Hannah, but the girls were determined to keep walking. The Lovelies gave in, wishing them well, even though all three of them expressed concern. The forecast was for another day of blazing heat. But what could they do? They were independent girls after all.

Putting their worry aside, the Lovelies enjoyed a rest day. They took care of what little errands they had, then lazed over a long, sumptuous lunch, before heading back to their albergue to indulge in naps in the afternoon. When they left for dinner, just after seven, the room had remained empty but for the three of them. Aubrey considered it a stroke of good fortune.

But when they arrived back at nine, the room had been invaded by what looked to be self-indulgent teenagers. At least that's what Pam had called them. Open suitcases, tiny slips of lace underwear, hairdryers, and hair straighteners were strewn across the floor of their room.

"The bathroom is a pigsty," Georgina exclaimed, walking back into their room. "It's worse than in here." Aubrey popped her head in and saw make up and beauty paraphernalia everywhere. With all the albergues they had stayed in, they had never come across such blatant disrespect for others. These women, girls, were not pilgrims.

They went to bed around ten, all falling asleep quickly. Around one in the morning, their dorm-mates returned, drunk, giggling and talking loudly. Contrary to hostel etiquette, the lights came on. Pam yelled out to them to 'turn the fucking light off!' They complied, but after a few minutes of whispering loudly and shuffling around in their suitcase, one girl climbed into bed while the other two ran out, howling with laughter.

At four, the two girls returned, drunker than before. Again, they turned the lights on, then stood in the doorway and stuffed their faces with cream pastries, spilling the contents all over the floor. Pam yelled out again to turn the light off, but they ignored her, mocking her instead, spitting pastry on the floor as they tried to sound coherent. Aubrey poked her head out from her pod and stared directly into the eyes of the nearest one and said in a very icy, very pissed off tone, 'turn the fucking light off, and shut the fuck up.' They switched the light off, but said something to her in Spanish, something Aubrey could only interpret as unsavoury given their tone. Then they stumbled together to the shared bathroom. Defiantly, they kept the bathroom light on with the door open, while they showered and giggled, and did god-knows-what for forty-five minutes, including flushing the toilet ten times. Aubrey counted.

After bumping and weaving their way to bed, it was all quiet by five, snoring notwithstanding. That was until one of the girls ran to the bathroom to throw up. Aubrey would discover later that the girl had not made it to the toilet.

Just after six, someone's alarm went off. When it was still going after a minute or two, Pam yelled out 'Oh! For fuck's sake. Turn the fucking alarm off!' When the alarm continued to be ignored, Aubrey got out of her pod to investigate. The phone was next to the passed-out girl's head. Her friend saw Aubrey and scrambled down from the top bunk. With apologies, she switched it off. Aubrey went back to bed, exhausted.

Fifteen minutes later, the alarm went off again. Pam yelled, 'Jesus fucking Christ! Get a fucking hotel room next time!' She unzipped her sleeping bag and noisily began packing up. Aubrey and Georgina followed suit. Since the bathroom was now in a deplorable state, they had no choice but to grab their stuff and find another bathroom.

Pam, livid, was the last to leave the room, turning the light on and slamming the door on the way out. They were relieved to find a single bathroom in the communal area. They all took turns in the small space and left before dawn had even broken.

The antics had left them all so consumed with turmoil and exhaustion that they left Logroño on an empty stomach and without coffee. They knew they had a thirteen-kilometre hike, primarily uphill and with few services, but they were all so agitated they looked like three women marching toward war.

They were relieved to find a café open at the top of the hill. It sat on the edge of a community park, beside a large lake. They ordered breakfast and sat at a table outside in the sunshine. They went through the motions like zombies. Aubrey noticed the sunlight dancing across the water, causing a sparkling effect. It calmed her.

"I can't even speak, I'm so angry. The selfishness of those girls!" said Pam, slamming her coffee down on the table. Aubrey had to agree. She had never experienced behaviour like the girls in their room. Not even with her own kids.

"Lucky Lee wasn't with us," said Pam.

"Can you imagine how this would ignite her?" Aubrey said. She saw a smile form on Pam's lips. "She wasn't happy with the scene in Puente La Riena. The girls last night would have her spitting chips until Burgos!"

Pam nodded at that, but the smile had disappeared. She could sense Pam was regretting her words to Lee.

"I don't think they were pilgrims," said Georgina, picking up her coffee cup.

"No, I reckon they were in for the party scene," Pam said before taking a bite of her bread.

"I'm glad we had a rest day yesterday. Can you imagine if we hadn't? Need to look at the positives and let the angst go," said Aubrey.

"I'll get there. Just need to have a grumble first," said Pam. Georgina nodded in agreement.

"Seeing that Michelangelo in the Cathedral yesterday was a surprise," said Georgina as she took a sip of her steaming coffee. It didn't matter if the coffee tasted nasty this morning. They needed the caffeine to spur them on to Navarrete.

"The forum strikes gold again with their useful information," said Pam. Aubrey noticed that the conversation about the Camino seemed to be calming them all. Food and coffee also worked wonders.

They took their time to enjoy breakfast and to admire the awakening landscape surrounding the lake. When more pilgrims began filling the place, they took it as a sign to keep moving. Georgina bussed the table and carried the dishes inside. Aubrey offered to help, but Georgina refused, insisting it was merely professional habit. Aubrey found it a considerate gesture. The staff inside always seemed to appreciate it too.

They continued up the hill and soon they were walking through beautiful vineyards, the vines were just beginning to bud. Georgina restarted their conversation and talked about the differences she'd observed between the mentality of cyclists on the Camino versus pilgrims on foot. Just as she was describing her surprise at the lack of cyclist notification, two cyclists came flying down the hill toward them. The girl in front began wobbling. She was soon out of control. Aubrey was close enough to see fear in her eyes as the girl barrelled toward her. There was nothing they could do but jump out of her way. The girl crashed right in front of them, banging her head on the ground when she went down. Thank god she was helmeted, thought Aubrey.

They threw down their trekking poles and rushed to help the girl. Aubrey and Georgina lifted the bike off, while Pam told her to stay still and rest. The rider's boyfriend grabbed for her arm and tried to pull her up. Pam encouraged her to stay. She removed her backpack and reached in for her first aid kit. The girl had a serious gravel graze on her left arm. Georgina wanted to call for an ambulance, but the girl insisted she was fine. The fall had embarrassed her more than anything she said, apologising to them in broken English, over and over.

After ten minutes, the cyclist thanked them for their help and encouraged them to continue on. Reluctantly, they left. At the top of the hill, Aubrey looked back at the scene. The girl was lying down again, although now on the other side of the path. Aubrey quickly began walking back towards her, but the girl waved them on.

"She might have a concussion," said Pam, when they continued walking. "If not, at least a terrible headache later." Georgina started second guessing whether they should have gotten help, but Pam reminded her they offered all they could. It was the girl's choice.

"What a fucking day," said Pam. "I'll be happy to make it to Navarrete at this point!"

They followed the highway, keeping to their own thoughts, when Pam broke them out of their revery.

"See that up there?" she asked, pointing to a giant metal silhouette of a bull at the top of a hill. Pam explained that these bull structures had once featured in advertisements for an alcoholic drink across Spain, but the advertising was now banned.

"So why do they keep the bulls?" asked Georgina.

"Popular demand. Apparently, they were deemed 'nationally renowned'," Pam said. "I read that on the Australian Camino forum yesterday. They dropped the advertisement but kept a handful of bulls to appease the community. Fantastic, isn't it?" The sarcasm wasn't lost on Aubrey.

They came to a fork in the road. A town was off in the distance, but there were no visible yellow arrows on how to reach it. Aubrey stared uselessly at Google Maps, while Pam studied her online guidebook, both trying to determine which way to go. After ten minutes of increasing agitation, a young couple riding bikes stopped and graciously pointed out the right way. Aubrey pointed to a yellow arrow, hidden by a dip in the road once they'd picked up the trail. Bloody hell, Aubrey thought. Will this day ever end?

By the time they'd reached Navarrete, it was one in the afternoon.

All three readily agreed to call it a day. Pam found a small private albergue for them, but it was still too early to check in. All they wanted was something to eat and a long nap. They discovered a restaurant in the shade above the piazza.

"How far was Ben walking today?" asked Georgina, taking her backpack off.

"Not sure," Aubrey said and looked down at her phone to see if he'd mentioned it. She saw a second message from him. "Oh, this is interesting. There's another message from Ben. I didn't see it before. He said Hannah and Marinka decided on a rest day in Logroño after all. They got to the other side of town and turned around. They stayed in the albergue where Ben and Paolo had moved to."

"Well, that's good," said Georgina, with a confused look on her face, reflecting Aubrey's own questioning thoughts. "Hannah needed a rest day. But I wonder why they didn't come back to us?"

"Shame they didn't," said Pam. They all nodded in agreement. Their night would have been a much different experience.

"I'm ordering a beer," said Pam. "Anyone interested?" Both Georgina and Aubrey nodded quickly. Georgina surprised Aubrey by not looking at her watch.

"I'll take a look at what they have on their menu while I'm in there," continued Pam and wandered inside.

"And look who it is," Aubrey said, as she leaned her backpack against the wall. Ben walked into the piazza along with Paolo, Marinka and Hannah. "We were only talking about where you guys may be stopping today."

"Did you just arrive?" Ben asked. Aubrey nodded. "We left super early this morning, but you know us, we're slow."

"Plus, we helped that girl who fell from her bike," interjected Georgina. Aubrey nodded. It was true. They'd stopped for at least thirty minutes to help her.

"We left around seven," said Ben, "We had a noisy dorm last night." Ben and Paolo moved another table over so they could sit together. Paolo and Marinka took a seat at the far end, while Hannah sat next to Aubrey.

"That sun was too intense to take our time today," Ben continued.

"It's getting too hot to walk now." He looked over to Hannah, then back at Georgina and Aubrey. "How did you guys do?"

"We had disruptive roommates last night too, so we left before sunrise," said Georgina, as Pam placed a beer in front of her.

"Roommates from fucking hell!" announced Pam and, once everyone had drinks, Pam relayed the story.

"Wow. You guys win, hands down," said Ben then delved into a conversation with Pam of the dreadful Camino stories they'd read on the wider Camino Facebook group. Aubrey nudged Georgina, nodding toward Paolo. He was seriously flirting with Marinka. Marinka just shook her head at his antics.

"She seems flattered by the attention," whispered Georgina.

"They've been like that for about two days now," Hannah said, leaning in. She looked down at the end of the table. "Marinka said nothing will come of it. She's heading back to Germany in a few days. She believes he's just playing with her."

"But he'll still try," whispered Aubrey, smiling, taking a sip of her beer. She placed the drink back on the table. "How are you feeling Hannah? Any better?"

"The rest day helped. I guess I need to rest more," Hannah said, looking down at her stomach.

"Oh?" Aubrey said, feigning any knowledge of her condition. Hannah looked up, over to Georgina and again back to her. She glanced quickly at Ben then looked back at Aubrey once more.

"I'm pregnant," she said in an almost inaudible voice, clearly embarrassed.

"Oh," Aubrey said.

"Unplanned. Obviously," said Hannah. Aubrey reached for her hand. She was surprised Hannah took it.

"How are you feeling about that?" asked Georgina with a deep look of concern. It was a relief to have it out in the open. Now they could offer her some advice.

"Stupid," said Hannah, an embarrassed smile formed on her lips while a blush spread across her cheeks. "I feel even more stupid because it's like, one of those things I never thought would happen to me. We were careful, you know?"

"These things happen, no matter how cautious you think you are," Georgina said.

"I just don't know what I will do now. I found out right before I started the Camino. It's why I'm walking. To work out what to do." She picked up the cool lemonade Paolo had bought for her and took a long drink.

"And the father?" Aubrey asked. Hannah looked forlorn.

"He doesn't know yet. I need to call him. He started college in the fall last year and I was taking a gap year before I started school. I planned a fun year, just for me." She sighed. "Yeah, not much fun at the moment," she said with a rather anxious look on her face.

"Do you have morning sickness? Was that what was going on when Pam and I helped you, before Torres del Rio?" Aubrey asked.

Hannah nodded. "Yeah. I just feel, I don't know, extremely tired and nauseous all the time."

"Are you able to eat anything?" asked Aubrey. "You're walking long distances and in the heat. You need to be sure you're eating. And drinking plenty of water too."

"I can drink the water fine," Hannah said, "It's the food I can't deal with. I'm eating bread. It's all I can keep down at the moment."

"Try to add some cheese to that if you can," suggested Aubrey. "It'll at least give you some protein and calcium." Hannah nodded, but Aubrey could sense they were pushing her too hard even with that limited advice.

"I'm keeping an eye on her, making sure she eats and gets rest," said Ben, nudging Hannah with his shoulder. "These mother hens are just concerned about you, kiddo. We all are," Hannah smiled at him. Aubrey had the feeling that this girl trusted Ben. That was something.

18

MOTHERS

NAVARETTE TO SANTO DOMINGO VIA NAJERA

THEIR DAY STARTED EARLY from Navarrete. But now, in Najera, Aubrey's feet were on fire. They sat by the river, an umbrella shading them from the sunshine, her feet propped up in Paolo's lap. He'd offered to give her a foot massage, and she'd taken him up on the offer with glee. As Paolo methodically stretched the muscles in her left foot she relaxed instantly. She thought of Brendon. He had never rubbed her feet like this. But then, she'd never asked him to.

Aubrey looked around. They were a strange group. Pam and Georgina, her lovely Amigas, sat chatting with Ben, Hannah, Marinka and Paolo. They were from all walks of life, but somehow, they clicked.

After finishing her beer, Pam announced she wanted to look through the Monastery of Santa Maria la Real, built into the hills behind the town. She looked to Georgina, but Georgina responded she had no intention of moving anytime soon. Aubrey responded with 'same' when Pam looked at her. Marinka said she was interested and asked if she could join her. Pam nodded and off they went across the plaza, disappearing into a laneway. Hannah headed back to the albergue for a nap. Poor love. She was really feeling run down. Aubrey felt better knowing she was taking better care of herself in the early days of her pregnancy.

Aubrey thought about her chat with Georgina a few days earlier. Georgina questioned why the younger ones were sticking with them. They'd each found something in each other that connected them, Aubrey had said. Georgina asked what she meant by that.

"Ben reminds us of the son we'd love to have, or the son we already have at home. He probably sees us all as mother figures, or we remind him of ones he misses. Marinka has stuck with Hannah, becoming fast friends from day one. And now, Hannah needs support and guidance, so she's stuck with Ben and now with us. She knows we will take care of her," said Aubrey.

"And Paolo hangs around because of Marinka, that's obvious," said Georgina.

"Yeah, he admitted that he had given up on his quest to get laid by as many women on the Camino as he could," shared Aubrey.

"You can see the adoration in his eyes when he looks at her," Georgina had said. That was the truest of all statements.

Aubrey sat with her eyes closed, tuning in to the conversation nearby.

"It's like she is a goddess on my path," she heard Paolo say.

"Marinka? Seriously?" asked Ben and he laughed. "Sorry man. I'm just really surprised. I mean, dude, Hannah is more your type from what I saw only a week ago." When Paolo stopped rubbing her feet, Aubrey opened one eye. Paolo now held his head in his hands.

"She hates everything about me. She has told me this. I don't know how to talk to her."

"She is very shy Paolo. You've got to cut her some slack, man," said Ben. "You're very…"

"Exuberant," Aubrey piped in. She took a drink of her beer since Paolo had relinquished her feet for the time being.

"What is exube…" said Paolo, taking up Aubrey's other foot to massage.

"It means alive, spirited, excited," she said, reaching over to put her beer back on the table before he resumed the foot massage. "You're all of those things."

"Yes," said Ben, "and for a shy girl, that can be a little too much to handle."

"Ah, si. I understand. But I don't know how to change…"

"You need not change," Aubrey said. "If she likes you, she will see the kind-hearted man I know you to be and will accept you for who you are." She laughed out loud when Paolo blushed.

BEN PLAYED HOST AT DINNER THAT NIGHT. HE SAT HANNAH WITH Georgina, in the middle of the table, Pam with Paolo at one end and then took a seat at the other end, next to Marinka and across from Aubrey.

As they delivered wine to the table, Ben poured for everyone. She'd seen him doing this now at every meal they shared. Aubrey loved this quirk of his, so she asked him about it as he poured.

"It's a habit from Kanmi's restaurant. If the restaurant is extremely busy, I help out. Seating guests and pouring wine eases the burden for the regular staff. It keeps things flowing," he said, standing behind Pam's chair now, pouring wine, one hand behind his back like he was waiting on their very own table.

"Fortunately for us, I host most nights," he added with a chuckle. Ben was a natural.

"I could learn a lot from you Ben, for my café," said Georgina when he poured her wine. He smiled and squeezed her shoulder.

When their main course was delivered, Ben was deep in quiet conversation with Marinka. She looked down the table at Paolo and blushed. Aubrey could overhear their conversation and what she heard was interesting indeed. Marinka said Paolo's antics irked her, but she had a crush on him too. She just didn't know how to handle him. She had met no one like Paolo before. She saw how sweet and attentive he was, not only with her but to everyone. The problem was, she admitted, she didn't like the flirting.

Ben then explained that his husband was the same way. Aubrey's ears perked up. He said he had been put off, even offended, when Kanmi started hitting on him, like he was just another conquest. Only when Kanmi made a grand gesture did Ben realise that Kanmi was genuine in his feelings. Ben explained to Marinka that not everyone expresses love in the same way. Sometimes people do small, seemingly insignificant things to express how they feel. Others prefer to make grand gestures.

Aubrey had never thought of love that way. She had grown up in a household where marriage was stoic, but she saw love too between her parents, even if it was only within the walls of their house. Her father was a very traditional Englishman, never letting his emotions show, but he had a major soft spot for her mother. He would bring her roses from the garden every morning when they were blooming. In winter, he'd bring her a cup of tea in bed every morning. For her parents, it was the small gestures. Outside of the house though, they were a unit. They showed no romantic overtures in public. It just wasn't done.

But Aubrey had learned over the years that marriage was one of the hardest things she'd ever experienced. It had many, many shades of compromise. She'd always believed, thanks to the untold number of Mills & Boon she'd read growing up, that romance equalled forever and without it, no relationship could exist. Ben's comments made her think of her ex-husband, Brendon. Grand romantic gestures were his thing. Small acts of kindness never occurred to him. He was all show. No substance.

After dinner and too much wine, they settled the bill. Ben helped Pam from her chair, as Paolo did for Hannah. When Ben held the door open for everyone, Aubrey went through last. Just as she passed him, he gestured over at Marinka, then wiggled his eyebrows. She flashed back to the conversation earlier in the day with Paolo and suspected Ben was playing matchmaker. Was Marinka ready though? That was the question.

"I PLAN TO STAY AT THE PARADOR IN SANTO DOMINGO," PAM announced, as they made their way back to the albergue. Georgina, Pam and Aubrey were straggling behind the others. "It's my dream to stay in a grand hotel on the Camino, and Santo Domingo de la Calzada seems like the place to do just that."

"Can I tag along?" asked Georgina. "I'm eager to do something like that for myself."

"Sure! Everyone's invited. Just not in my room!" said Pam. "How about you Aubrey? Want to join the party?"

"Oh yes! Especially if there is a bathtub!" So, they agreed, for the following day, no matter how fast or slow they walked, the Parador was their reward.

WALKING OUT OF NAJERA, AUBREY REACHED PAM AND GEORGINA AT THE top of the hill. Aubrey had stayed behind to stretch, knowing she was likely to catch them. But now, she was out of breath from the steep hill. It looked as if Pam and Georgina stopped to catch their breath too, but also to take in the expansive views.

"That's one way to kick start the day, don't you think?" Pam said to Aubrey as she approached them. Pam somehow looked as fresh as spring daisies, sitting on a rock off the trail, while Georgina took photos of the flat landscape beyond them. Aubrey could only nod until she caught her breath.

"You know, I was just thinking of my mother," said Pam, popping her water bottle back into the side of her pack.

Pam's stories of her parents were not positive, so Aubrey didn't expect this to be a wonderful memory either. She reached for some of her water and took a long sip. It was still cold from when she'd filled it a little earlier.

"Hannah's pregnancy made me think of her," said Pam. "I was thinking about when I told my mother I was pregnant."

"Hannah said she hasn't told her parents yet," said Aubrey. She tightened her pack around her hips. She'd stopped wearing her belt a week before. It kept getting in the way of her pack. "I get the sense that we are the only ones who know at the moment."

"I get that impression too," Pam said, standing when Georgina finished with her photos and was ready to walk again.

"What did your mother say?" Aubrey asked as Pam double tapped her poles.

They found their pace quickly, but Pam stumbled slightly, quickly correcting her step. "My mother told me it appalled her. That she was utterly embarrassed, and that I was an absolute disgrace to the family."

"Wow, that's harsh. You were pregnant, not a criminal," said Aubrey.

"It's the same thing in the eyes of the Catholic church. Unmarried girl, pregnant. So, she did what she thought she had to. She made me marry the father," said Pam.

"Mick," stated Georgina quietly, shaking her head.

"Yup. Mick the Dick. My father thought he was the son he never had. Little did he know the night I got pregnant," she began, as she hitched her backpack up on her hips, tightening the belt a little, "well, that night, he took things too far. I told him no. Many times. By the time I found out I was pregnant, I had only had sex with him that one time. That's all it takes to get pregnant. In hindsight, I probably should have gone to the police, not gotten married."

"Geez Pam," said Aubrey. "You were..." This woman, she was learning, had some deep shit going on in her life. This had to be the source of the underlying anger she'd been picking up on, back in Torres del Rio. No question now.

"Yeah. He was a winner on so many levels," said Pam. "I think he was trying to play the situation."

"How? What did he hope to gain?" Aubrey asked.

"Status. That's all he was looking for really. Position. Power," Pam replied.

"I just can't imagine how hard that life was for you Pam," said Aubrey.

"My father gave me no choice. It was a different time back then," she said.

"It's amazing you've come out the other side with your sanity," said Georgina.

"Well, let's not get too hasty," Pam smiled. "Some would question it based on my decisions. And, considering I was a first-grade teacher and I swear like a sailor..."

"Justified," said Aubrey.

"What was your relationship like with your mother?" Pam asked

Georgina. Georgina hesitated. She seemed to be reeling from Pam's admission, just as Aubrey was.

"It was good. A lot different from yours by the sounds of things. Mine was loving and very supportive," Georgina laughed. "She loved my father like a giddy schoolgirl. That kind of love was lovely to grow up around. But she was also strong and very opinionated. She stood up for things she really believed in. They always adopted stray animals. And, I suppose, stray people. Christmas was always an amalgamation of odd people from all around. But with me and my brother, she was fierce. With me, it scared her to think I would stay and be a young mother, reliant on my husband. She told me I needed to go to the mainland to get my degree. And she convinced my father that was the right thing for me. He was so in awe of her, he agreed without hesitation."

"Sounds like a wonderful mother. Is she still with you?" asked Aubrey, picking up on Georgina's use of past tense when she spoke of her.

"Yeah, she was. But no, she's gone now. She died young," said Georgina, sadness in her voice.

"How old was she?" Pam asked.

"Forty-five," Georgina said and took a deep breath. "She and my father died together in a car accident."

"Oh, fuck Georgina!" said Pam, stopping to look her in the eye. "That's young." Georgina nodded and waved her forward.

"I'm so sorry George," said Aubrey. "That must have been awful."

"It was. I still miss them to this day, but it was a long time ago now," she said. "I was halfway through my second year of University when it happened."

"You were still young," said Pam.

"Yeah. My brother was on the mainland, working in the mining industry. He'd gotten an apprenticeship at seventeen and was well on his way to starting his life by the time it all happened. I had an aunty who was living in Hobart. She helped arrange everything until we could get home. But still," Georgina said, wiping the tears from her eyes. "We were all reeling. For a long time. I took a year off from Uni until my aunty reminded me that I had to finish my degree for my mother."

"Takes a lot to deal with that kind of grief," said Aubrey quietly. Georgina nodded.

They walked for some time in silence. The path was long and dusty, with the wind picking up enough to make it uncomfortable. The sun's rays were intense, making it challenging to walk the long slow hill toward Cirueña. There was a picnic area with huge shady trees, so they stopped and rested beneath the trees for a while. Aubrey took her shoes off and let them cool in the breeze. It felt amazing, but all too soon, Pam was getting antsy. The sun was burning hot today and the quicker they were out of it, the better.

"Come on," said Pam. "Let's go. We still have six kilometres to go and there's a luxurious room with my name on it." Aubrey groaned, but Pam was right. They refilled their water and reloaded their packs.

When they reached Cirueña, the place looked deserted. The village was half built. They saw a few cars, but many houses looked abandoned under construction. There was a beautifully lush golf course doing a bustling trade though. The rest of the town looked sad, almost haunted.

"It's eerie," said Georgina. Aubrey had to agree. Aubrey felt the sense of doom as they walked the deserted streets, following the ever-present yellow arrows.

"I think this is the town where the builders went under during the Global Financial Crisis," said Pam.

As they continued toward Santo Domingo, the canola fields appeared again in abundance. Fields of golden yellow enveloped the rolling hills for as far as they could see. Georgina took a selfie with Aubrey and Pam with the gorgeous gold as their backdrop. Even with selfies, Georgina knew what she was doing. She promised to share, blushing when Aubrey told her how great the picture was. The six kilometres they had remaining seemed to stretch on forever in the heat.

"Aubrey. Your turn. What was your relationship like with your mother?" asked Pam. Aubrey welcomed the conversation. It helped pass the time.

"It was okay," Aubrey said. "I mean, typically English I suppose."

"What does that mean?" asked Georgina.

"Well, she was loving behind closed doors, but it was like I was on parade in society as soon as we stepped out the front door. I grew up in Notting Hill, which is a fancy part of London. My father was in finance and my mother has links to the Royal Family, so societal status is a real thing. I was put in pretty dresses and lacy socks with Mary-janes, bows in my hair. It was very much about appearances."

Aubrey continued. "But my experience was similar to yours, Georgina. My mother died young. When I was twenty-five."

"Suddenly?" asked Pam.

"Not suddenly like Georgina's parents, but relatively quickly. My mother had renal cancer and it spread quickly. I was already living in Australia when it happened. That was hard." She took a breath, trying not to remember the vision of her mother's body lying still in the casket. The vision had stuck with her.

"When I was young, at boarding school, we did quality things together when she'd visit. Mummy would take the train to see me twice a month. We would go to the library, sometimes shopping. We'd linger over high teas for hours. We'd talk about school or whatever was going on at home. Sometimes, we'd spend the day playing gin rummy in her hotel room. I loved that game as a child. We usually played it when it was raining, which was often. She was very attentive, but I think she believed boarding school was better for me in the long run."

"I'm sorry to hear she died young. She sounds lovely," said Pam quietly.

"Me too," said Georgina, knowing what that felt like. "Why is it the good ones die young?"

"And the nasty ones linger…" said Pam. Aubrey laughed.

"That's my mother-in-law," said Aubrey. "She's still alive and kicking at seventy-five. She's a nasty piece of work."

"Mine was too," said Georgina.

"My ex-mother-in-law was, is, like a product of her generation. She lives in Sydney. In America they would call her very 'June Cleaver'," said Aubrey. "She always has her hair done and her makeup on. She likes to give advice whether you ask for it or not. She's the queen of gossip. But I will add, she is downright vicious if you behave in a manner than is, and I quote, 'unbecoming'," Aubrey hesitated for just a moment. "She thought, being English, I was perfect for her son. But her version of societal class differed greatly from the version I was raised in. My mother-in-law sees motherhood as a role, not a relationship."

"I know the type," said Georgina. "My sister-in-law is that way with her children. She's not the mother I am. I don't understand it myself. Children should be loved, cherished. Not put on a stand, like a trophy you own. That's what my sister-in-law does."

"Yes, exactly," said Aubrey. "Maybe your sister-in-law and my mother-in-law are related?"

"Scary thought," said Georgina.

"And your ex-husband is close to his mother?" asked Pam.

"Oh, a total Mummy's boy. He believes she walks on water and God help you if you rock that boat. I said something to her a few years ago, bucking her opinion on something. I don't even remember what it was, but what most would consider a healthy difference of opinion. But she had a heart attack shortly afterwards and so his family blamed me for her heart attack. Didn't matter that she had three blocked arteries. Then later, when I refused to conform to the family ways, my mother-in-law told me she would do everything in her power to protect her family. The 'from you' was heavily implied. This was, of course, when we were alone. The vicious comments were always when we were alone. But on that day, my husband walked in right after her threat and you'd think I was having tea with the bloody Queen. Which, I can attest, my mother-in-law is nothing like. The woman turned swiftly from downright sour to sickly sweet."

"Far out!" said Georgina.

"Oh, I should have known early on," said Aubrey. "There were red flags all over the place. I took her shopping with me when I was looking for a wedding dress. She had two boys, so I thought it would be a gracious gesture. I was standing in front of her, wearing the dress I was considering, and she informed me I should not be buying a wedding dress at all."

"Why not?" asked Pam.

"It was my second wedding. I was briefly married when I was young and silly. My parents were mortified. I eloped with the boy I was in love with, at nineteen. He was everything my family wasn't," Aubrey laughed. "It was so cliché really. He was in a rock band, and not a good one, mind you." She laughed.

"Anyway, because of that, my mother-in-law said I should look for a cocktail dress, or a fancy ballgown, but not a wedding dress. You could almost hear the words 'used goods' coming from her lips, but she didn't say them. She didn't need to. The implication was enough," Georgina gasped. Pam stopped and stared at Aubrey.

"Are you fucking kidding me?" said Pam.

"No. But don't worry, I bought the wedding dress!" Georgina laughed.

"Good," said Pam.

"There were enough red flags, even back then, that we had a pre-nuptial agreement. That was unusual in those days, but my father insisted. Now, according to Simon, Brendon's family are in shock because when we divorced, all Brendon got was his car and half of our joint bank account, which was only set up to pay bills. I guess his family weren't aware of the pre-nup."

"Didn't you have a house in Melbourne?" asked Georgina.

"Yes, but my parents technically owned it," said Aubrey. "It was our wedding present, but the house was still in their name. I think my father had an inkling about Brendon even back then."

"Good!" said Georgina.

"Indeed. I supported Brendon's relationship with his family one hundred percent, but eventually I set my boundaries. I couldn't take the toxicity anymore. Brendon grew up believing in perfect families..."

"There's no such thing as perfect," Pam said, shaking her head.

"Agreed," said Aubrey. "When my mother-in-law announced that her goal in life was to be perfect, I laughed. But it explained so many things." Pam stopped suddenly in her tracks.

"Wait." Pam didn't move. Aubrey turned around.

"Are you okay?" she asked.

"Yes. Yes." Pam stared at her, shaking her head. "But wait. I want to understand this. Her goal in life is to be… perfect? Are you fucking serious?" Pam asked.

Aubrey laughed. "Yes. Her goal is to be perfect in everything."

"So unattainable. And your husband grew up with this ideal?" Pam continued.

"Yes," Aubrey smiled at Pam. She knew the goal was ridiculous. She watched as they played these roles of that picture-perfect family. But Aubrey saw how deep the cracks ran.

Pam shook her head. "Girl, the fact that you stayed with him for so long with all of that bullshit tells me you have more strength than most."

Aubrey just smiled. "Just as you do. I'm only relieved I'm out of that completely."

"Sounds like this is the perfect time for a night of luxury ladies and looking at that," Georgina said, pointing ahead as they made their way down a long hill toward Santo Domingo, "looks like we are almost there."

"I still want to hear your mother-in-law story Georgina," said Aubrey.

"Another day. It'll be worth the wait, believe me."

19

OVERCOMING FEAR

"THERE ARE THE CHICKENS," said Pam excitedly, as they stared up at the birds in the glass enclosure, high in the Santo Domingo Cathedral. "You know, the ones that came alive."

Pam shared the miracle story, as she positioned it. The folklore went that an eighteen-year-old German boy was walking to Santiago with his parents in the 14th century. A local girl made advances toward him, but he rejected her. At this point in the story, Pam pointed out that the kid either had to be gay, or on his way to becoming a priest, because what eighteen-year-old boy would reject a girl coming on to him, parents or not?

She continued with the story. The girl, angry at the rebuff, hid a silver cup in the boy's bag. She informed the authorities that the boy had stolen it, so they sentenced to the gallows.

"To hang!" Pam exclaimed, with much drama.

The distraught parents examined their son's body still hanging on the gallows, when they heard his voice. He told them that Saint Dominic had saved his life. His parents, believing any idea that their son was alive, made their way to Santiago de Compostela to see the magistrate. It had to have been weeks, Pam said, but when they got there, the magistrate was eating his dinner. He laughed at their story and told them: 'Your son is as alive as the fowl I was feasting on before you interrupted me.' And in that moment, the chickens leapt from the plate and crowed with gusto. Pam had done a little chicken dance at that point, which had Aubrey and Georgina laughing uproariously. And here they stood, staring at the miraculous chickens.

"Do you believe that story Pam?" asked Aubrey, chuckling along.

"It's a fantastic story," Pam said, "And until I saw the backup chickens out the back of the cathedral, I would have wondered how those chickens survived."

"Ah, maybe they are just the descendants of the originals?" offered Aubrey.

"Party pooper," said Pam.

"It's a great tale," said Georgina, "but those chickens don't look happy to me, nor are they singing with any kind of gusto. My chickens certainly don't look like that!"

"Well, you wouldn't be happy or full of perky song if you were seven hundred years old!" said Pam, looking cheeky. "Come on, let's go find this Parador."

They headed out the door and back to the square to look at their app, only to discover there were two Paradors in Santo Domingo.

"Which one did we book?" asked Georgina.

"The cheaper one…. let me find the email. Bernardo de something," said Pam.

"Oh look! There's Lee," Aubrey said, waving to her. Lee looked at Aubrey and, when about to wave, looked over to see Pam and Georgina hovered over Georgina's phone. Lee's face changed quickly from happiness to hurt then to anger. She quickly dropped her hand and kept walking.

"Well Pam, I think you really stomped on Lee's toes." Pam looked up to see Lee walking away from them. She looked after her with remorse.

"I hope I have the chance to apologise," she said. "I mean, what I said wasn't that offensive, but…"

"It was the way you said it though, I think, that has her so angry," Aubrey said, softly. Pam slowly then returned to the phone.

"There it is," Pam said, her voice a little more sombre, handing Georgina back her phone. "Okay, let's go."

"I can hear the bathtub calling me from here," Aubrey said.

After they checked in, they darted from one room to another, gushing over the luxury. Pam suggested they meet back at seven for dinner. Georgina looked at her watch and announced it was just after four.

"Good. I'm planning a long soak and a delicious nap," said Aubrey with an enormous smile on her face.

"SHOULD WE CALL PAM? MAYBE SHE IS STILL ASLEEP? I'D HATE TO MISS our reservation since the Parador made it for us," said Georgina, looking down at her watch for the fourth time in as many minutes. They stood in the lobby looking out into the dark night.

"You know how Pam is," said Aubrey. "She faffs around, but she'll get here eventually. We agreed on seven and it's only a little after."

"Our reservation is quarter past, and truth is, I'm starving!" whispered Georgina, rather loudly.

"Good, me too. Let's go!" said Pam as she strode into the lobby. Georgina rolled her eyes. Aubrey laughed.

"Do you have the directions to the restaurant Georgina?" asked Pam.

"Yes. It's back over by the Cathedral. A few blocks," said Georgina. "Here. Take my phone," and handed the phone to Pam. Georgina knew, as did Aubrey, that Pam liked to be in control of the directions.

"I texted Ben earlier," Aubrey said. "Apparently Hannah found her appetite, so they made pasta and salad in their albergue. He said to have fun and that he'd see us tomorrow."

"Oh, I'm glad to hear she's doing better!" said Georgina.

"I think it helped they left early today. Maybe it was an easier day to walk for her," said Aubrey, stopping to wait for traffic. As they made their way to the restaurant, they passed several small shops. They turned left, then right, then left again. Aubrey was glad she wasn't navigating. The town was a maze. She was surprised, no, shocked, when Pam announced they were at the restaurant as she handed Georgina her phone back.

Santo Domingo was a major stopping point according to the guidebooks and this place reflected that. There were a few locals drinking at the bar. The Spanish didn't eat this early. For them, it was time for a friendly drink before they ventured home. The restaurant was full of noisy pilgrims. She heard the faint sounds of music coming from somewhere, but the chatter overwhelmed any clear melody.

The waiter appeared and handed them menus. He quickly returned with a carafe of wine and a basket of bread. Georgina and Pam dove straight in. Aubrey poured a glass of wine for each of them.

"Another day," she said, raising her glass.

"Did you notice this place has a Michelin star?" Georgina asked. Pam shook her head, but Aubrey had noticed. "It's amazing. And I can't believe we're dining here.

"Our options look better than the standard pilgrim meal too," Aubrey added, salivating as she scanned the menu.

"I have to say, it wasn't an unpleasant day all around. Just long," said Georgina. The waiter took their orders. Georgina continued, "I'm so happy to be eating something other than a tuna salad and dried out pork."

"And the Parador, to top it all off. That bathtub was nice. I was like a kid staying in a hotel for the very first time," said Aubrey. "But afterwards, I got on Instagram and saw your posts Georgina. You have published some gorgeous photos." Georgina looked down and picked something off her shirt.

"Georgina, when are you going to get over this discomfort over compliments? What are you afraid of?" Aubrey asked.

Georgina looked up. She ran her hand through her hair, fluffing it up, since she had left it down tonight. It was a gorgeous silver, Aubrey thought, the colour suited her perfectly.

The waiter placed a plate in front of Pam, who then nudged Aubrey and pointed to the one giant stalk of asparagus sitting on her plate. She grinned. It seemed the asparagus had survived Pam after all.

Pam looked toward Georgina.

"Well?" she asked.

"Don't gang up on me. I'm not afraid," Georgina responded defensively.

"What is it then? You clearly have an eye. You have exceptional talent and it'll be a waste if you don't do something with it," said Aubrey, thanking the server when they placed a plate in front of her.

"Well… maybe I am not in the position to do something with it at the moment," said Georgina, picking up a spoon to delve into her creamy soup.

"Fair enough, but when will you be? What are you waiting for?" asked Pam.

"It's kind of hard at the moment with the café and Patrick's stuff," said Georgina.

"We're talking about you. Not Patrick," Aubrey said. "I get it. His stuff may take a lot of energy, but Georgina, you have a gift. And the café? You've already talked about handing that over to your daughter." She was lucky her daughter was in the wings, ready to take over.

Georgina was quiet for a few moments as she ate her soup. She seemed to contemplate the questions.

"I guess I am afraid," she said quietly, then looked up. "I don't see the talent that you do. I don't think I'm good enough for it to go anywhere." She took another spoonful of soup. Aubrey could see her hand was shaking a little.

"Can I tell you a story then?" asked Aubrey.

"Please do," said Georgina, in barely a whisper, before reaching for her wine.

"My shop in Melbourne started out small. I took it over from a woman who wanted to move back to Perth. The shop wasn't that successful at the time. I was new to Australia, fresh out of business school in London and newly married. So, I bought the shop. I thought, I'll give it a year. If I couldn't do anything with it, I'd sell it." She broke off some bread and took a small bite.

"The shop carried mainstream wares, which I knew would not suffice in the market. So, I did something that few had done in Victoria. I brought London and New York to Melbourne. I created a high-end designer shop. My clients were wealthy and well-travelled. I adapted to the client's taste. And it worked. I didn't have to carry many items. If a client wanted something, and I didn't carry their size, I went to the fashion house and custom ordered. I carried the stock on consignment from the designers. It was cheaper than buying outright." She looked up and found Georgina and Pam spellbound by the story, just as the waiter served their main course.

"I took a huge risk, but it paid off. It's only recently that I sold the shop, and it sold fast. It wasn't an easy decision but there were things that made the decision necessary." Aubrey took a breath. She hated the reasons and quickly moved on. "Now, I am free to pursue something that I have wanted to do for a long time. I didn't do it before, because, well, to be frank, I am scared shitless. And yes, it may sound silly, given the success of my shop, but my fear is because I have been told over and over that my dream job isn't a career. And, if I pursued it," she paused, "I would fail."

"So, what's the dream job?" asked Pam, looking at her over the edge of her wine glass. Aubrey took another deep breath. She was glad no one had seen her confidence slip. She was good at wearing the mask. She closed her eyes.

"I want to design jewellery," said Aubrey but felt herself lighting up just by saying it.

"Now, that makes sense," said Georgina. Aubrey looked at her, surprised. Georgina continued, "I could never really picture you in high-end fashion. I mean, look at you. You have this amazing bohemian vibe. A pierced nose. A tattoo. I saw it on your ankle, by the way. High end? It's not the Aubrey I have come to know."

"I couldn't see it either," added Pam, taking a huge bite of her bread. "I mean, you've got the posh accent and everything, but the rest of you… it doesn't fit."

"That's because I let that life go. I finally figured out who I really was, and it wasn't the snobby English rose I was raised to be. I'm more comfortable with who I am now. I went through a lot of therapy to get to this point, to accept who I am. But the jewellery thing, I don't know. I mean, when I sold the shop…" She shook her head. She didn't need to talk about that. And she needed to get the conversation back on track. She looked back at Georgina. "I'm not saying it's easy to take the leap. I guess my point is, I gave myself permission to pursue the shop, to make changes. To do something different than what was the norm. Yes, it was a risk, but I knew that if I didn't try, I had already failed. But you have to give yourself permission first."

"Permission. I hadn't thought of it like that," Georgina said.

"Yes. At least give yourself permission to look into it," Aubrey said, looking Georgina in the eye. "You could sell your photos to travel agencies or even as stock photos. But I think you should go upscale. Your work is phenomenal Georgina. Sell your photos in a gallery. Isn't Salamanca a draw for tourists? I stopped there. There are some amazing galleries in there you could sell to."

Aubrey saw something cross Georgina's face that thrilled her. Acknowledgement. It was the first step.

"Dare to live the life you've always imagined, George. You really do have the talent," Aubrey said, as she sat back in her chair and sighed. She wished she could find that gumption to pursue her own dream. But she wasn't ready yet. She wasn't sure if she'd ever be, after the mess she made of her professional reputation.

"I don't want to leave," said Aubrey. "I had another bath when we got back last night. It was too inviting not to."

"Such a luxury," agreed Georgina, "I don't think I've ever spent that much on a hotel room, but it will be something I will remember. Thanks Pam."

"Better than spending four hundred euros in Santiago for the same experience," said Pam.

"Seriously?" gasped Georgina.

"Yeah. When I looked into it before I left, I discovered that Santo Domingo was the cheapest place on the Camino to stay in a Parador," said Pam.

"It was a splurge even in the movie *The Way*, right Georgina?" chuckled Aubrey, looking over at Georgina.

"It was!" She laughed, giving Pam a nudge with her walking stick. "I still can't believe that out of all of us Pam, that you have not seen that movie!"

"Get over it," she grumbled, as they stepped on to the bridge to cross the Rio Oja out of Santo Domingo.

"Oh, look at the storks!" said Aubrey. On the left of the bridge, three poles had massive stork nests perched on top. Georgina whipped out her phone and captured the moment, with one photo capturing a stork in flight, coming in to land.

THEY TALKED MOVIES FOR A WHILE, COMPARING WHAT THEY HAD SEEN, what was good on streaming services, and what movies they had grown up with. The conversation was light and comfortable.

They stopped in Redecilla del Camino for second breakfast. While they sat in the bar, Georgina pointed to the hotel owners as they buzzed around their customers. It was impressive to see two people managing such a large crowd with a constant, genuine smile.

"Did you see that? Their chemistry was amazing," said Georgina when they were putting their packs back on outside. "That was customer service at its best."

"I did. They were a well-run machine," said Aubrey.

"And your Tortilla de Patatas looked damn good too," Aubrey said to Georgina as they waited for Pam to finish in the bathroom.

"It was so good," said Georgina, a broad smile across her face as she patted her stomach playfully. Pam returned, mounted her pack in silence and double tapped her trekking poles.

They walked past more fields blooming canola although these looked to be growing with the help of steroids, they were so tall. Georgina took a photo of Aubrey alone, standing amidst the blooms as a reference to show how tall the canola was.

"You're the tallest of us, so I can explain through your height just how tall the canola is!" Georgina had explained. They inhaled the scent of every rosebush they passed like they were junkies looking to get high. It was a gorgeous day. The sun was out, the birds were twittering along with them and they couldn't believe just how beautiful this countryside was.

They stopped in Villamayor del Rio for a toilet and another coffee when they found Ben, alone.

"Hey stranger. Where's your posse?" asked Aubrey.

"They left early, about six I think?" said Ben, pulling his pack away from the chair so they could sit down at the table. "I stayed until the dorm emptied. It was easier. Everyone seemed to leave at the same time this morning."

"So, Hannah had more energy?" asked Georgina.

"Oh no. She was still dragging," he said, "but Paolo read there's a swimming pool at our next place in Belorado, so he was eager to get going. Since it was still cool, Hannah and Marinka joined him." Aubrey nodded, thinking that sounded just like something that would get Paolo fired up. "Surprisingly though, he insisted on breakfast before they got walking, so I think they are in safe hands with him."

"That's good," said Pam. "It was a long way before food this morning." Ben nodded.

"Marinka told me last night that she now knows why the Camino called to her," Ben said.

"To meet Paolo?" asked Pam.

"No. I thought that might be her answer too. No, she said it was to be here for Hannah," said Ben, smiling a kind smile.

"She's a lovely girl. I hope Paolo is good to her."

"Oh, he's smitten," said Ben. "Maybe for the first time."

They continued walking with Ben for the last five kilometres to Belorado. Thank god it was mostly downhill, Aubrey thought. Her feet were killing her. Even with the stretching she was doing, there was not much she could do with tired feet. She'd look at getting better insoles in Burgos, she decided.

They found Cuatro Cantones easily. It was hard to miss the albergue with the giant pilgrim mannequin out the front.

"Message from Paolo," said Ben, as they all stood in line to check in. "Grab a cervesa," said Ben, laughing as he looked up to relay the next part of the message, "from the vending machine," and looked down to finish the rest of the message, "then come out to the pool."

"I want a shower before anything else," said Georgina.

"Same. And I'm not drinking a beer from a vending machine. Surely there's a bar around?" asked Pam.

"I'm with them," Aubrey said to Ben, nodding in Pam and Georgina's direction. "Shower and a real beer."

"Okay. Then I will let them know we're all here and we want more than vending machine beer," he said, typing with a smile.

AFTER WANDERING AROUND THE TOWN, AUBREY, GEORGINA AND PAM found a bar in the piazza, with tables lined up in a row outside. At one end, under an enormous shade umbrella, a group of American pilgrims played cards with pitchers of beer on the table. At the opposite end, they found Ben with Paolo, Marinka and Hannah and some additional chairs ready for them.

"Hi kids," said Pam, rubbing Hannah's shoulder with affection. "How was the pool?"

"Great," said Hannah, looking much better than before. "Marinka and I only stuck our feet in. We didn't bring swimsuits with us, but Paolo wasn't shy. He stripped down to his briefs and jumped right in."

Marinka blushed. She was such a sweet thing. She looked over at Paolo, a cheeky grin splashed across his face. Aubrey shook her head. Bloody rascal.

"I'm on the beer run today. Who's in?" asked Pam.

"I'll help," said Aubrey. They strolled inside. The place was empty but for a couple in the corner writing in journals with beers in the centre of the table.

"Ugh," Aubrey said, nodding at the couple, "I've been so bad about writing in my journal. I really need to. Most of my energy has been zapped by the time we stop walking though."

"I've managed it every day, but I'm sure I'll regret not going into as much detail as I should," said Pam.

"It's hard when there's happy hour every day," said Aubrey.

"Yeah, but just as rewarding," said Pam. "I am loving our little group. I'm not sure I would have given these kids the time of day in my other life. But you know, I feel connected to them. It really feels like they are my own kids. I know that sounds, I don't know… strange?" said Pam, as they waited for their drink order.

"Not so strange. I've had the same thought. Being with these kids is kind of...." Aubrey stopped herself. She wanted to say healing, but that would reveal too much.

"Comforting?" asked Pam.

"Yes," she said, relieved with that explanation. It was close enough. Pam nodded and picked up as many drinks as she could carry. Aubrey grabbed the rest.

The group enjoyed a peaceful afternoon in the sunshine. Aubrey chatted with Marinka while Paolo kept trying to butt into the conversation. Aubrey asked him to move to the other end of the table, explaining she wanted to get to know Marinka better. Paolo hesitated. Marinka looked at him and simply said: 'shoo'. So he did. Aubrey laughed, realising Ben was right about Paolo. He was smitten.

"You've walked the Camino before?" asked Aubrey.

"Yes. A little," Marinka said. "I walked from Saint Jean Pied de Port to Pamplona last year. I only had a week, so that is as far as I walked. That's why I started there. Many Europeans do it this way." She took a sip of her beer, looking up the table to find Paolo. She smiled.

"He's smitten with you. You do know that?" Aubrey asked, following her gaze to find Paolo watching Marinka, waiting for permission to return to her.

"I think so," said Marinka. "I don't know. He is a boy."

"What about you? How do you feel?" asked Aubrey. "You will leave us soon and then what? Where do you return to?"

"I will go home to Berlin. Paolo will continue on and find another girl," Marinka said. Aubrey could hear the disappointment in her voice.

"Maybe. Maybe he will keep in touch and maybe walk another section of the Camino with you next year?" said Aubrey. Marinka looked down into her lap.

"I doubt it. He will forget me," said Marinka, sadness heavy on her words.

"If you find it to be love, you will find a way," said Aubrey. Marinka looked up in surprise, as if love hadn't even crossed her mind. "What will you be returning to, in Berlin?"

"School," said Marinka. "I am a teacher. I teach grundschule," Marinka said and hesitated. "Ah, for you, elementary?"

"Primary school," said Aubrey, "Primary is Kindergarten through Grade Six in Australia."

Marinka nodded. "I teach Grade Two."

"Did you know that Pam was a teacher before she retired? She taught six-year-olds," said Aubrey.

"No, I did not know this," said Marinka, looking over at Pam. "Really?"

"Yes, she surprised Georgina and me too. Doesn't seem the type, does she?"

"I disagree. Now I know how she can manage Paolo so successfully!" said Marinka with a quick laugh. Aubrey laughed too and wondered whether more would eventually develop between these two beautiful people.

20

GRIEF IS A CURIOUS THING

BELORADO - VILLAFRANCA MONTES DE OCA

AUBREY WOKE early to snorers trumpeting various tunes in the very crowded dorm room. The silicone earplugs she bought in Logroño couldn't come close to drowning out that music. She checked her phone, five-thirty. Too early to get up, but she knew there was no return to sleep either.

She snuggled under her blanket and considered the people they had met so far. Lean and Mean immediately came to mind. No, not Lean and Mean. Lee, that was her name. Aubrey remembered her walking away angry in Santo Domingo. Pam had been harsh to Lee in Villamayor de Monjardin, and Aubrey knew Pam was remorseful for what she had said. She admitted that to Aubrey, when they walked back from dinner in Santo Domingo. She should have apologised when they'd seen her earlier that day. Still, conversation had to happen for things to improve and they had plenty of opportunities for that on the Camino. They just had to see Lee again for Pam to do that now.

But just like she'd felt with Pam, Aubrey got the sense something else was going on with Lee. She knew, somehow, that it was something deeper... her intuition was speaking to her once more.

Both Pam and Georgina stirred. Aubrey caught their attention, indicating that she was heading to the bathroom. Nodding, they quietly followed.

"Good Morning," Aubrey whispered once they were out of the dorm room. "How did you sleep?"

"Okay, once I got there. At least enough to keep me going. Just glad it's not a long stretch today," said Pam. "Happy about that. Tomorrow will be a beast though." Aubrey nodded and they silently got ready for their day.

They strolled through the streets of Belorado. Georgina snapped photos of the incredible murals covering the stone walls along the path. She asked if they could circle back to the piazza so she could photograph the murals she had missed yesterday afternoon. The amazingly detailed murals depicted everything from flowers to snails to old cars. Aubrey managed a few photos of her own, which she promptly emailed home to Simon.

When they finally reached the outskirts of town, Aubrey looked up to the multi-storey apartments, always curious about the people who lived in these towns and hamlets along the way. This morning, she saw two women. One stood front and centre at her window on the top floor, looking down sternly. Another woman stood two floors below, waving exuberantly and blowing kisses when she met Aubrey's gaze. Aubrey returned the kisses in kind, feeling happiness at the love being shared. When the air kisses ended, she looked back up to the woman on the top floor. She now wore a deep scowl on her face and her arms were tightly crossed. When they were almost past the building, Aubrey blew a kiss to the stern woman and gave her a wave, surprising the woman enough that she uncrossed her arms, raised her arm slightly before retreating from the window.

As they crossed the bridge out of town, Aubrey pondered the stories of the two women. It was true, she thought, you really didn't know someone's story. Maybe the stern woman had lived her entire life, trapped in obligation, jealous of those who had the freedom to walk the Camino? Whereas the woman below may have run an albergue, or maybe she had even found love on the Camino? She let her imagination run wild.

Soon enough, the younger ones caught up with them, all excited at the gorgeous day. They stuck together for a while. Before long, the young legs of Paolo, Marinka and Hannah allowed them to break ahead. Ben stuck with them, happily reporting that Hannah seemed to have some energy again. They walked in silence for a while, then Aubrey began chatting quietly with Ben about winters in New York. She compared it to places she'd lived. Georgina added her two cents from behind. Pam was walking further behind. She seemed reflective. After a while, they walked in silence again. It seemed no one was in the mood for talking today.

When they stopped for water, Aubrey broached what was weighing on her mind.

"I was thinking about Lee earlier this morning," Aubrey said. "I am confused by her reaction when we saw her in Santo Domingo. But I've been considering the idea that we really don't know the extent of someone's story."

"I've been wondering about that too," said Pam. "I realise now I was quite... terse with her in Villamayor de Monjardin."

"What did you say that had her so offended?" asked Georgina. Aubrey remembered she wasn't with them that night.

"I told her to suck it up," said Pam. "She was a bundle of negativity and I guess I'd just had enough of it. I was rather mean about it though."

"Oh?" asked Georgina in disbelief. Pam's behaviour that night did not reflect the woman they both had come to know.

"She may have a valid reason to be upset," said Ben, putting his water bottle back in his pack. Ben gave Aubrey a knowing look.

"Are you aware of something?" Aubrey asked. Ben didn't answer right away. When Pam turned towards him, looking for answers, he looked sheepish.

"She's dealing with stuff," Ben said. "Grieving. That's all I'll say."

"How do you know that?" asked Aubrey.

"She was staying at the same albergue in Logroño," Ben said. "She and I shared a beer together, and she told me the reason she's walking."

"Well, fuck," said Pam. She picked up her pack, double tapped her trekking poles, and started walking. They tried to give her space, but she was slow, even at her determined pace, so they caught up quickly.

"Now I feel like a complete bitch," she said out loud about ten minutes later.

They could say nothing to make the situation better, so they continued in silence. They passed through a small hamlet where a sign showed they still had over five hundred kilometres to walk before reaching Santiago. Georgina pointed at it, groaned, and took a group photo to mark the occasion. After many kilometres, the path eventually went downhill to a single file trail. They came to a small bridge spanning a babbling brook, then headed uphill to reach Villafranca Montes de Oca, navigating the very narrow path edging the busy road. Their albergue was at the top of the hill. Of course. It was the perfect end to what had had been an interminable day of walking.

The albergue offered single beds separated by a partition, quite the luxury in the land of bunk beds. But Aubrey's head wasn't into the accommodations. While most of the group headed to the bar after showers, Pam took a nap. Aubrey found a quiet space out the back of the albergue, happy to have some space of her own. She needed to spread out, write, and do some yoga. She was feeling the intensity of Pam's anger like it was her own. She needed some time to work it out.

At dinner, Aubrey sat next to Ben and asked discreetly about Lee. With a shake of his head, he said Lee had her own stuff to ponder. She had probably forgotten about Pam's outburst anyway. But the look on Lee's face in Santo Domingo haunted Aubrey. Pam's words had hurt Lee. And if Lee was grieving, she was already in pain. She decided to try and talk to Pam about it and hoped that they would see Lee again. Aubrey knew others would see her as meddling, but this was something causing Pam distress. Aubrey knew because she could feel it. Her time outside had not eased the premonition she felt.

At dawn, Aubrey was packed up and ready to go. While she waited for Pam and Georgina, she walked outside to feel the air. The weather had turned. Sleet hit her face.

"Shit!" she exclaimed and dashed back inside. Pam had warned them about the weather forecast the night before. Turned out, she was right. She stopped in the bathroom before warning the others. When she returned to the dorm, Pam and Georgina were gone.

"Where did the Lovelies go?" Aubrey whispered to Ben, still in bed in the pod next to her. She pulled on her windbreaker and put her poncho on the outside of her pack.

"Pam assumed you wanted space, so they left," he said. She turned to go but Ben called her back.

"You don't have to carry the weight of the world on your shoulders Aubrey. Everyone has their own stuff. That's why we're all here, to work that out. Even you I suspect. Everyone else will be okay," Ben said. Aubrey nodded, warned him of the sleet, grabbed her beanie and gloves, and headed out.

Between the frigid air and the steep hill, it was slow going. She saw Georgina and Pam stopped about halfway up the steep incline. They had bundled up against the cold. Hearing her approach, Georgina turned and waved, but Pam continued facing forward. She'd not said a word to Aubrey all night and then they left without her this morning. She knew something was up for sure.

"Morning Lovelies," she said when she caught up.

"Morning," Georgina said. Pam mumbled something inaudible. She double tapped her poles signalling time to move.

"You okay?" Georgina asked her. Aubrey nodded, smiling at Georgina but Georgina looked worried.

"Are you, Pam?" Aubrey asked. Georgina shot Aubrey a side glance.

"Yeah, I'm fine. Just a lot on my mind," Pam said, and continued her pace. They walked in silence, which wasn't unusual for them in the early mornings, but the vibe was different today. Something was definitely up with Pam. Aubrey pondered going ahead when Pam spoke again.

"I have been thinking about Lee and my own lack of grief. I don't know what happened with Lee, or who died, but I feel like shit," said Pam as they continued up the Alto. "And the look on her face in Santo Domingo, now that I know she was grieving. I can't get that out of my head."

"Are you...are you talking about Mick?" Aubrey asked. Pam nodded.

"I..." Pam hesitated, then stopped and looked behind her, as if she didn't want anyone else to hear what she had to say. Aubrey followed her gaze and saw a lone figure off in the distance. Only then did Pam continue.

"I celebrated when my husband died," her whisper barely audible. "Clearly Lee has lost someone close to her and I feel an utter bitch by saying what I said. If she's at the angry stage in her grief, she has every right to be bitchy."

"We all react in different ways. Don't be too hard on yourself," said Aubrey. They reached the summit. Around them, emerald green moss clung to trees and wildflowers popped out of the lush grass below. Newness sprung all around her, but Pam's burden was more like a laden blanket of snow than the first buds of spring.

"It was a lot different for me," she said. "When Mick died, I never grieved. I grieved years ago when I realised my marriage was a sham. There was never love with him. I was... happy when he died."

"Was it really that bad?" asked Georgina. Pam chortled. Aubrey heard footsteps behind them, and Pam turned to identify who it may be. It was a young South Korean pilgrim they'd seen in their dorm the night before. He waved as he hiked on by with a chirpy "Buen Camino!"

"Buen Camino," they chorused, plodding on before Pam finally answered Georgina's question.

"Yes, it was that bad. I told you about losing the baby not long after we married." Aubrey opened her mouth to say something, but Pam continued.

"After that, he wanted nothing to do with me. People asked me constantly about having babies. Back in those days, that's what women did in the country. Stayed home, had babies." Pam was clearly angry.

"But you have to have sex to have babies. We didn't. The first time wasn't really, well, a loving experience either."

"Yeah, you said you were..." whispered Georgina. "And I don't mean to make light of that. I mean, to be forced into a marriage with your..." She didn't finish the sentence.

"Yes. I know what it was. I haven't told anyone this before. I tried to tell my oldest friend Sue, but she wouldn't hear it. And, before long, I was a married woman with a baby on the way with this.... dickhead."

"After I lost the baby, we didn't have sex again until about two years later. He came home drunk one night and demanded sex. It was as sloppy as you can imagine, he was so drunk. I was raised to believe that I was there to please my husband. It was my duty as his wife. He told me the next morning that I didn't satisfy him, so why bother. As the years went on, it only got harder. He ignored me for the most part. It was hard to be his wife. Mick became highly regarded in the community. Everyone looked up to him. Revered by all the men, admired by the women. He was good looking, I suppose. He looked a bit like John Travolta I've been told. I heard rumours of an affair with a woman in a nearby town, but he quashed it every time I brought it up. It was not something spoken about and, when I did, that was cause for another beating. He was very careful about those too. The bruises were always in places I could cover. He constantly told me that I was never good enough. I was never pretty enough. I was never..." Aubrey could feel the emotion build, breaking into Pam's voice. "I was never enough for him."

"Pam..." Aubrey said

"There's more..." said Pam. Aubrey saw Georgina shake her head in anger and disbelief.

"Jesus," Aubrey said.

"The woman he'd been having an affair with came to my house one day. I must have been thirty. She was probably the same age, possibly a few years younger. She told me she should be the one he married. I looked at her and told her she could have him and slammed the door in her face. Then I cried, because as much as I wanted that to be the case, I recognised it would never happen." Pam stopped on the trail and took a drink of her water. The hills were a bitch and walking and talking took some extra chutzpah. Georgina and Aubrey followed suit but said nothing. Pam was on a roll, so they stayed quiet for her to continue.

"When he died, I was... relieved. He died in a car accident on the way back from spending a week with her. He hit a kangaroo and lost control of the car. My reaction differed from Lee's grief. There was no grief for me, only relief."

"The woman, Heather was her name. She came to the funeral. I allowed her to sit on the pew on the other side of the aisle, at the front. It was funny really. I was his formal life, and she was his secret one. When people asked me who she was at the funeral, I realised then he was dead and that meant I no longer had to cover for him." Aubrey looked over at Pam, but her head was down. Her eyes were focused on the ground. Their pace had quickened.

"So, when I got up to give his eulogy, I told them exactly who she was. All of it. How he had only slept with me twice in our marriage because he'd been having an affair with Heather for thirty years. How he'd carried on this secret life with this woman. How he'd even had two children with her. I told them how he'd been abusive and even rolled up my sleeves to show them my latest bruises, although they were a bit faded by then. I even played the 'remember when I broke my arm three years in a row?' game. Nodding heads. That's all I saw. They all knew the truth. But they did nothing to help."

"Then I told them how he'd lied in his business affairs," she continued. "How Mick was telling them one thing but doing another. Nothing illegal. He seemed careful about that. It was more stuff the Church would frown upon, immoral kinds of things. I told them about the Thai women he sponsored to come into Australia, to work in the massage place in Newcastle he opened. Okay, so maybe he was into illegal stuff. I heard they gave something called 'happy endings', which I can only imagine..." Aubrey chuckled.

"Yes. That was probably illegal," said Aubrey.

"You were gutsy," said Georgina.

"I suppose. I just felt I had to tell them the truth. I was sick of hiding his lies," said Pam.

"So? What happened? Was there any repercussion?" asked Aubrey.

"Heather was his sole beneficiary. He had over a million dollars in debt. Apparently, he'd filed for a divorce and filed formal separation papers the day before the accident. I didn't know about that. But the farm was in my name only. The day after the funeral, I put the farm on the market, all ten thousand acres of it, and left town. My lawyer made Heather sign a document saying she wouldn't come after the farm sale and she signed it. Idiot. I sold the farm to a winery about four years ago. It was prime cattle grazing land, but the vineyard offered me three times as much as the graziers, so it was my last-ditch effort to show the town my middle finger. I gave Heather's kids twenty thousand dollars each because they, too, were collateral damage."

Aubrey stopped. Raw emotion and pain radiated from Pam. Aubrey began laughing. Pam stared at her, dumbstruck then angry.

"What the fuck? Why are you laughing?" Pam yelled. Georgina smiled in understanding.

"Because you deserve a medal for putting up with that shit for so long!" said Aubrey. "Do you know how much gumption you have to say all that at Mick's funeral? How strong you had to be—and still are—to survive all of that? I am amazed that you have such a positive outlook on life after being treated that way. I am only sorry that you couldn't get out of it earlier. I'm so, so sorry for that."

"Me too!" said Georgina.

"Do you know what got me through every day?" Pam said, her voice quiet.

"Please tell me," Aubrey replied.

"Seeing twenty-five smiling, hopeful faces. Those children in my classroom were my lifeline," said Pam, her face softening.

Aubrey stepped forward and hugged her. Georgina followed suit.

"Let's go. I really need to pee," Pam said, after a few minutes, her tone and step much lighter.

21

I MADE IT THROUGH THE RAIN

VILLAFRANCA MONTES DE OCA – BURGOS

IT HAD BEEN a hard slog for two days through torrential rain. Aubrey's Gore-Tex hiking shoes kept her feet dry, while her poncho worked for the rest of her. Marinka had worn waterproof shoes and had head to toe rain gear, but the other young ones weren't so prepared. Ben's blisters were flaring up once more. The rain had done a number on Pam's knees and even Georgina, who never complained, said she was sick of being wet.

They stopped in Agés to get out of the rain for a while. They found an inviting restaurant that looked straight out of a history novel with its dark wooden beams and unlevelled floor. A roaring fire burned at one end of the room. Aubrey took a bite of the homemade apple cake and groaned with pleasure. It was incredible. Even Georgina lauded the coffee. There was a silver lining to everything, Aubrey thought. Looking at her guidebook between bites of her cake, Pam suggested that they walk as far as Atapuerca, then call a taxi and ride into Burgos from there.

"The main walk into Burgos is quite industrious from what I read. According to the forum, it's several kilometres through busy traffic areas and blocks and blocks of concrete. Add in the rain and that will be fucking miserable. A more scenic route exists, but it's not well marked, and the rain would make it difficult to navigate." Pam's insight into the Camino hadn't let them down so far, so Aubrey, Georgina and Hannah readily agreed. Marinka, Ben, and Paolo decided to walk.

"Are you sure you want to keep walking Ben?" asked Aubrey, worried about his blisters.

"I am," Ben replied, looking toward Marinka.

"Marinka is worried about being alone with Paolo," Hannah whispered to Aubrey, out of earshot of everyone else a few minutes later. Aubrey wasn't so sure he was a threat to her, believing Paolo would walk over fire for Marinka. But Marinka seemed inexperienced. Ben continued to impress her with his generosity and kind spirit, even if it wasn't in his best interest. He'd be nursing those blisters for days. Pam chuffed him, told him to at least dress the blisters and double up with dry socks. He nodded like a scolded schoolboy and followed her direction.

On the walk to Atapuerca, they stopped at an enormous sign beside the trail that showed a sketching of what looked to be a Neanderthal. With the rain stopping for a spell, Pam read from her notes that it was the site where they'd discovered the first human remains in Europe.

"The remains are reported to be over seven hundred and fifty thousand years old," she said, her voice reflecting her amazement. It boggled their minds.

"Yes! They have the remains on display in the Burgos Museum of Evolution," Georgina said. "I read about this. It was the one thing that stood out in my mind when I was researching the Camino." Georgina was as excited about it as Pam. Aubrey noted that nugget for later.

Getting a taxi felt weird at first. Aubrey had not been in a car for weeks. She felt guilty, like she was cheating her pilgrimage by fast forwarding. But Pam reminded her that pilgrims, back in the day, would not have dealt with semi-trailers barrelling down the highway or kilometres of concrete. They likely hitched rides on carts or donkeys at any opportunity. As the taxi drove toward the centre of Burgos, they passed through a warehouse district. Steam billowed from exhaust pipes. People walking on the footpaths were getting drenched when passing cars hit puddles on the road. Aubrey dismissed any anxiety about cheating the walk. Pam was right. The walk into Burgos might have done them all in.

When the taxi dropped them off, Pam, Aubrey and Georgina insisted on walking with Hannah to her albergue. She'd suffered morning sickness again; the mother ducks were back to cluck mode. Once assured Hannah would rest for the afternoon, they continued to their hotel.

Aubrey was looking forward to her own room, a long hot shower and hopefully, some decent sleep. Since losing one of the silicone earplugs two nights prior, sleep had eluded her. She was glad they had all agreed to stay in Burgos for two nights.

She walked into her room and found a king-size bed covered in luxurious bedding. The room was dry, and the heating worked. Fluffy fat towels hung in the bathroom. A rain shower with hot water was available whenever she wanted it. She was more than happy to spend the hundred euros for two-nights of indulgence. The price of this simple luxury was a bargain.

After a hot, revitalising shower, she washed the mud out of her hiking pants and hung them over a chair near the radiator to dry. Then, dressed only in underwear, she lay down on the gorgeously comfortable bed and fell asleep.

Two hours later, when the sun finally broke through the gloomy clouds and straight into her eyes, she got up, washed her face, dressed, and headed out to deal with her errands. She navigated her way through the bustling streets. Siesta was over and there were pilgrims everywhere. She found some nuts and muesli bars in a small Supermercado near the bus station, then popped into a nearby Farmacia. She needed replacement earplugs as well as shoe inserts to relieve her aching feet. As she walked out of the Farmacia, she was startled to see Lee, walking in.

"Hi Lee!" she said, but seeing the confusion on Lee's face, she continued, "I'm Aubrey. We met a week or so ago, in Villamayor. How are you doing?"

"Oh, yes. You're walking with Pam and another woman...?"

"Georgina," she said, helping her.

"Ah, yes. That's right," said Lee.

"I have been thinking of you. Well, worried about you to be honest, since..." Aubrey said. She couldn't explain more without offending Lee. "I haven't seen you since Santo Domingo. And you looked upset."

"Yeah? Well, I'm okay. I've been walking on my own mostly. I mean, I've walked with others, but I'm happy on my own."

"Look, what Pam said to you in Villamayor," Aubrey began. Lee nodded, looking down. "You should know, Pam feels awful about it."

Lee looked straight up into Aubrey's eyes from her five-foot frame. "Well, let her suffer a little more. Her words cut me." She paused for a moment, then sighed. "But tell her I'm okay."

Her eyes told another story, but Aubrey let it go. She paused while she considered her next move. "I'm about to find a coffee somewhere. Would you like to join me?"

"Sure," Lee blurted. "Let me get a few things in here." Lee said, pointing inside the Farmacia. Aubrey nodded, surprised she'd taken her up on the offer.

"Great. I'll wait for you just outside."

They stopped at a lovely chocolataria. They found a table outside, partially shaded from the intense sunshine. A waiter approached them and they both ordered hot chocolate and churros.

"I've always wanted to try them," said Lee when the waiter walked away. "It's not coffee as you suggested, but this is something I had to try while in Spain." Aubrey was surprised to see how relaxed Lee seemed. This was not the woman they had met so far.

"I'm happy to try it too. A place in Melbourne, where I used to live, sells churros. But these look far more delicious. I'm sure I won't be going back there once I have tried these," said Aubrey, just as the waiter placed fresh churros and mugs of hot chocolate in front of them. "This chocolate looks absolutely decadent." Lee dipped her churro in, the thick mud of chocolate coated just the tip. Aubrey did the same. When she bit into the churro, the crispness crackled before melting against her tongue.

"Oh, my goodness," said Aubrey. Lee looked up at her with a

knowing smile. "It's a relief I'm walking eight hundred kilometres. The calories are adding up with every bite, but I don't care. This may be the most delicious thing I've ever eaten. Chocolate wise anyway."

"It's incredible," said Lee, revelling in her own chocolate world.

When they were both three churros down and half their chocolate mass devoured, Aubrey smiled and leaned back in her chair. "I can't eat anymore." Lee continued eating hers but slowed down considerably.

"I guess I should explain why I reacted the way I did," said Lee. "I've heard Australians can be blunt. I suppose I wasn't quite in the right headspace to be told to 'suck it up', as Pam put it." Aubrey nodded. "I was being negative. No, angry. I get that. Maybe fed up, I suppose. You see, my Camino experience so far isn't what I hoped it to be. The timing of Pam's attack didn't help."

"It's true," said Aubrey. "Australians can be blunt. It took me a while to get used to that when I moved there thirty years ago. And they don't hold anything back, either. But, having said that, Pam knows she didn't approach it well either. She's had to deal with a lot of negative stuff in her life too, so that may help to explain things." A puzzled expression crossed Lee's face for a moment.

Lee continued, "I guess I'm tired of watching these damn kids treat this walk with such disregard. It's supposed to be sacred. And people should be respected."

Lee's attitude still surprised Aubrey. Ben mentioned she was grieving, but Aubrey wasn't sure of the cause. She had assumed that she had lost someone, but what if it was something else? Perhaps she'd lost out on a job to a younger person?

"We've been walking with some younger pilgrims. I would say they are very respectful. Ben is one of them. You met him in Villa-mayor with us, and then in Logroño too, I think he said?" Lee looked surprised, then nodded. Aubrey sat back in her chair. "Everyone has their reasons for doing this Camino."

"What's your reason?" Lee asked. Aubrey hesitated, remembering Ben's words about carrying the weight of other people's issues. She considered giving Lee a vague answer or at least the 'change of life, a change of scenery, a new adventure' line. But she felt compelled to be honest with Lee.

"I want to figure out what I want from my life," said Aubrey. "I've dealt with… change in my life in recent years, so it's time for a new direction."

"And have you discovered what you want yet?" asked Lee.

"Creativity. Friendship. But I want more than that. I'm still working through that. And you? What was it you are expecting?" Aubrey asked.

Lee reached for another churro, dipped it in and stopped before taking a bite. "I lost someone I loved deeply. I believed this pilgrimage would help with the healing."

"I'm sorry to hear that. And you don't feel the Camino is helping?" Aubrey asked. She understood the healing aspect all too well.

"No. I'm just… angry," Lee said, finally taking her bite. When she was done, she continued, "Angry she's gone. Angry that I'm doing this walk alone. Angry that I can't run anymore. Angry at… well, everything."

Aubrey decided that the easiest way to defuse the growing tension was to ask a simple question. "Did you used to run a lot?"

"Yep. Ten miles every day. Ran up into the canyon behind my house. The quack says I can't do it anymore. My joints can't deal with the pounding. God, I hate getting old." Aubrey studied this petite woman. She estimated her to be only a few years older than she, putting her around fifty-five.

"May I ask how old you are?" Aubrey asked. "You don't seem too old to be running to me. I mean, I'm not a doctor but…"

"I'm seventy-three," said Lee.

Aubrey leaned forward in shock. "Really? Oh my! I thought you were twenty years younger!"

"Ha!" barked Lee. She saw Aubrey's stunned look, "Oh! You're serious…" Aubrey nodded. "Well, thank you. Sadly, the pounding has taken its toll. Arthritis in my left hip and both ankles. I've run every day for almost sixty years. There's not a damn thing they can do about it. Now I have to… walk."

"You're in the right place for that," said Aubrey with a smile. But

Aubrey felt the anger still coming from Lee, so she took a breath and eased the conversation away from the harder questions.

AUBREY ENJOYED THE QUIET OF HER ROOM FOR THE REST OF THE afternoon. She wrote a long email to her son Simon about the journey so far, then wrote in her journal. Her pen moved smoothly and quickly across the paper. She described the varying landscapes and the troubles with the rain. She wrote about how deeply she cared for these two amazing women she had been walking with since the beginning of the walk. Then, she described the flirtations between Marinka and Paolo. As the pen flowed, her mind kept going back to what Pam had shared about her marriage. Aubrey considered what her own marriage was like.

Every marriage had its challenges. Like Pam, she'd experienced the anguish of infidelity. Pam's resilience to survive such a horrible situation amazed her. She now understood Pam's hurt, her anger, but she also got a strong sense of Pam's damaged self-worth. Aubrey felt it all. It pained her deeply. But Pam was right, young children brought joy with their laughter and she could see how much strength Pam took from that.

Finally, Aubrey put her journal down. She was exhausted thinking of other people's woes. Her eyes were heavy, so she moved her journal and phone to the far side of the bed, pulled the blanket around her, and snuggled down as the sun set outside her Burgos window.

22

REALITY SEEPS IN

BURGOS

AUBREY DREAMED OF CASS. Her daughter had been lying on a single bed in a long, dark room, sobbing. She had been naked but for a white sheet draped over her. When Aubrey walked into the room, Cass looked directly into Aubrey's eyes and muttered two words that shook Aubrey to her very core: 'I'm sorry.' She repeated the words, over and over. Aubrey stood frozen, but finally she nodded, then turned and walked out of the room. It was only then that the crying ceased behind her.

As the morning light filtered in through the window, she felt like an elephant sat on her chest. It was a familiar sensation. The dream made her angry. She didn't want Cass to be sorry, she wanted to understand why. Tears drifted down her cheeks and she tried to gather herself. Therapy had shown her there was nothing she could have done differently. The doctors, even Cass' therapist, had assured her of that. Aubrey had come a long way to get to this place, a place of peace. She had already been down a very rough road mentally and emotionally. But now, she needed to leave the guilt behind.

Aubrey needed to look forward now. She needed to start her next chapter.

She left the comfortable bed and stood for a long time in the shower, allowing the tears to wash away. When she was dressed, she looked outside the window. A rainstorm had passed overnight. The morning sunshine looked inviting. Time to let the dream go. She had the day to herself, so she decided to spend it exploring.

When she talked about her journey with her son, now an architect, he begged her to visit the Burgos Cathedral, a UNESCO World Heritage Site, so she headed there first. Standing in front of it, she found herself reluctant to go in. She thought of the limitations the Catholic Church had put on Pam's life, and how religion had bound her. Pam's thoughts on churches echoed in her head. All Catholic Cathedrals should be known as 'The Mockery' Pam said one night after a few too many wines.

But that was Pam's story, not hers. Besides, she thought, Pam was a lover of architecture. She'd mentioned that when they'd visited Zabaldika. That alone made Aubrey wonder if Pam would visit the Cathedral. She made a mental note to ask her later.

She paid the pilgrim's entrance fee, which included the audio tour, but popped the audio equipment into the nylon bag she carried. She didn't need a guide to appreciate the beautiful architecture. She missed Simon's presence though. Aubrey wandered the marble floors, knowing Simon would point out intricacies in the naves and chapels, even points the audio guide might miss.

When the clock struck eleven, she noticed a gathering at the far end of the Cathedral, close to where she was standing. There, in the upper corner of the Cathedral, was the Papamoscas Clock Simon had told her about. Aubrey remembered the story vividly.

Made for the King in the 14th Century, the clock was considered a masterpiece. The King had it custom-built to honour his love for a woman he'd seen but had never spoken to. They made eye contact every day inside the church, but she always ran away, knowing he was the King. One day, as the woman was walking home, she dropped her hand-kerchief. The King picked it up and handed it to her, but she turned and quickly returned to her house. As she entered the abode, the King heard a loud and painful scream, a unique sound that stayed with him for years to come. He never saw her again. He tried to find out what happened to the woman he'd fallen for but was told only that she had died. Years later, he saw her image in a forest as wolves threatened him. She saved his life when she let out her unique scream once more, scaring the wolves away.

The clock was the representation of her beauty. But it also represented her screams. Sadly, because the King could never quite describe the woman or her scream precisely, the clockmaker created an odd-looking robot-like figure that moved strangely and emitted a hideous sound. The clock was eventually silenced out of respect for this sacred place.

Now, with the mouth ending its silent screams, the crowd moved on.

Aubrey wandered further around the Cathedral. She came to the 16th Century Golden Staircase, made of marble with black and gold fixtures. Standing in front of it, she felt ill because of the opulent use of gold. How could they justify this, she thought, when the villages they'd walked through struggled every day to make a living? Especially when hamlets relied solely on pilgrims to make ends meet. How was the church helping to support those people, especially those on the brink of destitution? Many pilgrims walked the Camino because of their religion, and she wondered if the church was helping those Camino businesses at all? She sincerely doubted it. She knew she should not judge but seeing this, it was hard not to.

The church's dictation of how to live a life, especially when she thought of Pam, seemed antiquated. Aubrey walked the marble floors with increasing distress as she passed relic after priceless relic. Soon, it became too much for her and she looked around for a place to sit and clear her mind. The Cathedral was busy. Tourists clicked and talked around her, their audio guides on the highest level. Thankfully, she found respite in the chapel and closed her eyes to the surrounding noise.

She guided her thoughts to her children. Simon brought a smile to her lips. They had studied this Cathedral in great detail. She imagined him here now, describing the intricacies of the Sacramental Door. Her mind went to Cass and a pain stabbed her heart. She missed Cass the most. She brought her hands together on her lap and squeezed. It was a technique her therapist had taught her when her emotions took over. She breathed in and then out, focusing her mind on the present. Soon, she could hear the noises invade her space again and decided the Cathedral was best left explored by others.

Aubrey walked back into the bright sunshine, cupping her eyes from the harsh rays. She needed to settle her thoughts and searched for an outdoor café.

She strolled a short distance across the piazza to the first café she came to. A waiter showed her to a table facing the Cathedral. She ordered a beer and when the waiter brought it to her, it was served with a dish of fresh green olives. As she looked to the Cathedral, she ran her fingers down the glass, feeling the coolness from the condensation. She felt compelled to write about her Cathedral experience and bent to retrieve her journal from her bag. That's when she noticed a young woman sitting nearby. The woman held her hands in her lap, her head slumped, her shoulders shaking, as if she were sobbing.

The woman looked up. Aubrey gasped. Hannah. Their Hannah, with tears streaming down her face. Aubrey waved her over at once. Hannah hesitated, her eyes darting around for an escape.

"Hannah. Sweetness…," Aubrey called. Hannah stood and walked toward her reluctantly. Aubrey stood and took Hannah into her arms.

"Come. Sit. What's going on? Are you okay?" she asked. Hannah finally sat heavily into the nearby empty chair. The waiter reappeared, and Aubrey ordered Hannah a cool drink.

"I'm sorry. I didn't mean to disturb you," Hannah said, looking down and seeing Aubrey's journal now sitting on the table. She made a move to stand.

"Stay. You aren't disturbing me. How may I help?" asked Aubrey. Hannah picked up her drink, took a small sip and then looked up at Aubrey, tears brimming her lashes again. Hannah took a deep breath.

"I just talked to my parents." Ah, thought Aubrey. "I haven't talked to them in, I don't know, maybe a month? I've sent texts. I mean, I have let them know I'm okay. But I just couldn't talk to them before now. I guess it was time. I told them that I'd ditched my friends in France and that I was walking the Camino. Then I told them I was pregnant."

"How did they take the news?" asked Aubrey.

"Not happy about it." A tear broke free from her lashes, and she hastily brushed it aside. "I told them that Brett, that's my boyfriend, the father, was no longer talking to me. They were mad about that. He's a football god in our town, so my dad said he was going to hunt him down." She started crying more with that news. Aubrey leaned back in her chair, not knowing how to help her. Ask questions, she remembered from therapy. Ask straightforward questions.

"How do you feel about that?" Aubrey prodded.

"I don't know. Angry, sad. But, good, in a way. Glad my dad's going to talk to him face to face. He's responsible too, right?" Hannah asked, although Aubrey understood the question was more rhetorical than anything.

"And what are you thinking, now your parents know?" Aubrey continued.

"Confused. I am still trying to work out what to do. I know they are worried, but I've told them all about our Camino group here. That I'm okay. That people are watching out for me." Aubrey glanced at the Cathedral, considering what to say next.

"Would it help if I talked to them? Reassure them? I'm happy to do that." Hannah hesitated. "We have your back Hannah."

"I don't know if that would help really, but I guess it wouldn't hurt. Would you mind?" She seemed to contemplate the idea as she took another sip of her drink. "Maybe tonight when we are all together, we can do a video conference with them? It might help for them to meet y'all. You have all been amazing friends to me here, more than my school friends. I guess that way, they'll know I'm not alone." Aubrey recognised the pleading of hope in Hannah's eyes.

"We're with you all the way, whatever you decide," said Aubrey.

"Thank you," Hannah said. "That's nice to know, especially now Marinka is going home."

"Hello girls!" Pam approached their table with a broad smile on her face as if relieved to see familiar faces. "Mind if I join you?"

Aubrey looked at Hannah, who nodded, showing she didn't mind and pulled out the chair next to her. Aubrey smiled and said, "Have a seat."

"Hannah? Are you okay?" Pam asked, as a waiter approached their table once more. Pam and Aubrey looked up at him, as Pam ordered, "Una cervesa, por favor." Pam looked back at Hannah for her answer.

"I'm okay. I just called my parents. Told them I was pregnant." It looked like reality was sinking in for her, Aubrey thought.

"Were your parents angry with your news?" Hannah shook her head.

"Not angry. Upset. Disappointed probably is more like it." Hannah hadn't looked up since Pam sat down.

"They'll get over that. It's good they weren't angry," Pam said.

"Are they at least supportive of you?" asked Aubrey when Hannah finally looked up. She smiled at Hannah. "You know, apart from your dad's hunting expedition."

Hannah smiled, then nodded again. "Yeah, they were. They told me to come home. I told them I wanted to finish the Camino first."

"That's got to be scary for them," said Pam. "As parents I mean. We know you're okay. But they don't know that."

"I offered to call them. Reassure them," said Aubrey, recognising Pam's concern. "We were just talking about doing a FaceTime with them tonight when we are all together. Let her parents know she has a group of us walking with her."

"That's an excellent idea," said Pam. "You know, I was about your age when I got pregnant too." Aubrey caught Hannah's eyes go wide. "My parents weren't as supportive as yours."

"They weren't? What happened?" Hannah reached for a tissue from her pocket.

"They made me marry the father. The problem was that I didn't love him, and turned out, he didn't love me either." Pam looked to the Cathedral. "But we were Catholic, and back in those days, that was what you had to do. Oh, I'm sure it happens now, in deeply religious families, like mine. And because I was under the age of twenty-one, I had to legally comply with my parent's wishes."

"Well, I thought I loved Brett," Hannah said. Pam nodded. "But, given his reaction to this, I don't know if he's the guy I thought he was."

"Maybe it's good that you're figuring that out now? With some distance?" suggested Pam. Aubrey had to agree.

"What did you have? A boy or a girl?" said Hannah. Aubrey heard Pam catch her breath. Hannah's question was innocent enough.

"I don't know. I lost the baby not long after I got married." Hannah gasped.

"Did you have any more children?" Pam shook her head no.

"I'm sorry," Hannah said. "You would have made a great mom."

"Thank you. But I managed a classroom full of happy, beautiful six-year-olds for thirty years. That was enough love to last anyone a lifetime." Pam smiled at Hannah. "And to be honest, I'm happy I didn't have any children with my husband." Hannah looked at her with uncertainty.

Pam elaborated, "He wasn't the kindest person."

"Oh," said Hannah, self-consciously.

"What is your intuition saying about your pregnancy?" Aubrey asked as she saw Pam look over at the imposing Cathedral. She scrunched her nose, as if smelling something putrid, before turning her attention back to Hannah.

"You have choices. You understand that, right?" said Pam. "No matter what your upbringing, you have choices." Aubrey looked to Pam with respect, knowing her history.

"I know. I think I'm too young to be a mother but, god, I just don't know what I want to do," Hannah said, picking up her glass and taking a long sip.

AFTER SOME TIME, THEY WENT THEIR SEPARATE WAYS FOR THE AFTERNOON. They'd already agreed to meet up for dinner. Aubrey took in the Museum of Human Evolution where she found Marinka walking the halls. Marinka was giddy, taking copious amounts of photos. She explained to Aubrey that she was excited to take the experience back to her classroom.

At six, Aubrey got a text from Ben.

Casa Pancho, tapas bar, reservation at 7.

The staff welcomed her into the bar like a long-lost friend. A plaque on the wall stated that the bar had been around since 1958. It was clear to Aubrey why it had enjoyed such longevity. The place was packed with people. Paraphernalia and photos lined the walls of the narrow room. The vibe was intoxicating.

Ben waved from the table where he, Paolo, Marinka and Hannah were sitting in the side restaurant. She returned the wave, ordered a glass of wine and walked toward the saloon door, just as Georgina and Pam walked in.

"It looks like everyone is inside here. Grab a drink from the bar," Aubrey said as she continued through the doors. She took a seat next to Hannah. Ben rose when Georgina and Pam came in, then took the seat next to Aubrey. He nudged her and discretely pointed a finger toward Marinka and Paolo sitting together, holding hands. Aubrey nudged him back, eyes wide in wonder that Marinka had succumbed to Paolo's courting ways.

"She's leaving in the morning. Why bother?" she whispered to Ben.

"Who can explain it?" said Ben, raising his glass as a bon voyage for Marinka's journey home. The group offered her many cheers.

"We will miss you Marinka. No one more than Paolo, I am sure," said Ben, a cheeky grin on his face. Paolo blushed. "Hannah too, of course. We will all miss your smiling face."

Marinka's eyes zeroed into Hannah with concern blazing through them before she met Ben's eyes.

"We'll take care of her, I promise," Ben said. "She'll be okay. Besides, she has the mother hens here. The cluck fest will be a riot." Aubrey slapped him playfully.

Marinka nodded and responded with a soundless 'Thank you'.

"We need to do a quick video conference with Hannah's parents. Did she tell you?" Aubrey asked. There was a collective nod from the group.

"Paolo. You need to behave," said Pam. "We need to assure her parents she's in safe hands."

"Why are you all picking on me?" he said, before leaning over to kiss Marinka on the cheek. She blushed.

"Shhh. Go time!" said Aubrey as Hannah connected.

"Hi Mom. Hi Dad," said Hannah. A round of hellos and introductions ensued. After spending fifteen minutes getting to know Hannah's parents, Aubrey and the hens managed to put their minds at ease. Hannah, too, appeared relieved and relaxed. Her parents were delighted to learn that three of them had extensive first aid experience. Paolo took it a step further when he disclosed that he had just finished medical school. Everyone sat stupefied for a moment with that piece of news.

"Why didn't you say anything?" said Georgina, patting his cheek like his Italian Mamma when the call was over.

"Why murder the fun? It is better to be carefree and enjoy life! No?" He looked at Marinka. Aubrey realised that he must have shared that nugget with her already, which probably resulted in her finally trusting him.

By ten o'clock, they reluctantly called it a night. Marinka was flying home the next day and they were all continuing on. With hugs and reassurances, they said goodbye to their shy German friend, with promises to keep in touch. Aubrey watched as Paolo and Marinka walked slowly away, hand in hand. Ben and Hannah trailed behind at some distance.

Walking back to their own hotel, Aubrey shared her news of Lee with Pam and Georgina.

"Oh? And how was that?" asked Pam, as they left the laneway and walked into the piazza.

"Enlightening," Aubrey said. "You two need to chat."

23

LAUGHTER CAN MAKE YOUR CHEEKS HURT

BURGOS TO HONTANAS

THE FOLLOWING morning was cold and drizzly when the remaining six met at the Cathedral at seven. Pam declared she wasn't keen to walk on hard pavement for an entire day. Hannah continued to battle her morning sickness and wasn't too keen on the pavement idea either. Ben expressed concern about making his flight home given their slower pace.

"Seems like we need to consider fast forwarding," Aubrey offered. So, after huddling in a café over breakfast, they decided as a collective to taxi to the next town.

By the time they reached their destination of Tardajos, the first town outside of Burgos, the rain had stopped, and the sun was shining. They were sad to leave Burgos, but they were happy to be back on the Camino and heading west. They were about to begin their second stage, known as the Meseta. This was the section renowned for endless plains, few trees, and a lot of time to think. The first stage, the first two hundred and seventy-odd kilometres, since St Jean Pied de Port, was the physical stage, a stage they had all felt in some way. Aubrey wasn't eager to walk the Meseta. She had originally planned to skip it. She didn't need the thinking time. That was the last thing she needed, but she was happy to be walking again, and happy to be with the Lovelies. She didn't have much time to spin into the abyss while walking with this beautiful group.

Their happiness was short lived. The wind was brutal, biting cold and unrelenting. Hannah was already dragging, so Pam stuck with her. They were two turtles together, Pam joked. Ben and Paolo pushed forward at their faster pace.

Conversation was difficult with the wind, but as they'd found over the last few weeks, conversation helped ease the kilometres. Aubrey and Georgina talked about where they first heard about the Camino. Georgina shared she'd first read about the Camino on a woman's blog and something in it had caught her attention.

"Maybe just the fact that the Camino was a long way from Tasmania," she admitted. Aubrey knew that feeling of wanting to flee her life. She told Georgina that it was Simon who'd told her about the Camino. He had a couple of friends in Melbourne do it the prior year. Said it was the best experience of their lives and they had recommended the movie, *The Way*. It was a good introduction. It had helped her find a focus again, especially after the last few years. Simon kept nudging her until he finally gave her a book about the pilgrimage at Christmas. She said she'd booked her flights before she even got to the end of the book.

They walked on for another few kilometres in silence. The wind was really howling and talking was difficult. But not talking seemed worse over the long stretches of wild grass and little else.

"Tell me about when your parents died. You said before that you returned to Tasmania after University? That had to have been hard for you without your parents there?" asked Aubrey.

"Yeah, it was. My parents left everything to my brother and me, so I at least had somewhere to live. I travelled a bit first, but then I went home. It was harder when my brother died, about ten years later, in a mining accident. I really felt alone in the world then."

"I'm so sorry. I didn't know your brother died as well. That must have been painful."

"It was twenty years ago. Patrick and I were married by then, but he was out of state. It was a hard time, yes, but I try not to dwell on it. It was harder when Patrick decided to stay on the mainland and not come home for the funeral." Aubrey thought to say something, but Georgina's look of concentration stopped her. "Patrick worked for the mines then and was locked into a contract. So, that excused him from dealing with the funeral," This surprised Aubrey. Why couldn't he have flown home to support her? It was obvious to Aubrey that Georgina would have needed the support. Before she could ask, Georgina continued.

"Patrick's mother was still around then. He offered her help in his absence. But my mother-in-law was not the maternal type. She was so different from my own mother. My mum was that woman who would hand out hugs to anyone. She'd take on our friends like they were part of the family, rescue an animal if it wasn't in the right environment. She was a thoughtful person, generous with both her time and her love. We had no doubt that she loved us deeply. But my mother-in-law was, well, different. She was cold and suspected everyone," Georgina said. "She didn't like my friends. Didn't think I did the funeral arrangements correctly. I ordered the wrong flowers. I didn't provide enough food. She was the least supportive person I could have, but Patrick offered her as his stand in."

"Our mother-in-laws sound a lot alike," said Aubrey. Georgina stopped and took some water and tucked a loose strand of hair under her beanie. Aubrey turned and looked for Pam and Hannah, now far behind them. Aubrey waved. Pam waved back. Satisfied that they were okay, she turned and started walking again at Georgina's determined pace.

"I could tell you some glorious stories about my mother-in-law," Georgina said, with a quick chuckle. "I suspected she was a lesbian at one point. I mentioned it to Patrick, and I was surprised he agreed. She was soft around her best friend, but hard with every other person, including him."

"Did she ever come out?" asked Aubrey.

"God no. That would admit she had a personality. She was terrified to reveal who she really was," said Georgina. "No, she cared about appearances above all things."

"Hmm. Did you ever tell Patrick how hard it was, or lean on him for support, even remotely?" Aubrey asked. "How soon did he come home after the funeral?"

"He stayed on the mainland for two months, buried in work. By the time he came home, I had adjusted to the new normal. Patrick just slid himself right back into it, as if nothing had happened." Aubrey could understand this. Brendon had been the same when times were tough. She knew how hard it was to feel unsupported by the one person who was supposed to be there for you.

"And now? Have you told him how you've felt?" asked Aubrey.

"No, but I'm thinking it may be time I tell him what I need from our marriage. I don't want to be in this marriage alone anymore," Georgina said. "I want to decide what I want, rather than letting things happen to me." Aubrey nodded but before she could say anything more, the winds picked up and changed into a merciless headwind. It felt like they were walking in slow motion as they struggled to move forward. Aubrey had to wonder if they'd ever make it to Hontanas when the trail dipped, and a village seemed to appear out of nowhere.

"Let's get the hell out of this cold. Time for a coffee," shouted Aubrey.

"Always," said Georgina with a smile.

AFTER THEIR SECOND BREAKFAST OF COFFEE AND A CHOCOLATE CROISSANT, Aubrey walked ahead with Hannah. Hannah wasn't very talkative, but Aubrey nudged her, asking about what high school had been like, and what she envisioned for her future.

"It's hard to think about that. I have this huge decision that will affect the rest of my life."

"I have been in your shoes before," Aubrey confided, her voice just loud enough for Hannah to hear against the wind. "I know it's difficult."

"You have?" Hannah asked. Aubrey nodded, slowing down her pace. Trying to talk and battle the wind was a grind, but she really wanted to share this with Hannah.

"I was seventeen. I fell pregnant to a boy I met at boarding school.

Oh, we'd been careful. We'd used protection but, well, things happen. I was about three months along before I realised. I had to decide what to do," she said. Hannah looked at her with wide eyes.

"So, when I say I know that this decision isn't easy for you, I mean that. We're here for you," Aubrey said.

"That video conference with my mom and dad? It made me realise that. I think it shocked them I was walking with older women, but I know they were relieved too. It helped a lot," Hannah said. "And it helps me too, knowing you are all here."

Aubrey moved the pole from her right hand over to her left, then reached out for Hannah's hand. They walked hand in hand for a little while.

"So, what are you thinking? If you take the father and your parents out of the equation, what do you want to do?" asked Aubrey. Hannah hesitated.

"Honestly?" Aubrey nodded. "I am leaning either to abortion or adoption. I know I am not ready to be a mother." Aubrey squeezed her hand reassuringly.

"Those are both tough choices. Pros and cons for each." They continued talking for quite a few kilometres, weighing the options. By the time they reached the bar in Hontanas, Aubrey felt she'd helped, if it was only to talk to someone who had been through the same experience.

The bar was packed with pilgrims escaping the wind. The space was the size of a narrow living room, with the large, enclosed bar taking up much of the space. The bartenders were continuously moving, pouring beers, passing food, and taking names for reservations for the albergue upstairs. It took Aubrey and Hannah a minute to take it all in. Miraculously, they found an open table off to the side to wait for Pam and Georgina. After dropping their packs, Hannah turned and hugged Aubrey, whispering 'thank you' in her ear.

They agreed a hot drink sounded good, so Aubrey went up to the bar to order two hot chocolates. While she waited for their order, her mind wandered into a place she was hesitant to go. Maybe she was ready to go there, she thought. Being with Hannah was therapeutic. Aubrey only wished she could have this kind of conversation with her own daughter. But, before going deep down that spiral, she considered her purpose on this Camino. Maybe it was to help Pam move past the grief she denied she was carrying? Not the grief about losing her husband, but of the years she lost being married to him. Or was it to help Hannah find the right choice for her? Or, to help Georgina work out her future? Maybe all of these reasons? Maybe none? She had her own stuff to work through, she knew, but it seemed like everyone had something and talking through it was cathartic. Thinking that, it made her wonder what was holding her back from sharing her story? Was it shame? Embarrassment? Fear of judgement? That last idea stung.

Before she returned to Hannah, Aubrey inquired about private rooms. After the wind today, she needed rest. And Hannah, she looked beyond exhausted. Aubrey reserved two rooms, both with two single beds. She returned to the table, drinks in hand and asked Hannah if she was interested sharing a private room with her. Hannah's relief was palpable. Aubrey smiled, just as Pam and Georgina barrelled into the bar, windswept and out of sorts.

After they were shown their rooms and Aubrey had showered, she went in search of Ben and Paolo, since they'd walked ahead. She found them stretched out in the dorms. She was happy to know they'd all arrived.

"Let's go get a drink you two," she said, not waiting for a reply before she turned to round up the others.

Thankfully the wind had died down. They could finally converse without shouting at one another. They found a table out in the sunshine. After a round of drinks were ordered, Pam announced she was about to lose a toenail.

"But you're the one telling us what to do! How is it you have issues with your feet?" asked Ben, teasing her. Pam just shrugged, her cheeks turning pink, which made them all laugh.

Music was playing from somewhere, maybe the bar, Aubrey couldn't tell. She closed her eyes, feeling the warmth of the sun thaw the chill that had stayed with her all day. She swayed to the simple beat. She couldn't remember being so relaxed with herself in a long time. Oh, she knew she looked a mess. Hell, she hadn't shaved her legs since she left Australia. Her hair, a tangled mess of curls, was bundled on her head. She could feel it moving as she moved to the beat of the music. The song changed to something more upbeat. She opened her eyes to reposition herself in her chair, static making her skirt stick to her leggings beneath. Yes, a mess was a good description. But she didn't care. She was comfortable and happy.

She gazed around the table, stopping at Georgina. She admired how chic Georgina looked, leaning back in her chair, laughing at something Ben said to her. Georgina was so oblivious of her beauty. She had gorgeous green eyes, the colour changing with her moods. Aubrey had noticed they changed to a smoky-grey when she was angry or upset. And her hair shone a million shades of silver in the sunshine. Aubrey made a mental note to tell her again, just how beautiful she was.

She looked to Pam. Their own pet turtle, Pam had joked. The woman was tiny, yet fierce and determined. But Aubrey would also describe her as soft and generous, amazing considering her horrible history. Most would think that would make her hard and bitter, but she was neither of those things. When Pam laughed, the world lit up inside her. Aubrey made another mental note to get Pam laughing more.

She put her head back against the chair, angling her face toward the sun and closed her eyes once more. It felt so good and, this time, when she opened her eyes, Paolo was in front of her, arm outstretched, asking her to dance. She didn't hesitate.

"Oh! I haven't danced in years," she said, jumping up to take his hand. "I am not sure I'm good anymore."

"It does not matter, belladonna," he said, taking her into his arms and whipping her around the stone path. He was truly a master at his game. Paolo was fast and light on his feet, and it surprised her she could keep up with him. She threw her head back, laughing loudly as he whirled her around. She didn't recognise the sound she made; it was as if it was coming from someone else. She felt alive, happy, free, as she kept up with the dance steps, realising she hadn't felt this good in years. The group clapped in time with the music and soon Ben took Pam's hand and danced with her. Georgina looked like she could not sit still either. After Hannah declined, Georgina roped in an older man sitting alone, who had been tapping his foot to the music and clapping at the frivolity. Too soon, the song was over and a slower one took its place.

"Oh wow, that was great. Thanks Paolo," Aubrey said, reaching for her beer to quench her thirst. She fixed a piece of her messy bun that had broken free. "I had forgotten how much I love to dance. It's been so long."

"Then we shall dance all the way to Santiago," he exclaimed.

"Now that Marinka has gone, the flirt returns," teased Pam.

"Ah no. My heart, it belongs to Marinka," Paolo admitted, hand over his heart, "but I still promise to bring joy to those who have brought joy for me on my pilgrimage." He flashed a dazzling smile at Aubrey.

"Speaking of pilgrimages," said Ben. "There's a Pilgrim Mass at six-fifteen before dinner at seven. Who's in?" Georgina looked down at her watch, announcing it was almost six already.

Georgina looked over at Aubrey. She shrugged.

"There will be flames if I go," Ben exclaimed, "I will need help to douse them." Aubrey laughed, agreeing this would be the case for her too. Pam remained silent and sombre. Aubrey looked at her with concern. Her jaw dropped open when Pam announced that if she was going, they were all going. She let Hannah off the hook since she needed a nap, but the rest, she said, they were all fair game.

They walked down the hill to the church together. At the left turn toward the entrance, they found two heavy wooden doors hinged together by equally heavy wrought iron work, tucked into the weathered stone building. The church was unadorned. When they stepped inside, it felt welcoming. Rows of solid wooden pews, worn from centuries of use, lined the centre of the open space. A table to the right was covered with mass pamphlets in many languages. Off to the side, hung on the stone wall, was a shrine with images of saintly people, their frames backlit. Sitting on the floor beneath was a low, circular pot filled with sand, supporting candles of people's prayers. Nearby, bibles rested in various languages, available for the pilgrim's contemplation.

Pam walked down the centre aisle, directly to the front pew as the rest of them took in the surroundings. Surprised, Aubrey hesitated, not sure if she should join her. But, before she could make a definitive decision, Georgina grabbed her hand and pulled her to the back row where Ben waited. Paolo joined Pam in the front, winking at them as he passed by.

"He was a choirboy in his youth," said Ben. Aubrey and Georgina laughed out loud. Heads turned back at them with deep frowns at the disruption.

While there were candles and lighting, creating a warm ambiance, the place still felt like an icebox. Aubrey felt Georgina shivering beside her, having forgotten her jacket. When she noticed a stack of blankets nearby, she nudged Ben to grab a few.

When the service began, they found themselves respectfully quiet. But with all the kneeling and standing, Aubrey jokingly whispered that she was 'getting her squatting exercises taken care of with this service'. They couldn't stifle the giggles on that one.

After that, it became a whispering free-for-all among the three of them. Georgina predicted the priest was wearing jeans, hoodie and tennis shoes underneath his robe. Ben wondered if the priest had scheduled the service earlier than posted because he had a poker game lined up afterwards. Later, when communion started, Ben whispered, 'Now, if they gave us a glass of wine to wash down that wafer, I may consider converting!' Georgina hooted. More heads turned. Their antics were all very innocent and not meant to offend, and it helped lighten the ominous tone of the Spanish Catholic service. As they waited for the mass to end, Aubrey reached up and felt her cheeks. They were hurting from laughing so much. She'd missed that kind of joy. It was time for more of that in her life.

2 4

WHAT ARE YOU?

HONTANAS TO CASTROJERIZ

AUBREY SNUGGLED UNDER HER BLANKETS, cocooned in an upstairs room she'd shared with Hannah. She heard voices, mixed with a howling wind outside. It would be another interesting day of walking. She looked over at Hannah's empty bed, but her backpack still sat in the corner.

Aubrey reached for phone, quarter to eight. Fuckity, fuck, fuck. Eviction time was eight. She tossed the covers back, grabbed her toiletry kit and raced down the hallway to the communal bathroom. Hannah turned at her approach.

"Good morning sunshine," she said to Hannah as she pulled her unruly hair into a messy bun. Hannah smiled as she finished tying off the second of her two neat, blonde braids, a style that made her appear much younger than she was. "How are you feeling?"

"Hi. Doing okay. Better than yesterday." Hannah took her toothbrush out, loaded it with paste and began brushing.

"That's good to hear. That weather... ugh. It'll make for a rough day today," Aubrey said, as she grabbed the travel size face soap from her bag. Hannah nodded and finished brushing her teeth while Aubrey washed her face.

"How far are we walking today, do you know?" asked Hannah.

"Not far. Ten kilometres or thereabouts. Destination is Castrojeriz, I think? Something like that."

"Yeah, okay. That name sounds right. I just couldn't remember how far. Some days it feels like we've been walking forever," said Hannah.

"And only about five hundred kilometres to go," teased Aubrey. Hannah groaned and started packing up her belongings into her small toiletry pouch.

"I'll see you down in the bar. Pam and Georgina are there already, getting some breakfast," she said.

"Sounds good," Aubrey said, her toothbrush loaded and ready to go. "I looked in their room when I walked past. I'm surprised I didn't hear Pam faffing around like she usually does."

"She was when I went past. Georgina looked impatient," said Hannah, with a slight smile.

"Yes, she drives Georgina nuts, but George deals with it like a champion," then seeing Hannah move toward the door, she added "I won't be long. Five minutes. Max." Hannah nodded and headed back to the room.

THE TEMPERATURE WAS SHOWING THREE DEGREES CELSIUS, BUT THE WIND chill pushed it much lower. Aubrey was glad the walk was short today. Ben suggested they stop for lunch in Castrojeriz, then stay in Itero del Castillo, which was another nine kilometres further. But, when Pam looked at it, she reported the albergue Ben had mentioned received awful reviews of late. They had reported bedbugs for the last two nights in a row. Aubrey was grateful once again that Pam kept up with the happenings on the trail, keeping them safe. Pam's paranoia about bed bugs had definitely been to their advantage. None of them had come across any yet, and she would be just as happy not to.

As they walked out of Hontanas, Aubrey realized she forgot to swap out the inserts she bought for her shoes. Even with two days of rest in Burgos, her feet ached badly.

Within an hour, the wind had died down, but the temperature stayed cold. The sun was rising, taking the temperature with it. Still, it seemed to be a very slow process. Ben texted earlier that their dorm room woke at five, so he and Paolo planned to meet them at the albergue Pam had reserved for them.

They got into a peaceful rhythm, Pam and Hannah walked together behind her. Georgina walked just ahead. After a while, Georgina stopped to wait for Aubrey, who was trailing about thirty metres behind.

"Doing okay?" Georgina asked her. She knew Aubrey's feet were bothering her. Aubrey nodded. "How about some conversation to keep the mind off the pain?"

"Conversation would be good," she admitted. It always helped.

"Tell me about leaving Melbourne. Have you decided on where you want to be?" asked Georgina.

"I think so. It's been a slow transition finding a place, but I'm thinking the Victorian Highlands. I like it there. Once I arrived in Bright, it felt right. I don't expect the physical move will take long. I have very little in the way of possessions anymore. After the divorce, I couldn't stay in the house…" she trailed off. She didn't want to flash back to that image today, nor did she want to talk about what had happened in the house.

"So, with the house sold, I donated all the furnishings to bushfire victims. Brendon didn't want any of it. I stayed with Simon for a few months, but that was just hard. As much as I love my son, we're a lot different in how we like to live," Georgina nodded, understanding.

"It's the same with Nicole. I have no influence anymore," said Georgina.

"Exactly," said Aubrey, "So I bought a campervan and started driving around. I wasn't sure what I was looking for exactly, just a place I connected to. Eventually, an old friend recommended I take the Great Alpine Road. I followed his advice and stopped in Myrtleford. I liked it, but I kept going back to Bright. There's something about the place that resonates with me."

"I remember travelling through there when I was at Uni. There's a river that goes through the town, isn't there?"

"Yeah, there is. I was looking online at properties while we were in Burgos. I've found a property I may want to buy. It backs up to that river."

"That's exciting!" Georgina said, with an enormous grin. Aubrey smiled. She was cautiously optimistic about it.

"It's like the Universe was waiting for me to decide. You know? I emailed the real estate agency about it."

"And?" Georgina asked.

"Simon will look at it this weekend for me. The agent is fine with that, knowing I'm here," said Aubrey. "If we can do a FaceTime, great. But if the time difference doesn't work out, I trust Simon knows what I'm looking for."

They walked in silence for a little while, then Georgina stopped, turned and looked at Aubrey.

"Can I ask you a very personal question?" Georgina asked.

"George, you can ask me anything you want," Georgina paused a few beats, taking a breath before plunging in.

"Was there more to the story of why you divorced?" Aubrey's breath hitched, but she was quick to control her reaction. Georgina didn't wait for her reply, she turned and started walking again as Aubrey considered the question.

"Apart from the affair, you mean?" Georgina nodded. "Well, I guess our divorce was inevitable. For twenty-three years, our marriage was a rollercoaster with crazy work schedules and social lives. We never took the time to really get to know each other. But his true nature, the character I had ignored for so many years, surfaced about two years ago."

"Something happened with our daughter back then," she ploughed through, knowing this was the only way through this part of the story. "Brendon brushed it off, like 'that's life.' But then, about a year ago, I was sitting in his mother's living room in Sydney. There was a report on the news about a tragic incident. Brendon and his mother started laughing about it. They found the incident funny somehow. When I questioned his mother about it, she looked at Brendon, who was still laughing along with her, and said that I would never understand because I wasn't really a McLaughlin." Georgina gave her a questioning glance.

"Their family name," Aubrey said. Georgina nodded in understanding. Aubrey continued, "I just found it…"

"Heartless. Cold," said Georgina.

"Yes," Aubrey whispered. She walked on for a little while, thinking back on that day. The day that changed everything.

"Later that night, I told Brendon I was going home to Melbourne. I couldn't stand his mother's insensitivity. Nor his. He told me he was staying in Sydney. For business, he said. But I suspected he was having an affair. He then told me I was too fat. That I had embarrassed his mother with my weight gain. He called me sad and lazy."

"Seriously?" Georgina asked, looking at her in disbelief.

"Yes. It broke the relationship for me. An affair is one thing. In hindsight, this was a pattern for him. When times were tough… he strayed. But to behave as he did. To treat this awful thing as a joke. That was what did it for me. As for the comment about my weight gain, I coped with what happened with our daughter by dropping the abnormal conventions of society. The notion that appearances matter. I stopped worrying about how I was perceived," Aubrey could almost see the steam coming out of Georgina's ears.

"Now we're divorced, Brendon is in Sydney living with his mother. It makes life easier on all of us. Even my son admitted he feels better without his father around. Simon came out when he was fifteen, and when he did, Brendon told him never to tell his grandmother because it would disgust her." She remembered those words, shocked at the brutal way Brendon had said them and the sad reality of the truth behind them. She knew then that Brendon felt the same way as his mother. She should have known then how gutless he was.

"I'm trying to think of what to say to that, but there are no words," said Georgina. Aubrey nodded.

"That's only scratching the surface," Aubrey said. She was ready to change the subject.

"Have you seen Brendon since the divorce?" Georgina asked.

"Once," Aubrey said. "At Simon's graduation last year."

"And?"

"Oh, he had his mother on one arm, and his blonde-haired, size zero, twenty-something girlfriend on the other. When he saw me, dressed so differently from the successful business owner he knew – now with my nose pierced, my hair bunched like I wear it now – he looked at me and said: 'What the fuck? What *are* you?'"

"What did you say?" Georgina asked.

"I wanted to slap him, but by then, I just said: 'Happy'."

Georgina guffawed, "Well done."

"I almost feel like there was this other person inside, waiting to come out. I was such a people-pleaser for a long time. My husband, my mother-in-law, that lifestyle, perception was what they were all about. Keeping up appearances and the wrath of judgement was all they cared about. It wasn't me."

Aubrey was quiet for a bit. "You know what's funny about all of it, and I just realised this myself, on this walk. I was happier in that Campervan just driving around, listening to music, having conversations with other travellers, than I ever was in Melbourne. It was like Superwoman, finally coming out of the business suit. I relaxed. I became me. And now? Now, I am happy."

WHAT ARE YOU AFRAID OF?

CASTROJERIZ TO BOADILLA DEL CAMINO

THE ROOM WAS BUSTLING with people packing up, including Pam and Georgina. Aubrey lay in her bed, cocooned in her down blanket. Ben and Paolo were also deep in their sleeping bags on the other side of the cavernous room. None of them wanted to face the frigid air just yet.

"Where's Hannah?" Aubrey asked Pam. Her bed was made, and she didn't see her backpack.

"She's having breakfast," said Pam. "Come on, lazybones. Time to get moving. It's a shortish day, and it's already after seven. They provide breakfast, thank god, so there's still time to eat before we go."

Man, she was militant, thought Aubrey, especially for a woman that would be faffing around for another twenty minutes at least. Still, she was glad she had time to dawdle.

"I'll join Hannah," Georgina said. She offered a knowing smile to Aubrey. Pam always had the best intentions. She diligently organised herself the night before and then she muddled around like an old lady in the morning. But she could walk the feet off of the rest of them. Aubrey's especially. There had been more asphalt than she'd expected yesterday. Her feet had been sore again last night, even though she finally remembered to change the inserts she'd bought in Burgos. Paolo had graciously rubbed her feet, which had been amazing. Lucky Marinka. The man had magic fingers.

With Pam finally finishing up, Aubrey realised it was time to get going. She tossed back her blanket, put her bare feet on the tiled floor, then yanked them up quickly.

"Holy shit!" she said. Ben poked his head up. "The floor is freezing."

"Doesn't it get cold where you live?" asked Pam, about to head out the door.

"Yes, but I've always had underfloor heating. I'm not an idiot," she said, and slipped her feet into her sandals for some protection against the icy floor. Pam clucked and left the room, leaving Aubrey with the boys.

"Come on you two. Time to go."

"We will catch them," said Paolo, speaking the truth.

"Yes, but they will kick us out soon and I'm sure you'll want food," Aubrey said and smiled at Paolo. The guy could devour copious amounts of food at an alarming rate. Pam had nagged him only yesterday to slow down, like a grandmother would her grandson. Ben had even been on to him, instructing him to savour what he was eating.

Thirty minutes later, Aubrey, Georgina and Hannah walked out of the albergue together. Pam shocked them all by leaving the building first.

"I'm slow on the hills," she said. "No one needs to watch me huff and puff." She was like the little blue engine. She had the 'I think I can' mantra down. And with that mantra she'd most likely be to the top before Aubrey would. She needed to take it slow. She was thankful when both Georgina and Hannah said they'd be happy to walk with her. Hannah was feeling okay, following her usual pattern. She would be fine for a day or two before the nausea returned. Morning sickness, she remembered, could be a vicious cycle.

As they approached the bridge at the base of the Castrojeriz hill, Hannah talked about the last conversation she had with her parents. It had consumed and confused her. Her parents expressed their disappointment, understandably, but also their willingness to support her whatever her decision. But they were pressuring her too, on what to do, and she acknowledged she had to decide soon.

"Before this happened Hannah, what did you see yourself doing? You were taking a gap year, then going to NYU, right? They accepted you?" asked Georgina.

Hannah stood up from adjusting her shoelace. "Yes. That was the plan."

"So, with a baby, how does that change your plan to pursue NYU?" Georgina asked, putting her phone back into her hip pouch. She had taken photos of the long narrow bridge they had just crossed.

"I've decided that keeping the baby is not the right thing for me to do. But I thought adoption might be?" Hannah said and loosened the hip belt on her backpack a little.

"Have you talked to the father again?" asked Georgina, setting the pace again as they made their way up the incline.

Hannah looked over at Aubrey, looking for a save, but Georgina must have recognised the look.

"I'm sorry Hannah, I don't mean to push. I only want to help you find the right path," Georgina said, with a supportive glance toward Hannah.

"I understand that. And yeah, Brett texted me the other day. He said he's willing to marry me. Apparently, my dad and his both flew to L.A. and sat him down together. But I don't want to marry him. I love him, but neither of us is ready for marriage! I'd never even thought of marriage before this," Hannah said as they meandered up the hill. They were all quiet for a while before Georgina spoke up again.

"Never settle," Georgina said. "Life is shorter than you think and if you don't do what you love, be with who you love, life will be miserable. Hell, you may wake up forty years later, wondering what you are doing with your life." Aubrey looked over at Georgina, wondering if she was thinking of what happened with Pam. But Georgina wore a faraway expression on her face.

"Is that what happened to you?" Hannah asked. Georgina looked up quickly. Hannah hesitated, then spoke again, "Sorry. But you seem serious a lot. You always have this intense look on your face."

Georgina was quiet for a little while. "I didn't realise that. But no, I'm happy enough, but I do have regrets. I don't want you to be saying that same thing when you are my age." Aubrey had to wonder what those regrets may be. Was it that she regretted marrying Patrick? Or maybe staying with him? But Hannah was right. Georgina did look intense much of the time and she didn't seem happy, no matter what she said otherwise.

"Okay, so here's a question my therapist asked me," said Aubrey. "If you were told you would die in a year, or let's say two, would you change anything in your life? And if so, what would that be?"

"That's a question full of punch, isn't it?" asked Georgina.

"It's a good question," said Aubrey, "Made me sit up and take stock of where I was in my life."

"I can answer that if I knew for sure I would die," said Hannah. "I wouldn't want to be looking after a baby. I would want to be doing things I loved, around people I loved." She smiled the innocent smile of one so young. Aubrey remembered when life seemed to be so straightforward.

"Sounds like you've decided at least one thing then," Aubrey said to Hannah. Georgina was quiet, pondering Aubrey's question.

"I guess the follow up question is: What are you afraid of?" Aubrey asked, looking over at Georgina. Still quiet, Georgina nodded.

Ben and Paolo bounded up behind them. Ben put his arm around Hannah.

"Hello girls. How's the walk so far?"

"Slow! But we're getting there," said Aubrey.

Georgina looked back at the boys and stopped.

"Look at those views!" she said. Ben and Paolo's presence had snapped her out of her head. The early morning sunshine beamed down on the hills behind them, its rays splaying out in all directions. With an outstretched hand, Georgina gestured out to the countryside like she was a model on a game show. "Beautiful!"

"Bellissimo! Like your eyes Georgina," Paolo said. Georgina blushed. She swatted him with her trekking pole.

"Paolo, you are such a flirt. You need to stop that if you're serious about Marinka," said Georgina. "I have meant to ask you what you are going to do about that?"

"I have not decided. She has returned to Germany and I am here," he said in his stilted English. He looked down and mumbled, "I miss her." Aubrey's heart went out to him. He was definitely love-struck with the shy German.

"So do I," said Hannah softly. "But it's still good to walk with y'all," she quickly added. Aubrey and Georgina smiled.

"I was thinking Hannah," said Ben, his arm around her as they trudged up the last of the hill. "It looks like I'll be heading to Texas every few months over the next year, so I can visit you."

"Are you wanting to check up on me?" Hannah asked. "Seriously, you are the big brother I've never had. But I'm not sure I'll be staying in Texas." Ben looked at her anxiously, but Hannah caught his concern. "I just don't know what's next is all."

As they reached the top, Pam was waiting for them.

"Took you guys forever," she said, sitting on the low stone wall, eating a banana.

"Did you run up the hill?" Ben asked her, "Because you didn't leave that much earlier than we did."

"Must have found my mojo," she said, popping the banana peel into a side pocket of her pack. "I waited so we could take a group picture. I mean, look at those views. What a great background. Hell, I must have learned something from Georgina too!"

Georgina positioned them for a group selfie, getting the vast Meseta background behind them, just as the sunlight shined down onto Castrojeriz. Georgina showed the photo around. They all agreed it was a keeper and asked for her to share it.

"We need to send it to Marinka too," Hannah said. Georgina nodded. "I'll send it on to her. I have her info," she said and looked over at Paolo, who also nodded, his face reflecting his loss.

"Did I hear the host wish you a happy birthday this morning Ben?" asked Pam, while they all took a water break.

"Ben!" exclaimed Aubrey, looking over at him as she worked to get her water bladder positioned correctly in her pack. "It's your birthday?"

"Yeah, well, it's no big deal," he said, looking down at his water bottle, suddenly shy. Paolo laughed then tackled him with a colossal hug.

"It's your birthday. It's an enormous deal!" said Pam, walking over to hug him.

"We will celebrate tonight in Boadilla," declared Aubrey, giving him a hug too.

"Time to go. We will not have time to party if we're lolly-gagging around here," said Pam as she led their descent as a group. "Despite my momentum up that hill, going down is worse on the knees, so I'm going slow." Pam used her trekking poles to lessen the burden on her knees.

"Watch the bikes!" called Pam a few minutes later. "They are flying down!"

They all stepped to the side as the cyclists zoomed past on the steep descent. They all yelled 'DING-DING' to remind the cyclists to use a bell. It was one thing they had discussed often over the last three hundred-odd kilometres since they'd started. Too many times, they had to jump off the path right before a cyclist came through with no warning. After swearing and yelling with little reaction, they agreed that DING-DING was universally understood with the cyclists. Sometimes they got a wave in return. Most times they were ignored, but they hoped their efforts made an impact for other pilgrims in harm's way.

Pam chose to walk alone much of the day, content with her own thoughts. Aubrey felt the same way. She reflected on her conversation with Georgina the day before. She wondered if it was time to tell the group what happened two years ago. But it was all still very raw and some days it felt like it had happened yesterday.

She was deep in her thoughts when she heard parts of the conversation behind her between Paolo and Hannah. They were talking about love. Hannah shared Brett's proposal with him. She wasn't surprised when Paolo dissuaded her from marrying him, even with her pregnancy to consider. What did shock her was when she heard him say that he was experiencing a deep pull towards Marinka, and how in love he was with her. Was he thinking of marriage? Now that was an idea that surprised her.

She wondered if she'd missed her chance for true love in her life. Aubrey remembered how love could be so carefree. She missed that sensation. She missed being in love. If she was honest with herself, she was jaded enough not to believe in fairy tales. Ben glowed when he spoke of his husband. That's how it's supposed to be, she thought. She shook her head. It was no good thinking about what others had. Sure, she would love to have a partner to share her life. Someone to experience the good and the bad. Someone who had her back when things were rough. She knew there would be more rough days ahead. But she wasn't interested in romance anymore. Brendon had cured her of that notion, with his ridiculous grand gestures. Now, she wanted, needed, depth in her relationships. But she was fifty now. Was it too late for that one love?

She stopped for a drink and saw Ben and Georgina a fair distance behind her. They were deep in conversation. She didn't stop for long and continued walking alone. She didn't mind. The haunting memories stayed away when she had other people around. She had more positive things to think about. She thought of destiny. Of people coming into her life for a reason. She reflected on each story of her Camino Family for a long time. With these people around her, she believed she had found her place again in the world. She felt content.

Paolo stopped ahead abruptly. When Aubrey caught up to him, he took her poles and handed them to Hannah. Aubrey looked at him quizzically. He took her hand, placing it on his shoulder, and led her in a waltz down the trail. They both laughed as they spun awkwardly, their backpacks bouncing, barely able to keep their feet. Her friends, her family, were laughing with them. They looked silly, but she didn't care. This was fun. She hadn't felt so good in a very long time and for that she was grateful.

THEY CHECKED IN TO THE ALBERGUE IN BOADILLA AFTER A LONG, DUSTY walk in the intense sunshine. The reservation allowed them to bunk in the same room. After showers, they made their way back to the bar to celebrate Ben's birthday.

"Beers for us, and a lemonade for Hannah," requested Aubrey to the server, after they found a large enough table to fit them all. Paolo led a chorus of people in singing happy birthday. Aubrey snagged Ben's phone and connected via FaceTime with Kanmi, who led his restaurant in singing along too. Ben was mortified at the attention, but as she looked at her blushing friend, she thought how wonderful it was that he had so much love in his life. Yeah, she wanted that. But how?

2 6

DISTRACTIONS FROM THE HEAT

BOADILLA DEL CAMINO TO LEON

"I AM SO sick of this heat," Georgina said. "I will be ready for Leon. Remind me again why we didn't skip the Meseta?" They had been grumbling for days. At first, they'd experienced freezing weather with strong head winds. The last two days though, Mother Nature had challenged them with an oppressive heat.

Hannah decided to fast forward to Leon with Pam. The Lovelies convinced her it would be better for her to do that, considering the rapidly changing conditions they had been facing. Pam admitted that walking the Meseta was never part of her Camino plan. She'd had enough of treeless plains to last a lifetime, she had said, so she and Hannah caught a train from Fromista to wait for them in Leon. Pam booked a private hotel, not wanting to bounce from albergue to albergue with their one-night limitation. She invited Hannah to stay with her. Grateful, Hannah accepted. Aubrey knew Pam would take care of her and suspected Hannah did too. Her morning sickness had hit her with a vengeance once more. This time, all she wanted to do was lie in bed all day.

With Ben, Georgina and Paolo, Aubrey walked the trail that never seemed to end. They passed through crusty villages covered in dust. The track, Aubrey shared, was just as sparse and barren as Australia's outback. Conversations over the days ranged from their daily lives, what they loved about their hometowns, all the way to politics. When the conversations turned to relationships, Paolo surprised everyone when he announced he was leaving in Leon. He said that as much as he wanted to lay his stones at Cruz de Ferro, a Camino tradition of laying one's burdens, he longed to see Marinka more. Aubrey was shocked to see him so shy when admitting this, but then his cheeky smile broke through. The boy wasn't altogether gone, but the man was emerging.

"I have not known this way before," he admitted, the day they walked out of Sahagun, the halfway point of the Camino Francés.

"What does Marinka think?" Georgina asked, as Aubrey hung on for the answer.

"I do not know, not really," Paolo admitted, "but I would like to find out." He looked fearful at the thought of rejection. Aubrey wondered if a woman had ever rejected him.

"I read a great line recently, online somewhere," Georgina said to Paolo, "It was: 'Destiny speaks to those who choose to hear.' It sounds like you've listened."

The comment stayed with Aubrey. For three days, she considered the path the universe had taken her on so far, of the people who'd come into her life. Some were to show her an idea, a unique path, an original opinion. Others were there to teach her a lesson. Now, she felt she could add to that list. She realised that people also came into her life to remind her what love was. To remind her that she was safe and free to be whoever she wanted to be. To be authentic.

For so long, she held on to the notion that Brendon was the one for her, while she ignored so much along the way. Georgina and Aubrey had talked about the red flags in their marriages. The things they had ignored or looked past. Georgina had admitted that Patrick's aloofness resulted from his upbringing. His father had been the same. He'd never really had a role model to show him it was okay for men to show emotion, or to ask for help. It was something that had bothered her immensely, Georgina finally admitted, especially given her own father had not been that way.

Aubrey explained that much of Brendon's upbringing was materialistic. He didn't know that life could be more than what you possessed. There were many times she felt like a possession, a trophy he had won. He knew her family were wealthy. He admitted to her one drunken evening that he was waiting for her parents to die so he could retire and enjoy the benefits of the inheritance he assumed he would be part of. Aubrey laughed when she told this story.

"Why are you laughing? That's a horrible thing to say!" said Georgina, aghast.

"Because my father explicitly stated in his will that Brendon is never to inherit from him. Brendon never read the details of our prenuptial agreement either. He assumed my 'personal wealth' was just the house in Melbourne. Had he read the document closely, he would have known my personal wealth included a robust trust fund from my parents. He never had access to any of that money. Nor will he."

They talked about their pre-walk anxiety. Georgina had admitted to having an actual panic attack, calling her daughter and asking her what the hell she was doing. She was embarrassed when she relayed the story. Nicole had reminded her that she would never live it down if she returned home with a 'I quit on the first day' story. Aubrey had laughed uproariously, telling Georgina about her anxiety-ridden conversation with her son Simon, who had told her to 'shit or get off the pot'.

By the fifth day of walking together on the Meseta, they were punchy. All four of them recalled the ten best movies in every genre they could think of, just to forget the heat.

"What's the most embarrassing thing you've ever done?" asked Ben on the day they were walking into Leon.

"Hmm. Nothing I would want to admit to," said Aubrey. "What about you, Paolo?" deflecting the question.

"Easy. Being caught by Mamma while I was making love to a girl I was courting. She just stood there next to the bed and kept talking while I lay on top of the girl." He looked almost embarrassed, but he was obviously proud that his mother had caught him in the act.

"Courting? Really Paolo? We know you better," Ben laughed. "But yeah, being caught by your own mother having sex is up there. What about you, Georgina?"

"Hmm. Probably passing out on a toilet, pants down around my ankles," she said.

"Wow. Yeah, that would be embarrassing. What happened?" asked Ben.

"I had just given birth the day before and I still had super low blood pressure. There was a nurse nearby who literally caught me as I fell, which only added to my embarrassment," she explained.

"When you factor in the context, it loses embarrassment points. But we'll give it to you anyway," said Ben, throwing her his gentle smile. "Okay Aubrey, your turn." Georgina did a quick curtsy, with a look of relief to have the attention off her.

"Okay. Well… so many to choose from I must admit. I guess it would be marrying a wannabe rock star. That was pretty embarrassing, especially to my parents."

"Yeah, but was it embarrassing for you?"

"Not at the time. Now, a bit. But he was very cute."

"Try again," said Ben.

"You have to remember; I was raised to not bring embarrassment to my family. They even sent me to deportment classes," she shared.

"Okay, now that's embarrassing. Did you have to learn how to hold a teacup with your little finger raised? How to greet guests? How to walk around with a book on your head?" teased Ben.

"Honestly? Yes. I even had ballroom dancing lessons and came out to society," she laughed. At that, Paolo swooped her up and danced a few steps with her poles flying. It was enough to make Georgina duck when they almost took off her head.

"Now Ben, it's your turn. Most embarrassing moment?" said Aubrey, hoping to move on. While she wasn't embarrassed by her upbringing, she knew, in these times, it was all a bit ridiculous.

"Hmm. Fine, for now," he said. "Okay, mine was joining the mile-high club on a flight. An old woman caught us waiting her turn for the toilets. I was so embarrassed! Kanmi was still zipping his pants when he walked out behind me. I expected to be scolded by her, except," he chuckled, "this little old lady, she must have been in her eighties, just smiled and winked wickedly at me." They all laughed at the image. "With a giggle and a pip, she walked into the bathroom and closed the door."

"Well, that's pretty embarrassing being caught out by a grandmother!" said Aubrey.

"Right?! I assumed we were being stealth. We waited until most of the plane was asleep to slip away to the bathroom together. Guess that saying about how the old never sleep is true. The rest of the plane was snoring. Granny was not."

"I could never imagine having sex on a plane," said Georgina. "The germs alone. And the space. There's no space for two people."

"And that is why your most embarrassing story is about passing out," said Ben, giving Georgina a nudge. "You should try it. It's rather risqué."

"And quite fun," added Aubrey.

"Oh my god Aubrey! You've had sex on a plane before too?" said Georgina, even more shocked.

"Yes. I thought everyone has. Granted, mine was in first class on an Air France flight to Paris," she winked at Ben.

"Paolo?" Georgina prodded. It was hilarious just how shocked she was. Paolo held his hands up, like he was caught too.

"Have you done it since getting caught Ben?" asked Georgina, the expression making Aubrey giggle.

"Oh yeah. Couple of times," said Ben, with a naughty smile.

By the time they arrived in Puente Castro, it was three o'clock in the afternoon and the heat radiated off the road. They had been walking on, or beside pavement for too long. They were only a short distance from Leon, but they were all feeling defeated by the heat.

"What do you all think about taking a bus or taxi to the old city from here?" asked Aubrey. They were sitting in the first cool bar they came to after arriving in the village.

"I'm in," said Georgina, not hesitating. Aubrey looked over at her. She looked hot, sweaty, and about as fried as Aubrey felt. Her feet were throbbing.

"How about you guys?" asked Aubrey. She noticed Ben looked wilted for the first time. Sweat soaked his shirt from where his backpack had been. Paolo guzzled the rest of his water and asked the bar for a refill, which he downed just as quickly. Aubrey looked at the weather app on her phone. The temperature was in the mid-thirties. No wonder they were spent. Aubrey would even go so far as saying she was experiencing some heat exhaustion. She was going with or without them by some transport and, if it had air conditioning, that would be a bonus.

"Yeah. I'm in too. The old pilgrims would have hitched a ride if they could have, so why not?" said Ben. He looked over at Paolo, who remained quiet.

"Paolo?"

"I am seeing my Mamma's words in my ear," he said. Aubrey laughed at his phrase, clearly trying to convey his mother's guilt. "I am already quitting in Leon. It's like I'm, what's the word... cheating?"

"I think she would excuse you, Paolo. Besides, there's a beer with your name on it in Leon. I'm sure if we let Hannah and Pam know we're almost there, they will meet us and have beers waiting."

"On it," said Georgina, typing into her phone.

"Okay, okay. Let's go!" Paolo said, hopping off his stool.

They picked up their packs, while Ben inquired at the bar about transportation. He came back and said, "We're in luck. There's a bus stop right outside and a bus due in five minutes."

"Brilliant!" said Aubrey. With a "Gracias!" to the bartender, they walked outside and waited for a bus to Leon, feeling the spirits of past pilgrims bless their decision.

27

LOOKING INWARD

LEON TO VILLAR DE MAZARIFE

GEORGINA AND AUBREY walked into the Correo Bar in the old city in Leon, the meeting point for the group. Pam and Hannah sat in the corner booth, looking as if they'd been there a while. Pam had her journal in front of her, writing manically, while Hannah held her phone in her hands, her thumbs flying over the keyboard.

"Hello Lovelies," said Aubrey, her greeting rewarded with enormous smiles from both Pam and Hannah at the sound of her voice. Pam jumped up and hugged them both, Hannah following. "It's so good to see you!"

"We're happy to see you too!" said Georgina. "The boys aren't here yet?"

"They were, then dashed out for something. They'll be back shortly," said Pam.

"Good. It's been a bloody long day," said Georgina, settling in as the waitress approached the table. They placed their drink orders.

"It has been a long day, but I feel almost human after that shower," Aubrey said, nudging Hannah. "You wouldn't have wanted me sitting here beforehand." It was wonderful to be amongst the girls again.

"I agree. All I have dreamt about for the last two days was a bath. So, we're sharing a room that has one," said Georgina. "What I didn't expect was the five kilos of dirt that came off me."

"Ew!" said Hannah.

"Yeah, I'm not kidding when I say the bath water was brown when I got out. I had to take a shower afterwards. It was disgusting." They laughed at the image. "I think it will take days for it all to come off me."

"Be glad you didn't walk it," said Aubrey. "It was brutal with the cold, which hit us first, then the ferocious wind..."

"... and then the heat!" said Georgina, finishing her sentence.

"I'm grateful I didn't walk it," said Hannah. "Ben was telling us how dry it was."

"And how boring?" said Pam. "Ben said he was happy for the company. He said there were stretches where you all just walked on your own, lost in your thoughts." Aubrey flashed back to those few days on the Meseta. Her thoughts weren't as dark as they'd been when she started the Camino.

The server delivered the drinks to the table.

"Cheers! Another day on the Camino!" said Aubrey, raising her glass.

"Nice to see you've kept the tradition going," said Pam, clinking her glass with the others.

"Of course!" Aubrey said, taking a long drink of her beer. "Oh, that's good." She was parched, despite drinking copious amounts of water on the track.

"I'm itching to walk," said Pam, taking a sip of her beer.

"I'm not walking any more today, that's for sure," said Georgina. "But I'm not sure I want a rest day yet either. I'm happy to walk with you tomorrow."

Aubrey hesitated. Like Georgina, she wasn't sure she wanted a rest day, but the thought of walking anywhere seemed torturous just now.

"I'm on the fence. I'll let you know later tonight if I'm walking tomorrow," said Aubrey.

"I'm not going anywhere," said Hannah. "Not yet." Aubrey cast a glance at her. She looked pale. "The morning sickness has been kicking my butt and I've just been so tired. I'll rest another day or two before I walk again. I don't know. It may be time I went home."

"Just take your time. Will you be okay if we go ahead?" asked Pam. She and Hannah looked to have formed a tight bond while stopped in Leon for five days. It was good to see. Ben had worried about Hannah, texting her constantly, but she'd assured him Pam was keeping her company.

"I'll be okay," Hannah said, looking at Pam fondly. "If I feel better the day after tomorrow, I'll walk. You never know, maybe I'll still catch you." She gave Pam a teasing smile.

"Probably will. But don't walk until you're ready. Okay?" Pam prompted.

"Yes, Nana," Hannah added, laughing as Ben and Paolo walked in.

"You guys seem fresher than you did earlier," said Aubrey. She'd noticed that Paolo had had a haircut. It had only been three hours since they'd last seen them. He'd been busy.

"We wanted to get Hannah something since we're both leaving tomorrow," he said, handing a bag to Hannah. "This is from Paolo and me."

"Wait. We know that Paolo is going to Germany to chase down Marinka, but you too? Where are you going?" Pam asked. Aubrey was stunned. He had said nothing earlier.

"I'm heading to Oviedo to walk the Primitivo. I had planned on doing that from the start. It'll be hard leaving you guys though," he said. Sadness washed over Aubrey. The band was breaking up.

Suddenly Hannah laughed. She pulled a Camino de Santiago onesie from the gift bag.

"You may not keep the baby, but we wanted you to remember this journey," Ben said, "we are so lucky you shared your story with us." Hannah stared down at the onesie in her lap, trying to control the tears.

"Thank you," Hannah's voice cracked. "Y'all mean so much to me." She took a deep breath, regaining her composure.

"I've decided," Hannah began, as she looked at Pam, "to put the baby up for adoption. I'll stay with my parents until the baby comes, then I'm headed to NYU. After talking about how adoption has been a part of your story Aubrey, and for you soon Ben, I know that there are wonderful people in the world wanting babies. And I will love this baby until it's born, but it's not the right time for me."

"I think it's a brave choice Hannah," Aubrey said. "I know it was not an easy one to make. But I've felt that desperate need of wanting my own child and I know you will change someone's life for the better." She reached over and pulled Hannah into a hug, while tears flowed down both their cheeks.

"You know I'm here for you, kiddo. All the way. You can call me anytime you need anything. Okay? Even if it's just to chat. You have my number," Ben said. Hannah looked to Ben and nodded, as Aubrey watched him wipe his tears away.

The following morning, they all met for the last time, indulging in their favourite Camino breakfast of bacon and eggs. Ben looked down at his watch and announced he needed to go. He had a bus to catch to Oviedo to start his Primitivo Camino into Santiago. Paolo announced it was time he had to go too. He was heading to the train station. With hugs and tears, they said goodbye to the boys. They'd made sure to exchange information. They would stay in touch, but this was the end of their Camino journey together.

All too soon, Aubrey, Georgina and Pam stood. It was time for them to continue walking. Hannah assured them all that she would be fine. She was going to enjoy the hotel room for another night, Pam's treat, and then decide if she wanted to continue the pilgrimage. They clung together in a group hug, tears freely flowing, and Hannah promised to let them know when she left Leon.

"FUCK, THAT WAS HARD!" SAID PAM, WIPING TEARS AWAY AS AUBREY, PAM and Georgina followed the yellow arrows out of the city. "It's like I'm letting my kindergarten kids go all over again!"

"It was more emotional than I was expecting. Imagine, we only met them a few weeks ago," said Georgina. "What's it going to be like in Santiago for us?" An uncomfortable silence followed. Aubrey didn't want to ponder the end of the Camino yet.

They walked through Leon and took a left at the fork after Virgin del Camino, taking the scenic route. But the winds were howling, and the wind chill cut through them. They ploughed through to get to Villar de Mazarife as soon as possible.

The views were expansive. It reminded them of home in Australia with the wild grasses thrashing in the wind. But it was the red poppies lining the track that excited them the most. They had seen them earlier on the Camino, but here, the trail was lined with the bobbing red flowers. The flowers were abundant and despite the cold wind, they stopped to take photos. Georgina, between taking her shots, offered them tips on how to show the flowers with the landscape and trail in the background. Aubrey was happy with the results, thinking she may even frame one photo she took. It captured the essence of the Camino for her.

"See Georgina?" Aubrey showed the photo to her, "This is why you need to be a professional. You know what you're talking about and can even teach others how to do it. Something else to add to your repertoire." Georgina smiled. It was the first time Georgina had not shown embarrassment or dissuade from Aubrey's suggestion when it came to her photography. Progress, Aubrey thought.

They continued in silence for another few kilometres. Once the winds died down a little, they could talk again. It was still cold, but they had warmed a little from the walking. Aubrey asked Pam how the stop in Leon was for her.

"I sorted through a lot of shit about Mick, truth be told," Pam said.

"Oh?" asked Aubrey.

"I guess I realised it's not right to celebrate someone's demise and I was feeling guilty and ashamed about that. But, thinking it through, I finally figured out he was just a fucking horrible person and he had it coming to him. Karma and all that shit." Aubrey was glad to hear that Pam was sorting through the anger. She had sensed her demeanour had calmed a lot since meeting up with her again.

"So, to hell with him," she continued. "The misery he inflicted is on him, not me. Did I tell you about when he got arrested for a DUI while on a business trip? That's a magnificent story."

"No, I don't think you shared that one," said Georgina. She looked to Aubrey, and she shook her head. She didn't remember that one either. "Tell us the story."

"Okay. He was working for the mines and had to go to some union thing in Brisbane. On the last night, Mick went with some of the boys he worked with to a pub nearby. The story goes that he left the bar with the boys around eleven. But the blonde bartender had caught his eye. So, when they left, he got into his rental car, like he was going back to his hotel. But instead, he circled the block and returned to the pub. Later, when he left the bartender's place around three, the police pulled him over for drink driving and hauled him to gaol. He didn't call me. Didn't call his girlfriend either. He just sat there in his gaol cell. So, when he didn't show up for the meetings the next day, the boys tried calling him. No answer. That's when they started to worry. Someone finally considered how much they had been drinking, so they called the hospital. Not there. Then they launched a search party. They checked in at his hotel. No Mick. They even looked behind skip bins at the pub. Eventually his boss' secretary, clearly the smart one in the outfit, did some digging and learned of his arrest. His boss went down to the gaol, bailed him out, and told him to go home. Then, the boss pulled everyone who'd been looking for him into a meeting room and told them to forget it ever happened. Somehow, Mick got a promotion not long after that. Hell if I know how. And the interesting part of all of it? He never said a word about it to me."

"Are you serious?" Aubrey said. "What the hell?"

"My guess is he was having an affair with his boss. She swept it all under the rug," said Pam. "Yes, another woman in his bag of tricks. It's the only thing that explains how he got away with it."

"How did you find out?" asked Georgina, surprise in her voice.

"Someone he works with told me." Wow, Aubrey thought. The audacity of it. But then, she suspected Brendon had had his own batch of similar stories. For him, it would have been Mummy Dearest and expensive lawyers cleaning up his mess.

"So, I sorted through all those memories," Pam said, "and I considered the only thing holding me in that marriage was religion. And now, I'm thankful he's gone. I can stop feeling trapped and stop feeling guilty about my feelings. I can stop being drawn down by it all. Fuck, I was so tired for so long. What they say is true. Mind over matter. If he hadn't died, and hadn't filed for divorce, I would not have lasted much longer."

"What? Without killing him?" said Aubrey. "The thought would have tempted me."

"No, I mean depression. I was very depressed. I see that now," said Pam. Aubrey wanted to say something, but Pam quickly continued. "I considered what Ben said about Lee and her grieving. I wish I loved Mick enough to feel that kind of loss. But the sad fact is, I didn't. I never did. Mick was just a man I married. But I wonder about that kind of love that Lee had. What it's like to love someone that intensely."

"I thought about that too, on the Meseta," said Georgina. "I don't know what it was, but the Meseta gave me the head space to consider my marriage to Patrick. What we have, but more importantly, what we don't. I'm at a crossroads. I realised that I'm not over him, but I'm over the situation. Something has to change. I want more than what we have."

"Sounds like we've all been reflecting on relationships these last few days. Ben has inspired me. From what he told me, he struggled to find that kind of love in his life. He's helped me realise I don't have to give up on love yet," said Aubrey.

"Well, look at us. The Camino provides, as they say," said Pam.

When they arrived to Villar de Mazarife, they took photos of the beautiful mosaic at the village entrance, then found their albergue to the right of the trail. They walked up the garden path and stepped into a compact room, no larger than a closet really, where a small wooden table stood front and centre, ready to welcome pilgrims. On the table sat a book and a bell. They considered just knocking on the closed door, but decided the bell was there for a reason. Pam picked it up and gave it a quick shake.

The hospitalero came through the door after a few moments. He welcomed them, checked their passports, and stamped their credentials in turn.

"Would you like to share a private room or sleep in the dorm?" he asked. They decided on the dorm. He gave them a quick tour of the facility before showing them to their assigned beds. They were tucked into a corner in the expansive dorm room. The setup was comical. The bunk beds were pushed together, two by two, giving the illusion of a king-size bed, top and bottom.

"Looks like we have the deluxe bunk beds," chuckled Georgina. Pam had scored big time with an empty bed next to her.

"I read the dinner here is homemade and delicious," said Pam, as they unpacked their gear.

"Hello ladies," Aubrey turned to see Lee, aka Lean and Mean, standing at the head of their bunks. Although, she had to admit, she didn't look very mean at the moment. "I'm happy to see you all." Lee wore a huge smile. She looked almost... free, thought Aubrey. Lee waved at Pam, who was standing on the opposite side of the bunk bed. Pam walked over to her slowly and after hesitating for just a moment, embraced her. Lee, taken aback at first, softened, and hugged Pam hard in return.

"I'm so sorry," Pam said.

"Me too," replied Lee.

What were the odds? Aubrey never thought they would see Lee again.

28

IT'S WHAT YOU DO

THE FOLLOWING MORNING, Aubrey noticed a missed call from Simon. She texted him quickly, mostly to make sure everything was okay at home, but also because Pam and Lee were already packing up.

Hi love. Everything okay? xx

The response from Simon was immediate.

Just checking in. Haven't heard from you for a few days.

All okay here. Still walking with P & G. On to Hospital de Orbigo today. No rest day in Leon. U OK? xx

She knew she needed to get up and get going. Breakfast was served at seven. Georgina, in the bunk next to her, opened one eye, looked around and then closed it again, mumbling, "Looks like we have about ten more minutes."

"Come on Georgina. We don't want to miss brekky. It's a long wander to Hospital with no food. Pam said she read it was a good offering." She thought she heard Georgina grunt next to her, but realised it was her phone buzzing.

All okay here. Just wanted to hear you were okay. Love you Mum. Face-Time me when you have a chance (aka good connection). x S

Relieved to know all was okay at home, she put on her pants and bra, then grabbed her toiletry bag and headed to the communal bathroom.

"Let's go George," Georgina grumbled, but Aubrey heard her unzip her sleeping bag as she walked away.

At dinner the night before, Aubrey and Georgina chatted with a group of Dutch women at one end of the table, while Lee and Pam kept to themselves at the other end. Something happened with those two over that conversation, Aubrey thought, and for the better. Georgina's jaw nearly hit the floor when Lee asked if she could walk with them today.

After breakfast, Pam reported, "It's two degrees but feels like -2. Better rug up in this wind."

"What's that in English?" Lee asked.

"Bloody fucking cold," Pam replied.

By the time they reached Villavante, the sunshine was warming, but the wind was still brutal. They stopped for some coffee, mostly to wrap their frigid hands around the warm cups.

"So Lee, we didn't get to chat with you last night," said Aubrey. "How's your Camino been? How did you do with the Meseta? We didn't see you at all."

"I biked the Meseta and then spent three rest days in Leon," said Lee. "Riding a bicycle was therapeutic for me. I really enjoyed the speed. Walking is just too slow." Aubrey smiled, remembering their conversation in Burgos that Lee hated having to give up running.

"That sounds like fun," Aubrey said. "Georgina and I walked it with Ben and Paolo."

"Oh great! Lovely boys," Lee said, taking a drink from her cooled coffee. "What happened to them?"

"Ben is walking the Primitivo. Paolo went to Germany to find out if he was truly in love, or just infatuated," said Aubrey.

"We are hoping it's love," said Georgina.

"With the German girl?" asked Lee.

"Yes. How did you know?" asked Georgina.

"Oh, you could see it in his eyes whenever he laid eyes on her. I was sitting drinking coffee with Ben and Paolo in Logroño, when the girls showed up. His entire body seemed to melt. It's as if he'd been waiting for her his entire life," Aubrey sat back and realised that's exactly how she would describe Paolo around Marinka. She only hoped Marinka didn't reject him.

"And how was walking the Meseta?" Lee asked. "There were some days when the wind and cold were pure hell." Georgina nodded.

"Worse than this morning, for sure," Aubrey said, "but we kept our minds distracted with some great conversations. Conversation was the only way to not go mad."

"I appreciated the Meseta. It helped me sort through some stuff in my head. I don't think being distracted would have helped me. I needed that time to sludge through the grief."

"Grief?" asked Georgina.

"I lost someone close to me," Lee said. Aubrey and Pam nodded while Georgina sat looking a little stunned. Aubrey realised she had not told Georgina about that part of her conversation with Lee while in Burgos. She suddenly felt guilty she hadn't told her earlier. "Truth is, I lost my partner of fifty years, Amelia. We were like Paolo and the German girl. We were each other's first loves." Lee looked down at her lap. "She died a year ago."

"Oh!" said Aubrey. Ben had told her she'd lost someone but didn't realise it was her life partner.

"I'm so sorry," said Georgina.

"Thank you," Lee said. "It's been hard. This Camino was something we talked about doing together. So, I thought doing the walk on my own was the best way to honour her. While I was at it, I could try to deal with my grief. It took a while, but I finally got off my ass and flew over here," Lee smiled. "I have felt her presence with me every single day."

"I don't doubt that," said Aubrey.

"I had a dream about Amelia the night after Sahagun. She told me I needed to suck it up and get on with life," Lee chuckled. Aubrey was shocked, remembering her reaction when Pam gave her similar advice. "I guess I should add that Amelia didn't hold back. She was very much a tell-it-like-it-is kind of gal. Kind of like you Aussies, I realised later. Anyway, the weather was beautiful after that dream." The smile on her face was soft, her eyes watery, as if she knew Amelia had something to do with the weather change.

"I hate to cut off this conversation but are you ladies ready to continue on to Hospital de Orbigo?" asked Pam. Aubrey suspected she mostly wanted to leave this conversation behind. Pam didn't believe in the supernatural as she did.

"I'm ready when you Lovelies are," said Aubrey. Georgina piled all the cups and saucers and took them inside. Aubrey noticed the look of confusion on Lee's face.

"She does that. She owns a café in Australia," Aubrey said, reaching for her backpack.

"Oh! Okay. I've just been leaving them," Lee said, putting her backpack back on. "Seems inconsiderate now."

"I'm sure we would have too, but we noticed it stressed Georgina out to leave them, so we take turns," Aubrey said, as Georgina re-emerged.

Lee and Pam walked ahead a little. Aubrey watched them as they walked, deep in conversation, crossing the bridge and turning left. The trail followed along the railway line, taking them past a rural albergue, the yellow arrows showing them the way.

Aubrey was at odds and felt her anxiety bubble. She trusted these women implicitly, even Lee, but somehow the words she needed to speak most failed her. What was preventing her from revealing her truth? She knew exactly what Lee was referencing when she spoke of her partner's presence. So why couldn't she tell them who'd been walking with her?

2 9

FINDING YOUR WEIRD PERSON

HOSPITAL DE ORBIGO TO ASTORGA

AFTER A LENGTHY DINNER and copious amounts of wine, they ventured back to their albergue, San Miguel. They were assigned a spacious private room, hosting two sturdy wooden bunk beds with chequered linens. Georgina and Lee claimed the top bunks, which now, with a few wines in, Aubrey was grateful for. But just as she settled in, she remembered Lee was twenty years older than she. She got up and tried to give Lee the lower bunk, but Lee was adamant. She refused to relinquish her top bunk, and given Lee's determined look, Aubrey wasn't going to argue. She wondered though, if they shouldn't all just sleep on the tiled floor.

"I snore when I've drunk a lot of wine," said Lee. "I'm warning you all."

"I doubt it will bother any of us. We'll have the walls bellowing in and out tonight between the four of us most likely!" said Pam as she puffed up her pillow and buried herself into her sleeping bag.

The following morning, Pam's phone alarm blared at six-thirty. Georgina mumbled, 'shut the fucking thing off!' which was rare for Georgina. She was usually up and going for the sunrise. Aubrey considered it a minor miracle that they were out the door by eight, with coffee and food in their bellies. They were all dragging with hangovers this morning.

Pam seemed determined to set a good pace, despite their slow start.

"Geez. What's your hurry?" asked Georgina.

"It will be hot today," said Pam, "and I don't want to be walking in it. The heat is not for the weak."

"Or the hung over," said Lee. True statement thought Aubrey. The heat wasn't something she was keen on either. The Meseta cured her of ever walking in the heat again.

As Lee and Pam scooted ahead, Georgina and Aubrey walked together in silence, giving Aubrey time to reflect on Lee's story, which she'd shared over dinner.

She'd met Amelia fifty years before at the hospital in Albuquerque. Amelia was working in the Emergency Department as a receptionist at night. Lee was a nurse straight out of school. Their connection was instant. For weeks, they went to restaurants and galleries together, but just as friends. One night, they took it a step further. The chemistry had been brewing and, as strongly as Lee understood she was gay, Amelia wasn't so sure. But, Lee said with a smile, Amelia took a risk. It had been Lee's first serious relationship and, as it had turned out, it was for Amelia too. They decided to marry three years before, once it was legal, although they'd been partners for almost fifty years already. That was, until Amelia died a year ago after a long-suffering battle with breast cancer.

"I was just thinking about what Lee was saying last night about her life with Amelia," said Aubrey, following some distance behind the other two. "I can't seem to stop."

"Me either," said Georgina. "I see the love when Lee describes her relationship and I realise, I don't have that. I want that. I love Patrick, I do, but I can't help but think something is missing. If I'm honest, I've felt like that for a long time. Our lives are going down a path that feels, I don't know, like a dead end. Something has to change."

"If you could sit and talk with Patrick, at this very moment, what would you say to him?" asked Aubrey, looking over to her. Georgina wasn't her usual chic self today. She looked kind of pale. Her hair was a mess too, pulled haphazardly into a low ponytail, her wide brim hat skewed on her head.

"I have kind of been doing that," said Georgina. This revelation surprised Aubrey. "I've been emailing with him." Aubrey realised that Georgina had been typing a lot on her phone in the afternoons.

"Turns out," Georgina continued, "he kept asking Nicole if she'd heard from me, so she told him to email me directly. He told me when I left that I shouldn't ring him. Too expensive, he said. We never considered email."

Pam and Lee were still ahead, taking photos with a mannequin dressed like Elvis.

"Should we stop for our own photo op?" Georgina asked.

Aubrey nodded. "I need water anyway." They stopped for a little while to pose with Elvis. Pam and Lee were antsy, so they continued walking ahead of them.

"So, how are the emails going?" said Aubrey, picking up the conversation.

"Okay. It's weird. He writes like he talks," said Georgina. "It's like we're having a conversation in person. But it seems, well, he may miss me? The lack of communication may have helped us."

"Why do you say that?" asked Aubrey, as they walked through a scrappy grove of trees. The shade felt wonderful, a welcomed reprieve from the intense sun. They stopped for more water.

"I suppose me being here has given us some distance," she said. "Ugh...obviously. I mean, I know we've had the distance thing with his contract work on the mainland, but this, I don't know, this is different. I have the space to reflect on what has been going on and what I want. Because of you guys, I've found my courage to talk to him about that."

"What do we have to do with it?" asked Aubrey.

"Ben's marriage to Kanmi, Lee's relationship with Amelia. They positively glow when they talk about their partners. I see how it can and should be. I know now that I want a true partnership like they have," Aubrey looked thoughtful. Georgina gazed up toward Pam.

"And then..." Georgina looked ahead and quietened her voice

slightly, "I understand why Pam stuck to the status quo, because of her religion, but the way she was being treated... Unless you're in such a position, you probably don't know how you will react. I'm not judging her, not in the least. But I know, if I was treated as she was, I would not have stayed. All I know is, I have put up with a lot of stuff over the years that I shouldn't have. And Pam's situation has made me sit up and ask why? I've asked myself that question over and over. I've finally realised it's because it seemed easier. Easier than standing up for myself. Standing up for what I need in my own marriage."

"It's good that you recognise that," said Aubrey. "He hasn't physically..."

"Hit me?" Aubrey nodded. "No. Nothing like that."

"I just don't want to be the 'little woman' anymore," Aubrey groaned but Georgina continued. "Yeah, I know. Patrick has called me that many times, mostly to his friends. I'm his partner, not just his wife," she said, her voice finding its volume again.

"And you've said this to him? In your emails?" Aubrey asked.

"Yeah," said Georgina. "Finally."

"And how did he take it?" she asked. She motioned for them to stop to remove a stone from her shoe.

"He asked me if that's how I honestly felt," Georgina said, holding her arm out to help Aubrey keep her balance. "I explained that by not treating my business as part of our income, by not having conversations with me about managing the property, I felt that he was not respecting me, or my opinions. He said he didn't know what to say to that. Apparently, his mother said something to him about not involving me in the family business. She told him I should be busy enough with my 'little café'. He believed she made sense, so he went with that."

"Little café?" said Aubrey, while she re-tied her shoe. She stood up. "That's insulting," she said, noticing Georgina turn a slight shade of red.

"Yeah, I thought so too," said Georgina. "It surprised me he listened to her." She shook her head. "No. It pissed me off. I can't believe he took her advice."

"And did you tell him that?" Aubrey said, re-hitching her pack.

"Yes, after I gave myself some time to cool down a bit," said Georgina. "I told him that my little café, as he put it, was pulling in some decent money. Enough that I invested the profits into a house over by the beach as a source of rental income. He was rather shocked by that and asked me why I didn't tell him. Of course I told him. It's quite possible he didn't listen because it's..."

"... your little business," said Aubrey.

"Exactly," said Georgina, her walking style becoming closer to stomping.

"Sounds like you've been level-headed with business decisions," said Aubrey, impressed with Georgina's acumen. She was much more business-savvy than she had revealed.

"I think he's beginning to realise that. I've been trying to tell him for years he needs to sell off some of his prime beachfront property. He'd make a small fortune. Enough to keep the family farm running comfortably. But he ignores me because I'm not talking about sheep. If it's not directly sheep related, he doesn't consider it. But he doesn't even run the sheep near that land, so what difference does it make?" Aubrey could see clearly how upset Georgina was. Her face was flushed, and her knuckles were white around her trekking poles.

"Do you feel he'll listen to you now?" Aubrey said, trying to snap Georgina back to the here and now.

"He said he would," Georgina said. "We'll see."

"And what about the rest? Is he willing to talk to you about other stuff? The personal stuff?"

"Well, let's not get ahead of ourselves," Georgina snickered. "He said he has stopped drinking." Aubrey gave her a raised eyebrow, not understanding. "He was drinking heavily for a while. Drowning out the stress, the pressures, the anxiety, I imagine."

"That's a start. Does he suffer from anxiety attacks?" Aubrey asked. Georgina paused a beat.

"Yes, but he doesn't like to talk about that. That part will take time. He needs professional help. His father did a number on his mental health. His mother too. She always expected perfection," said Georgina, then looked at Aubrey. "Maybe it's generational? Didn't you say your mother-in-law expected perfection too?"

"Yes. The unattainable goal, as Pam said."

"I think his father did more damage though," Georgina said. "He expected Patrick to be a man's man, to never show his emotions, or show weakness. His father expected him to be strong and just soldier on, no matter what. But when you have a mental health issue mixed in, that can be awfully confounding."

"I know counselling helped me," said Aubrey. "I had anxiety issues on top of my depression. Simon, my son, has had anxiety issues for much of his childhood. Counselling helps. They teach you techniques to manage it. Patrick can learn how to put his father's words in his head aside and focus on how to be the man he wants to be."

"I hope so," Georgina said, wistfully. "But he has to figure that out for himself. I've suggested counselling before, but his first step is to realise that the land is his now, to do with as he wants. It's not the same as it was twenty years ago. His sisters have given him total control. As long as they get their cut, they don't care what he does. I'm damn sure if he made it viable again, they would not be complaining."

"Most definitely," said Aubrey.

"But I've learned with Patrick," Georgina said, "at least in the past anyway, that he needs to feel as if he came up with the solution for it to work. If it's my idea, it's dismissed. I told him that too."

"What was his reaction to that?" asked Aubrey, as they approached a fruit stand set up off the side of the trail.

"Surprised? Then defensive," Georgina said. "That was the last thing we talked about, so I'm giving him the time to let that sink in."

"Good for you," Aubrey said and pointed to Pam and Lee enjoying some fruit in the shade. They made a beeline to them.

"Hello Lovelies. What have you found?" asked Aubrey, as she took her pack off. Her sweaty back was cooled by the gentle breeze.

"There are some fresh strawberries over there. Pay by donation." Aubrey looked over to the stand. A good-looking Spaniard rested one foot up on a wooden crate while conversing with two younger Asian pilgrims. The guy caught her eye. Aubrey was taken aback by his piercing blue eyes boring straight into hers. He smiled, waved, welcomed them, and returned to his conversation.

"Lovely, isn't he?" whispered Pam, biting into a strawberry.

"Mmm," said Aubrey, bringing her attention back to Pam.

"Come on, that fruit looks too good to pass up," said Georgina, nudging her. Aubrey grabbed some money from her top pocket and followed Georgina to the stand. The owner said hello in Spanish in a husky baritone. Then, switching to English, he invited them to take whatever they wished, then walked away, wishing them a Buen Camino. The donativo stand was filled with all kinds of goodies, from fruit to juices to slices of cake.

They returned to Lee and Pam in the shade. The four of them sat enjoying fresh strawberries and slices of juicy watermelon. As they munched away, Aubrey watched the owner weave his way through the pilgrims, welcoming them all as he continually replenished the stand.

"Aubrey and I were saying earlier, we've been thinking about your love story with Amelia," Georgina said to Lee. "I'm curious what made your partnership so successful."

"Curious minds want to know," said Aubrey, taking another bite of watermelon with juice running down her hands.

Lee laughed. "Heck, I don't know. Respect?" Her face glowed as she thought about the question. "Laughter too I suppose. We had a lot of fun. Our motto was always: 'Sure! Why not?!' We would try anything once." She explained that Amelia was the yin to her yang. She could talk her into anything.

"I guess too, we shared the same values and," she laughed again, "we were both just weird enough for each other."

Aubrey thought about that. She didn't remember a lot of laughter with Brendon. It sounded like it had been a long time since Georgina had laughed or had fun with Patrick too. She considered the Spaniard with mesmerizing eyes.

Yeah, she wanted to find her weird person too.

30

LAYING THEIR BURDENS

ASTORGA TO EL ACEBO VIA RABANAL

AUBREY WAS happy to walk with Georgina while Pam and Lee set the pace ahead. She was finally opening to the idea of taking her photography seriously. Georgina admitted that she had thought about selling at Salamanca markets in Hobart before. She knew she needed to expand her portfolio first and find a quality printer and framer. She just couldn't quite get out of the 'considering it' stage. As they talked, they came up with a solid plan for when she got home. Georgina seemed really excited at the prospect.

By the time they reached Astorga, they found Pam and Lee sitting at a table in the piazza. Aubrey's mouth watered when she saw the juicy burgers on their table.

"I want that," said Georgina quietly next to her.

"Me too!" whispered Aubrey. "May we join you?" she asked, not waiting for an answer before sitting. Georgina sat opposite her as a waiter approached their table.

"Dos, por favor," said Aubrey, pointing at the burgers with a ravenous look.

"Cervesa?" asked the waiter, nodding at Pam and Lee's beers, pen raised to his pad, ready to add to the order.

"Oh! Si! Si! Gracias!" said Aubrey. Georgina nodded her acceptance. "Those burgers look too good to pass up." Juices ran down Lee's chin. Georgina handed her the extra serviette sitting in front of her.

"Thanks. It's so, so good," said Lee. "We would have waited, but I was ready to pass out." The waiter placed their beers on the table.

"Cheers!" said Aubrey, clinking with Georgina. She had to wait for Pam and Lee to drop their burgers to clink with them too. "Another day done on the Camino!"

"Lee said she's not taking a rest day. She's walking tomorrow," said Pam.

"Oh, that's too bad," said Aubrey. "Georgina and I didn't have a rest day in Leon, so we're ready for a break. You don't want to chill with us?"

"No, I rested plenty in Leon. I need to keep going since I have limited time. I have one more rest day planned and that will be in or around Sarria," said Lee, before taking another bite of her burger. Lee had mentioned in Hospital de Orbigo that she had a flight already booked back to the States.

"We're sorry to see you go," said Georgina. Aubrey agreed. Lee had brought lightness to Pam's step, that was for sure.

THE FOLLOWING MORNING, THEY WAVED SLEEPILY TO LEE WHEN SHE LEFT them at dawn. When the door closed, the Lovelies each rolled over and went back to sleep. It felt good to do that. Aubrey had been ready for a rest day. They booked a private albergue that allowed them to stay two nights. Pam had been antsy the night before and said she was considering walking with Lee. But by the end of the night, she decided she was happy to keep in step with Aubrey and Georgina. Aubrey was relieved. It was hard enough to not be walking with the youngsters, but without Pam, it would be odd. It felt like something major was out of place when they'd walked the second part of the Meseta without her.

After a relaxing breakfast, they spent the rest of the morning exploring the Gaudi Museum. Georgina played tour guide this time, providing information she learned in high school of the architect and his background.

"Geez Georgina. How can you possibly remember back that far?" Aubrey teased.

"It's a little ostentatious for my liking," Pam commented, as they wandered through the overly decorated palace. Aubrey had to agree.

"We called the architect Gaudy back in high school," Georgina said "mostly to piss off our art teacher. She was an enormous Gaudi fan."

"Gaudy sounds about right," agreed Pam. Aubrey was impressed with all Georgina had remembered. She would have been more likely to forget about this architect.

THEY LEFT EARLY THE NEXT MORNING, HAPPY TO BE LEAVING IN THE mellow dawn light. They kept to the routine of a quiet thirty minutes or so before Pam began their day's conversation, relaying news about a murder on the stretch between Astorga and Rabanal.

"Oh shit! Is Lee okay?" exclaimed Georgina, a little paler than she had been minutes before.

"Oh! Not now. This was years ago," said Pam, much to Aubrey's relief. She'd read something about that episode too. She would hang up her boots if it had happened again.

"She's okay. She told me about it in a text last night. Said she had walked with another American woman she'd met in Santa Catalina de Somozo. They had walked to Rabanal from there together."

"Oh good," said Georgina.

"The woman approached Lee as she was leaving the café," Pam shared, "asking if she could tag along. The woman said she was nervous to walk alone on that stretch, after reading about the murder in her Camino guidebook."

"I remember when we first saw Lee," Georgina said. "She wasn't interested in walking with anyone. Ha! She wasn't very approachable at all. She's changed."

"I think she has changed," agreed Pam, setting their pace. "Or maybe she was like this all along? That dream, where Amelia came to her, helped put a lot of her angst behind her, she said." Aubrey thought of how relaxed and funny Lee had been these last few days. Turned out, she had a wicked sense of humour and more of a potty mouth than she imagined. It was no wonder she and Pam got along so well.

The landscape was barren and mundane as they walked toward Gonzo. The path was lined with scrub brush. As they walked, Georgina filled Pam in on her photography plan. She would set the wheels in motion when she got home, assuming her daughter would agree to run the café.

"I've already dropped some hints," Georgina said, "She seems eager to continue running the café, which is great. But I haven't shared why with her yet. And I want to talk to Patrick too. It's only fair."

Aubrey had emailed Simon the night before, asking if he'd be willing to help Georgina set up a website. He had made extra cash building websites while he was attending University.

"You'll be in reliable hands," said Aubrey, after sharing this with the Lovelies. "He worked as an IT guy for bloggers, so he is well-versed in working with creatives already."

"I will pay him for the work," insisted Georgina.

"No you won't," replied Aubrey. "He's happy to help you for free." Georgina looked at her with suspicion.

"Seriously, he said he was happy to help. He's a geek at heart. And he's probably relieved his Mum finally has actual friends!" she joked. Little did they know how true that statement was.

When they reached Rabanal, Georgina was talking a mile a minute about website design. They were booked into a boutique casa rural, which looked old and rustic. Walking in through the tall gate, they found an airy courtyard in the centre of a two-storey house. Upstairs featured a wrap-around verandah which connected the rooms, and downstairs held reception and the breakfast room. It was old world and full of character. In their room, Aubrey opened the window to let in a cool breeze to offset the late afternoon sunshine. Pam lay on her bed and announced she wanted to stay longer, but Georgina nixed that idea.

"We can't stay. Big day tomorrow," said Georgina without saying why.

"I'm not ready," Pam replied, her voice sounding very unsure.

They attended vespers later that night after dinner. The reality of where they were on the Camino almost brought Aubrey to her knees. The ceremony turned her introspective. At the end of vespers, she sat, breathless, knowing what was to come the next day: Cruz de Ferro. The day they would lay their burdens to rest. She was looking forward to and dreading it at the same time. For Aubrey, this was a major part of her Camino journey.

She told Georgina and Pam she wanted to walk a little before heading back to their room. She needed to calm her racing heart. She knew, in this moment, she had been wrong not to share with Pam and Georgina what had happened two years ago. She felt the weight of it even more than usual and decided it was time. But first, she needed to lay her stones at the cross. She needed to do this for herself.

THE FOLLOWING MORNING, THEY HAD BREAKFAST IN SILENCE. THEY SPOKE only when tasks required it. The mood was edgy. While they waited on Pam, Aubrey explained to Georgina that the reason she'd come to Spain was to lay her burdens at Cruz de Ferro.

"I read about it right before I left," said Georgina. "I didn't know about it before. I had to scramble the day I left Tasmania to find a rock, and I've been working that rock ever since. It definitely holds my burdens now."

Aubrey hadn't shared what her stones represented. The three of them kept that information to themselves. The stones and their meanings were sacred, held tight until released.

The weather turned for the worse as they walked the narrow path. Sleet stung their cheeks, like tiny needles going in and out. Talk was difficult, not that anyone had much to say anyway. Only the huge patches of bright purple and yellow flowers, standing in stark contrast to the steel grey sky, evoked awe and wonder from the trio. Eventually, the sleet turned to snow, creating a winter wonderland.

Pam, first in line, stopped on the track, raised her face to the sky and let the snowflakes land on her beaming face. Aubrey did the same but stuck her tongue out to catch the flurries. Georgina took pictures of her two friends, laughing at their wacky antics. It was enough to lighten the mood for a while.

They stopped in Foncebadōn, the last town before Puerto Irago, better known as Cruz de Ferro. Foncebadōn was, at first glance, a quaint hamlet. A cross stood in the middle of a concrete footpath guiding pilgrims in. But with a few steps, the hamlet became a jumble of rambling, rundown buildings on either side of a snow-covered dirt track.

On the left, there was a decrepit stone building, with a patchwork of corrugated iron for the roof, and slate rock holding the sheets in place. Aubrey mused that it was probably held together with rusty nails and duct tape. Georgina squealed with delight.

"It has so much character," she exclaimed, whipping out her phone. Aubrey wondered how it was even standing upright.

While Georgina stopped for photos, Aubrey and Pam went looking for the nearest bar. Aubrey was freezing. She'd not grabbed her gloves and was eager to wrap her hands around a hot mug containing something yummy, like a hot chocolate. She suspected they were all delaying the inevitable too. Thankfully, they discovered a bar on the left doing a roaring trade.

After an hour of defrosting, they gathered their gear, and grudgingly stepped out into the elements. The snow had ceased, turning into a drizzly mess. The path was quickly becoming a mud pit. They navigated around a group of Asians studying their guidebook, looking lost, with rain dribbling beneath their hoods. Pam gave them a thumb bump, pointing them to the café. She received smiles and a quick two thumbs up as they acknowledged her advice. They muttered 'Buen Camino' and hurried inside. With a double tap of Pam's poles, they continued up the hill.

Aubrey was baffled by the simplicity of Cruz de Ferro when they approached. She expected to see a monument standing regally on top of a mountain. Instead, they were looking at a five-metre wooden pole, with an iron cross mounted at the top, standing in centuries of stones laid by the many pilgrims before them. But the surprising part was that this monument, the place they were to lay their burdens, was in the middle of the trail with a carpark off to the side. This is a bit of a letdown, Aubrey thought. How is this ever going to work?

But the magical part came from the rocks they lay. Painted stones, stones wrapped with paper and secured with a rubber band, and simple pebbles held the prayers, words of sorrow, and memories of all that had passed through here. This moment was regarded by many as the most spiritual on the Camino. For Aubrey, the moment was as immense as the massive stone pile.

Aubrey stood standing a distance away from the cross. She wasn't ready. She saw Georgina and Pam ahead of her. They turned and looked back at her.

"Do you mind if I say a prayer?" Pam asked. "It's a pilgrim prayer."

"No, not at all. I'd like to hear it." Aubrey said and slowly stepped forward to join them.

Pam pulled up her notes from her phone.

"Lord, may this stone, a symbol of my efforts on the pilgrimage, that I lay at the foot of the cross of the Saviour, one day weigh the balance in favour of my good deeds when the deeds of my life are judged."

The prayer was from the movie *The Way*, Aubrey realised. Ironic that Pam would find that prayer to recite since she'd never seen the actual movie. But the words spoke to her. She caressed the stones in her hand.

"That was beautiful," said Georgina. She looked over at Aubrey as if to say something, but hesitated, then looked down at her hands.

"Do you mind if I go first?" Georgina asked.

"Not at all," Pam said.

"Would you mind taking my photo before I lay my stones?" she asked. Pam took Georgina's phone and snapped a few shots, both candid and staged. Aubrey was still in her own world but heard Georgina step forward and scramble up the rocky hill to the base of the cross. She looked up a few minutes later to see Georgina lay a stone, then heard a quick sob escape her. With her head bent, focused on her footsteps, Georgina slowly made her way back down. Aubrey and Pam hugged her ferociously.

Pam broke away, nodded with purpose, and turned and crawled her way up the hill. Aubrey watched Pam bow her head as if in prayer, then cross herself, a gesture of Catholicism she had not seen Pam do the entire Camino. Then she raised her head, paused, and shot her middle finger toward the sky defiantly. Aubrey smiled. It was very much a Pam thing to do.

When Pam returned, there was another round of hugs. Aubrey hesitated.

"Aubrey?" Georgina asked softly, a few minutes later.

"I'm not ready," she whispered. "I don't know if I can."

"Take your time," said Pam, just as Georgina said, "You don't have to…"

But she did. She had to do this. She walked up to the edge of the pile and slowly navigated her way over the rocks, careful not to twist an ankle. When she reached the top, she pulled out her first stone.

"This stone represents my marriage," she whispered. "While it gifted me with the immense love of my children, I am glad that part of my life is over. I wish Brendon well, but here, I leave the burden of the marriage and of the man I was married to." She bent down and placed the stone on the pile. She stood and took out the second stone. This one was harder. She rubbed the stone between her fingers. It was worn smooth from many months of her fingers rubbing the surface. Her throat constricted. Her tears flowed freely. Her heart was tight. She held the stone in both hands in front of her heart for several moments before she raised it to her lips and kissed it softly. Finally, she bent down to place her stone gently on the pile.

With that effort, the floodgates opened. She let go of the howl within her. Her knees buckled and she fell onto the hard edges of the stones beneath her knees. She had to let her go. Cass. She could no longer keep her with her. It had been Cass' decision to leave. That was Cass' burden, not Aubrey's. But the guilt was hers and she needed to let that go.

The emotion poured out of her like molten lava, the force fierce and hot, more than she could control. She put her head to the base of the cross and hung there for a moment. She balled her hands into fists, collecting stones. She could feel in the stones all the pain and anguish from the pilgrims that had come before. Her own grief overpowered them all. She howled, over and over, until her throat was raw. She couldn't find the will to stand. She was losing herself to the grief, when she felt hands rubbing her back and her name being whispered in worried tones.

"Aubrey," she heard Georgina say as if she were at the other end of a long tunnel. "Are you okay?"

"Come on, let's get you down," whispered Pam in an authoritative tone. Suddenly, Aubrey heard Cass' voice and she lifted her head. Cass, singing "Let it go", the song from *Frozen*, something she used to sing when she was in a playful, joyful mood. Aubrey started laughing softly. Georgina and Pam, looking at her like she'd gone around the bend, helped her to stand on her wobbly legs. Aubrey wiped her tears and the snot that was trickling out of her nose with the sleeve of her shirt.

"One more," she breathed. After a moment, she looked down at her third stone, nodded, then tossed it on to the pile. She looked up at the cross above her and exhaled deeply. She'd been holding on for too many months. The moment was more powerful than she'd imagined it would ever be.

They didn't speak when they reached the bottom. Aubrey wasn't sure she could anyway, but her mind was back in reality again. Aubrey was so grateful for these two women. She would have been fine walking on her own for the last five hundred kilometres. But today, they mattered more than she could ever say. She couldn't explain why she felt so strongly about them, but it didn't matter. They were her family.

"I need to explain," she said, pulling away.

"No, you don't. The experience is yours, and yours alone," said Pam.

"Says the woman who flipped off God!" teased Georgina.

"We all have our burdens."

"My burden was, well, it's about my daughter, Cass." Aubrey looked down, not sure how to go on. When she looked back up, Pam pointed to a picnic table sitting in the middle of a field of wild daisies, separated from the trail and Cruz de Ferro by a rustic wooden fence. Aubrey nodded. When they were all seated, Pam offered them some chocolate she had pulled from her pack. Aubrey opened her mouth, then closed it again. Then, with a deep breath, she plunged into the dark, murky water.

"My daughter Cass committed suicide two years ago," she said and looked straight at Pam, knowing she'd be the stable one out of the two. Georgina gasped next to her.

"She was seventeen. By the time she was fifteen, she was an addict. At first, when she died, we thought it was from an accidental overdose, but that wasn't the case. She committed suicide." Aubrey knew she was just spewing the words, trying to get them out but not stopping long enough to worry if she was making sense. "When I talked to her therapist later, we learned she suffered from severe depression. I thought it was just normal stuff. Stuff teenagers deal with. She never let on just how bad it really was." Georgina and Pam were quiet, letting her speak.

"We tried everything we could. Treatment. Lots of treatment. Love. Even tough love."

"That must have been hard for you," Pam said, keeping her eyes on Aubrey.

"Yes. It was beyond challenging some days," said Aubrey, flashing back on a gruesome day. "Cass was a sweetheart when she was clean. Well, even when she was high. She had an absolutely beautiful soul and she was wicked smart. She could have done some amazing things with her life. I look at you and your daughter, Georgina, and I have to admit, I was jealous at first. I'm so sorry about that."

"Oh Aub, I'm sorry if I said something that made it hurt more for you."

"No. I wasn't ready to say anything, and really, I wouldn't have wanted you to change what you were saying anyway. You have a beautiful relationship with Nicole. Please, cherish it." Georgina reached for her hand. "I wish I had that with Cass. But her addiction made her unpredictable. So many things set her off. When she died, I didn't know what to do. I thought her addiction was from lack of attention and too much time on her hands."

"No," said Pam simply.

"No. And, I know that. Now. At least in my head. I went through a lot of therapy. But my heart…"

"Was this what you were referring to when you talked about the major thing that happened?" asked Georgina. "When you talked about the ending of your marriage?" Aubrey nodded.

"Yes. That was my first stone. My marriage. That life."

"Good," said Pam.

"I'm really sorry I didn't say anything before," Aubrey said, reaching for a tissue out of the top of her pack. "I should have said something to you both before now. I just…"

"Don't worry about it. If you remember, I told you that I haven't told anyone but the two of you some of the truths about Mick. I get it," said Pam. "But, Aubrey, that guilt, that pain. That's a heavy thing to carry. I'm glad you have told us."

"It's not that I didn't trust you both, please understand that," said Aubrey, her cheeks heating. She was sorry she hadn't said something before this and yet, she wasn't sure she could have.

"Didn't even cross my mind."

"Mine either," said Georgina.

"Well, Lovelies, we still have ten kilometres to walk today," Pam said. "Shall we head down the mountain?" Pam looked directly at Aubrey when she asked the question. It was up to her. She nodded. She could share more later. They knew her truth. But for now, they needed to keep walking.

With the snow and rain behind them, it felt like Mother Nature agreed that they had overcome their own storms. They had snow-capped mountains cocooning them as they walked toward El Acebo, following a narrow trail bordered by spectacular fields of blossoming wildflowers. As she navigated the path, Aubrey felt lighter and freer than she had in years.

Now she just had to tell Pam and Georgina what the third stone represented.

3 1

TAKING THE LEAP

EL ACEBO

EL ACEBO WAS BUILT on a mountaintop overlooking Ponferrada. Knowing they would need some quiet and time to reflect, they each reserved a private room at the Casa de Peregrino. Aubrey walked into her room feeling this could very well be a five-star suite. She wondered if Pam or Georgina had noticed a similar shift in what luxury meant. Clean sheets, fresh towels, and a bathroom all to herself went a long way towards extravagance these days. She sprawled out on the firm queen bed, staring at the ceiling. This is no Parador, but she was glad for the private space so she could decompress.

She smiled when she thought of their descent. Once she told them about Cass singing "Let It Go" to her, Pam began singing the song from the very beginning. Aubrey only knew the chorus, but Pam sang the entire song on her own, making them laugh. Pam said she'd heard the song every day for an entire year from a gaggle of five-year-old girls. The song was now etched in her mind forever. And not in a good way either, she'd joked. That was the moment that made the rest of the descent lighter. She would be forever grateful to Pam for that.

She decided not to linger too long in her room. She wanted to spend some time with these women who had truly been her Camino Angels today. She had broken at the top of that pile, but they were there to pick up her pieces and carry her down the mountain. She felt their love like never before and needed to be around them. She quickly showered, grabbed her dirty clothes and headed downstairs. Georgina was already sitting in the bar.

"Pam said she'll be five minutes. That was ten minutes ago," Georgina said. Aubrey smiled and kissed Georgina on the cheek, surprising her.

"Thank you for today," she said.

"Of course," Georgina said with a gentle smile. "Are you okay?"

"Yes. I feel, I don't know, relieved in a way."

"I do too. Who knew laying a stone on a pile of others would do that?" Georgina said. They both knew it was more than that. They'd walked five hundred kilometres and sorted through a lot of mental anguish to get to this place.

Pam walked in and announced she'd secured the washing machine. She just needed their clothes to add to the load. Georgina and Aubrey happily passed theirs over. Aubrey ordered a beer for her and they found a table outside inside the large outdoor gazebo.

"So, I want to be nosy and ask you both what your stones represented?" Aubrey asked, when Pam re-joined them. "And if you don't want to share, that's fine."

"I'm okay to share," said Georgina. "I was curious too but didn't want to ask while we were there." Pam nodded agreement.

"Shall I go first?" Aubrey asked. "I want to add to what I said earlier." With a nod from Georgina, she continued.

"The first stone represented my marriage. I held on to a lot of angst, a lot of anger. Not only toward Brendon and his behaviour after Cass died, but also his lack of willingness to put us first before his mother. In hindsight, there were three of us in the marriage. His mother, Brendon and me. I was emotionally strangled with her presence every single day." She took a sip of her beer before continuing.

"I wrote in my journal last night about what I want in future relationships. The process allowed me to identify everything wrong with my marriage. Seeing it in black and white made me comprehend just how many things were wrong. So, today, I let it all go. I want to move forward."

Aubrey was ready to say goodbye to the negativity that clouded her since ending her marriage, something she wasn't aware of before this Camino journey. She understood now, she would never compromise or settle for anything less than what she wanted. And she knew she was finally ready to open her heart again.

"I wrote stuff down last night too, about my marriage," said Georgina. "But go on. I'll talk about that when it's my turn."

"The other was about letting go of the guilt of Cass' death. I've been hanging on to the idea that I could have saved her, despite the months of therapy. But being here, having the conversations I've had, I realised that I did everything I could." She laughed. "When we were in Orisson, I told you the reason for my walking was 'a change of life, a change of scenery and a fresh adventure', but it's more than that. I knew the change of life was to move on from my marriage. The change of scenery and fresh adventure were simply a way to forget about the past two years for a while. It's been excruciating at times. I didn't know my reason for walking until today. At one point, I thought it was to be here for everyone else. To help Hannah, and the two of you, through your own issues. But my reason for walking is to let go of the guilt I've been hanging on to. To be okay with who I am and to be okay with the decisions I've made. And now, I understand, truly understand, that it was Cass' choice to make. Her decision to die. They were her burdens. Ones she could no longer carry. Not mine. So that was my second stone."

"And the third stone?" asked Georgina.

Aubrey hesitated, wondering if she wanted to admit the last one openly. What the hell, she thought. It was all part of it.

"Yes, my third," she said, her head bowed. She looked at her friends in turn while taking a deep breath. She smiled, embarrassed by what she was about to admit. "The third stone represented my fear. Letting go of my fears to move forward and do something different with my life." She stopped, took a drink from her beer, hoping to find some gumption, then jumped into her admission.

"I told you about my dream of being a jewellery designer in Santo

Domingo," she said in a quiet voice. "When Cass died, I had a major breakdown and made some very bad business decisions. My reputation in the business world suffered. Maybe to the point of no return. I don't know. But it was bad. I burned a lot of bridges."

"And, if I'm honest, I am terrified of stepping back into that world. I know I need to get over myself and trust in what I am doing. I've created some designs already and I have a few contacts who didn't want to burn me at the stake. But, until now, I've been afraid to send my ideas to any of those people."

"You have to do it," said Georgina. "Being a jewellery designer makes sense for you."

She looked sheepishly at Georgina, "What if I fail?" she said. Georgina snorted, trying to hold in the belly laugh threatening to explode. Pam sat back in her chair, whistling thru her teeth.

"But what if you don't?" said Georgina. "Isn't that what you've been saying to me about my photography?" Aubrey nodded, looking down to wipe the condensation from her glass. They had caught her in her own trap. She could dish out the encouragement, the push for others to pursue their dreams, but doing it herself was another matter.

"Aubrey... I will do you a deal," said Georgina. Aubrey looked at her with raised eyebrows. "I will leap if you will." Aubrey saw her fear reflected in Georgina's eyes. How could she not, she thought? She talked the talk, now she needed to walk the walk.

"Fine," Aubrey said, taking a huge drink from her beer. It was now or never.

"Good, because otherwise that would have been a waste of a stone I laid down," said Georgina.

"What do you mean?" asked Aubrey.

"I laid two stones. One was about the conflicts with Patrick. Our separation, my marriage woes. What I wrote last night, well, is my realisation that we need to throw out the traditional marriage ideals and all those stupid expectations. We need to create a marriage that works for us. We could have the marriage we both want. He's expressed some stuff in our recent emails that I wasn't aware of. What he wants is not traditional, that's for sure, but it's not outlandish either. We don't have anyone whispering in our ears telling us what we should be and what they expect us to be anymore. The question remains whether we can find our way to that place. From what I've learned from my Camino Family," she continued with a smile and tears in her eyes, "is that I need to speak up for what I want."

"Well done. That's a positive first step," said Aubrey. "And the other stone?"

"Fear. My fear of going after what I truly want professionally. I have built a successful business with the café, but I'm not excited by it anymore. It's now Nicole's dream to follow. Now I want to pursue my photography."

"Finally!" said Pam.

"Oh, I have wanted to for ages," she said, a blush so pink it could have burned her skin, "but I am so scared of failing. What if I look like an idiot? What if I am not as good as you guys keep telling me I am? What if I invest in this business and it fails?" said Georgina, her voice cracking under the pressure of her own expectations.

"As a wise woman asked me recently: But what if you don't?" said Aubrey.

"Yes. That's why I made the deal with you. If I'm putting aside the fear, you can too." Georgina said, determination replacing the fear.

"Okay, okay. I'm in," said Aubrey, then looked toward Pam. Georgina followed suit. "Your turn."

Pam took a deep breath. "I had only one stone. That was to leave my sad excuse of a marriage in the past and start living life on my terms. Since Mick died, I've just been existing, going through the motions. I appreciate now that life can be fun, loving and supportive. You guys have helped me remember that. So, I will take a leap too."

Then she told them about a man named Jack.

3 2

ADVICE FOR YOUR YOUNGER
SELF

EL ACEBO TO CACABELOS

"WHAT ARE YOU GOING TO DO?" asked Georgina.

Jack, it turned out, had been the boy Pam had been dating before Mick had bulldozed himself into her life. Jack had recently contacted her through Facebook.

Pilgrims were stacked, shoulder to shoulder, along the long wooden tables for dinner. The surrounding noise was muted by their focus on Jack's story.

"It sounds like he really wants to connect with you," said Aubrey. Pam was quiet for a minute.

"I don't know," Pam said, filling their wineglasses from the carafe on their table. She took a gulp of wine. She was already tipsy from the two beers she'd had earlier. "He kind of popped up out of nowhere."

"Sounds like he's looking for an answer based on his message," said Aubrey. Pam had told them how her parents had forced her to drop all contact with Jack when they discovered he wasn't Catholic. They were not at all pleased and demanded she end it.

"I suppose he does deserve an answer," Pam responded quietly. "It was just so long ago. Over forty years. That's a long time. Things were different back then."

"It has been a long time, but it sounds like you and Jack were happy. Parental intervention can be lethal," said Aubrey.

"Remember Pam, it wasn't your choice to walk away," said Georgina.

"The thing is, Jack doesn't know the full story," Pam said. "I only told him I couldn't see him anymore."

"It sounds like it'll be good for you both to get the truth out there," said Georgina.

"And once he knows the truth, it may be beneficial that Mick is dead, especially if you tell him everything," said Aubrey. Pam looked confused. She continued, "You know, once he knows what happened in the back seat of Mick's car, and the reason your parents insisted you marry him. He may be furious. I know I am that that happened to you. Are you ready for that if you tell him the entire truth?"

"I don't know," Pam said, stabbing her salad like it was Mick's heart. "If I respond to him, how can I not tell him the truth? What's the point otherwise? I just don't know. It's such a long time ago."

"How did you feel about Jack back then?" Aubrey asked. A look took over Pam's face like she was ready to throw her walls up. "Honestly."

Pam sighed. Her face softened, something Aubrey had rarely seen. "I..." She took a sip of her wine.

"I... I was in love with him," Pam whispered.

"Would you regret not responding, years from now, when you knew you had the chance?" Aubrey asked. Pam hesitated, then nodded.

"Then you should reach out to him," said Georgina, taking her hand and giving it a quick squeeze.

By the time dessert came around, they had given Pam some sound advice on how to respond to Jack. Georgina said that she and Aubrey were about to take scary leaps, so why not join the party?

· · ·

THE FOLLOWING MORNING, AUBREY STOPPED AT THE RECEPTION DESK AND ordered a taxi. They'd already passed some lavender growing wild on the way into El Acebo and Aubrey was allergic to the flower many considered calming. For her, she wanted to scratch her eyes out and couldn't breathe around the stuff. Lee, who was now two days ahead, warned them that it was prolific all the way down the mountain into Molinaseca. Aubrey didn't want to be tramping down the mountain and have her throat seize, no matter how much antihistamine she inhaled. Pam admitted her knees had been rubbery after their walk from Rabanal and Georgina wasn't keen to walk down on her own. So, they agreed to skip ahead via taxi.

They were unexpectedly entertained on their ride down to Ponferrada. Their exuberant driver played tour guide. Since he only spoke Spanish, he used Google translate on his iPhone to communicate. He educated them on the names of wildflowers, even slowing to point out a certain flowering tree to Pam in the front seat. It was rotten luck to suffer this allergy, Aubrey thought, as she saw the gorgeous lavender and other wildflowers growing abundantly around them. Pam cringed and tightened her hand around her seatbelt whenever they took the tight, hairpin turns. But the driver was used to the narrow, winding road. She admitted later that she was totally freaked out, but Aubrey found it to be a glorious way to spend thirty minutes as they zipped through the switchbacks and into the valley below.

When they were dropped off in Ponferrada, they had coffee in a café facing the imposing Templars Castle. It was a grand fortress built in the 13th Century by the Knights Templar, Pam read to them from her phone, rumoured to be full of Templar symbols. Today, it housed the Templars Library. Pam asked if they wanted to check it out. When they saw the entrance fees and, Georgina her watch, they collectively passed.

They followed the path past the soccer fields and continued up the long hill out of town. After crossing the bridge, they walked along the undulating dirt track bordered by fields of robust looking grape vines.

"Okay, question time," announced Aubrey with excitement in her voice. Georgina groaned.

"What kind of questions?" Pam asked.

"I have a list of questions I brought with me. We started them on the Meseta, but we only got through about ten of them," said Aubrey.

"Okay," said Pam.

"They're good questions," said Georgina. "Some a bit embarrassing, but it made for an enjoyable distraction, that's for sure." Aubrey smiled over at her.

"Okay, here goes. What is the one piece of advice you would give to your younger self?" asked Aubrey.

"Easy," said Pam. "Don't marry Mick. He's a dick." They all laughed at that.

"Too obvious Pam," said Aubrey.

"Yeah, didn't think I'd get away with that," Pam said with a cheeky grin. "Okay. Don't allow religion to dictate your life. My Catholic upbringing is so engrained, I'm still battling it. Had I loosened the apron strings I wouldn't have married Mick. Fuck, I would not have stayed pregnant! But that's religion restricting you too. So, I suppose I'd tell myself to stay the hell away from the church. Or at least, go in with your eyes open. Your turn, Georgina."

"Yeah, I saw your finger salute at Cruz de Ferro," Georgina said. Pam smirked. "Aubrey should go next," Georgina said, distracted by the field of red poppies they'd come to. Georgina stopped to take photos. Pam stopped and turned her pack to Aubrey, signalling a need for her water. It had become a request that no longer needed words.

"No. You're going next Georgina," Aubrey said, taking a drink herself. "I'm still pondering."

Georgina rose from her crouch.

"Okay," she said, thumbing to the direction of her water. Aubrey handed her the bottle. She took a swig.

"Then I will say," she said, pausing a beat, "don't be afraid to speak up when something is important." She passed her water back to Aubrey, who replaced it into Georgina's side pocket. "I mean, I can say that, now I've walked five hundred kilometres and I have only just put that advice into play, but I realise it's time I stop being a doormat. Sometimes it's okay to let things go, but other times, when it's something important, like with Patrick and the farm, or when he disrespects my business, those kinds of things are when I need to speak up. And I haven't until now. Okay Aubrey, now you."

"Hmm. I would have to say trust my instincts. If something seems off, it's because it is. Trust my gut. And…" she hesitated, not sure if she should admit this part out loud, "well, you'll think I'm nuts, but what the hell, you probably do already anyway. Trust the vibe you're reading from a person or situation. Listen to that and not what the person is saying. It can be very telling."

"I have a question for you," said Georgina, looking at her quizzically. "Are you an empath?"

"A what?!" said Pam, looking utterly confused. "What the fuck is an empath?"

"Yes, I suppose I am. I've had three random people call me that since I was a teenager."

"Nicole is too," Georgina said. She turned to Pam. "An empath is someone in tune with the spiritual world. They can read how others are feeling even before they realise it themselves. It's like super-duper intuition when they tap into it. Many even see or feel spirits, but some ignore it all together. Nicole researched it a lot." She smiled at Aubrey as if understanding.

"It took me a long time to recognise it in myself," Aubrey said. "I ignored it for most of my life. Clearly. I would have figured out Cass's issues had I been in tune with it. I didn't give it room until I started travelling in the campervan to be honest. Once I gave it room, it became obvious. I finally accepted it's part of me."

"Wow. I had no idea that was even a thing," said Pam. "I guess spirituality is something different to everyone. For me, spirituality is part of your religion. My parents raised me to believe that you find your spirituality by going to church. I'm not sure I accept that anymore. I walked away from my religion, but I can't say I've walked away from my spirituality."

"Yeah, to me spirituality and religion are not the same thing," said Aubrey. "You don't have to go to church to be spiritual. You don't even have to be religious to be spiritual. You can have peace and a sense of being anywhere. Here, on the Camino, I am in touch with my spirituality. I can't always say the same when I'm in a church."

"Same," Georgina said. "My parents didn't raise me within the bounds of any religion. My dad used to say he found God, or whatever it was, out on his boat in the early mornings. Mum said she found it in her garden. For me, I think I'm more like my dad. I find myself connected spiritually, early in the mornings, with the sun beginning to rise. I find an overwhelming sense of peace and I guess freedom too. It's where I can be whoever I want to be and that's okay."

"As long as you have love, whether you believe in the Universe or God or Mother Earth, love is the key," said Pam, smiling as they came into Cacabelos. "But tonight, ladies, we sleep in a church! Let's hope it doesn't get struck by lightning!"

Pam cackled a laugh they had not heard in its raw form. It was a beautiful, carefree sound.

33

HOW DIFFERENT THE ALBERGUES ARE

CACABELOS TO TRABADELO VIA VILLAFRANCA DEL
BIERZO

A COLD FRONT hit the town just as they settled in for the night at the municipal albergue. The accompanying rain made everything inside feel damp. Since municipals were the cheapest places to stay, they expected the room to be bare bones, but the stone walls and tiled floors made the rooms seem as cold as a freezer. Aubrey was thankful for the extra blankets the albergue had provided.

Aubrey rose before sunrise, stiff from the cold. Had she had a roommate, she may have suggested sharing a bed, she had been that cold. The blankets, it turned out, had been as threadbare as the room.

She touched her hiking pants hanging over the simple wooden chair. Still damp. Shit. She had slept in her leggings and now it seemed she would wear them to Villafranca de Bierzo. It was not the fashion statement she preferred to make, but that was what she got for having a lighter load in her backpack. She was lucky she hadn't had to do this before now.

"Morning," she heard Georgina say, as she snapped together the last of her pack's buckles.

"Morning George. How did you two do last night?" Aubrey said, dropping her pack to fish the safety pins out.

"Bloody freezing. You?" asked Georgina, crossing her arms to the frosty morning.

"Same. I think I slept in everything I had dry last night," said Aubrey, pinning her pants to the outside of her pack, hoping the sun would find them.

"Yep. Us too. A nice hot breakfast will warm us. I'm thinking bacon and eggs," Georgina said. Aubrey thought that sounded great as she stretched her back.

"Thank goodness it's a short day. Only eight kilometres, right?" Aubrey asked. "I'm looking forward to that!"

"Yeah, me too," Georgina said, then poked her head back into their room. "Pam, are you ready yet?"

Aubrey rolled her eyes. She could only hope this would be the one day that Pam would hurry. It was too cold to be standing around waiting for her.

It was almost ten when they set off up the hill out of town with bellies full of eggs and coffee. They were walking through vibrant green vineyards just coming into bloom. In the valley, they passed through a small derelict village that seemed without services. By now, the coffee had kicked in. Pam was literally hopping in place, desperate to find a toilet. They finally found one tucked in behind an unoccupied café. While Aubrey and Georgina looked around for someone to ask, Pam rushed around the corner, the door banging shut behind her.

Making their way through the rest of the village, it seemed impossible to Aubrey that many of the buildings were still standing. Georgina took a photo of a house with its walls collapsing. The rest was held up by a steel beam. When they saw movement within, they were amazed to see that someone still lived there.

Leaving town and into the countryside, they walked toward a beautiful stone house on a hill overlooking a fruitful vineyard. The owner had planted gorgeous princess-pink rose bushes at the end of each lush row of vines. Aubrey bent to smell a rose and found the scent so pungent it was heady. With such a gorgeous setting, they knew Georgina might be a while, prompting Pam to find a shady spot to wait. She invited Aubrey to join her and they shared a handful of dried fruit.

When they reached Villafranca del Bierzo it was just after noon, too early to check in. They left their packs just inside the door of their albergue and wandered through the village. They each bought more magnesium tablets at the Farmacia and easy snacks for the trail at the Supermercado. At one, they returned to their albergue. Their host welcomed them inside, offering a cold lemonade. She asked for their passports and credentials and then invited them to relax while she processed their check in.

After settling in, they walked to a restaurant in the piazza, shaded by the stone portico and an umbrella. The day had warmed, but not uncomfortably. They ordered burgers and cool drinks. Aubrey looked around and noticed many locals enjoying the day, drinking beers or cocktails, while watching their children play football in the square.

"What day is it?" asked Georgina, after the server delivered their food.

Pam looked down at her phone. "Saturday," she said.

"Ah, that explains why there are so many locals out and about today," said Georgina. "Geez, I have completely lost track of the day, not to mention the date. How long have we been walking?"

"I noted in my journal yesterday that it was day thirty-six," Aubrey said. "Is that right?"

"Yep," said Pam. "My journal says the same."

"Did either of you sense a presence at the albergue when we were there earlier?" asked Aubrey. She took a sip of her cola. "I've felt spirits before. Cass often visits me. She did at Eunate. But this was different." She wasn't shy about sharing her experiences anymore.

"No," said Georgina. "Did you?" she asked, before taking a bite of her burger.

Aubrey nodded. "I did. And this time it wasn't Cass. It seemed like, I don't know, maybe an older gentleman?"

"I hate to admit this," said Pam, "but before showers, I swear I put my comb on the chest of drawers in the corner with my other things. When I returned, it was lying on the floor on the other side of the room. Everything else was still on the chest. I was the last one out and the first one back in. The door was locked in between so no one else could have touched it. I don't believe in that stuff, the supernatural, but I know you guys do. Thought I'd mention it."

"It was definitely something," Aubrey said, taking a bite of her burger, juice dribbling down her chin. Pam was eating an ensalada mixta, a tuna salad, with a little more grace than she and Georgina were managing with their burgers.

"Speaking of journals," Pam said. "I want to take some time to write today. I'm way behind." Georgina said she wanted to wander more and take photos, which allowed

Aubrey to feel less guilty about trying to do some yoga. It had been a few days since she'd had a good session. They'd passed the river on their earlier wander and the park looked to be a promising place to stretch out. So, with an agreement to go their separate ways for the afternoon, they finished their lunches and headed in various directions.

When Aubrey returned to the albergue, she explored the beautifully restored three-hundred-year-old house. She couldn't shake the sense of a spirit and was curious who's spirit it was. Maria, the hostess, found her staring at a painting on the wall. She knew the spiritual presence wasn't the man in the portrait, but another male who had been in the house. Of that she was sure. She asked Maria about the painting and her family's history. Maria shared that her grandfather, the man in the painting, created a beautiful and successful vineyard that the family had owned for years. He was also a well-known musician in the region. The home was always full of laughter and music, she said. A few years earlier, they decided to turn their family home into an albergue, in hope that the pilgrims coming through, would experience the same joy the house had provided the family.

The mystery was solved when Aubrey learned Maria's father had passed away fairly recently. Aubrey knew then it was the father's spirit still present in the albergue. She didn't mention it to Maria. She didn't want to upset her. She would instead share this information with Georgina and Pam and put their curiosity to rest.

· · ·

AFTER A SIMPLE BREAKFAST THE NEXT MORNING, THEY SET OFF AT A leisurely pace to Trabadelo. It was only eight kilometres again, but most of their walk followed the road and the pavement was hard on Aubrey's feet. The last inserts had helped, but when she hit asphalt, the pain returned with a vengeance.

They continued following the yellow arrows, eventually coming to a smaller country road lined with chestnut trees, their husks covering the road. Amongst the trees were piles of freshly cut logs and kindling. Georgina exclaimed that would keep her house warm for years!

"There it is. See the Aussie flag?!" Pam did a jig and then giggled like a schoolgirl. She'd been telling everyone about Casa Susi's for days.

"You have to stay at that albergue," she'd say. "It's run by an Aussie girl."

Aubrey was eager to meet Susi. Pam explained the woman had sold her flower business in Sydney and, after walking many Caminos of her own, decided to open her albergue on the Camino Francés. She scouted far and wide for the perfect place, eventually finding a derelict building in Trabadelo that she restored into what was now a beautiful, simple albergue.

Since they were too early to check in, they found a bar and had a second breakfast comprising of café con leche and homemade carrot cake. Georgina had turned her nose up at the coffee but praised the cake like it was the best thing she'd ever eaten. When one o'clock rolled around, they walked down the road to Susi's who promptly stuck her head out of the upstairs window and said, "You three have got to be The Lovelies!"

"Yes! That's us!" said Pam, with an enormous grin. Pam had clearly booked them in under their moniker.

"I'll be right down!" said Susi, poking her head back through the open window.

Moments later, the barn door opened and out came Susi with her partner Fermin, hugging them all as if they were lifelong friends.

"Welcome!" Susi said, "It's always nice to have Aussies stay. We have four others staying tonight, along with two Americans, an English girl, and two Koreans. It'll be an interesting night!"

After check-in and a long chat, Susi showed them the enormous room at the back on the ground floor, where single beds lined the walls.

"Woo-hoo! Single beds!" said Aubrey. "Nice change from the bunks."

Pam dug into her backpack, then turned to Susi.

"The Australian forum suggested bringing you something from home," Pam said. She handed Susi a small packet. Susi looked at it with curiosity.

"It's ground wattle seed! It's delicious when you put it on roasted vegetables and a must for a veggie lasagne!" Pam explained. Susi got teary at the gesture. Aubrey recognised homesickness anywhere.

The night turned out to be a comedy of errors. The Americans, friends of the four other Australians, played dress up by donning American Pilgrim outfits, while their Aussie friends handed out leis and other Hawaiian paraphernalia. The English girl looked a little stunned at first, but quickly snapped to and ran to her backpack for smiley face stickers to hand out. When the Korean gentleman placed his stickers all over his face, Pam followed suit. By the time Susi and Fermin came downstairs with the homemade pilgrim dinner, the party was well and truly underway.

Before they could enjoy the delicious vegetarian meal, Susi announced they'd like to do a round table: everyone should state who they were, where they were from and whether this was a first, or tenth, Camino. Susi started the discussion and told the story of her very romantic meeting with Fermin. It turned out, Fermin, a Spaniard from Pamplona, had been Pilgrim Number Thirty through the Casa Susi doors. He promptly returned after making it as far as O Cebreiro before turning back. He was sure there had been a connection with Susi. Luckily it had been mutual, because here they were, partners in life and partners in their albergue business.

The round table was as chaotic as the attendees, all laughing, getting up in each other's stories. But when it was the Korean's turn to speak, the table quietened. He cleared his throat before continuing.

"Hello. My name is Kim. This is my wife, Li. I speak little English. She speaks zero," he said, turning to his wife, before turning back to the table. "But I want to say I love my wife very, very much," then he reached over and kissed his wife's cheek. They all watched her blush. And with that, he shook his head and gestured to the next person. The simplicity of the words and the gesture brought tears to Aubrey's eyes. She saw the love and the connection, not only with this couple but also with Susi and Fermin. It was this kind of love she wanted to find for herself.

The next morning, most pilgrims left at sunrise. The three of them took their time. When they reached the front room, the breakfast Susi and Fermin had laid out for them the night before, filled the kitchenette. They had thoughtfully included a jar of Vegemite. As they ate, they reflected on what a great time they had the night before. They swapped information with Helen, the English girl from Exeter, who had provided some solid recommendations based on her previous Caminos. By seven, they were out the door, with the barn door clicking behind them.

It seemed an interesting process to run an albergue, Aubrey thought. She had listened while Pam chatted with Susi and Fermin the afternoon before. Susi described how she found herself in Spain to look for an albergue, and then the process to set it up. It seemed like an interesting life. Aubrey knew it was not the life she would enjoy, but she wondered if it would be for Pam. But a seed had already been planted without Aubrey's help. As they headed out of Trabadelo, Pam was playing the 'what if' game, pondering what it would be like to move to Spain and run her own albergue.

34

BRINGING OUT THE QUESTIONS

TRABADELO TO O CEBREIRO VIA LAS HERRARIAS

THEY WERE SITTING in the shade outside a café in Vega de Valcarce, sharing a piece of Torta de Santiago, the cake of St. James, the official cake of the Camino. Its origins dated back to the Middle Ages. It was the first time they had seen it offered on the Camino. Georgina was excited to try it. She took a bite and her eyes rolled back into her head. Words of ecstasy mumbled from her very full mouth.

"Are you guys still okay with stopping before O Cebreiro?" asked Pam, taking a piece of the cake before Georgina devoured it all.

"Oh yes," Aubrey said. "I'll be happy to stop to be honest. This road walking is killing me." Aubrey knew reaching O Cebreiro would be a climb.

"It's always a slim chance to get a bed up there, but it would be for sure if we kept walking today. I think we're better off going up in the morning," said Pam. Georgina was still digging into the cake while nodding in agreement.

"Yeah, I read up on O Cebreiro last night," said Aubrey. "I'm excited to see the mountains."

"Should we consider riding horses up?" asked Georgina, holding her hand in front of her mouth since she still had cake in her mouth. She swallowed, then continued her train of thought. "Sorry. I read before I came to Spain, that it's a possibility."

"I'm not too keen on horses anymore," said Pam. "A horse threw me when I was in my thirties and it kills the urge to ride again."

"Same. I had a horse throw me when I was ten," said Aubrey, "but go for it, if you want to do that Georgina. Don't let us stop you."

"Nah, I'd rather stick with you guys," said Georgina, going for another bite of cake. "This cake is delicious by the way. You should have some before I finish it. I am going to find a recipe and add it to the café menu."

"Brilliant idea!" said Aubrey, "I'd buy it." Georgina grinned.

"Okay, I need to call and make sure we can get into the place Helen recommended at Las Herrerías. I forgot to do it last night," said Pam. "I hope they can understand my butchered Spanish." Much to their relief, Pam managed to secure the last three beds at Albergue Lixa.

AT SEVEN THE NEXT MORNING, FOG LINGERED IN THE VALLEY AND FROST covered much of the paddocks, a chilly reminder that they were already at elevation. The air was crisp and cold. They hadn't layered up too much, knowing they'd be spending the day climbing a mountain.

"I was looking on the forum this morning," said Pam, as they set out. "They say you must arrive in O Cebreiro about an hour before the Municipal opens for any chance of getting a bed." Their boots crunched under the frost-covered ground as they walked out of the village, passing the horses awaiting their pilgrim riders. Georgina patted one, then took its photo, before catching up again with Aubrey and Pam. They'd slowed for her but had not stopped. They'd learned that Georgina would catch up eventually.

"What time does the Municipal open?" asked Georgina, looking down at her watch. Aubrey smiled when she realised that it had been a while since Georgina had done that.

"One," said Pam, checking the note on her phone.

"Oh shit. We're out of luck then," said Aubrey.

"No, I don't think so," said Pam. "It's only just after seven now. It's only eight kilometres. Even though it's all uphill, I think we can swing three kilometres an hour. If we can, we'll make it in plenty of time. I bet staying in Las Herrerías last night put us ahead of the pack."

"Let's hope so!" said Aubrey.

"Wow, it's such a beautiful morning," said Georgina as they turned left just outside of the village. They continued quietly, enjoying the sounds of the morning as they made their way through a lush chestnut forest. When they approached the rocky switchbacks, Georgina groaned.

"It will be a hard slog, but I came prepared!" said Aubrey. She pulled out the folded paper from her side pocket.

"How? Did you hire a Sherpa?" asked Pam. She was already like a little blue engine in her own rhythm. Aubrey was walking behind her.

"With the two hundred questions sheet," shared Aubrey, shaking out the page. "This will get us up the damn mountain today!" Georgina snorted.

"We'll see how we do," said Pam. "I'm going slow, but I'll get there eventually. Just call me a turtle."

"I'll call you 'Turt Russell', how's that?!" Georgina said, winning a laugh from them all.

"Okay," said Pam. "Bring on the questions."

Aubrey shook out the paper in a grand gesture. "Okay, first question: What do you have doubts about?"

"Geezus. Fuck," said Pam. Aubrey and Georgina both let out a quick laugh. "Way to start easy there Aubrey."

"Ah, there's the Pam I know and love," said Georgina. "I was wondering where the drunken sailor had gone. You haven't been swearing much of late."

"I was trying to be good," said Pam. "Okay, my answer is getting up this fucking mountain in one piece today."

"Fair enough. I'll let you off easy since it's the first question," said Aubrey. "Georgina. What do you have doubts about?"

"Can I repeat an answer?" asked Georgina slyly.

"You can, but I'm not letting you off that easy," said Aubrey.

"Okay. Fine." She hesitated before adding, "Oh! Simple answer. I doubt I'll be successful with my photography, considering the talent already out there," said Georgina.

"Hmm. It's not true, but okay," said Aubrey, knowing they'd both taken the simple way out. "I'll answer easy then too. I doubt I will ever be a size eight again, but then again, I don't want to be."

"Okay, next?" Pam said, taking a quick break, determining how to navigate the rocky path.

Aubrey looked down at the sheet, taking advantage of Pam's break. "What gets you fired up?" she asked. "As in, what pisses you off? Pam, you're up."

"Fired up," repeated Pam. "Okay... lying, arrogance. And opulence, when there is so much poverty. Did you see the Burgos Cathedral? So wrong," Aubrey realised she'd forgotten to ask Pam if she'd visited. They had been too caught up in what was going on with Hannah and Marinka's departure back to Germany.

"Don't go to the Vatican then!" said Aubrey.

"Oh?" asked Pam. "Why? I haven't been."

"Because when I visited, the tapestry room alone made me feel ill," said Aubrey. "There is so much money in those works that you could sell one or two in a Sotheby's auction and resolve a third world country's poverty. It made me angry that the Catholic Church has so much money in art and artefacts, yet there are people in Catholic-dominant countries dying from starvation and sanitation issues."

"Now we know what gets Aubrey fired up!" said Georgina.

"But as a Catholic Pam, you need to go at least once," said Aubrey. "It is worth it. Despite the overwhelming opulence, the architecture is beautiful, and I know you would appreciate that."

"From an artistic point of view," said Georgina, "it awakens your senses. When I went to the Vatican, I spent three days walking around taking photographs. It really awakens the creative self."

"Yes, that's true. Good point George. But three days? Really?" Aubrey asked Georgina. Georgina shrugged. "Well, Pam, I guess you will just need to go and see it for yourself."

"I'll consider it when I'm done with the Camino," said Pam. "I was thinking of heading to the U.K. for a few months then on to Italy and France before I go home. I am in no rush."

"Dream trip," said Georgina.

"I'd go straight there," Pam said, "if it weren't for the bloody Schengen Agreement restricting us to our visit of ninety days! Didn't they consider people flew halfway across the world on a once in a life-time trip to see these places?"

They hit the next switchback and pulled aside to admire the view, just as some other pilgrims passed them. It was beautiful walking through the forest. The questions made the climb a little easier than focusing on the walk alone. Aubrey couldn't imagine the mental strain of doing such a climb without the conversation to distract them.

"Okay, Aubrey. Anything more to add on what gets you fired up?" asked Georgina.

"Yes," said Aubrey. "Mental health does not get the same priority as physical health in the medical system. There are too many hoops to jump through to get help with a mental health issue. It's disheartening. I guess I have a major issue with dishonesty too. But I have a softer side for people with mental illness who lie. I wonder sometimes if they don't realise that they are lying because of their addiction, or their illness?"

"I think it's different when it's a lying sack of shit who's sleeping with another woman, versus someone who feels they have to lie to survive," said Pam. Aubrey couldn't agree more.

"It's a fine line, I suppose," said Georgina, "I mean, lying is lying. It still hurts, but sometimes people have no other choice, or feel they don't."

"Good point," agreed Aubrey. "Okay, next question," she said, reading the page. "Oh, this is good. What do you feel is the best thing about yourself?"

"Oh shit, I don't know," said Pam. "Someone else. I have to think about it."

"Okay. Georgina, you're up," said Aubrey.

"Gee, thanks Turt Russell!" said Georgina, taking some time to ponder the question. "Okay. I think it's my sense of loyalty. I am a shy person, but if I trust you, if I'm friends with you, I will be loyal to that friendship until proven otherwise."

"Hmm... good answer," said Aubrey. "I would say the same, although I don't have a large circle of friends." She stopped, realising Pam had slowed down considerably.

"Wait for me," said Pam, looking like a little caboose, huffing a little, trying to keep up the pace. "I don't want to miss the answers!"

"Sorry. We'll slow down," Aubrey said. "Water break?" Everyone agreed.

"Aubrey, you were saying?" said Pam, as they began again, this time taking it slower.

"Okay, I would say my best thing is my intuition," Aubrey said. "Now that I have learned to listen to it. I can read a room, read a person, sense when something is not right. It took me a long time to believe that about myself."

"Loyalty is a good answer for me too," Pam said, answering the question. "I was very protective of my little ones in my classroom. But I would say perseverance is my best quality. I keep slogging through it all. I don't quit easily."

"Even when you should!" said Aubrey. Pam nodded. "Do we need a longer break? There's a village just ahead."

"Should be La Faba," said Pam. "I could use a water refill."

They followed the yellow arrows until they came to a café and a communal water fountain. After refilling their water, they set their packs against the nearby stone wall and Pam took out some trail mix to share.

As Aubrey focused on working out what had been digging into her back, she heard Pam mumble, "mmm...fine specimen." Aubrey looked up and saw a tall, lean guy refilling his water from the public fountain. She guessed him to be around her age, his blonde-red hair cut short. He mounted his backpack as if it was empty and placed his wide-brimmed hat back on. He reached around and popped his water bottle back into his pack's side pocket, a limber gesture he made look easy, then readjusted the hip belt. He glanced over and looked away quickly, before looking back at her again. He touched his hat and smiled, his laugh lines cutting deep into his cheeks. He wished them a Buen

Camino, then followed the arrows pointing up the hill. She and Pam stared after him, mumbling Buen Camino in reply, just as Georgina reappeared from the café's bathroom.

"Damn, what did I miss? The expression on your faces tells me it was something good," said Georgina, popping a roll of toilet paper back into her top pouch.

"A fine specimen," Pam repeated, before shaking her head. "Yet young enough to be my son, no doubt."

"Oh, I don't know about that," said Aubrey, standing to hoist her backpack on. The guy was younger than Pam, that was true, and he was lovely. His eyes were smiling, one slightly larger than the other she'd noticed, the colour of clear blue water. He'd looked right into her, like he could see her for who she was. Her heart was still racing from his glance.

"Come on. Let's keep going," said Pam. "Maybe we'll catch up to him and Georgina can check him out too."

"You know," Georgina said, "Ben would remind you it's sexist or something, ogling a guy like that and calling him a fine specimen."

"Probably. I don't care," said Pam. "I wouldn't actually say it to the guy. I'm only saying it to you two. You know, those I trust. Remember what we just talked about, about loyalty and all that?" said Pam. Aubrey laughed.

"Scolded!" said Aubrey, poking Georgina like a precocious teenager behind Pam's back as they continued up the trail. "He was cute though."

"Yes, and he definitely noticed you too," Pam said. You couldn't put anything past Pam. The double take and the tip of the hat kind of gave that away.

"Okay, what's the next question?" said Georgina. "Let's keep those questions going. They are definitely helping with this walk today. And they are good questions."

Aubrey pulled the piece of paper back out from the pocket on her thigh.

"Okay. Let's see. Here's a dreamy one. If you had no financial worries, what would your dream life be like, and why?"

"Interesting." said Pam. "I don't have any financial worries anymore and I'm still trying to work out what's next for me. Living in Spain, running an albergue, that sounds good. But I've been thinking of something else for a while. Maybe writing a book. I don't know, I'm still mulling it around. But, if I did that, I'd like to be living in a cottage overlooking water. I'm done with the country life. I want a nice little cottage with a large open pergola, covered in something like jasmine. Beneath that, I'd have an enormous wooden table where I could sit outside and enjoy the weather and write. Then, when company stays, we'd enjoy dinners outside with flowing wine and great conversation. And up the back, or off to the side, whatever, I'd like a little writing studio. One with a potbelly stove for the cold rainy days and maybe a little kitchenette too, so I can make a cuppa without having to go back to the cottage. But the studio would have picture windows that open to views of the water. Or maybe bi-fold doors with a little verandah to let the cool breeze in on the days I want to be writing inside."

"Gee Pam. Doesn't sound like you've given this dream much thought before," Aubrey said, tongue firmly in her cheek. "Sounds amazing though. Will you have a guest room available?"

"Yes! And an open invitation!" said Pam. Her smile was infectious. It was a dreamy idea. If it were hers, she would use the studio to make jewellery.

"I love your vision Pam. I'd like to come and stay for a month or two!" Georgina said.

"Well, let's not get ahead of ourselves. Spain is now in my head. I guess it's more realistic at my age to find the cottage. I'm still looking for the right location," said Pam.

"So, this is happening?" asked Aubrey.

"I think so. I've been searching for a while now. I may extend my parameters. I'm just not finding what I want in New South Wales. Besides, it's too expensive. I may have the money, but I refuse to pay that much!"

"You know Pam," said Georgina. "I may have the piece of property you're looking for. Well, Patrick might. You'd have to build on it, but there's a flat section overlooking the bay that would be perfect for a cottage and writing studio. It's remote, an hour from Hobart, so I'm not sure if you'd like that part, but it could be perfect for you."

"It's something to consider," Pam said, a smile forming on her lips.

"We can talk about it later. I can show you pictures," Georgina said. "I have some on my phone I believe and, if not, I'll email Patrick. We go over there to watch for whales during the season. It's a beautiful spot."

"Okay Aubrey, what about you? What's your dream without worrying about money?"

"My life has been nice already, materially anyway," she said. "I want for nothing. But maybe a lovely spot to set up a home, like Pam, but I'd like something with about five acres. I'd like to have chickens and maybe a goat or two."

"Wasn't Simon looking at a property for you?" asked Georgina.

"Yes. And he did. He said it's been on the market a while. It may work, but he thinks I should view it first before I make an offer. The real estate agent said the sellers aren't in a rush, so if it's there when I get back, I'll check it out. If not, it's not meant to be. Once I have the place though, I want a nice, quiet life. A simple life. If there's nothing else I've learned from this Camino, it's to live with honesty and with minimal things. I can see myself living out the rest of my life as a jewellery designer. But I'd like a nice little place for when my hands cripple up. I don't need a lot to be happy. How about you Georgina?"

"The happiness question has been lingering in my mind for weeks now," she said. "When I started my Camino, I found myself, I don't know, I guess lost. Pam asked me if I was happy. That spun me out for a while. It's why I spent two days walking by myself." Aubrey nodded.

"I feel I am at an age where I should have the life I want," Georgina continued. "And I do. Kind of. But my marriage needs work. And, yes, it's time I got off the proverbial pot and pursued my photography," Georgina said, to cheers from Pam and Aubrey. She continued, "but I like simple. My life is simple, and I want to keep it that way." She stopped for a minute before adding, "I mean, take this view. I could stay here for days and photograph that!"

They stopped and looked around. In the distance, a rust-coloured mass of wildflowers covered the rolling hills. They decided it must be wild heather covering most of the mountain range. In the valley below, the farmhouses looked like specks, their cars like ants, while the fog still lingered in the deep nooks of the valley.

"I wish I had my camera with me," Georgina muttered, turning to walk. "Okay! Ready for the next question."

"I have a harder one. Are you ready for that?"

"Let's hear it," said Pam, trailing Georgina on the narrow path.

"Okay. How would you like to be remembered?" asked Aubrey.

"That's easy," said Pam. "As a kind person."

"Yeah, that's an easy one for me too. Kind. Loyal. Loving. Supportive."

"Well, fine. I'll ask a harder one then," said Aubrey, and searched for a question she knew would send them deep into thought.

"Maybe wait? I am hoping there's a bar up ahead because I need a bloody toilet," said Pam.

They walked into what the guidebook claimed to be a village. It looked more like a rundown farm. The living quarters were above the barn area, which, to their surprise, held livestock and the smell of pure, unfiltered manure. Aubrey couldn't imagine living with that smell coming into the kitchen and house daily, but everyone was different. Further along sat the only bar in the village. The sun had peeped out from behind the clouds, so they voted to sit outside. Georgina joined Pam to order coffees and use the toilet, while Aubrey waited with their backpacks, holding the table. It wasn't busy, but it was clearly a prime spot for a break. She sat down, retied her shoelace, then sat back to people watch.

"You're up," said Pam, coming out with a coffee and croissant. She sat down in the chair opposite Aubrey after placing her goodies on the table. "Not the friendliest service, but it's efficient at least."

With coffees and a pastry each, they enjoyed the sunshine in relative silence, listening to the accents all around them. They said hello to a pregnant German woman they had met at their albergue the night before. The woman reminded them of Hannah, so Aubrey sent her a quick message. Hannah responded quickly, saying she had found her energy and was continuing with her Camino. They were pleased to hear that.

They continued up the mountain and reached a point where Pam asked if they'd rather take the road or the trail. Both led to O Cebreiro, but with Aubrey's tired feet to consider, they stayed on the trail.

"Okay, what's this hard question you have?" asked Pam.

"Let's try this one: What has been the hardest day in your life so far?" Aubrey asked. Both women were deep in concentration. "I can go first. For me, the answer is straightforward, and one I'm sure you both can already guess. It's the day Cass died. I couldn't get to her fast enough. Simon called and told me. I hated that he was the one that found her and the one who had to call and tell us. It will always be a horrible memory for him. I remember the moment I saw her. I had an out-of-body experience. I was in shock I suppose, but I remember looking down at myself holding her, crumpled on the floor, rocking back and forth, saying over and over, 'I'm so sorry. I'm so sorry.' That was the worst day of my life," Aubrey's voice cracked, and she felt Georgina reach out for her. She took her hand, comforted by the gesture.

"For me, it's a tie," Pam said after a while. "The night in the back of the car with Mick, the day I married him, and the day I lost the baby. I was angry and sad at the circumstances around the pregnancy, but I also wanted the baby like nothing else. So, I made the most of it. I decided I would be the best mother I could be and nothing like my own. I remember taking up knitting and was halfway through a baby blanket when Mick beat the baby from my body."

"Bloody hell ..." Georgina said. They walked a hundred metres with no sound but the crunch of their feet on the gravel.

"I can't imagine the pain you suffered," Georgina said. "Both of you." She took a deep breath and continued, "I had a miscarriage before Nicole. I mean, I know it wasn't the anguish of a beating or losing my child later in life, but I understand the heart-wrenching pain of losing a child. It was our first baby and a baby I desperately wanted. Patrick was just as devastated as I was. I was nineteen weeks along and we had just found out it was a boy."

"I was twenty weeks along," said Pam. "I get it. My baby was a girl. I named her Rebecca. Hannah asked me that question in Burgos, whether I had a girl or a boy, but I couldn't bring myself to tell her that part." Pam's pace seemed to increase after that, but then she reeled herself in and slowed back down.

"Fuck. That was a hard one. We need a light question now."

"Agreed," said Aubrey. She remembered an easier question on her list, without needing to get it back out from her pocket.

"What's your favourite movie?" and with that change of subject, the discussion got them into Galícia and to the village of O Cebreiro.

35

THE UNIVERSE SPEAKS

O CEBREIRO

"That climb wasn't half as bad as I imagined," said Aubrey.

"Interesting conversation helps," responded Georgina. She looked at her watch, "and it's only a quarter to twelve."

"What do you think?" asked Pam. "Should we go in search of our albergue? They open at one. I wouldn't want to miss out on getting a bed."

"Me either," said Georgina, "We can explore afterwards. This village is amazing." Aubrey could already see Georgina's fingers itching to take photos.

"We also need to get something to eat," suggested Aubrey, her stomach rumbling. Pam looked at her app before leading them out of the primary part of the village. They found the Municipal easily, on the left overlooking the mountains, as the trail left town.

"I'm warning you both," said Pam. "I've read it's bare bones. Lots of bunks in one room. Be sure to wear your earplugs tonight."

"It's one night and we get to stay in the village. I'm game," said Aubrey. Pilgrims were already lined up to enter the albergue as they approached. They dropped their packs at the end to hold their place.

Aubrey stretched while they waited. Georgina shared a bag of dried fruit to tide them over until lunch.

A little past one, they handed over their credentials and payment. They found three beds together near the far wall, away from the door. But, with the amount of bunk beds in their room, sleep would be scarce.

After completing their chores, they headed back toward the village to find something to eat. They were famished. Pam declared bacon and eggs sounded good to her, even though it was now almost two.

"You know Pam. You ought to open a café in Spain and only sell bacon and eggs during Camino season. You'd make a fortune," Aubrey predicted. Pam laughed.

"It's not an insane idea. But I think I'd like an albergue more. I like what Susi and Fermin have done at Casa Susi. That would be more my style," Pam said as they walked into the bar for lunch. She stopped so suddenly that Aubrey, distracted by the architecture, smacked into the back of her.

"Well, look who it is," Pam whispered, slowly and deliberately. Aubrey looked around. The guy they'd been ogling in La Faba sat at a table in the corner of the bar. His plate of octopus was half eaten, and he had a nearly empty glass of beer nearby. He looked up when Pam made more noise than necessary, then zeroed in on Aubrey with a beaming smile.

"I'm ordering at the other side of the bar," announced Pam. "I may chat to the fine fellow seated over there. What would you all like to drink?" Georgina laughed. Aubrey was embarrassed and nervous.

"Beer please," she muttered, looking over at the Fine Specimen. He wasn't what she would call classically handsome. Rugged was the word that popped into her head. His arms were muscular and tanned, the light hairs on them reflecting in the streaming sunlight. She watched as he moved the fork towards his mouth. His mouth was…

"You're staring," whispered Georgina, snapping Aubrey out of her daze. Aubrey flushed, quickly looking towards Pam who placed their drink orders in her terrible Spanish accent.

Aubrey groaned inwardly as Pam turned to say hello to the Fine Specimen. The guy glanced at Aubrey before turning his attention to

Pam. His face broadened into a smile. He wiped his mouth with his napkin before speaking. Polite. Thoughtful. She picked up the Irish lilt from across the room, but their conversation was hard to make out. She heard snippets of 'where are you from and where did you start?', the usual Camino chit chat. Moments later, Pam picked up their beers and carried them back to the table. He followed Pam with his eyes while taking a sip of his beer. Aubrey smiled over at him when Pam placed the beers in front of them. He smiled back. Oh, those laugh lines…

"His name is Tom. He's Irish. From Cork. I don't know Ireland at all. He said it's in the south," said Pam, matter-of-factly. Aubrey stared at the napkin in her lap, wanting to break the spell.

"Nice. Well sorry to interrupt this information session, but I'm starving. What do you want to eat? I can order at the bar," Georgina asked, ignoring Pam, as she glanced over the menu. Aubrey was grateful for the distraction.

"I'm getting soup," Georgina said, placing the menu down on the table and stood, reaching for her purse. "And bread."

"That sounds good to me. Would you mind ordering some for me too?" asked Aubrey, handing Georgina some cash.

"No problem. Pam? Bacon and eggs for you?" Georgina asked.

"Yes, thanks."

Aubrey could sense a tension in the room suddenly. Something she wasn't expecting and something she didn't welcome either. Tom had finished his meal and was now walking toward them.

Fuck, fuck and fuckity fuck, she thought. Why was she feeling this way? Why was she so damn nervous?

Before she knew it, the Irishman was standing at their table.

"Hello. I'm Tom," he said and reached out his hand toward her. Aubrey stared at it.

"Her name is Aubrey. She's not usually an idiot," said Pam. Aubrey stared at Pam for a moment, jaw agape, but it was just enough to bring her back to reality. She took his proffered hand. The electricity was undeniable. "And I'm Pam. But you knew that already."

"Hi. Sorry. I'm Aubrey. You're Irish?" she managed to squeak out. God, I'm babbling, she thought. Now was not the time.

He nodded at her. "Aye. And you're Australian too?" He looked over at Pam who, Aubrey noticed, looked back and forth at them like she was sitting in the bleachers at Wimbledon. His eyes were so blue she wondered if she'd ever seen that colour before. His eyelashes, long and thick, curled in a way it looked like he'd used an eyelash curler. But that was silly. He seemed too masculine to do something like that. She blinked, willing herself to focus.

"English actually, but I live in Melbourne. You?"

"Originally from Dublin but live in County Cork. Did you start in Saint Jean too, with Pam here?"

"Well, not together. We met the first night in Orisson, along with Georgina," she said and pointed toward the bar as Georgina finished placing their orders. She willed her to return quickly so she'd have someone else to carry on this conversation. Pam wasn't helping. She looked to be rather enjoying this little meet-cute.

"My son is moving to Australia soon. He plans on staying a while. A bricklayer, he is," said Tom, as Georgina reached the table and handed Pam and Aubrey their change.

"He won't have trouble getting work, I imagine," said Georgina, who promptly introduced herself.

"Grand to meet ya. Well, ladies, I best be gettin' on. I have some washin' needing some attention. Are you staying in the village tonight?" He looked at each one of them.

Pam and Georgina looked directly at Aubrey. She nodded.

"Then, I'll be seeing ya," he said, looking at Aubrey. And with that, he left. Aubrey caught her breath again.

"I don't think I've seen you blush so red. You've certainly never been so quiet," said Pam, with a glint in her eye, a smirk curled on her lips around her beer glass.

"No thanks to you!" Aubrey said, glaring at Pam. "What was that? The 'Let's Put Aubrey on the Spot' show?" she said and stared after the door. She'd never had a reaction to anyone like that in her life.

Until now. She felt like a silly schoolgirl. But with Tom, she could feel the energy radiating from him.

She was quiet while Pam enthusiastically shared the history of the yellow arrows as they ate. She was glad Pam had slipped into her role as Camino Information Guide.

"A priest, from O Cebreiro, was the one responsible for painting the yellow arrows. He said he was preparing for an invasion which, when you think of how many people are walking now, rings true. He began painting yellow arrows along the Camino roughly forty years ago. Now, the arrows are the symbol of the Camino, and I, for one, am glad he had the foresight!"

Aubrey listened to Pam as she told the story, but found her mind returning to the blue eyes she'd been gazing into not too long before. By staying in the village, would they bump into each other again? She wondered how she would react next time.

"Well, that was good," said Pam, placing her knife and fork neatly together on her plate. "I think I will visit the church. Lots of history there. May take a walk around the village. You're both welcome to join me. But I warn you, I plan on spending a little time in the church." Pam was working through her grievances, one church at a time now.

"I'm going to wander a little myself," said Aubrey. She needed to clear her head.

"I'm eager to take photos, so I guess we'll meet back at the albergue later?" asked Georgina. They nodded, grabbed their day bags, and returned their dishes to the bar.

"I'll see you Lovelies later," said Aubrey, desperately needing some breathing room to take in this unfamiliar feeling. She wanted to grab her journal from her backpack and find a quiet spot to write for a while.

Ten minutes later, she found a place to sit on the other side of the church, outside the boundaries of the village. A lush, grassy hill flowed down into a deep valley, revealing the massive overpasses they had only walked beneath the day before. The overpasses looked like a miniature play set at this height. The clouds, puffy like cotton balls, drifted by, nearly close enough to touch. The undulating mountains were shades of blues and greys, as they gradually faded into the distance. Aubrey sat cross-legged on the grass, meditating, hoping it would recentre her. She thought of where she was, and the journey taken so far. But, before long, her mind wandered back to Tom. Who was he?

"It's spectacular, isn't it?" The Irish accent made her jump. She turned, but the sun proved a little too bright to be looking directly at her visitor. "Don't worry, I'm not stalking you. I was doing a bit of exploring and saw this view." Nodding, she stayed silent.

"May I?" gesturing to a spot next to her.

"Yes, of course," she moved her journal to the side, making room for him.

"Am I interrupting your journal time?" he asked, indicating he did not wish to intrude.

"Oh no, I haven't gotten to writing yet. Please, have a seat," Tom sat close but not intimately so.

"I won't stay long," he said, placing his bag to the left. "Are ya enjoying the walk?" She could feel his presence intensely, in a spiritual sense. Her intuition was on high. Had she met him before?

"Yes. I feel lucky to have met Pam and Georgina. I had planned on walking alone, but their friendship has meant a lot."

"Aye. I was walking with a young lad early on. He had to go back to Sweden. After that, I walked with an American, but we didn't quite get along, so I bid him goodbye and walked a little faster. He was an older man, set in his ways, if you know what I mean."

"Yes, we met an American woman who rubbed us the wrong way when we first met her," she said, remembering her first meeting with Lee. "She was a tough nut to crack, but once we got to know her and her story, she was lovely."

"And what's your story, Aubrey?" Tom asked. Hearing her name on his lips gave her butterflies.

"My story? Oh, not much to tell," she said as she pulled her knees up and wrapped her arms around them.

"Everyone says that, but it usually turns out they are a fascinating sort. Go on then," he nudged.

"What would you like to know?" she asked, knowing she wasn't about to tell this strange man, one who held such immense power over her, her life story in their first proper conversation.

"Married?" She shook her head. "Kids?" She nodded, told him two. "And what do you do when you're not conquering mountains?"

"I used to be a business owner. Now I'm a jewellery designer," she said, trying that idea on for size and found it sounded good.

"See, now that's fascinating," his accent made her smile. She found it… enchanting. "A business owner, you say," he said, looking off into the distance, "but you don't say what, although you're specifically a jewellery designer?" He looked her in the eye.

Her cheeks flushed. "Well, I'm in the beginning stages of being a jewellery designer. I owned a dress shop in Melbourne but sold it. Now I'm dabbling in my next career."

"Aye, see? Fascinating," he said, scanning the views beyond. "So, you're creative, beautiful." He looked at her pointedly and smiled, "and successful, I would imagine?" She blushed at his flattery. She smoothed out the wrinkles in her skirt to avoid his gaze.

"And, what about you? What's your story?" He hesitated too. "Same questions."

"Okay," he agreed. "Divorced. Two boys. Too independent for my liking, but that's okay I suppose. I write mysteries, but I was in the tech industry for a long while."

"So, creative. Good looking. And successful?" she said, grinning, throwing his words back at him.

"Ha! Creative, aye. Good looking? No. I'm a funny-looking lad. And successful? Well, my tech job set me up to be a writer today. Still not published. Working on that."

They sat talking for another two hours. He was a compelling man. They compared their views of the curiosities of the world, the travels they had done and shared stories of the people they had met along the Camino. Ironically, she discovered he'd walked with Lee for a few days. She told him about Pam and Georgina and shared their stories, the ones she'd heard them tell other pilgrims a million times over.

A COOL BREEZE PICKED UP AND GOOSEBUMPS FORMED OVER HER ARMS. SHE rubbed them, realising she had not brought her jacket.

"It's getting on. I didn't mean to monopolise your time," he said, picking up his daypack.

"That's okay," she said, knowing in her mind it was time to head back, but not wanting to. He stood while she continued to gather her things. "I enjoyed the chat."

"Where are you staying?" Tom asked, "I'll walk with you, if that's okay?" He came across as a pure gentleman.

"The municipal on the other side of the village," she answered. He looked surprised.

"Me too," he replied, then helped her to her feet. The touch was electric, like grabbing a live wire. Both quickly pulled their hands away.

"Huh," Tom said, beaming at Aubrey. "Did ya feel that?"

36

CONNECTIONS

O CEBREIRO TO TRIACASTELA

AUBREY AND TOM stopped in the church on the way back to the albergue. She didn't want to miss it. Tom gave her some space as she walked around. It soon became her favourite church on the Camino. The design was simple in style, missing the usual opulence she'd experienced in other catholic churches she'd visited. She noticed the bibles lining the walls, written in various languages, all open to the same psalm. This touched her. It was if the church was saying, 'We are in this together. We are one'.

"This church has an incredible history, you know," Tom said, eventually joining her. "The story goes that the Holy Grail is buried here. Over the centuries, many miracles have occurred within these walls." She had to wonder if Tom popping up was not one of those miracles.

She lit a candle for Cass, as she had in every church she'd been in since starting the Camino. As she did, Tom walked discreetly past. The flame flickered, almost going out, then returned strong as ever.

Did you send him? Her inner voice asked, reaching out to Cass. The light flickered again. She smiled. Well, thank you for that, my sweet. It's a delightful distraction. The flame suddenly extinguished. She lit it again. Not a distraction? The flame flickered strongly. Then it stilled. If not a distraction, then what?

She returned to where Tom stood at the back of the church.

"I think this is the loveliest Catholic church I've ever been in," he said, as she approached him. "And I've spent many an hour in the church."

"Are you Catholic?"

"Aye. Well, lapsed now. Religion and I don't really see eye-to-eye anymore. But the Camino is giving me the time to reconcile with that."

"You should speak to Pam. She is of the same opinion. Religion had a major impact on her life," she said as they walked out of the church, back toward the village. As they neared the albergue, a large group of people walked toward them. She looked around, trying to work out where they were heading.

"Time for Mass," Tom said quietly.

"Not going yourself?" she asked.

"No. I had my time in the church today. I don't need some fella in a fancy robe pushing grandiloquence I don't need to hear. I've heard it all before. I know what I need from religion and it's not that." The intensity in his words surprised her.

"Sorry," he said, his smile genuine, his blue eyes dazzling in the soft light. Her stomach fluttered. "As I said before, the church and I don't see eye-to eye."

"THERE YOU ARE. WE WERE GETTING WORRIED," AUBREY FOUND Georgina laying on her bed and, upon seeing Aubrey, sat up.

"Sorry," Aubrey said. "I found a spot just outside the village on the other side of the church. It was beautiful, and the views were spectacular from there." She sat down opposite Georgina on Pam's bunk bed.

"Pam's attending mass. She left a few minutes ago," Georgina said.

"I'm surprised she's going," said Aubrey.

"I was too. But I think she's finding some peace with it."

Aubrey looked down and picked at her broken nail. "I invited Tom to join us later, if that's okay." She felt like a schoolgirl, asking Mum for permission to see a boy.

"Oh?" said Georgina, picking up on Aubrey's hesitation. "Are you okay with it?" Aubrey nodded quickly. "Then that's good with me. Pam and I were just talking about dinner. I told her I'd wait for you, then we'll meet her in the bar when Mass is over. Figured we can get a table while the crowd is otherwise occupied. I'm ready to head there now, if you are? Did you set a time with Tom?"

"No, just told him we'd grab him on the way out. He's staying here too. I was chatting with him on the hill," Aubrey said, sounding so unsure of herself.

"Are you ready then?" said Georgina. "I could use a wine!"

"Yes. I'll pop into the bathroom, then I'll meet you at the door," Aubrey said. "It's getting chilly. You'll need your jacket."

"Okay. I'll grab Tom and we'll meet you there," Georgina said. Aubrey needed a moment to herself, to catch her wits. She wanted to freshen a little too. She felt flushed despite the cool breeze blowing through the place.

It was a night of great conversation. Pam and Georgina asked Tom a million questions. She felt sorry for him, but he bounced the questions back when he needed a break. When prodded by Pam on his marital status, he was open about his divorce, admitting he would not have married the girl in the first place, had he had the full picture. It turned out the woman had targeted him. After seeing her for six months, she showed up and announced, in front of his parents and the parish priest, that she was pregnant. She had planned it all, she admitted later. From there, Pam and Tom discussed their woes with the Catholic Church.

"Ah, the Camino," Tom said, walking next to Aubrey, when they made their way back to their albergue. "It brings out all kinds of conversations. I would not have shared that information with another soul at home in Ireland. It's just too personal. But here, it's like this place, this journey, it opens up the soul and brings out even the most vulnerable information."

"I agree," she said. "I've had some intense admissions in my conversations with Pam and Georgina." He reached out to her and pulled her to a stop. Pam and Georgina continued walking ahead of them.

"I know this is mad but, as we agree, it's an unusual place. I can't explain it and I don't think I could if I had the words. But I like you and I would like to continue this conversation with you."

He reached for her hand and took it in his. The moonlight illuminated the connection.

"I like you too. But..." She'd only met him that afternoon. She couldn't explain it either.

"So, we take it one step at a time," he said, chuckling. "We'll walk and talk."

"I'm not wanting to step away from Pam or Georgina at this point," she said. "We've come too far together. And we walk a slower pace than most."

"I'm happy to walk your pace. Or, if you'd rather, I'll wait for you in Santiago?" She hesitated. "I don't want to push you, but I see something between us. I want to explore that a little more."

He looked deep into her eyes and she felt the moment was right to kiss him. She leaned toward him and felt his soft lips meet hers. It was a chaste kiss, but it was enough to experience the spark between them. He then raised her hand to his lips and kissed it gently, before walking in silence back to the albergue.

At the door, he kissed her on the cheek and bid her a restful sleep. Fat chance, she thought, her mind already reeling. She'd kissed a perfect stranger, but she knew too that she was not unhappy she had. For now, she was thankful for Pam's pushy nature.

GEORGINA, PAM AND AUBREY LEFT AROUND SEVEN THE NEXT MORNING. Audrey popped her head into Tom's room, but it was empty. Disappointed, she joined Pam and Georgina, and reminded herself that she and Tom had not made a plan. Ready to go, they decided to wait for breakfast in Liñares, the next village.

Continuing down the trail, the layer of thick fog was nestled in the valleys below. The surrounding mountains peaked just above. They were walking in heaven, Aubrey thought, with reality obscured below the clouds.

The winding path rose and fell gently outside the village. The fog slowly lifted, but the views of green mountains and deep valleys continued forever. Georgina stopped constantly and took photo after photo. Pam and Aubrey found they couldn't resist the postcard-worthy opportunity either. Pam pointed out the bridges below, the same ones Aubrey had noticed herself the day before, peaking out through the clouds as they got closer to Liñares.

There, they had tortilla and coffee for breakfast. Pam was devastated she couldn't order bacon and eggs. As they reloaded their packs outside, a herd of cattle ambled toward them, their bells ringing gently from their necks. Aubrey pulled out her phone to record the moment. The cows nudged closer toward her and when she backed up to get out of their way, she stepped straight into a patch of stinging nettles. She felt the sting almost instantly. Before long, the itch became overwhelming. Pam offered help, but Aubrey told her she had some tea tree antiseptic cream in her pack that would do the trick. While fishing it out of her pack, she felt someone come up behind her.

"Are ya having some trouble there?" It was Tom. She figured he was long ahead of them today, since he wasn't in the albergue when they left.

"Oh! Hello! I just stepped into stinging nettle getting out of the herd's path," as she continued her search for her tea tree cream. "I'm looking for my antiseptic cream."

Tom started hunting in the grass. What on earth is he doing, she wondered. It was an odd reaction to her concern, so Aubrey asked what he was looking for.

"Dock," he said, matter-of-factly.

"What?! What's that?" she asked, now pulling everything out of her pack. She grabbed her medical kit from the very bottom. Tom continued his search, while Pam and Georgina stood nearby holding Aubrey's poles for her.

"It's a long, broad leafy weed that grows next to stinging nettle in a symbiotic relationship. It serves as the antidote to stinging nettle. Works a charm," he said, as he continued looking along the path.

"By crushing the leaves of dock, vein-side down, and running it across the irritated area, you get instant relief," he explained, his hands running through the tall weeds. Desperate for relief, Aubrey joined the search.

"Ah ha!" Tom raised his hand with the prize. As he crushed the leaves, Aubrey whipped up her pant leg. Tom rubbed the leaves vigorously into her leg.

"Oh! That's so much better," she said, the itch subsiding almost instantly. "It works!"

"It's like watching a weird kind of porn," Pam whispered. Georgina giggled. Aubrey whipped around, giving Pam a scathing look. Pam was already on a bend to tease her this morning. She had seen Aubrey and Tom kissing the night before, she confessed. Aubrey was mortified. She felt like a teenager caught by her parents.

"Thank you, Tom," Aubrey said, the pain subsiding as she rolled her pant leg back down.

"My pleasure," he said. His smile melted her. He turned to Pam and Georgina. "And how are you ladies this morning? I was hoping I would catch you. You're further along than I thought."

"I thought you'd be way ahead by now," said Aubrey. "Your room was empty when we left."

"Aye. I left around six-thirty but got a hearty breakfast in the bar. Bacon and eggs. There's nothing like it to get you started in the morning," he said.

"Oh fuck! I missed it!" Pam said. Aubrey laughed at the look of horror on Tom's face.

"It's alarming the first time you experience Pam's potty mouth," she whispered. "I should have warned you."

"May I join you on your walk today? I really enjoyed our chat last night, although truth be known, it felt a little like an inquisition at first," he looked pointedly at Pam who just smiled, double tapped her poles and turned. The four of them continued, talking about what was next after the Camino.

Georgina shared her decision about becoming a photographer. Aubrey was surprised that Georgina went into such detail, talking about her hesitations, as well as her plans.

"You have to do what's right for ya. What makes you happy in life, that's the key. What makes your heart sing? What lights you up when you talk about it?" Tom said. "Aye, but I admit, it took a long time for me to figure that out."

"That's what we've been telling her," said Aubrey. "She shines when she talks about her photography. You can see it on her face, hear it in her voice when she talks about her photography."

"I snuck out this morning," admitted Georgina. "The sunrise views were... almost ethereal."

"Aye, they were," said Tom. Surprise touched Georgina's face. "I saw you but didn't want to disturb ya. Pure magic this mornin'," Tom said turned to Aubrey. "And I see what you mean about her demeanour changing."

"Right?" said Aubrey. "And somehow, she doesn't think she has what it takes."

"If she has that kind of passion for it, she has it," Tom said, "and if she doesn't yet, she will."

"I'm standing right here you know," said Georgina, looking embarrassed. "I get it, okay? I already said I'd do it!"

Further along, Tom asked Pam what her plans were.

"I'm thinking about writing a book," she said. Aubrey asked if she'd consider writing a book about the Camino. Pam looked contemplative. Georgina and Aubrey joked that she should call it the Camino Information Guide. Pam snorted.

"Well Pam, you know a lot about the Camino," Georgina said. "The book would be helpful to novices like us. My app certainly doesn't explain half of what you've shared with us. You need to write that book."

"Sounds like you have a task ahead of ya," said Tom.

When they stopped for a second breakfast in Fonfria, Tom asked them if it was all right if he tagged along for a while. He didn't wish to encroach on their walk. He was just happy for their company.

"You know, we've walked with others. Ben and Hannah from the U.S., Paolo from Italy, and Marinka from Germany," said Pam. "So, you're not encroaching on us at all. We've just been together since day one, and you know, it's good to have fresh conversations."

"Don't forget about Lee," said Aubrey. "Tom walked with her too, at one point."

"Did you tell him you called her 'Lean and Mean' when you first met her?" asked Pam, while she looked through her guidebook to find an albergue for them to reserve.

Aubrey felt herself blush, "Um, no."

"I can kind of see why you would," said Tom, putting his hand on Aubrey's shoulder. "She has that kind demeanour at first meet." He smiled over at her as he rubbed his hand over her shoulder. She bowed her head and smiled. His touch sent shock waves through her veins.

After Fonfria, Tom and Aubrey spent a good hour walking by themselves. Their conversation moved into deeper topics. They talked about relationships they'd had in their lives and what their marriages had been like. She'd given him a sense of what had happened with Brendon, but not everything.

About six kilometres before Triacastela, a group of people stood at a fence, mesmerised by something in a paddock. Curious, they walked over to check it out. Aubrey saw a cow cleaning a calf. By the time they reached the crowd, one pilgrim, an Englishwoman, whispered to her, "It must have been born about an hour ago. Isn't it brilliant?!"

"Actually, more like ten minutes ago by my estimation," Aubrey said. The Englishwoman looked at her like she was an idiot. Aubrey shrugged and the woman left them to it.

"How do you know that?" Tom asked, his admiration apparent.

"My grandfather had a farm, down near Surrey," said Aubrey. "He taught me all kinds of things. See how the mother is licking the calf's face, and there's still a lot of goop over it?" Aubrey said to Tom, "She's clearing its air passage so it can breathe." They watched in fascination as the cow moved on to lick around the calf's legs. She licked with such force the calf nearly rolled over.

"Now she's trying to get him up and walking," she continued, speaking in a soft tone. "The faster she can do that, the better it is for the calf." A few minutes later, the crowd dispersed, either bored with the show or wanting to continue to their next stop.

"It's fascinating," Tom said. "I have never watched a calf being born before." He took out his phone and started recording the scene, just as the mother delivered the afterbirth. "Now that? That was something I didn't need to see," Tom said, chuckling. He turned the video off. "Let's give her some privacy, shall we?"

They continued walking, surprised that Pam and Georgina hadn't caught up yet. She sent Georgina a message. The reply was quick. They had stopped in the hamlet just before so Pam could use the toilet.

Let's meet in Triacastela at the albergue.

"Looks like we're on our own for a bit," Aubrey said, putting her phone away.

They talked about how they grew up. Tom was a city boy. After he finished at the University in Dublin, he moved to Cork for work. He seemed spellbound by Aubrey's life. She told him about moving from London to Australia and the childhood holidays at her grandfather's farm. As they walked past a field of blooming dandelions, she stopped to admire the cluster.

"I've never seen so many dandelions in my life," she remarked. "They're gorgeous."

"That there? That's called a field full of wishes," said Tom. She loved that. She took a photo of the field to remember the moment. Tom suggested a selfie of the two of them with the flowers set as a backdrop. She readily agreed.

When they reached Ramil, they took photos of the eight-hundred-year-old chestnut tree. Tom dropped his pack and gave the tree a big hug. He said he watched a documentary featuring Dame Judi Dench called *My Passion for Trees*. He described the absolute joy on Dame Judi's face when she recognised 'her tree'. He told Aubrey he felt a special joy with this eight-hundred-year-old beast.

"It's a gnarled old thing, isn't it?" he said, his fingers trailing the bark. "Just imagine the centuries of tales it holds."

They talked about friendships. She learned Tom had three very close childhood friends, who'd been with him through everything. Aubrey was embarrassed to admit that she never had such close friends.

"You know, I love this journey on the Camino," Aubrey said. "I have been craving deep connections all my life. I haven't had these kinds of conversations with anyone before. Pam and Georgina have become closer to me than anyone. I've divulged information I've not told another soul. Most of my friends in the real world have not been interested in the deeper conversations. It's all superficial stuff. I've always thought that odd. Isn't that a major benefit of a genuine friendship, to have people in your life you can trust enough to bare your soul to? Or to have conversations that make you think outside of the box? Maybe they weren't the friendships I thought they were?"

"Aye," said Tom. "I have that with one of my oldest friends. It seems with men, at least the ones in Ireland, talk only of topics which include sports or politics. And they are always over a pint. I have to wonder if they are afraid to have an emotional conversation, thinking they look weak?"

"Is it as simple of not having the time to invest, or are they afraid to be vulnerable? That goes for both men and women," said Aubrey. "Is this how the world is now? No one invests in true friendships anymore. Rather, it's about amassing social media connections. It's quantity, not the quality. I find that depressing."

"Aye," said Tom, "I wonder if they are afraid to say the wrong thing. Or is there no connection to begin with? Only circumstance?"

Aubrey stopped at the top of the hill. She looked down into Triacastela in the distance. The connection, she thought. We have it. Tom stopped and turned back to her, his wild blue eyes making her catch her breath. He smiled and she stepped forward and kissed him. At first, it was chaste, but knowing this was something different with him, something she'd never experienced before, it soon became deep and soul-clenching. Aubrey was no longer afraid to hold anything back.

37

FAIRYTALES

TRIACASTELA TO SAMOS

Tom and Aubrey checked into the albergue in Triacastela, securing bunks for their group. After showers, they shared a load of laundry, their clothes hanging side by side on the line outside. It seemed rather intimate to Aubrey. She had a deeper relationship with Tom, after only twenty-four hours of meeting him, than she'd ever had with Brendon. Twenty-three years wasted, she lamented.

They waited for Pam and Georgina, sitting in the sunshine nursing beers.

"Hello!" said Georgina, finally reaching them after what seemed to be hours.

"Hi," Aubrey said. "It's been a while. I was beginning to worry. Are you okay?"

"Oh yeah. Just took our time," said Georgina, reaching over and grabbing Pam's pack for her. It was like watching a synchronised ballet with these two now. "You two must have hightailed it. You look very comfortable sitting there. Have you, wow, showered already?"

"Yeah. We've been here about an hour and a half, maybe two?" She looked over at Tom. He checked his watch and nodded his agreement. "We didn't walk fast though. In fact, we even stopped to watch a Mum and her newborn calf for a while."

"We went slow down the hill," said Pam, pulling out a chair to lean on. "It did a number on my knees. Figured they'd be used to it by now."

"I was thinking about that when we came down. You okay?" asked Aubrey. Pam nodded. "We grabbed a bunk for you in the albergue. We put stuff on them so no one else would grab them. You just need to show your credentials. They're expecting you."

"Okay, we'll go check in and meet back up with you," said Pam, looking at Georgina for agreement. "Have you done laundry already?" Aubrey nodded, feeling her face blush. Pam smiled knowingly. She grabbed her pack and walked toward the albergue.

"They know," said Aubrey to Tom, her eyes following Pam and Georgina as they walked towards the dorm.

"Know what?" he asked, taking her hand across the table.

"That we kissed," she whispered. He chuckled. "It's embarrassing!"

"Why? Is Pam your mother?" he asked. "Do you need her permission?"

"Well, no. Of course not," she played with his fingers.

"So, let's take it as it is," he said, returning her finger play.

"Will you come with us to Samos? Pam seems intent to go that route," she said, reaching for her beer with her free hand. "It's supposed to be rather picturesque."

"If you like. As long as Pam and Georgina are okay with me joining you."

"I will ask them later," she said.

"It may be the last of day of walking with ya, since I'm meeting my son in Sarria." She looked up suddenly. "I'm sorry, I thought I mentioned that already?" She shook her head. "My younger son is meeting me. We are walking to Santiago together."

"No, you didn't say," she said, feeling his absence already. "But that's great. How old is he?"

"He's twenty-three." His three sounded like tree, which she found endearing. "He's a bit of a lost dog. I thought this would be a brilliant opportunity for he and I to talk some stuff out." He sat back in his chair, breaking the bond of their hands.

"I had that same thought a few weeks ago," she said, "about walking the Camino with my daughter, Cass."

"Will you plan another Camino with her?" Tom asked as he reached for his beer. She went quiet.

"No. It's impossible now," she said, astonished she hadn't told him about Cass already. She took a deep breath. "Cass died two years ago."

"Oh. God, I'm so sorry," he said, concern etched across his face. "Ya didn't say."

"It's okay. I'm... dealing with it a little better now. She was seventeen." She took the plunge. "She committed suicide."

"Ooof. That's rough. I'm so very sorry to hear that. That must have been hard for ya." He reached for her hand again, but she moved it to her lap.

"It's okay. It's just hard to say it out loud to people. It's not a secret. Most people in my life are aware. But, at times like this, I miss her." She took his hand again, realising the message she would send him by avoiding his gesture.

"Aye. I'm sure ya do." They were quiet for a little while, lost in their own thoughts, observing pilgrims strolling past. It was the first time since their two-hour chat on the mountain at O Cebreiro that the silence felt uncomfortable.

"Tell me about your son. Why is he a lost dog?" She tossed the ball back into his court.

"Oh, he's a young pup, trying to find his way in the world. He's the one about to go to Australia. Seems a bit unsure now, leaving his mates behind. But I think it'll be good for him, ya know?" She nodded, happy to take the spotlight off her and her grief. She plied him with more questions since he seemed happy to talk about his boys.

· · ·

When Pam and Georgina returned, they relayed how they'd laughed when they saw Tom's bright yellow towel with a four-leaf clover on their bunk. They were sure which bunk was theirs once they saw it.

"So Irish!" teased Pam.

Tom asked, as a sincere gentleman, if they would be okay if he walked with them another day.

"I am enjoying your company," he said.

"Ours or Aubrey's?" Pam quipped, nudging Aubrey.

"I have enjoyed Aubrey's company today, but it's you two I'd like to walk with tomorrow, if you'll have me?"

"Ignore her Tom," Georgina said. "It's fine for you to walk with us. Besides, it's refreshing to have another person to chat with. Listening to Pam prattle on about historical elements of the Camino all day... it gets really old!" she said, tossing the barb in Pam's direction.

"Thanks. It'll be only one day, I'm afraid," he said. "I'll be meeting my son in Sarria the day after. He's biting at the bit. He arrived yesterday."

"Are we delaying you?" asked Aubrey, concerned.

"No," he said, giving her an intimate smile, a smile she was sure Pam and Georgina could not have missed. "Not at all."

The following morning, the walk out of Triacastela was rather dodgy. They walked single file down a busy road. Semi-trailers zoomed by so close, Pam was nearly blown into the ditch. But soon they came to the trail, lush with vine and gnarled old trees, ancient cobbled stoned walls guiding their way.

A hunched old man, arched over his wooden staff, herded his docile sheep into a large paddock by the creek. He then turned on his heel and returned in the direction he had come. This completes the fairy tale, Aubrey thought dreamily. It was all so fitting with the environment. The shepherd inspired nostalgia for farm life in the group. Pam regaled how her dad used to whistle to give their working dogs instructions. Georgina explained that Patrick used an ATV on his sheep farm. Aubrey said her grandfather was more like this old shepherd with his old-fashioned ways. Tom jokingly told them that his version of farm life was herding his kids, with bribes of ice cream, through the city of Cork, bringing laughter to them all.

They passed over creeks that flowed under ancient stone houses. Georgina had a field day snapping photos with her phone, but it soon turned to grumbling under her breath of how she missed her camera more than ever.

"I'm coming back," Georgina announced. "And next time I'm bringing my damn camera with me!"

That spurred a discussion about walking the Camino again in a few years. And why not? It was a beautiful walk. They followed a gently flowing river and passed crumbling stone walls covered in foliage that created miniature gardens of their own. Community gardens grew on the edges of each hamlet. Old and distorted trees lined the path, their large branches arching across, providing shelter from the blistering sun.

Before long, they descended a hill lined with an imposing stone wall, scaled much higher than their heads. When they came to the other side, they saw their destination. The monastery nearly encompassed the entire valley. The massive building dwarfed the quaint village that surrounded it. Following the path, they made their way around the building to the municipal albergue, a part of the Monastery.

They entered through the wooden framed door and looked around the room. One by one, Aubrey, Georgina, and Pam turned on their heel and walked outside. No one said a word. Tom hesitated, looking confused as to what had just happened, before joining them outside. Pam spoke what they'd all been thinking.

"Nope. I know we agreed on staying at the monastery, but no. I'm not staying there," she said. "Besides, I could not get my bum up to that top bunk if someone paid me. From what I could see, top bunks were the only ones left!"

"Did you notice there were no ladders leading up to the bunks either?" Georgina asked. Pam nodded. Aubrey shook her head. "I mean, I could climb up there if I had to, but I'm with you Pam. No."

"I just don't get it. The monastery is huge. Why would they squeeze forty beds into such a tight space?" asked Pam.

Tom remained quiet, looking lost.

"I'm sorry Tom. Did you want to stay there?" Aubrey asked.

"Ah, no. It's fine. I think I'm just a bit gobsmacked that you all realized it was a hard no, without saying a word to each other," he said, looking at each of them with appreciation. Aubrey smiled.

"Let's find somewhere else, shall we? Maybe there's a room we can share?" suggested Aubrey.

They could only find two separate rooms, situated across the hall from each other, in an albergue nearby. Pam and Georgina simultaneously gave Aubrey a knowing wink when Tom offered to find another albergue for himself. Aubrey looked at him, considering her next move.

"I'm game if you are?" she asked. Tom nodded, and all too soon Pam sang a somewhat more adult version of 'kissing in a tree' while they checked in.

Pam and Georgina begged off for dinner, saying they wanted an early night. Tom and Aubrey knew they were being set up but didn't fight it. This would be their last night together before Tom began walking with his son.

Their albergue hosted a lovely restaurant upstairs. The atmosphere was intimate, and they agreed they needed a change from the pilgrim meal. Aubrey ordered steak and roasted vegetables. Tom ordered sea bass with grilled asparagus and a nice bottle of red wine. A Rioja, Aubrey noticed. Ben would be proud.

Over the course of the meal, she learned more about Tom's childhood and his friends. Sarah, he said, talked a mile a minute and was in love with her dogs more than her husband. She had been there for Tom through thick and thin. His other best friend, Sean, was a fisherman. A real man's man.

"But…" Tom shared, "show him a film with a dog, especially one in trouble or dying, and he's a sobbing mess. We went to see *The Fox and the Hound* when we were young lads. Sean refused to leave until the theatre cleared. He couldn't stop cryin'!" Tom laughed at the memory.

"Poor love," said Aubrey which made Tom laugh even harder.

His laugh entranced her. She loved hearing about the deep friendships he'd formed over his lifetime. She realised, once again, what she'd missed. She told him how she felt a deeper connection to Pam and Georgina than any other relationship she'd had in her life, except for her son and her mother. Even with Cass, she'd not had the relationship she thought she had. Through therapy, she admitted, she'd learned to cobble together the many pieces she missed about Cass' life.

She told Tom about Cass and Brendon and of the events of the last two years. Then, how she'd changed her life completely. She admitted to checking herself into a psychiatric hospital for in-house therapy. He expressed compassion and kindness, not pity or judgement as she was accustomed. His questions about Cass and her mental health touched her deeply. He explained he had someone close in his life who had had a mental breakdown and was in hospital for several months. He had the dignity and loyalty to not reveal who it was. She appreciated that discretion.

She told him about Simon and his struggles of coming out as a gay man. Tom's response was simple: 'Love is love'. He explained what it was like for his twin uncles growing up. One was gay in a Catholic world and committed suicide in his early twenties. His parents never accepted his sexuality. Not having their support caused an intolerable amount of pain.

By the end of the night, she felt she understood a lot more about who Tom was. He was compassionate, kind, charming, especially the way he humoured Pam's teasing, and was even a little old-fashioned. He was genuinely sincere, a quality that seemed rare in the world she lived in. She believed she would fall in love with him, if she allowed herself.

Alone in their room an hour later, Tom reached for her. The sexual tension had been building all evening. She returned his kiss with wild reckless energy. Her body hummed and when she leaned into him, deepening the kiss, her knees weakened. She braced her hand against the wall when he pulled her closer. She relinquished control. When he pulled away unexpectedly, she stumbled forward a little.

"Aubrey," he said, his voice hoarse. His hands held hers, but now he was holding her at arms-length. She ran her tongue over her swollen lips. "I don't want to hurt you, but I don't think we should…"

"Sleep together?" she finished for him.

"Aye. I care deeply about you, I do, but I don't want to hurt ya. I'm, well," he looked down at the folded towel sitting on the end of the bed, "I think I'm falling for ya, truth be told, and I want to see where this goes. I just don't want to make the wrong move. I don't want you to think I'm…"

"I understand. I want to see where this goes too," she smiled. "Thank you for being a gentleman." Aubrey kissed his cheek tenderly, then his lips softly. She then bent down, picked up her toiletries from the bed and headed to the bathroom. When she closed the door, she felt herself breathe again. What was it about this man?

THE FOLLOWING MORNING, TOM ROSE EARLY TO MEET HIS SON AT NOON IN Sarria. He kissed Aubrey one more time.

"I would have slept with you, you know," she whispered, giving him a wicked smile. With a shake of his head and a wave, he quietly left. She threw back the covers and caught a whiff of his scent. She missed his presence more than she wanted to admit. He said he would wait for her in Santiago since he did not have to hurry back to Ireland. She was excited at the thought of seeing him again.

With any chance of sleep gone, she packed her backpack and texted Georgina, figuring she was probably up. Georgina texted back right away. She had gone out to photograph the monastery, even snapped some shots of the fog on the river. She said she saw Tom too, hugged him goodbye. She added how she hoped to see him again. Aubrey did too.

Are you guys ready? Aubrey texted.

Just waiting on Pam, she replied. *Meet you down in the bar. Shouldn't be 5-10 mins, but you know Pam…*

Aubrey chuckled. She mentally closed the door gently on her two days with Tom and headed downstairs to wait. As much as she wanted him, she thought he was right that they didn't rush things. Sex too easily confused things and she wanted to see what might develop with a clear head. Besides, she was looking forward to walking with the Lovelies to Sarria. It was just a little over hundred kilometres until they reached Santiago de Compostela.

38

RECONNECTING WITH THE LOVELIES

SAMOS TO SARRIA

WHILE SHE WAITED for Pam and Georgina, Aubrey texted Tom, wishing him a beautiful day of walking. She thanked him for the memorable few days. He responded with only an XO.

"Guess it's just us from here!" said Pam, double tapping her poles to signify she was ready to go. "But I will miss gazing at the bum of that Fine Specimen." Aubrey ignored her.

"How are you doing Aubrey?" Georgina asked as they headed out of town. "You and Tom seemed to hit it off."

"I'm okay. I'm sorry to have abandoned you the last few days," Aubrey said.

"You didn't abandon us at all," Pam said, looking over at Georgina. "We left you alone on purpose. It looked like you were having a great time." She saw Pam nudge Georgina. She stayed silent.

"And did you? Have a great time I mean?" Pam asked. Aubrey felt heat flame on her cheeks. Pam laughed, "I'll take that as a yes."

They were taking their time today. They reserved at the Albergue Casa Barbadelo in Vilei, the village after Sarria.

"You know, it's a good thing we reserved tonight," Pam said, following the footpath out of Samos. "It would be hard to find a place in Sarria. It's the starting point for seventy-five percent of people walking the Camino."

"And so our Camino Information Guide informs us..." said Aubrey, in a mock radio voice, ribbing Pam. Georgina laughed. Pam simply shook her head.

Aubrey enjoyed walking in the crisp morning air. Georgina stopped them regularly, enraptured by the morning light. Just the thing to slow them down, Aubrey thought. She liked this pace. She could walk faster. She kept pace with Tom easily. But she appreciated that Pam and Georgina were more aware of everything around them, pointing out the minute nuances they found. Aubrey had missed Pam and Georgina's company.

"Can you believe that we only have a little over a hundred kilometres to go?" asked Georgina.

"We're practically home free!" said Pam. "It will be a walk in the park at this point. But, I admit, I'll need to go shopping when I'm done with this thing."

"God, why?" asked Georgina. "I couldn't think of anything worse. All those crowds."

"Well, it will be out of necessity! My pants are falling down," chuckled Pam. Aubrey teased her about finding her some trouser braces in Sarria.

"You mean suspenders?!" asked Pam, aghast at the thought. But, as she kept hitching her pants up, she began muttering how suspenders might be an excellent idea after all. They had all lost weight, despite their second breakfasts and wine indulgences.

Eventually they stopped at a small café, the only one they'd seen so far. Like Tom, they were walking the scenic path.

"It's a little unnerving that we've only seen one other pilgrim all morning," Pam admitted, grabbing some money from her top pouch. They had looked at Pam's Google Maps app more than once in the last three hours, checking to see if they were on the right track.

"Did you notice," Aubrey said, the last of them to grab her coffee and pastry, "the café requires you to order before using the bathroom?"

"I noticed that," said Georgina. "We've only seen that once, charging you to use the toilet." Georgina took a sip of her coffee but made no comment about it. Her obsessive attitude toward coffee was softening, Aubrey noticed.

"I would think they would rather you use the toilet, even if you aren't buying, than litter up the path with toilet paper," said Aubrey, breaking off a piece of her croissant.

"And we've seen plenty of that along the way," said Pam, taking a sip from her steaming cup.

"So, enquiring minds want to know," Georgina said, putting her cup down on the table. "How did it go with Tom?"

"It went... better than I thought," said Aubrey. "He's a very interesting man."

"Yeah, yeah. We know that part," said Pam. "We want to know if you slept with him and if you will see him again." She had the most devilish grin. If it were anyone else, even Georgina, Aubrey doubted she'd be as accepting of the question.

"No, and yes." Aubrey said, sitting back in her chair.

"No, you aren't seeing him again or no, you didn't sleep with him?" asked Pam.

"No, I didn't sleep with him. And yes, I will see him again. He said he'll wait for us in Santiago."

"Us, meaning you," said Pam, "You should have stepped aside. I'd have devoured him like a bag of hot chips. Frankly, I'm disappointed." She feigned annoyance. Aubrey laughed.

"I'm sorry to disappoint. We decided it best not to," Aubrey said, looking down at her lap.

"There's more to it, isn't there?" asked Pam, eerily intuitive on this. She would not let up, Aubrey realised. She was like a dog with a bone.

"Yes. There are feelings involved. And to be honest, too many questions about the future." Aubrey looked up. "Stuff we haven't talked about. Or maybe even admitted to yet?"

"Wow," Pam said and sat back in her chair. "Wow. It's love. Love on the Camino."

"I'm not sure about that, but I do like him. I wasn't expecting him," said Aubrey.

"Yes, you were," said Georgina, confusing Aubrey. "You put it out into the universe of what you were looking for. Remember? Back in Rabanal?"

Aubrey was wracking her brain.

"Your journal," Georgina prompted. "You wrote it down. You told me you wrote down what you wanted from a partner moving forward. Just like I had written down what I wanted from my marriage." Georgina scoffed. "If there is a marriage when I get back. Patrick's being weird again. But that's beside the point. You said you wrote it all down."

"Wait. You're right." She found her notebook and flipped through the pages. "I thought it was maybe Cass sending him my way for a brief distraction." She found the section Georgina had referenced and there, in black and white, was Tom in every yearned-for characteristic.

"Maybe Cass sent him, knowing he was the one that ticked all those boxes for you?" suggested Georgina. Aubrey thought that may be a stretch.

"That's just freaky," said Pam. "But go Cass!"

Aubrey decided it was a little too good to be true. A little too coincidental and changed the subject back onto Pam.

"How's the communication going with Jack? Did you respond to him? You haven't mentioned him in a while. I know you were nervous about contacting him," Aubrey pressed.

"I did when we were in O Cebreiro," she said. "Those questions you asked were enough to kick me in the bum. I prayed about it in the church and decided it was time. I lit a candle for the baby too. When I got back to the albergue, I responded to him."

She didn't say anything more for a while. As if sensing it from the other, both Georgina and Aubrey looked at Pam and, at the same time, asked, "And?!"

Pam chuckled and signalled to them to keep walking. Aubrey knew it was easier for Pam to talk about deeper issues when they were walking. It was easier than someone staring at you, waiting for an answer, as she well knew.

"I surprised him when I responded, I suppose," Pam said. "He seemed happy to hear from me though. He responded right away."

"And..." Georgina prodded.

"We've gone back and forth a few times since," said Pam. "I told him what happened, you know, with Mick, with my parents. He seemed okay with it, understanding even. I told him he need not be so understanding. That I was still trying to forgive myself, but well, our conversation went pretty deep about what happened back then."

Pam continued, "But it's confusing too. If I'm honest, I am over-whelmed by memories. I can only hope that the core part of what we had back then remains. I mean, he was my best friend. Sure, there's a lot I want to say to him, but I wonder if it's best that I don't? Let's face it. It's been a long time. We've moved on. He's happy with his life. He doesn't need me digging shit back up."

Aubrey looked at Georgina. Georgina nodded in quiet agreement to let Pam talk it out. It was clear she'd been thinking a lot since O Cebreiro. Aubrey started feeling immensely guilty for the time she had spent with Tom.

"But I also know," Pam said, "without that relationship I would not know true love. I would not know what a loving relationship looked like. Without it, I would not have felt like I could go beyond the farm fences and pursue the life I have now. I am who I really am because of him. He was, well..." Pam was quiet for a little while before she continued speaking.

"The struggles and uphill battles I've had have only strengthened me. But I also realise, those struggles made me put up emotional walls so I could not feel hurt or love. Being here now, with my past conversing with me with the same intensity as so many years ago, but still with so many unsaid words, I feel the walls cracking a little. But I'm afraid. What if that first crack in the wall will cause an avalanche. Maybe that's a good thing? Maybe I had to find that hairline crack to split me open?" She stopped and Aubrey watched as Pam pulled a tissue from her hip pack. She dabbed her eyes and then blew her nose. Aubrey embraced Pam, backpack and all. They stayed like that for a few moments before Pam pulled away.

"I miss the person I was that loved so deeply. The person who had wonder and joy. I miss the unfiltered laughter. I miss the simple things in a relationship like kisses that make you swoon, holding hands, playful banter, and sharing showers," Pam blushed. "I hope to have those things again, but first I need to open my heart, and myself." Pam took a deep, cleansing breath. "I think I'm ready to see Jack when I go home. He lives south of Melbourne now. He owns a five-acre hobby farm on the Bellarine."

"Is he married?" asked Georgina.

"No, widowed. Fifteen years," Pam said, blowing her nose.

"I think that's a great idea Pam. And you know that we'll be there if you want us to. For support," said Aubrey.

"Oh, hell no! I'm a grown woman and if I get lucky, I don't want to know that you guys are waiting in the wings. I'll just get more nervous!" She smiled and turned. Georgina reached into her pack and handed over her water bottle.

"I HEAR SARRIA AHEAD," PAM SAID, AFTER THEY WALKED UP AND DOWN undulating hills that seemed to go on forever. They passed by a few albergues, a sure sign they were close to the city.

"We need to make sure we get new credentials while we're here. Mine is almost full," said Georgina. Aubrey agreed. Hers was too.

"Let's stop and get some lunch. Hopefully by the time we're done, we can stop at a church and get a new one," suggested Pam. "I need a new credential as well because, from here on out, you have to get two stamps a day to get your Compostela in Santiago."

They navigated the city, passing shops, restaurants, markets and hotels. They groaned when the arrows led them to a ridiculously long set of stairs.

"One step at a time. Use your poles," said Pam. Like they needed reminding at this point on the Camino, Aubrey thought sarcastically. At the top, the rush of people stopped them in their tracks.

"Holy mother of…" said Pam.

"Wow!" exclaimed Aubrey. "Where'd all these people come from? I mean, it was busy in Leon, but this is…"

"Sarria," said Pam. "The start of the Camino for many. Come on, let's get some lunch, then get the fuck out of here!"

When they ordered burgers, Pam asked the waiter if he would

mind calling ahead to the albergue in Vilei to assure them they would be there. She was concerned that the albergue would give their beds away with the onslaught of pilgrims. While they waited for their lunch to be delivered, Aubrey looked down at her phone. There was a message from Tom. She opened the message and found Tom smiling, posed with a younger version beside him. Both men were beaming into the lens. Aubrey sighed audibly with a warm smile.

"What are you grinning about?" Pam asked. Aubrey showed them the photo of Tom and his son. It looked like it was in front of a Sarria sign, one they hadn't seen yet.

"Oh goodie. There are two. Maybe..." said Pam, a sassy smirk on her face.

"Ew. No," Aubrey said, picking up on Pam's train of thought. "Don't even think of it." She put her phone away. The timestamp on the picture read just after eleven, so they had found each other early. There would be no way she'd see him now. They'd be a day ahead from here at the very least.

They enquired when the church would reopen and were told around four.

"Well... Now what?" Pam said and, for the first time, Aubrey saw Pam perplexed at their situation. "We already passed the tourist information centre earlier in town. I'm kicking myself for not stopping now. I sure don't want to tackle those bloody stairs again!"

A couple overheard them and asked if they may help. They were an English couple and had arrived in Sarria the afternoon before. They had visited the Monastery of the Magdalena a little further along the way and had gotten their credentials from there. Pam thanked the woman, offering to buy their beers in return for their help.

"Oh, no, but thank you. You three don't look like you've just begun this Camino adventure," the woman said. "Where have you walked from?"

"Initially, from Saint Jean Pied de Port. But today? From Samos."

"You've walked from Saint Jean? Oh my! That's incredible. All of you?" She looked around the table. They all bobbed their heads with full mouths. The burgers were excellent.

"Yep, all seven hundred kilometres of it," said Pam, the first to finish her mouthful to answer.

Kay, the Englishwoman, was a Chatty Cathy, but so was Pam, energised by the nourishment and the enthusiasm of these kind people. As Pam regaled the story of their journey to the inquisitive couple, Aubrey and Georgina sat back and finished their beers. Aubrey reached for her phone and saw it was a quarter to three. They had time. It was nice to sit for a while and let the atmosphere and excitement of 'new pilgrims' wash over them. They were the seasoned pilgrims now.

But she had to wonder what the Camino would be like now, with all of these new people on the trail.

39

THE EFFECTS OF TOURIGRINOS

SARRIA TO PORTOMARIN TO VENTAS DE NARON

"Let's get our credentials and get the fuck out of this funhouse!" exclaimed Pam when they left the bar. Aubrey had to agree. Sarria was overwhelming. Hundreds of newly arrived pilgrims stood in large packs, with squeaky clean boots and shiny new backpacks, talking loudly to one another. The noise was alien to them now. Aubrey was curious to see how busy the trail would be the following day. She was relieved, now more than ever, they were walking between the stages noted in the Brierley's guidebook.

The hill climbing out of Sarria was tough. To manage the ascent, they talked about movies, naming their favourite rom-coms, comedies, thrillers, and dramas. By the time they got to the top of the hill they were laughing hysterically because of the offbeat suggestions that Georgina mentioned. She surprised them with a passion for gory horror films. Pam went in for action movies, but said she had a secret love for anything with Sam Elliott in it. It surprised no one when Aubrey admitted to her love for indie films.

"Let's settle in and then dip our feet in that pool," said Pam, once they finally reached their albergue.

"Looks like the millennials have taken over," said Georgina, as they looked over at party central by the poolside. "Lee would have a field day with this scene."

"I'll move them out of the way," said Pam. "I'm not shy." Aubrey had no doubt about that at all.

At dinner that night, they learned that there were three types of pilgrims staying at their albergue: The first type were the bed-runners, who walked hard and fast, chasing the next bed. Those pilgrims typically walked from Saint Jean Pied de Port to Sarria in under three weeks. The second type were the Camino Sprinters: they arrived at Sarria jet lagged and immediately started walking to the next town. They were mostly younger hikers with limited time or hubris to burn. Aubrey supposed they made up a third contingent, the slow strollers: The folks that respected the time-honoured tradition of the pilgrimage for what it was, a time to reflect and to grow spiritually. It worked for the Lovelies. And with the dorm asleep by nine pm, they appreciated the peace and quiet after such a hectic day.

The following morning, they were up before dawn to beat the heat. The forecast called for the temperature to top out at thirty-three degrees Celsius. They also wanted to beat the crowd. They walked in quiet contemplation for an hour before the onslaught from Sarria overwhelmed them in droves. Hikers were kitted out with headphones blasting in their ears, oblivious to anything that was going on, other than how fast the next foot would drop in front of the other. Even Georgina, as patient and calm as she was, expressed frustration when her friendly "Buen Camino" greetings were ignored or waved off.

"I don't understand it. Is it me or are they just rude?" asked Georgina when they stopped to the side to let a massive school group pass them by. She'd just been grunted at by a hiker on her last perky greeting.

"It's just the way they are, I suppose," said Aubrey. "Some see it as a hike, some a pilgrimage, others only see the physical challenge. It's their Camino too, remember?" Georgina scoffed at that.

"They must not have done any research about what it means," Georgina said. "Maybe they read about it somewhere and thought, 'Cool. I've got holidays coming up. I'll just go for a hike in Spain.' Ugh.

Sorry. I'm grumpy. I didn't sleep well, and they have rubbed me the wrong way."

Pam's quietness surprised Aubrey. If any of them would complain about this onslaught of people, it would be Pam. Georgina being the upset one was new.

"I'm not used to crowds or cities," Georgina said. "Crowds do me in."

"But you were okay in Burgos and in Leon?" said Aubrey. "Pamplona was just as busy."

"This is a different busy," Georgina said. "People were relaxed in Pamplona. This kind of determined pace, this rush, this aggressiveness," she said, as she inhaled deeply, "this is something else."

"Bloody millennials," grumbled a voice behind them. They swung around at the voice.

"Lee! Oh my god," Aubrey exclaimed. "We figured you'd be in Santiago by now."

"Nah. Threw out my back in Ponferrada," Lee said. "Had to stop a few days. That meant I had to change my flight home. No big deal."

"Oh, no! Are you okay?!" asked Georgina.

"Your backpack," Aubrey commented, noticing Lee was without hers. "Are you forwarding on?"

"Yes, and I'm regretting it at the moment," she said. "I'm considering picking it up, staying overnight and then fast forwarding. This shit is insane. I've never experienced so many rude people in my life." Ah, there was the Lean and Mean they'd met early on, although Aubrey kept that thought to herself.

"That's not a bad idea," said Georgina, moving out of the way for a tall man who seemed to be half walking, half running. He spat out a 'Buen Camino' as he raced by. Georgina just gave him a wave in return. His headphones would have prevented him hearing her reply anyway.

Lee stayed with them as far as Morgade. Her backpack waited for her there. She decided she would walk as far as Portomarin the following day, then fast forward to Santiago. She wasn't done walking though. She talked through her plan at length as they walked. She planned to take a bus to Finisterre, then walk back to Santiago via

Muxia. Georgina mumbled to Aubrey how tempted she was to walk with Lee, but Aubrey convinced her to stay with them.

"We'll get you through, Georgina," Aubrey said. "Maybe even help you keep your wits. These people are doing my head in too, but I keep thinking, we're almost there."

Lee hugged each of them before they left her in Morgade, promising to try to meet up with them in Santiago.

"The woman is pretty bad ass," said Aubrey, remembering the term she'd learned from Ben.

"But she's kinda scary too!" said Georgina. They laughed at that and talked about their initial impression of her.

"I still want to be her when I grow up," said Aubrey. "Maybe I can strive to be a creative like her. Did you know she's a successful artist?"

"No! Really?" said Georgina, shock making her voice rise.

"She was telling me when I was chatting with her in Burgos," said Aubrey.

"Yeah, she told me that too," said Pam. "An Avant Garde Georgia O'Keefe. That's what they called her in her local newspaper."

"She's from Santa Fe, right?" asked Georgina. "Isn't that where Georgia O'Keefe lived?" Aubrey confirmed with a nod.

"She told me she was both astonished and embarrassed by that description. That she could only hope she was half as good as Georgia O'Keefe," said Aubrey. "She truly is the bee's knees."

Just past Mercadoiro, the trio stopped at the iconic sign that showed them they had one hundred kilometres left to walk. Aubrey was appalled at the graffiti all over the sign. Pam asked if they'd recognised the change in the distances shown. She explained it had changed to a countdown to Santiago, rather than how far they had walked so far.

"Yeah, I wondered about that," said Georgina, as she tried to coordinate a group selfie. Aubrey fell on her bottom trying to scrunch down low enough to fit them all in the frame. They were all howling with laughter. It turned out to be one of the best selfies they'd taken on the trail.

"We need a selfie stick!" said Pam. Georgina reluctantly agreed.

Thankfully, there were plenty of other pilgrims on the trail willing to help, but their bungled selfie still turned out to be their favourite.

Further down the hill, as they closed in on Portomarin, they came to an intersection. They had a choice of route. They could either walk the easier way along the road or go via the historic path. Pam was concerned about her knees and voted the road route. The blurb on her app said there were some challenges to contend with on the historical, but Georgina and Aubrey were eager to try it. So, they split up, agreeing to meet at the bridge below. Aubrey and Georgina passed through a stunning array of colourful wildflowers. The aroma was intoxicating, which the bees seemed to agree with as they bounced among the hundreds of flowers, looking to absorb the abundant pollen.

"Are you sure this is right?" asked Georgina, when they finally reached the ancient stone steps, descending to the main road.

"Yes, I think so. I mean these stones look like they've been here for thousands of years," said Aubrey, taking her backpack off to toss it to the section below. There was no way she would get down the steps wearing it. The term 'challenges' in Pam's app was apt. It was going to be slow going, the steps were steep, but it didn't look impossible.

"Just imagine how many other pilgrims have gone before us!" Aubrey added.

Georgina led the way as they inched their way down the boulders on their bottoms, handing their backpacks to each other through a narrow passage and leveraging their trekking poles like they had when they descended the Pyrenees. With their feet safely planted on the road again, they took a selfie together with the boulders set in the backdrop. They celebrated their accomplishment of successfully navigating their way down with enormous smiles.

"Those rocks may not be bad for some of those fit kids we've been seeing, but I am not ashamed to say I went down on my bum!" declared Georgina.

Meeting back up with Pam, they crossed the bridge over the Miño River into Portomarin. At the end of the bridge, the trio stood at the base of the ascending stairs to the village. Aubrey, Georgina, and Pam let out a serious growl. They stared up at two teenage boys who sprinted up and down the steps like their asses were on fire. They flew up and down like it was nothing. To the Lovelies, it may as well have been Everest. Hills were one thing. Stairs were another. Stairs hurt.

Aubrey looked over at the other two. "Come on. Slow and steady. We can do this." She took the first step. Some young pilgrims passed them, but they didn't care. They took their time. One of the boys running up and down the stairs stopped and offered to carry Pam's pack to the top, but she shooed him away and, when she got to the top, did a Rocky dance. The young runners cheered and slapped her with high fives.

The climbing and heat had wiped them out. Today's walk was supposed to be nineteen kilometres, but the iPhone read twenty-four. Spanish kilometres, they joked. Somehow, the kilometres walked always tended to be ten to twenty percent further than the guidebooks showed.

The albergue for the evening was near the main plaza. The hospitaleros showed them to a room with five bunks lining the walls with another two bunks behind a heavy velvet curtain. He assigned them bunks closest to the curtain, tucked around the corner from the main door. The older gentleman spoke only Spanish, but they had enough experience now to understand the basics.

With the arrival routine complete, the Lovelies went in search of pizza. It took a bit of searching, but they finally found a place that offered what they were craving. They sat outside to enjoy the people watching. The sheer volume of people was intense.

"What do you Lovelies think about making reservations all the way through to Santiago?" Aubrey asked. "I estimate we saw close to three hundred people today and, at our pace, I worry we won't get beds. Did you notice we got the last three beds, and it's only just on three o'clock? Luckily we reserved!"

"I noticed that too," said Pam. "We need to be sure to stay in villages, rather than the major stops along the way. This is a major stage stop, according to the guidebook most pilgrims follow, which explains the crowds."

"I'm in," said Georgina. "I'm done with this shitshow. This is not what I imagined for the end of my Camino. I am finding the people way too stressful."

With that, Pam pulled out her online guide to look up places to stay. Georgina had paper and pen to take notes, and Aubrey was assigned to make reservations. She hoped to reach the albergues by either email or reserve online. Failing that, she had to make an old-fashioned phone call. When she had to call using her very basic Spanish, the other two laughed and taunted her mercilessly. By the time they'd finished their beer and pizzas, they had a clear itinerary that would take them all the way to Santiago. The icing on the cake was an Airbnb they had booked right next to the piazza in Santiago de Compostela.

By then, it was after six, so they ordered a bottle of wine and a round of desserts, finally able to relax.

AT QUARTER TO FIVE THE NEXT MORNING, FOUR SPANISH WOMEN SLEEPING in the bunks behind the velvet curtain started packing up. They whispered, zipped, rustled plastic bags and clipped repeatedly. Every time they left their room, their overhead light shone straight into Aubrey and Georgina's eyes. This went on for an hour. Aubrey lay there, willing them to turn their light off.

Pam politely asked them to be quiet in Spanish, but it fell on deaf ears. She repeated it in English, and they claimed not to understand. Bullshit, thought Aubrey, remembering one of the women answering a pilgrim's question in English only the night before. They treated the curtain as though it was a solid door, rather than fabric, oblivious to the other pilgrims still trying to sleep. Once packed, they walked to the kitchen on the other side of the albergue, leaving their packs by their bunks. Unfortunately, now their conversation was loud enough for the entire albergue to hear.

By six, the entire room was awake and packing up, including the three of them.

"Those Spanish women," said Pam, once on the trail again, "they know they fucked up. When they left, when you guys were in the bathroom, their heads were down. I told them in English, because I know at least one of them understood me, that they need to think about other pilgrims when staying in the dorms. Then I added for good measure that it wasn't just their personal fucking Camino experience!"

Aubrey chuckled. She was glad someone had spoken up.

"They really pissed me off. I felt I needed to say something. They were just so fucking rude," huffed Pam.

"There was no common courtesy this morning in our dorm," said Aubrey. "Even the French men came back and started banging on the front door. Did you hear them?" Pam and Georgina both shook their heads. Georgina had been in the kitchen, filling her water, Pam in the bathroom. "It's a wonder you didn't. They weren't just knocking. They were pounding on the door. It went on for quite a while. The twenty-something sitting by the door just sat, staring into her phone, ignoring the door completely. They were incessant! I was in the middle of putting Vaseline on my feet. Since no one else could be bothered, I threw my socks on and went to see what was going on. The girl didn't even look up when I went past her."

"Why were they trying to get back in?" Pam asked. "Was the door locked?"

"I suppose so. The gentlemen forgot their trekking poles. When I opened the door, they rushed in, strode to the pole stash, then walked right back out. No thank you. No acknowledgement. Just got their poles and left."

"Wow!" said Georgina. "I mean, even if they only spoke French, a simple smile or Merci would have sufficed!"

"Agreed. This is a different crowd, that's for sure," Aubrey said.

Attitudes continued to disappoint the Lovelies as they left Portomarin. The crowds seemed to grow bigger by the minute. They were all ready to give up and join Lee when a passing couple turned to them with beaming smiles and said, 'Buen Camino' so enthusiastically, it made them stop in their tracks. Seeing that made Aubrey feel some-what better. She loved their smiles and their attitudes. Unfortunately, the couple would be the anomaly of the day. They quickly gave up wishing anyone a Buen Camino who blazed past them. There was little point. After a while, they agreed many hikers were there just to check the Camino off their 'bucket list'.

They counted three school groups, one of them on bikes. They lost count of the tourigrinos but noticed a lot of tour buses parked at each bar. One bus group wore lanyards with "Ministries" written boldly on the label. Pam grunted in disgust.

"That's how they're doing a pilgrimage?" Aubrey said "Via a tour bus? I think they sorely missed the point of the Camino."

"It's a tourist destination, now that we're past Sarria," said Georgina. "I think that's an apt description, don't you?" Aubrey nodded. It sure seemed that way.

"I miss the Pyrenees!" declared Aubrey. Aubrey looked over at Pam. She was unusually quiet. She could almost see the cogs turning in her head. "Pam?"

"I think it's fair that I should talk about judgement here," said Pam. "There is an underlying sentiment to not judge others who walk the Camino. Everyone has their own way of accomplishing that goal. We walk slow while some walk fast. Others may fast forward. I mean, look at Lee. She hurt her back, so now she wears a day pack, sending her backpack forward. If we didn't know her and saw her today, we'd probably think 'tourigrino', right?"

"I agree. Most of that anyway," said Aubrey. "What I'm feeling, however, is many are missing the true essence of the Camino. Just remember the conversations we've heard in the last two days. That girl from England who did not know what the pilgrim shell represented? Or that conversation we overheard at dinner last night about how that woman didn't know the Camino had been a pilgrimage for centuries? The fact that she thought it was built fairly recently for," she said, indicating air quotes, "'a lovely hike'. There are people who just aren't aware."

"Or don't care. To those people, it is just a hike," said Georgina. "They don't wish anyone a Buen Camino. They aren't considerate of anyone around them. And I think that's where I find the most issue."

"You're right. The Camino is not a hike," said Pam. "And yes, I'm frustrated that people ignore, or are ignorant of the fact, that it's meant to be a pilgrimage. I mean, without touching on the religious part of the Camino, without feeling the true physical, emotional or mental strain, it feels like these people are diminishing the importance of it. Without the camaraderie with those around you, without the deep conversations, they are not fully experiencing it. And honestly, that saddens me."

"But not judging. Right?" said Georgina, sheepishly. "As you said, people are walking it for their own reasons."

Pam nodded and went quiet for a while. Aubrey agreed with Pam, but it was clear Pam had been pondering this. She had said little about judgement. She wasn't one to hold back most days with her opinions, but Aubrey wondered if this latest admission related to her Catholic upbringing. Tom had mentioned something similar about judgment in the text she'd received from him the night before.

"Maybe I'm judging people too harshly," said Pam. "Judgement is one of my biggest pet peeves in the world. Seriously, I hate it when people judge me. And yes, I see the irony."

"I hear what you are saying Pam," said Aubrey. "To be honest, I'm finding myself eager to finish this wander now. I am kind of over it at this point."

"I feel the same," said Georgina. "I was considering this last night. It irks me to no end that these rude, self-absorbed tourigrinos get the same Compostela that we do! The same sacred document that certifies we've met the requirements of our pilgrimage on the Camino de Santiago. It feels, I don't know… devalued to me."

"Well, they still have to walk one hundred kilometres to be eligible to receive the Compostela," said Aubrey. It wasn't a short distance, Aubrey thought, that was true, but she understood and agreed with Georgina's point.

"I know that," said Georgina. "My issue is that the Sarria crowd get the same Compostela as we do. It should be a different one."

"It's good to know I'm not the only curmudgeonly old hen!" said Pam. "As I said, everyone is entitled to their own Camino. Besides, we all have our stamped credentials showing our efforts. I reckon that document will be more sacred to me than the Compostela."

Pam began humming 'Let it Go,' from Frozen, an excellent reminder given their frustration.

"We need to focus on the beautiful things," said Georgina and for the next few kilometres, she pointed out the size of the wild poppies and the fields full of wild daisies.

Soon, they smelled every rose on the trail. Aubrey was grateful to Georgina for keeping them grounded and said as much to her.

The long, hot, exasperating day ended in Ventas De Naron around two o'clock. They stood at the entrance of their albergue and looked at each other. The place was grungy looking. Their anxiety increased when they saw a tour bus parked out the front.

Aubrey stared at the scene, second guessing their decision of booking ahead.

40

KINDNESS AND COMPASSION GO
A LONG WAY

VENTAS DE NARON TO PONTE CAMPANA TO RIVADISO

"It's now a thing," Pam declared, when they finally left Ventas de Naron. The woman sleeping in the corner bed of their dorm room started packing up at quarter to five. More zippers and plastic bags crinkling, in and out of the bathroom, but at least she'd left the lights off. The smelly man, sleeping in the bed next to Aubrey, got up right afterwards, but he'd made no effort to be quiet at all. What was it about packing up so bloody early?

"The noise makers must be part of the Sarria crowd," Pam decided as they left tired, frustrated, and without breakfast. Fortunately, the first open bar they found was only three kilometres along the trail. The food and coffee quietened their tempers. The warmth of the rising sun settled them further.

As Aubrey walked, eucalyptus trees appeared along the hills. She pointed them out to Pam and Georgina and commented how surprised she was to see them. Pam recalled the story of how the trees arrived in Spain.

"A Galician monk travelled to Western Australia as a missionary, then returned to Spain with eucalyptus seed. Apparently, the species adapted so well to the climate here, it spread rapidly. Now, it's considered a nuisance." They laughed. It may be a nuisance to Spain, but the familiar smell was making them homesick.

They stopped to smell the roses as they had before. The flowers added another layer of beauty to the picturesque scene before them. They decided collectively to focus on the positives around them, instead of the pilgrims pounding out the kilometres.

"It's a lot quieter today. Not nearly the population we saw yesterday. I'm loving it," said Georgina, after taking some gorgeous shots of blooming roses with her iPhone.

"We left from Portomarin during peak hour yesterday," said Pam. "But we stayed off the usual Camino stage last night, so I think we'll see a lot less today."

The day heated quickly. It was forecast to be in the high twenties, Pam reported. In Australia this kind of weather was mild, but the exposure to the intense heat was another story. At this stage of the Camino, they welcomed the relief of forests to walk through, and the sound of the cuckoos in the distance.

They arrived in Palais del Rei and enjoyed a cool drink in the piazza. None of them had any desire to hang around the city. They wanted to get back to the country as soon as possible, especially after seeing two women standing outside of a church getting signatures for something. Scammers, Pam called them.

"Why do you say that?" asked Georgina.

"They're gypsies who stalk people around churches, sometimes they even go inside, asking people to donate to fake charities but line their own pockets instead."

"They go inside the churches?" asked Georgina, shocked at the boldness. "I'd think they've be afraid of, you know, the repercussions. Burning in hellfire and all that."

"You'd think so, wouldn't you?" said Pam, navigating the busy streets between glances at her map.

"I mean, I'm not religious, but there's something to be said about not tempting fate," said Georgina. She pointed to a yellow arrow on a wall and sighed with relief. They'd lost track of them navigating the traffic. Pam nodded and kept following the arrow's direction.

"This is an awfully winding way out of town," said Pam, as they had finally exited a major part of the city. She compared her app to the yellow arrows which took them down through a residential section, rather than straight down the major road.

"Probably to keep the pilgrims from getting hit," said Aubrey. "I mean, look at that guy further down." She pointed to a pilgrim taking his time walking across the highway. "That truck will have to lay on the brakes if the guy doesn't hurry."

"Let's stick to the arrows," said Pam. "You're right, Aubrey. Seems like the arrows take us this way for a reason."

Near where the pilgrim had scraped by from being run down, Georgina pointed to a distance sign on the highway that read sixty-five kilometres to Santiago. She let out a loud whoop.

They set a leisurely pace as they strolled through villages. Pam pointed to the hórreos; ancient structures used to store grain.

"They look like little elevated cubby holes," remarked Georgina, taking photos as they went past the structures.

"Some are built using wood, some stone. They're raised off the ground to help prevent rodents from getting in. And the slits in the walls allow for ventilation. In the old days, some grain was used to feed pilgrims coming through. Most are abandoned now, but some are considered pieces of art. Only a few are still in use."

Soon, the trees took on an eerie presence and Pam began making up scary fairy tales using the branches as wicked elements. One was about a cluster of trees snatching children. Another was about the branches squeezing the life from evil pilgrims.

"Are you sure you were a teacher?" joked Georgina. "Those stories sound more like nightmares!"

"You do know the original fairy-tales weren't the Disney version?" replied Pam and shared stories even Aubrey wasn't aware of.

They arrived at their albergue in Ponte Campaña, a rustic old farm building nestled into the valley of an ancient forest. The albergue itself was a family-run operation. They were relieved to find their bunks tucked into the back of the dorm room, far away from the door. It was Pam's favourite section of a room.

After Pam and Georgina took their showers, Aubrey went in for hers. The stream of hot water was delightful on her tired muscles, but she screamed when the water ran bone-chillingly cold after about a minute. She washed in record time, shivering as she returned to her bunk. Two lovely Swiss ladies arrived just as she was heading to the bunks, so Aubrey thought to warn them. Later, at dinner, they told her the gas bottle had run out. They'd explained that they'd tried to find her earlier, to let her know the host had replaced it. She thanked them for thinking of her, then shared that she'd let Mother Nature warm her instead. In doing so, she'd fallen asleep in the hammock suspended under a grove of trees, only waking to Georgina's gentle nudging at dinnertime.

Dinner turned out to be one of the best meals they'd had on the Camino. The hosts served homemade vegetable soup as the first course, which contained actual vegetables, something lacking on the typical pilgrim menu. The second course was a culinary dream come true. It consisted of heaping bowls of green beans and potatoes accompanied by beef that fell-off-the-bone. It was so tender and juicy Aubrey went back for seconds. Sadly, dessert let it all down. Georgina looked just as disappointed as she felt. They served a meagre piece of leftover cake and a sliver of ice cream. Well, she knew she couldn't have it all.

USED TO THE EARLY RISERS NOW, THEY WAITED UNTIL THE EAGER BEAVERS departed and took their time packing up. They decided to have some breakfast at the café before they set off.

With Georgina and Pam holding a table outside, Aubrey went in to order for them. As she stood waiting, a group of tourigrinos descended upon her like locusts, shuffling her out of the way. The gentleman behind the bar smiled at Aubrey with a look of resigned bemusement. He pointedly ignored the swarming mob and apologised to her for the wait. She returned the smile and placed the order speaking completely in Spanish. Proud of herself, she was pleased when the guy nodded at her order, then turned and left the locusts to wait.

Aubrey knew that today's distance would be a push for them. Pam was most concerned and called their upcoming albergue in Rivadiso to reconfirm their reservation, letting them know they would arrive around four. She stressed that they were slow walkers, but they would be there. Pam shared what she'd learned on the Australian Camino Forum: It wasn't uncommon for the albergues to give away the beds of late arrivals. It seemed a few bad apples made reservations, just in case they needed it, but did not intend to stay.

By the time they finished breakfast, the locusts had devoured their meal and hit the trail, leaving a mass of destruction in their wake.

Pam seemed agitated.

"We'll be okay," Aubrey said, assuming Pam worried about reaching Rivadiso at a decent hour. "We have lots of time. Besides, we're stronger now than we've been. With the cooler weather after last night's storm, we can pick up the pace a bit if we need to." Pam looked at her phone again, her expression dour.

"It's not that," she said, as they started on the trail toward Melide.

"What is it?" asked Aubrey. "Are you okay?"

"Yes, yes, I'm fine. It's probably stupid," said Pam, pulling her backpack lower on her hips and pulling the waist strap tighter.

"Pam. Spill it," said Georgina.

"Ugh. Fine. It's Jack." Aubrey and Georgina looked at each other and stayed quiet. "I emailed him two days ago. He hasn't written me back. I thought things were, you know, okay. Better than okay. But now, I don't know."

Ah, thought Aubrey. She and Jack had been emailing like two lovesick teenagers since Pam had finally reached out to him. She told him she was in the middle of northern Spain, walking the Camino. He'd responded that he was 'impressed that she was doing something that sounded so fascinating'. So, she gave him a list of books to read and programs to watch, including *The Way*. Aubrey and Georgina giggled at that, knowing Pam hadn't seen the movie herself.

"What was the last thing he said?" asked Georgina.

"He asked about when I would finish in Santiago and what I had planned afterward," she said. "He said that he'd lived in Paris for five years, many years ago, and suggested some places to visit."

"And you haven't heard from him since?" Aubrey asked.

"No. And I'm worried," said Pam "I mean, his son was visiting him. But I've heard nothing from him since. I'm wondering if I said something to, you know, piss him off."

"Pam. They're probably busy. You'll hear from him, don't worry," soothed Georgina.

They stopped at the church of San Juan de Furelos, near Melide. Pam was lost in her own world. Aubrey asked what she could do to help with Jack when they mounted their backpacks outside.

"Oh, I'll be fine. I'm over it," said Pam. "He'll get back to me when he's ready. You're probably right."

"You just seemed quiet in the church," Aubrey said. Pam looked at her, confused, before she caught on.

"Oh! Oh, that has nothing to do with Jack," Pam said. "Catholicism took over. The unusual crucifix of Christ reaching down from the cross to help humanity really moved me. It's an excellent reminder for each of us to show kindness and compassion in a world increasingly removed from both. I may have little faith, but the symbolism struck me."

"I have been thinking about something along those lines myself," said Georgina. She had been rather quiet today too.

"I have felt affronted by the abruptness of those walking from Sarria. It made me realise that, for many, they may not have the same opportunities to take the time off work, or have flexibility in their lives," Georgina said. "Maybe they only have a week and when you think of it, the Camino is a good way to clear your head and gain some perspective in the world."

"You make a great point," said Aubrey. "Many have limited time. We've seen that with the Europeans. They do the Camino in stages. And it may scare people, women especially, to something like this on their own. I guess groups make them feel safer, or at least, they may see groups as more convenient."

"I get that. I second-guessed myself before I started," said Georgina. "But I think the Camino is easy to do on your own because, hello! You meet people!" she said, waving her arms to show their bond.

"I still don't get the headphones though. Personally, I do my best thinking when it's quiet and I only hear the sounds of nature. But everyone is different," said Georgina. "I think that's why the Portomarin stage almost made me quit. I couldn't focus on anything but the noise. That was a big trigger for me."

"Yeah, it was rather bad," said Pam. "We were so used to it being calm. And, even before Leon, people were looking out for each other. It changed after that. Kindness and compassion, I tell you."

"I KNOW WE ONLY HAVE SIX KILOMETRES TO GO, BUT I'M STARVING. YOU guys okay to stop?" asked Georgina. The others agreed. It was close to two in the afternoon.

"Somehow we've walked twenty kilometres today," said Pam, looking down at the app on her phone. "It's no wonder we're hungry. I don't know what measurement these guidebooks use, but they sure aren't modern ones."

"Spanish miles," Aubrey said.

With the humidity creeping in, the result of last night's rain, Aubrey knew it would be a hard slog for the last six kilometres.

They found a café and ordered burgers and cold drinks. Beside them, a mix of Australians and American women talked about the quality of the food. An American complained it was too bland. The Australian compared her meal to the fare at the boarding school she had attended. Aubrey smiled, but said nothing. Aubrey realised the snotty-sounding woman, the one who was louder than the rest, had been a regular customer of hers about five years before in Melbourne. Aubrey did her best to make herself invisible.

"Bloody Stepford Wives," said Pam after they'd left the women to their bitching. "Happy we were quiet over lunch. God help us if they knew we were Australian..."

"They wouldn't have pulled us in to their conversation," said Aubrey. "I mean, no offence, but look at us." Dust covered each of them from head to toe, their shoes were scuffed and muddy, and their hats were skewed and faded by the sun. So much different to the ladies wearing makeup, pressed shorts and clean shirts. Understanding came to Pam and Georgina, and they howled with laughter.

"We're pilgrims," said Georgina. "Those ladies were out for a five-star hike. Did you see how clean their shoes were?!"

"One of them used to be a regular customer of mine," admitted Aubrey.

"Really?!" exclaimed Georgina, shocked.

"Yes. Nancy. That was her name. Named after Nancy Reagan. Her father was from Houston, I believe. Anyway, she's just as obnoxious in person. I'm only glad she didn't recognise me."

"They were already three sheets to the wind," said Pam.

"Drinking Sangrias by the looks of it," Aubrey said. "The pitcher on the table was nearly empty too."

"I'm glad to be putting some distance between us then!" said Georgina.

They finally reached Rivadiso after a gruelling day. Crossing a bridge, they saw tired pilgrims soaking their feet in the river below. They recognised the pilgrims as American women they'd met in an albergue way before Sarria.

"Hey ladies!" one of the pilgrims called out, waving at them with a huge grin on her scorched face, "Come on down! The water's fine."

"Happy pilgrims. This is our kind of group," said Georgina. When they got to the water's edge, Pam dropped her pack, threw off her shoes and walked straight into the river. When she was knee deep, she turned around to face them.

"Fuck soaking our feet," she exclaimed, "I'm all in!" Then she flopped backwards into the water, fully clothed.

41

REFLECTIONS

RIVADISO TO O PEDROUZO

"Two more days Lovelies and this will be over," Aubrey said, experiencing a tightness in her heart knowing they were almost at Santiago. She was relieved in a way. She was ready for the walking to be over, but she didn't want the journey to end. She felt cocooned on the walk, like the outside world ceased to exist. Georgina, Pam, and the walk were all that mattered.

They agreed to get a head start on the day. The heavy morning fog cast a beautiful glow on the village. Only the echo of footsteps and hints of whispered conversation could be heard through the mist. In the eerie quiet, she sensed that they were all keenly aware that their time together was ending.

"This Camino has been good for me," said Pam eventually.

"Well, you're complaining less," joked Aubrey. "And not swearing as much."

"Yeah, yeah. I'm serious," Pam said. "I was tossing this over in my head last night. I started this walk full of anger and feeling rather lost in myself. I was looking for something, but it wasn't religion. I've had enough of that to last me a lifetime."

"Did you find what you were looking for?" Georgina asked. They walked through a muddy passage, sheltered by the sun by a canopy of trees. A rowdy group of pilgrims with a spring in their step passed them by. A young pilgrim, no more than twenty-five, sporting a pixie haircut and a dazzling smile, turned and waved as she walked by. Aubrey wished her a Buen Camino.

"I've determined I need to have faith in something bigger than me, whether that's God or whatever. And, if I do that, if I trust it, I will be happier. But to be clear, I won't succumb to the doctrines of religion anymore and I sure won't let it take over my life. That is not God to me."

"Sounds like you have found the right path for you," said Aubrey.

"The thing I was missing was trust in myself. I thought I would find that when I discovered that little dream cottage. But I've realised it's not about the house. It's what goes into the house that makes me feel whole. Love. Compassion. Friendship. Understanding."

"I think that's really what we all want," said Georgina.

"Yes," said Pam, hesitating for only a minute. "Yes, I suppose you're right." She went quiet again. "Except that I've never felt much of that in my life. Not until you two came along and reminded me what that meant. And I thank you for that." Georgina, teary, gently rubbed her shoulder.

"Anyway, that's what I've been pondering. It's been a challenging walk for me. I came into it wanting to be free of the anger. I didn't expect the rest. The support, the friendship, the love you have given me. Or by the others… Ben, Hannah, Paolo, Marinka. I have a connection to people again and I haven't had that in a long time. Not since…"

"Jack?" Georgina asked.

Pam nodded. "I am thankful," she said. "More than thankful."

They walked for a little while in silence, stopping to take photos of the wildflowers, of cows with their udders stretched painfully full of milk, of other walkers traipsing ahead of them through the mystic forest paths. They walked like soldiers, heads forward, backs straight, proud to know that they had come so far.

"If we're going to talk about what we've learned," said Georgina, "here's mine. I came on this walk trying to work out what I wanted.

With my marriage, my business, my life. I still don't know some of it, but this walk has been enlightening for me too." She paused. "It's been more mentally challenging than physically. I mean, I've never been so bloody sore but, other days, I've felt rejuvenated."

"Those would be the less than fifteen-kilometre days," joked Aubrey.

"Ha! You're right," laughed Georgina before becoming pensive again. "I have learned I can be quick to fall into a negative mindset, especially if I am tired and sore. I know that if I can do this, then I can do anything. It's about perseverance and tenacity."

"You have a lot of gumption," said Aubrey.

"Yeah, I've realised that too. I can stand up for myself. Before, I just went with the flow. Did what was expected, but not necessarily what I wanted. I have had amazing emotional support from you two, which has completely bowled me over. I didn't expect that, and it's made me realise how much I've missed that in my life, especially in my marriage. I came here not realising how much I missed deep, emotional, heartfelt conversations."

"You're welcome to have those with me, anytime," said Aubrey. "I have missed that in my life too."

"I know this may sound out of left field, but what is happening in your marriage?" asked Pam, "You haven't mentioned that in a while."

"Yeah. You've been quiet about it," said Aubrey.

"Patrick finally got back to me," said Georgina. "He's been seeing a counsellor on the mainland. Part of his mining job provides mental health support, so he told me he'd try it."

"That's great," said Aubrey. Georgina nodded, but she still looked sad. "But it's not enough, is it?"

Georgina was quiet for a while as they walked through a trail full of grand old trees.

"He's saying the right things, but I'm not convinced," Georgina finally said. "It's like he's reading a guide on 'how to save a marriage'. I mean, I get that it's difficult with me being on the other side of the world. But I still feel like some of what he's saying is, I don't know, disingenuous."

"Do you think he's just trying to save face?" asked Pam. "From what you said, his upbringing was very much about appearances."

"I have been wondering about that. I just don't know," said Georgina. She stopped talking as they tiptoed their way over stone boulders to cross a creek. Cyclists politely waited for them to pass before they rode through the water. They thanked them for their consideration.

"What I know," Georgina continued, "is that I love him. I'm not ready to give up." She hesitated. "At least not yet. I'm willing to see what happens when I get home. But I've realised that if he's saying what I want to hear, but not doing the hard work, I'm strong enough to walk away. I know I'm strong now. It will be tough if I have to do that. I don't want to leave Orford, just as he won't, but that's another hurdle isn't it?"

"I believe you've always been strong Georgina. I just don't know if you knew that. It's good to hear you say so," said Aubrey. "And I'm here, anytime you need me.'

Georgina smiled.

"Me too," said Pam. "In fact, I think we should come and see you in Tasmania, just the three of us. Lee can join us later to do the Three Capes Walk.

"Yes. And we need to be there to help you launch your new business," said Aubrey. "You'll need help mounting those beautiful photos and we can help to get your website set up."

"You also need to look at our property, Pam. The area I have in mind, truly, it's perfect for your dream cottage," said Georgina. "Plus, it will mean keeping you close by." Pam reached over and squeezed Georgina's hand.

"Okay! Then soon?" said Pam. Aubrey wondered briefly how Jack would fit into Pam's dream.

"How about August?" suggested Aubrey. "My birthday is in August and I couldn't think of two people I'd rather spend it with."

"What about Tom?" asked Pam. "Why not bring that Fine Specimen with you?"

"Tom is still an unknown," replied Aubrey. "You guys are a certainty."

"No matter who comes to Tasmania," said Georgina, "you are all welcome anytime. And bring Simon. He's welcome, too. August sounds great to me. Just be sure to pack your winter woollies. It gets cold."

THREE KILOMETRES FROM O PEDROUZO, A RAINSTORM FORCED THEM TO scramble for their ponchos. They were seasoned now, only caring about protecting the contents of their packs. The shower passed quickly, and the green foliage looked fresh after the cleansing rain.

"Do you smell that?" asked Aubrey. The scent emanating from the eucalyptus trees was pure magic.

"Oh!" said Georgina. "I'm homesick. I want to hop a plane home to Australia. Like right now." She stopped and took a deep breath, inhaling the aroma of home.

"You still need to walk twenty kilometres Georgina. It's our last night my Lovelies," said Aubrey, as she stepped up to the footpath that led into O Pedrouzo.

"Do we know where our albergue is?" asked Aubrey, looking at the confusing mess of albergue signs posted on buildings and poles before them, while other pilgrims hustled through the traffic.

"Yep," said Pam, halting suddenly in front of a grand hotel positioned high on the hill. "Right here."

"That's our albergue?! It looks like a five-star hotel!" said Georgina as they stood shoulder to shoulder, looking up at the stone porticoed building.

"Come on, I'm ready to get out of this wet stuff," said Pam and bounded up the stairs with renewed energy. Aubrey and Georgina trailed behind, hobbling like they were twenty years older.

AT DINNER, THEY RAISED A GLASS TO TOAST THEIR LAST NIGHT ON THE Camino.

"To our last night. Saluté," said Georgina, taking a sip of her red wine. She sat the glass down on the table before adding, "It doesn't seem real. I mean, part of me is ready for it to be over. I'm wanting to wear a dress, for goodness' sake," she giggled. "And maybe even put some lipstick on. That's very girly, I know, but that's normal for me."

"I get it. I'm looking forward to being out of these clothes. I now understand why the pilgrims used to burn their clothing at Finistère," said Pam.

Aubrey was quiet. She too was ready for the walk to be over, but she was wondering about her future. Pam's comment about Tom nagged her as well.

"What are you looking forward to Aubrey?" Georgina asked.

"Fresh clothes. A nice long bath. Anything other than a pilgrim meal," she said. Their conversation from earlier had really made her think a lot about her journey.

"What's spinning in that head of yours then?" asked Georgina. She knew her too well.

"Too much," Aubrey said, hesitant to continue, but knowing the trust between them, she ploughed ahead. "I was mulling over our conversation about what you guys have learned," said Aubrey.

"And?" asked Pam, picking up her fork to move the tuna off her salad.

"I lost a lot of faith in the Universe, especially after Cass died. I was angry, furious really, with whoever was running the show. But now, after this walk, I have a sense of… I don't know. Peace? I didn't realise it until today. It feels strange that I feel that way. I mean, I will never be over losing Cass, but…" she played with the lettuce on her plate, "maybe I've finally accepted what happened was inevitable in a way. I mean, I did all I could, and I suppose, I have finally…," she said, sitting up in her chair a little more, "finally accepted that it wasn't my fault." She said it in almost a whisper. She felt Pam and Georgina looking at her but dared not look up.

"When I sat in my albergue room in Saint Jean," said Aubrey. "I was overwhelmed with self-doubt. I did not expect to finish this walk… Granted, we haven't yet… but I guess I'm in awe that we've walked this far."

"We will finish!" said Georgina.

Aubrey laughed. "Yes. We will." She took a breath. "I am so grateful I met you on that first day. I have enjoyed every step. Well, almost every step." They all laughed at that. "I mean, my feet have been incredibly sore. My knees have screamed at me at times. Even my hips have told me they've had enough around eighteen kilometres. But I've learned that slow and steady is the best course to take."

"Amen to that," said Pam.

"I guess what I'm saying is I know now that I am strong, physically, mentally and, like you," Aubrey said, looking over at Pam, "spiritually stronger. I feel more in touch with myself than I have in years. It's been an amazing journey and I'm glad to have done it with you two."

There were tears in Pam's eyes and it was enough to put her over. She started crying but quickly wiped the tears from her eyes.

"I'm glad to hear you've accepted it's not your fault," said Pam. "It's hard to get past the anger. That part I know. But I think this journey has been exactly what we needed to get past it." Pam reached over and kissed Aubrey on the cheek, then squeezed her hand.

"Here's to our beautiful lives from here," said Aubrey and raised her glass.

"To positivity, strength, and love," said Pam.

4 2

KNOWING WHAT YOU'RE
MADE OF

O PEDROUZO TO SANTIAGO DE COMPOSTELA

It was just after dawn when they began walking toward Santiago.

"I got a text from Ben last night," said Aubrey. They walked the empty streets of O Pedrouzo with only a handful of pilgrims about.

"Oh? Where is he? Will he be in Santiago?" asked Georgina.

"He's already there. With Hannah," said Aubrey.

"Hannah?!" exclaimed Pam, stopping in her tracks. "I thought she had gone home since we haven't heard from her."

"She left Leon two days after us, fast forwarding to Sarria. She's been in Santiago for three days, waiting for us apparently. Ben just arrived yesterday."

"She must feel better," said Georgina, "That's excellent."

"Yes. He said they'd wait for us at the Cathedral," shared Aubrey.

"Okay," said Pam. "Although, I kind of wish we could have walked in together. You know, our whole Camino family."

"I agree. They've been such an enormous part of this walk," said Georgina.

"You know, I've had Hannah on my mind for days. I have a feeling," Aubrey shared. "Not sure what it is, but it's a positive thing. I get a good vibe when I think of her."

"Your vibes are intriguing," said Pam. "I think it's an interesting part of you. Whatever it is, don't lose it."

"I doubt I will," Aubrey said, happy she was finally listening to her vibes.

They turned left from the road into another eucalyptus forest. The smell was intoxicating, and they each stopped, one by one, and inhaled deeply. Pam even walked over and hugged a tree, making them all laugh. Georgina said she wanted to capture the light beams filtering through the canopy, casting a sublime glow through the forest. It just had to be photographed.

"This is magical. Just listen," Pam whispered. "It's so quiet." There was a cuckoo counting down somewhere in the distance, but otherwise, the whisper of wind dancing across eucalyptus leaves was the only sound they heard.

"Where are all the pilgrims?" said Georgina softly. "I would expect this to be a highway of people this morning."

"Don't know. Don't care. I just want to take in this moment," said Pam. They stood in the middle of the track, soaking in the last moments of their walk. By the end of the day, it would be over. The thought weighed heavily on Aubrey's mind.

The cherished moment didn't last long. When they crossed the bridge out of Lavacolla, a stampede of pilgrims overran them. Thankfully, the mood had changed in this part of the walk. Everyone was excited to be so near the end. A few greeted them enthusiastically with an 'almost there!' Some walked with their eyes wide, soaking in the last morsels of their journey.

They stopped in the bar at Vilamaior for a second breakfast. They had eight kilometres to go.

"So, when are you leaving Santiago?" Aubrey asked Pam, as they enjoyed their last Camino coffee together.

"Day after tomorrow. What's your plan? Have you decided?" It felt weird to be talking about the actual world again. Aubrey wasn't sure she was ready for what was next.

"I am hanging around a few days, then taking the train to Madrid, I think. I don't know yet," Aubrey said.

"Is Tom still meeting you in Santiago?" asked Georgina.

"I got a message from him earlier. He said he'd be waiting for us. His son left this morning," Aubrey replied.

"Sounds like we have a crowd waiting for us with Ben and Hannah too. Should be a nice celebration when we get there," said Georgina.

"Should be," said Aubrey with a sadness seeping into her voice. She thought of Tom. He seemed so long ago. She wondered if the connection they'd experienced was real, or merely a Camino Romance. She feared the latter.

"Just have faith, Aubrey," said Georgina, picking up on her demeanour. "If he's still waiting for you, it means something." Aubrey nodded.

"How about you, Georgina? When are you off?" Pam asked.

"I have to check to be sure. A few days," Georgina said. "I'm not looking forward to the thirty-five plus hours it will take to get home."

"Yuck," said Pam. "That doesn't sound like fun. Which is why I'm delaying it. I should be home just in time for our get together in Tassie."

"Good timing!" said Georgina.

"But first, we have to finish this thing," said Aubrey. "Are you Lovelies ready?"

"Not really," said Georgina, sadness lacing her voice. But they headed outside and mounted their backpacks. Pam double tapped her poles for what would probably be the last time.

They rounded the perimeter of the airport. The thunderous noise of planes coming and going was a strange thing to hear after six weeks of near solitude on the trail. They walked single file. Others passed them by, eager to have their walk complete and to begin their celebrations.

They walked past grand houses with beautiful, lush gardens. The residents posted signs on their fences, warning the pilgrims not to stop. They continued toward Monte Del Gozo. When they came to a huge metal statue, signifying Pope John Paul II's visit in 1989 at the top of the hill, they caught their first glimpse of Santiago.

"There it is," said Pam, pointing at the distant towers. "The Cathedral."

They hugged each other. This was the last time that they would be together, The Lovelies, as one.

Aubrey looked at Pam, then Georgina. She held their hands as they stood ringed together.

"I know this is very corny, but I read a brilliant line in a book last year and I think it's appropriate to recite it today. 'I know who you are and what you're made of,'" she paused, looking at them in turn. "I hope you know it, too."

Tears flowing, they hugged once more. Then, continuing to hold hands, they walked down the hill and into the city of Santiago de Compostela.

"WELL, LOOK AT THAT," SAID PAM. THEY WERE CROSSING THE WOODEN-slated bridge at the base of the hill, across the busy highway, when they noticed two people sitting outside the first bar. They were deep in conversation. At the sound of Pam's voice, Ben looked up and sprang to his feet, engulfing Pam in a hug. Hannah followed.

"Hi! It's so good to see you. We thought we'd walk in with you, if that's okay?" asked Hannah. She looked healthy. Aubrey noticed her small round belly poking through her shirt.

"We'll give you space though, if you'd rather do it alone?" Ben said.

"No, we'd love that," said Aubrey. "We were just saying last night how we wish we were all walking in together. With you two, and Paolo and Marinka." After following Pam's lead stowing her trekking poles, Aubrey linked arms with Hannah, and they continued into the city.

"Have you heard from Paolo or Marinka?" Georgina asked Ben and Hannah. "How did it all go? I know it's none of our business, but I'm so curious!" Georgina sounded just as excited to reunite with them as Aubrey was. Aubrey flashed back to the moment she'd met Ben on day one. It felt like an eternity since that day.

"They are doing great," Ben said. "He's moving to Germany, in fact."

"Oh, it must have gone well then." Pam said, doing a little jig. They chuckled at her happy dance.

Hannah looked down, as Aubrey said, "And you look to be doing well too?"

"For sure. No more morning sickness, thank goodness. I have energy again. It's amazing!" She had the glow of a pregnant woman.

"How was the rest of your walk Hannah?" asked Pam. The excitement was bubbling between them. They had so many questions. The Lovelies, while glad to see Ben and Hannah, were eagerly anticipating finishing the walk.

"I skipped to Sarria," Hannah said. "Walked from there. I met another girl who was a bit older and we walked in together. But, well, it wasn't the same. She was only doing the Sarria to Santiago part. She was more of a hiker than, you know, one of us."

"Oh, don't we know all about that!" said Pam, throwing a look over her shoulder at Aubrey and Georgina.

Happy pilgrims jammed the streets of Santiago. The yellow arrows seemed harder to find but Ben helped them through it. The people they passed wished them a Buen Camino or an 'almost there'. One person offered congratulations.

"We're not there yet," grumbled Pam in response, which made Aubrey smile. She would miss Pam's ways.

"Is that the Cathedral?" Pam asked Ben repeatedly. He just smiled at her each time and shook his head. After the fourth time, Ben, with humour, said he'd start charging a quarter for each time she asked, but assuring them they were almost there.

Hannah and Ben slowed the pace. Aubrey looked at Ben, eyebrows raised in question. He pointed toward a tunnel ahead. The sound of bagpipes ricocheted off the walls.

"This is it," Aubrey whispered. Pam took her left hand. Georgina took her right. Together, they walked down the steps and into the tunnel. She could feel Pam shaking. Aubrey looked over and saw tears hovering on Pam's lashes. She felt emotion well inside of her too. She looked to Georgina, who was beaming. They took the last step and exited the tunnel. Aubrey inhaled deeply. She swept her eyes over the piazza. She saw several couples hugging. They looked like penguins with their backpacks swaying back and forth. Others simply sat staring up at the Cathedral or used their backpacks as pillows to do so.

Pam stopped and looked up to her left. She bent her head down to her knees, emotion overtaking her. Aubrey stepped forward and faced the Cathedral.

She'd walked eight hundred kilometres. She had made it to this place. Emotion overwhelmed her. A sob escaped her throat before she felt the tears on her cheeks.

Georgina walked over and embraced her, crying her own tears of joy into her shoulder. Aubrey looked to Pam, still bent over. Aubrey hesitated, uncertain how to proceed, when Pam stood. She exuded raw happiness. Aubrey held out her free arm and Pam joined the embrace. The Lovelies held on to each other tightly, relishing in their accomplishment. After a moment, they broke free. The Cathedral regally stood before them. They slowly walked further into the piazza, still holding hands.

"We did it," Georgina whispered.

"We sure as shit did!" exclaimed Pam. She let out a huge whoop and suddenly leapt into the air. They laughed at the sight of this small, grey-haired woman, her glasses sliding down her snotty nose. She did her little jig at the joy of walking eight hundred kilometres, her way.

"May we join in this party?" asked Ben, after giving them the space to celebrate.

"Of course!" said Aubrey, hugging him. "You were one of the first I met on the Camino. You are part of this! You and Hannah!" She looked up after her hug with Ben. "Oh my god. Look."

They all turned to see a smiling couple walking hand in hand coming toward them. The pair dropped their hands and started clapping, enormous smiles on their face, feeling the moment just as they were. Marinka and Paolo made it after all.

"What? You guys are here?!" said Georgina, hugging them. Pam and Aubrey finally dropped their packs on to the ground and hugged everyone unencumbered.

"We wanted to cheer you in," said Paolo. "You didn't think you'd party without us, did you?!" He picked Aubrey's hand up and whipped her into a waltz, as they had done many times. Overjoyed, she planted a huge kiss on his cheek. She was surprised to see him blush.

"Oh! I'm so happy. This is so, so great!" said Pam, doing another little dance. They took photos of the three of them. A pilgrim nearby offered to take a group photo of all of them. Aubrey and Georgina stood at the end with their hands raised. Pam, Hannah and Ben were between them. Marinka and Paolo sat on the ground in front. Aubrey felt stunned to know they were all together again. They had walked so much of the Camino together, sharing so many intimate details of their lives. These people truly were her Camino family. Each one of them meant so much more to her than those she considered friends at home. She now understood the true meaning of friendship.

"Oh," gasped Pam. She became very still. "It can't be."

"What? What is it?" Aubrey asked, as Pam started walking away. A few steps in, she stopped, turned to look at Aubrey, pointing to her backpack, silently asking her to watch over it, a gesture they'd made many times over the last few weeks. Aubrey nodded, then watched Pam walk toward the corner of the piazza. Where was she going?

"What is it?" asked Georgina, standing close to her, watching as Pam kept moving away from them. From the shadows of the piazza's portico, a man stepped out toward her, holding a gigantic bouquet of red roses.

"It's Jack," Aubrey whispered. The scene transfixed her. She felt like she was intruding, but she couldn't look away from the scene.

"Oh wow," replied Georgina, just as mesmerised as she. Jack's face grew from a tentative squint to a beaming smile as Pam got closer. In a flash, Jack embraced Pam, crushing the roses against her back. Pam's body folded into his, as if she were made for him all along. Aubrey and Georgina finally turned away.

"That was…" Georgina said.

"Beautiful," said Aubrey, breathless. Ben, Hannah, Marinka and Paolo were all looking over toward Pam, dazed and confused.

"Who is that?" asked Ben.

"Her first love," said Aubrey, looking back over her shoulder. Jack handed the roses to Pam, and she bent her head to smell them. "He must have flown from Australia to be here. She didn't know."

"Oh wow," said Ben. "That's love. Right there." Aubrey nodded.

THEY AGREED TO WAIT TO PICK UP THEIR COMPOSTELAS. THEY WANTED more time to celebrate their achievement first. Besides, the line would be too long at this time in the afternoon. They checked into their Airbnb, which overlooked the piazza with a grand view of the Cathedral. Pam declared it a bargain. The Parador had the same view and charged over four hundred euros per night. She knew this, she said, because Jack had booked a room there. For three nights. She would join him, she admitted sheepishly, saying she hoped it didn't put the other two out.

"Are you kidding? I'm happy to split this with Georgina!" said Aubrey. They skipped showers as they knew the others were waiting. They were just eager for a beer and to celebrate with their friends.

They joined the others at an outside bar, just off the piazza. Pam introduced Jack to everyone. He looked nothing like Aubrey imagined. Standing at Aubrey's height of five foot ten inches, he had dark blonde hair and a confident stance; and he didn't leave Pam's side. Aubrey noticed a look of awe, admiration and pure love plastered on his face whenever he looked at her. She wondered what else they had exchanged in those letters.

She texted Tom to let him know they had made it. Tom responded he was at his albergue, just behind the Parador, and was eager to see her. She invited him to join them. She was eager to see him too.

"Now there's the Fine Specimen!" said Pam, only minutes later. Aubrey turned and saw Tom approach and stepped forward to hug him. It was good to see him. He bent down and kissed her, immediately bringing the butterflies back.

Aubrey heard Ben lean over to Georgina and whisper, "Can I get the lowdown on this guy from you later?"

"Yes, but fair warning. I may be joining you in your albergue tomorrow night," she whispered back. "Three's a crowd if you get my drift."

"Well, look at this crowd," a voice said, and Aubrey looked over to see Lee approach the table. "Here are some familiar faces!"

"Holy shit!" said Pam, jumping up from her seat to embrace Lee. "You made it! We didn't see you after Morgade. I was hoping you didn't pack it in."

"Nah, as we talked about, I walked back to Sarria, then caught the train to Santiago," Lee said, while Jack found another chair for Lee to join them. "Those tourists were killing me. I then walked to Finistère, on to Muxia, and back to Santiago. So, I still got my hundred kilometres in to be eligible for my Compostela."

"It didn't turn out that bad," Georgina said, "once we started staying between stages."

"True," said Aubrey.

"That's what my son and I did. A lot fewer pilgrims that way," said Tom, in his Irish lilt. She missed his accent.

"I heard that's the way to do it, past Sarria," said Ben, and they began sharing their stories of the time they spent walking apart.

Aubrey smiled as she looked around the table. She started something she never thought she could accomplish. These amazing people she met along the way helped her do it. Her heart swelled when she looked at every face. This journey brought people together from all walks, she thought. Ben and Hannah, Paolo and Marinka, Pam and Georgina, each one special in their own way. Even Tom had surprised her. She reached over to him. He picked up her hand and kissed it, looking into her eyes with a feeling she could not put words to. Maybe it was love? She was keen to find out.

She was looking forward to the next chapter of her life now. The Lovelies had helped each other navigate the long road to Santiago. They found the strength and persistence in each other that they couldn't see in themselves.

As she had said to Pam and Georgina at the hill overlooking Santiago, she finally knew who she was and what she was made of.

EPILOGUE - CAMINO WANDERED

GEORGINA LOCKED the front door of the café, then leaned her head against the door and sighed. A roar of cheers went up. She turned to find flutes filled with champagne lifted in her direction. She smiled, though hesitantly. Her face didn't quite express the celebration that tonight should bring. Aubrey moved toward her.

"You have not made a mistake George. I can see doubt in your eyes. You had a great launch. You should be really proud of yourself, I am." Georgina nodded, but Aubrey knew she didn't believe her. Georgina held out her arm to her daughter Nicole, a mirror image of her mother but for the silver hair, when she slipped in to hug her sidewards. Nicole handed her a glass of champagne.

"You sold everything Mum," Nicole said, her face beaming. Aubrey wanted to laugh at the shock on Georgina's face.

"I knew you'd be a hit," Aubrey said to her friend. "You have worked so incredibly hard these last few months. You deserve this, Georgina. Although, to be honest, I still don't understand why you did a low-key opening at your own café."

"Just in case I crashed and burned," muttered Georgina, her face reflecting disbelief at her success.

"But wait until you hear the best part," continued Nicole. "There was a gallery owner here. He bought a shack in Orford just last month and saw the notice when he came in last week. He wants to do a showing for you in Salamanca. And another for his Melbourne studio."

"What?" Georgina's face paled.

"And see Merritt over there, talking to Sam?" Aubrey followed the direction Nicole was pointing in and saw the short voluptuous blonde woman in three inch heels. "She's talking about building an eco-resort and she wants your work exclusively for the lodge and all the cabins. I meant, she still has to build the place, but she's keen on commissioning you."

"Breathe Georgina." Aubrey pointed to the nearby couches when Georgina wobbled on weak needs. Nicole led her dumbfounded mother to sit.

"How am I going to do all that?" whispered Georgina. "I'm not…"

"Don't you dare say 'not good enough' because you are. And you'll do it, one step at a time, just like you did to walk across Spain. Although you may need an agent at this rate."

"I'm so happy for you, Mum," said Nicole, and clinked her own glass with her mother's. Georgina stared absently at her untouched glass.

"What's going on? You look like you've just been told you're having triplets, Georgina," Pam said, sauntering over.

"I…" Georgina just shook her head in dismay.

"She can't speak. Nicole just shared how successful the launch has been. All her photographs were sold, and she has interest from a gallery owner and that woman over there. She wants to commission her as well."

"Oh, that's fu…. Fantastic!" Pam said, sheepishly smiling, as she stepped into her excited jig. "I'm working on my swearing since Jack has a five-year-old grandson."

"I need to…" and with that, Georgina jumped up and ran toward the bathroom. Aubrey shook her head. She would understand how talented she was eventually.

"I need to help with clean-up and send the servers home," said Nicole and left them to it.

"She'll be okay. She has never envisioned the greatness we see," said Aubrey. She was so happy for Georgina's success and could only hope her own launch would be as successful. Between her travels with Tom in Ireland and then coming home to find a place to live, thinking about her jewelry designs had fallen on the back burner. She still worried about her professional reputation.

"I'm going to help Nicole," said Pam.

Aubrey knew she should pitch in, but she wanted to take a moment. She looked around at Georgina's café. No, she corrected herself, Nicole's café. Georgina had handed over the business only a few weeks ago, although the name would remain as 'Georgina's Café'. It was an amazing place with a huge open fire in the middle, with one end of the café hosting a mix of bold red tables and the other end with deep brown leather couches and armchairs, clustered around low coffee tables. On the walls hung Georgina's photographs. Every inch of wall space held gorgeous shots of Tasmania, some black and white, some colour. In the corners were more photographs propped up on easels. Every one of them had a bright yellow sticker on the frame, a sign that the photograph was sold.

Aubrey knew it was a team effort to pull off the event. The photographs had been carefully selected by Georgina and Aubrey. Tom, Patrick, and Jack had worked together to hang the professionally framed prints with Georgina's direction.

Aubrey saw Jack and Patrick conversing in the corner. No doubt talking about the property Jack and Pam had just purchased from Patrick. She wasn't sure where Tom had disappeared to. Probably helping cleanup in the kitchen. He was gaining a reputation as being the dishwasher.

She sighed, feeling a sense of helplessness overwhelm her. Pam and Jack were moving ahead with their plans. With Jack's property well established in Victoria, they were going to build Pam's dream cottage as their getaway. The plans she'd seen were stunning. They had designs of a quaint cottage, with a large, trellised patio overlooking Spring Bay, with a small writer's studio set further up the hill. Even the studio was being planned out to the finest detail. It included a smaller verandah, kitchenette, a tiny bathroom, and a cozy potbelly stove inside for the cold, wintry days. The house was every bit the dream cottage Pam had described on the Camino. Georgina and Pam had their shit together.

What's wrong with me? she chided herself.

Aubrey's phone pinged, interrupting her pity party. Unlocking it, she saw a message from Ben.

Well? How'd Georgina's opening go?

Major success. Facetime you tomorrow?

Great! Send our love to all and congrats to G. xx.

That's right, she realized, tossing the phone on to the table in front of her. Ben had his life worked out too. After a trip to Texas to see Hannah, Ben and Kanmi offered to adopt Hannah's baby through an open adoption. The time and space on the Camino gave Ben the opportunity to open to the possibility. And Hannah, still eager to attend NYU, knew adoption was her best chance. Aubrey bawled when she found out about their adoption plans. It was such beautiful news for them all. Now Hannah was living with them in New York with the baby due any day. It was the perfect arrangement. Aubrey knew Ben would make a great dad.

Her thoughts turned to Marinka and Paolo. They were talking about moving in together, much to his mother's dismay. And last she heard, from Pam, Lee was doing well in Santa Fe. She was painting again and walking miles in the mountains every day. She was still planning on travelling to Tasmania the following year to do the Three Capes Walk with them.

And yet Aubrey was still trying to get a firm grip on the reins of her life. None of the properties they looked at in Victoria seemed right. And being with Tom had thrown a spanner into the works, for sure. She wasn't altogether sure what she made of that. Unlike Pam and Jack, who had fallen back into step with each other like a well-rehearsed waltz, she and Tom were still fumbling their way around each other.

She drained her champagne glass and walked over to the counter to take the tray of empty glasses back to the kitchen.

"I WAS CHATTING WITH SAM, WHEN I WAS IN THE KITCHEN EARLIER," TOM said, as they were getting ready for bed. "She's a lovely lass, she is. She lives over in Fergus Bay. Anyway, she was telling me there's an area just southwest of Hobart we should look at. One that might fit the bill. What d'ya think?"

"Maybe," she mumbled. She was distracted. She wished she could summon some of the courage she had tried to instil in Georgina, but the doubts plagued her. She left the Camino very clear on her goals, but lately her issues around trust were bubbling. Her mind kept flashing back to Tom's recent trip home to Ireland in response to his younger son's car accident. She didn't blame him for leaving, not at all. She'd do the same in a heartbeat. Rather, it was the way he'd left. It nagged at her. Tom dashed back on his ex-wife's word with little information. When he'd left, they didn't know if Liam was alive or dead. But in hindsight, his ex-wife knew exactly what had happened before Tom had boarded the plane. Tom had called Aubrey as soon as he'd seen his son. He'd suffered a broken collarbone and, from Tom's description, a bruised ego. So why had his ex-wife caused that much strife? The only reasoning Aubrey could muster was because of Brigid's history of lies and manipulation. Aubrey had had enough of that to last a lifetime. So why was it eating at Aubrey now? Tom had returned to her.

She pulled the bedcovers back and eased into bed beside Tom. He held open his arms, and she moved easily into them, feeling his arms wrap around her and his lips on her temple.

"What's wrong, Grá?" She smiled. She loved how he called her 'love' in Gaelic.

"Nothing. It's just been crazy these last few days." She didn't lie. Not really. She was fine. She just didn't want to think about how fast he'd reacted to his ex-wife's call. Aubrey thought about what bad luck she had with men...two dead-beat ex-husbands, and now Tom seeming just too good to be true. She wondered if her bad luck would continue. Brigid just might be Tom's kryptonite.

"Are you regretting not buying the Bright property?" Tom asked, snapping her back to their conversation. "Sorry I was at home in Ireland for that." At home. That didn't sit well.

No. That's when he'd rushed back to Ireland.

"No, I'm at peace with it. I just couldn't shake the bad vibe I felt while I was there. I'm not sure I ever could. I mean, the property was great. It had everything I wanted, except the vibe I got of someone dying violently in the house. I felt it in my bones. The real estate agent said she had no record of it, but..." if she'd learned anything on the Camino, it was to trust her instincts.

"Aye." She knew it was a sound decision to pass on it. Except she still didn't have a place to live. Sure, she could rent a place, but where? Her time with Tom in Ireland had been great, but Australia was her home. Besides, this is where the Lovelies were. She didn't want to leave them now.

The following morning, Aubrey sat at Georgina's kitchen table while Tom was off on a Facetime call with his boys. Georgina was making another coffee, so Aubrey googled the area Tom had mentioned the night before. Huonville.

"I think you'd like that area, actually. It seems more like your kind of place. I don't know why I didn't think of it before," said Georgina. Aubrey zoomed through the listings, but one property stood out. She clicked in to view the details.

"Oh, wow."

"Did you find something?" Georgina asked over the whooshing sound of steaming milk in her beloved coffee machine.

"Yes. Look at this place. It has everything. Even the potential for a studio. Ten acres. Maybe a bit more land than I want. But..." Georgina came over and looked over Aubrey's shoulder as she flipped through the photos. The place was gorgeous. Her heart leapt. What was the catch?

"It's cheaper than the place in Bright," said Aubrey.

"Tasmanian properties are often cheaper than the mainland. You should call the agent quickly, though. It will go fast, I would imagine." Aubrey kept looking through the listing when Georgina sat, placing their coffees on the table.

"What are Tom's plans?" Georgina asked, sipping from her mug.

"I don't know. I've been hesitant to ask. We started talking about it, but then he got called back to Ireland and he hasn't mentioned it since."

"But you're still going ahead with buying in Australia?" The question surprised Aubrey.

"Well, yes. Of course. This is home."

"Yes, I know. But you are English, after all, and Tom's Irish, so we just figured..."

"We?"

"Pam asked me if I knew what your plans were. I said I didn't, and we thought you may move back to England, as a sort of compromise with Tom."

"I hadn't even thought of doing that. I haven't lived there for so long. This is more home than England ever was. Besides, you and Pam are here."

"Yes, but Pam and I can always come to you, and you can come to us." Should Aubrey consider it? Goosebumps sprang up on her arms and she shivered. Her gut told her no, but her indecision bothered her.

"I don't mean to complicate things for you. You haven't said how Tom fits into things."

"Probably because I don't know. And it's really weighing on me. His trip back to Ireland didn't help, and he was there for weeks longer than I thought he'd be."

"You don't have doubts about how he feels about you, do you? Because..."

At that moment, Tom walked into the kitchen.

"Sorry about that. Takes some juggling to get both the boys on a call simultaneously. Time zones and schedules are a pain in the arse," he said, kissing Aubrey on her head before he took a seat beside her.

"Coffee Tom?" Georgina asked, already rising to get it.

"That would be grand Georgina, if it's not a bother? You do make a great cup. You've spoiled me. I'll never be able to go back to the instant

I drink in Ireland." Aubrey's heart sank. So, he was planning on returning then.

"How are the boys?" asked Georgina. Aubrey was relieved Georgina was there to pick up the conversation.

"Well, it seems young Liam is talking of coming to Australia," he said.

"Really?" Georgina asked, turning in surprise. Aubrey was shocked. This was news to her. With both his sons here, maybe Tom would think of staying? Tom had mentioned that he didn't want to leave nineteen-year-old Liam alone with his mother.

"Aye. Now he's recovered from the accident, he wants to get out of Ireland. Away from his mother, no doubt. He's been talkin' to Declan, you see, hearing how easy he's had it finding work as a bricklayer. I think that's inspired him."

"What would he do here?" asked Georgina, pouring steamed milk into a leaf shape pattern in Tom's mug.

"Mechanics. He just finished his apprenticeship. He was out celebrating the end of it the night of his accident. Icy roads, they say. I only hope he wasn't stupid and drivin' while he was celebrating. I know how he and his lads like to put on the drink."

"He'd find work easily here I imagine. We're in need of talented mechanics," said Georgina, setting a steaming cup of coffee in front of him. "Aubrey seems to have found a great place in Huonville too."

"Have ya, Grá? Let's have a see then?" She pushed the phone toward him, the listing still front and centre.

"I guess I'd not considered Tasmania before. It certainly has everything I want," she said, as he scrolled through the listing.

"And it's by a river, too," he said enthusiastically.

"Yes, and it has two small sheds I could convert into studios or accommodations for guests. But I'd have to see what shape they're in."

"Then get on and call the estate agent. Let's go see this place," he said, passing her back the phone. "I'm going to take this coffee and head for the shower. See if the agent can meet us today." Tom seemed buoyed by the news of Liam moving out to Australia.

Once he was gone, Georgina returned to her grilling.

"So, Declan's here. Liam's coming. Sounds like there's more reason for Tom to stay," said Georgina. Yes, but Tom had said nothing about staying. How could she trust this?

"I suppose. It's just, when he was in Ireland and we Facetime'd, he talked about his writing. He doesn't here. He hasn't even touched his writing. It's like he's on holiday. Plus, he's not talking about properties like it's *our* place anymore either. Not like when he first got here. I mean, I'm the buyer, but I know that's only because he doesn't want to sell his house in Cork because it's the boys' home. And, until this news, Liam was still living there."

"Maybe he needed some time to decide how he wants to progress? I mean, it took the Camino for me to realise I'm happy to be independent. You can't say what Patrick and I have is a traditional marriage anymore. I like not living with him, but I also love going on dates with him again. It took me a while to determine that's what I wanted and to commit to that decision. It was a big step for me, and this is a huge leap for Tom. I guess my point is, maybe Tom is just trying to work out how to make his life work around what you have? You are a strong woman and you've never been shy about your independence. Being with Tom has been a big change for you too."

"Yes, I know, and you are probably right. I mean, I was happy on my own. Well, as happy as I could be, I suppose. But with Tom... it's like he's the final piece of my puzzle. I just don't know how to trust myself with this stuff anymore."

"Then you need to talk to him. Figure out a way that works for you both if that's what he wants too."

Later that afternoon, Aubrey stood on the verandah of the property in Huonville. It was everything she dreamed of. The house sat on ten acres of rolling hills overlooking a valley, with a river bordering the property. The house needed some work, but nothing Tom couldn't handle, he assured her.

"What's troublin' ya, Grá?" asked Tom, coming up beside her. Her imagination was going wild with all the changes she could envision for the place.

The real estate agent had walked off to take a phone call, but not before telling her there was another couple interested in the property.

She had to decide today. She wasn't sure now was the time for this conversation, but it was one she'd put off long enough.

"I am just thinking about what all this means, that's all," she said.

"About the house or somethin' else?"

"Well, I'm loving this house. I love the property. I love the location. I love that 'The Lovelies' are nearby, or at least when Pam and Jack are down after their cottage is built. I feel the creative vibe here. And I don't get a sense of doom. Instead, I'm gleaming hope and joy. But… well, I don't know." A sense of uncertainty crept up on her.

"What do you think?" she asked. She needed to hear what he wanted. What he envisioned.

"I agree with ya. This place is grand. It has everything you've been looking for and that creek is incredible. I can see spending time down there, at twilight, looking for the platypus the agent promises is there. I can see sipping wine on the porch. I can see parties in the house, with the fire roaring. I can see converting those sheds into space to create. Aye, it seems the right fit."

"Hmm," she mumbled, her mind spinning. Tom spoke of positive things, but he didn't mention himself in the scenario.

"But you're still unsure?" She looked away. She couldn't lie. She'd live here without him, but the truth was, she didn't want to. He stepped back behind her, giving her space to think.

"Aubrey?" She turned around at his voice after a few moments had passed. His eyes blazed blue, and his impossibly long eyelashes seemed to bat at her.

"I want to be here with ya, grow old with ya, see the days begin and end with ya. And I do think this is the place to do that, Grá. With the boys in Australia, it makes things easier, to be sure. But I've been thinkin' long and hard about the future." There it was. She knew there would be a 'but' coming. "I am not sure marriage is something either of us wants. But I love ya Grá, I do. So, I want to give you something."

He held out a ring nestled in his palm. She bit her lip, staring down blankly in confusion.

"This was my great-maimó's Claddagh ring. It's a traditional Irish ring which represents love, loyalty, and friendship. And that's what I'm offering you, Grá. My promise for all those things. I think we've

377

both been searchin' for each other for a long time." When she looked back up into Tom's eyes, she saw they reflected everything she was feeling. An uncertainty to trust but a willingness to take the leap anyway.

With his words spoken, Aubrey saw her future clearly. She turned to the real estate agent.

"We'd like to make an offer." She looked at Tom and beamed, finally feeling the smile reach her eyes.

"Ah, there's my girl. I've missed ya."

ACKNOWLEDGMENTS

How can I begin my acknowledgements without first thanking my own Camino Family? Thank you to Jerry, Sharon, Amanda and Helen. I know who you are and what you're made of. I hope you do too.

I also wish to thank the following:

My Camino Angels: Jerry, Sharon, Amanda, Phillippa, Maree, Vicky, Mike and Sarah (the amazing osteopath at Ultreia in Burgos). Without you, I may not have made it 800km the first time. To my husband Rich, with whom I walked a second Camino: Thank you for not leaving me in Burgos.

My fellow Camino Tragics who made my own Camino Wanders memorable: Agnes and Fe from N.Z., Nicki, Maree and Mike from N.Z., Vicky & Brian from the U.K., Jane and Kristy from Australia, Marion (R.I.P. Lovely) and Mary-Kate from Ireland, Missy & Brian from the U.S, Belinda from the Philippines, Marie (keep singing Love-ly!) from Sweden, Trish from South Africa, Mikey and Steve from Melbourne (Australia), Beth, Karen and Carole from the U.S., Heejin and Chong from the U.S. & South Korea, Sabrina and Reece from the U.S., Liam and Ella from N.Z., Li and Kim from South Korea and Ian from the U.K.

The beautiful Albergues I loved along the way: Casa Susi (thank you Sue and Fermin!), Gite Ultreia in Saint Jean Pied de Port (thank you Agitatx!), Orisson Refuge, Redecilla del Camino (Mumma!), and Albergue Leo in Villafranca del Bierzo.

My fabulous Beta Readers: Agnes, Seana, Jerry, Sharon, Angela, Meredith, Kim, and Judy. Thank you for your insightful, honest and encouraging feedback.

My Editors: Richard Marlow for his brutal yet honest red marks, who made my rants more decisive and words more vivid. And, Angela Garwood for being the spelling/ grammar police I so desperately needed.

My own circle of amazing, strong women (aka my Lovelies): Angela, Melissa, Pauline, Trish, Kim, Helen, Sharon and Ewa. You are amazing women whom I treasure immensely. Thank you for always being my cheerleaders.

My Tasmanian Camino and NaNo Writing Groups: Thank you for your friendship and your support. I can't tell you how much that has meant to me as a new transplant.

The amazing author Lori Oliver-Tierney, for the great line in her book, "Trudge": "*I know who you are and what you're made of. I hope you know it, too*". This line inspired me to stay focused on what was important for my book. I encourage you all to read Lori's book about her adventure on the PCT.

My daughter Natalie, who continues to be the sounding board for my crazy ideas and supports me in whatever I do. I'm immensely proud to be your mother.

My husband, Rich who is at my side no matter what path I decide to take, supporting me, pushing me to be better, and loving me intensely no matter what.

Lastly, to my mother, Gai. I can only hope she knew what she was made of, because she continues to inspire me every single day.

DISCUSSION GUIDE

Camino Wandering focuses on Aubrey, Pam and Georgina, as they walk the Camino Francés, an 800 kilometre trail across northern Spain. Not only do they struggle with their physical baggage, but also their emotional baggage too. Bringing other characters (pilgrims) into the story gives each of them different perspectives, but they question, too, why these younger pilgrims walk with the trail along with them. Soon enough, it is revealed. But along the way, all three women dig into why they are walking the Camino. It's not always as it seems. And it remains unknown whether they take that knowledge home with them.

DISCUSSION QUESTIONS

1. The novel is from Aubrey's point of view and it's her story that remains a mystery for much of the novel. Should Aubrey have shared her full truth with Pam and Georgina from the start?

2. How would the story change if told from Georgina's or Pam's perspective?

3. Both Pam and Georgina brought too much weight in their packs, while Aubrey was sure she brought just enough. How does the contents of their packs reflect who they are?

4. Was Tom's character necessary to Aubreys story? Why/Why not?

5. What do you foresee happening to the other pilgrims mentioned in the book? Why are their stories important?

6. What factors do each of the secondary characters bring to the story – Ben, Paolo, Hannah, Marinka and Lee?

7. Parenting is a theme that runs throughout the story - from The Lovelies upbringing, to Georgina's and Aubrey's relationship with their children, through to Hannah's decision. Why was this important to the storyline?

8. Is it right for Ben to adopt Hannah's baby? Why or why not?

9. Aubrey believes that her daughter's spirit guides her. Do you believe that is true? What source of hope did she have before beginning this walk? Why was her daughter's presence important to the storyline?

10. Could Pam have left Mick earlier? What bound her to stay with him and what kept her in the marriage? Why couldn't she leave? Do you feel Pam's anger at the Catholic Church is justified? Does she reconcile her anger by the end of the book?

11. Georgina's marriage to Patrick touches on underlining mental health issues. Discuss the stigma for men around mental health and how they may or may not be changing. Does that differ from how women manage it?

12. Addiction and depression were also things Aubrey has dealt with. Do you think these are issues we need to be more open in talking about and why?

13. While in Viana, Aubrey felt a malevolent presence. What do you think caused that? Have you ever felt that yourself?

14. What lessons do you think the characters took away from their interactions with one another?

15. What did Aubrey see as her "purpose" for walking the Camino? Did that change as they walked?

16. How did Aubrey's intuition influence her decisions throughout the story?

ABOUT THE AUTHOR

Tara Marlow is an Australian author of suspense and women's fiction. Tara was born in Sydney, and spent twenty of her early adult years living in the United States. In 2011, Tara ditched the corporate desk, emptied her nest in 2017 and travelled the world, full time for three years, working as a travel writer and photographer. Today, Tara lives in Tasmania, where she has pivoted her writing focus to fiction, writing about women overcoming seemingly insurmountable challenges, revealing who they are and what they're made of.

Mantra in life: She believed she could, so she did.

Visit Tara online at taramarlowauthor.com to sign up for her monthly newsletter.

For a copy of Aubrey's '200 Questions', visit Tara here:
www.taramarlowauthor.com

ALSO BY TARA MARLOW

If you enjoyed *Camino Wandering* you'll love these moving stories, also by Tara Marlow.

The Decisions We Make

"Lots of strong characters, lots of believable story lines, interesting plot points, twists, mini mysteries…"

- Shari Hamilton, Advanced Reader

Beneath the Surface

"Heartbreaking…heartwarming…sad…joyful…overwhelming! I can't say enough about this book. I would give it six stars if I could."

- Vickie Waters, Goodreads Review

Available where books are sold.

Made in the USA
Middletown, DE
22 September 2023

39061978R00219